Charles Fairfield

Some Account of George William Wilshere

Charles Fairfield

Some Account of George William Wilshere

ISBN/EAN: 9783337396145

Printed in Europe, USA, Canada, Australia, Japan

Cover: Foto ©Andreas Hilbeck / pixelio.de

More available books at **www.hansebooks.com**

SOME ACCOUNT OF

GEORGE WILLIAM WILSHERE

BARON BRAMWELL

OF HEVER

AND HIS OPINIONS

BY

CHARLES FAIRFIELD

WITH A PORTRAIT

London

MACMILLAN AND CO., Limited

NEW YORK: THE MACMILLAN COMPANY

1898

PREFACE

THANKS are due and are hereby given to sundry persons who lent letters from Lord Bramwell for use in this volume ; also to the proprietors of the *Times*, for permitting the republication of Lord Bramwell's many letters to the editor ; also to the proprietor and to the editor of the *Economist*, for a similar favour, as well as for other courtesies ; also to Mr. James Knowles, proprietor of the *Nineteenth Century Review*, who was good enough to allow Lord Bramwell's article, June, 1885, to be reprinted (pp. 264-274). The portrait frontispiece is reproduced by kind permission of Messrs. Fradelle and Young, 283, Oxford Street, W.

CONTENTS

ERRATA.

On page 4, 'ipsi,' *instead of* 'ipse.'

  „ 81, '1891' *should be* '1892.'

  „ 96, asterisk *should follow* 'Lords,' in line 1.

  „ 174, footnote, 'p. 320' *should be* 'p. 318.'

A MEMOIR

OF

LORD BRAMWELL

CHAPTER I.

LEARNER.

Monotonous faultlessness of our Judges—Their *apologia* never
  called for — None wanted in Lord Bramwell's case—
  Parentage—School-days—Clerk in a City bank—Early
  marriage—Studies law under a special pleader—Sir G.
  Bramwell's description of special pleading—Tries it for
  a while—Called to the Bar—Speedy success on Home
  Circuit, and large practice in commercial cases—A Judge
  at forty-seven.

THE memoir of each memorable Judge which Her
Majesty's public constructs for itself is : ' He sat
there and did what was right, and is dead.' The
reasons why Her Majesty's Judges are, of all the
nation's worthies, most readily forgotten may be
deemed honourable alike to those illustrious magistrates themselves and to the English and Scottish
people, immortality being so largely the ungracious
gift of a man's enemies, often remaining conditional
until made absolute by strenuous praise or apology

I

wrung from the dead great one's admirers. Thus, hate is the brine which preserved memory of Henry VIII., of the two Marys, the two Cromwells, Marlborough, Walpole, Pitt, of celebrities concerning whom vindications have been written—long enough for historical reaction in their favour to set in. Prince Bismarck can never be forgotten until the jaded French language will yield no more angry epigrams; Lord Beaconsfield until the last trespasser has annexed the last primrose root, and the last Conservative Government prohibits importation of these irritating flowers through the Custom House—to protect trespassers from cut-throat competition. English and Scottish Judges remaining singularly unhated, *hors concours*, are out of range even of newspaper attacks. In the introduction to a recent 'History of Trade Unionism,' the bare fact that it was Baron Bramwell who, August 21, 1867, delivered the charge in *Reg. v. Druitt and others* is coldly recorded. Vengeance is left to the collective conscience, although the principles Baron Bramwell laid down, that Trade Union pickets may not beat free labourers and that '. . . the liberty of a man's mind and will, to say how he shall bestow himself, his means, his talent, and his industry, is as much a subject of the law's protection as is that of his body . . .,' probably seem to the author of the work, and to his disciples, the quintessence of judge-made lawlessness. Also from the lowest story of the social edifice testimony is not wanting to popular appreciation of our Judges. A hulking labourer was once sentenced by the late Judge

Bodkin, for the second time, to penal servitude, for half killing a policeman.   As the batch of prisoners were going down the stairs from dock to cells, a pickpocket, who had just got a few months' imprisonment, cursed his honour the Judge audibly. 'Hold your noise,' said the labourer ; 'that toff in the klobber wig often and often defended my poor old mother, and arter the case was over he'd slip the fee back into her hand, and say, "'Ere, you want it more nor I do."'

All manner of men in the land, tacitly agreeing that none of Her Majesty's Judges can do wrong, take their revenge, so to speak, by speedily forgetting these their most faultless servants.   Mayhap the British public will condescend to talk about a legal celebrity if the first letter of his surname suggests an ugly alliterative nickname, if he was disbarred in later life, if his wife utters proverbs, if he was too partial to stimulants, if his father was a barber, or his sons got into disgrace.   Lord Bramwell left no enemies and made no mistakes ; that docks the length of the pleadings in his case. No awkwardnesses remain for indulgent friends to explain away ; no blunders, of the kind which gives the ingenious critic an opportunity of showing how much better he could have managed things himself. The rather cheap and obvious criticism of 'the School' represented by his great predecessor at the Exchequer has never been applied to Lord Bramwell's law.   He never gave the nation an ugly quarter of an hour, as the wittiest, most brilliant and most cynical of Chancellors did.   There was no dubious political romance, no domestic linen washed in public for the profession, the press, and the gossips to shrug their shoulders over and forget as quickly as possible, in consideration of other virtues.

From first to last Lord Bramwell owed nothing to 'interest' (a word of oppressive significance fifty or sixty years ago, when he tried his fortune at the Bar). He had at first no powerful friends nor family connections ; very little money. There is a legend that his grandfather was a tradesman in the City of London, an initial disability which required some surmounting, A.D. 1838. At Trinity College, Dublin, June 30, 1887, after Lord Rosse, Chancellor, had conferred the Honorary degree, Professor Webb, in the customary Latin oration, said of Lord Bramwell, *omnia sua sibi ipse debet ;* which was true in a wide sense. Further, he owed success, the physical power to struggle for success, very largely to his sound, healthy begetting. The *corpus sanum* which gave the *mens sana* so fine a chance all his life, he got from his progenitors—his father, a precise, conscientious business man of the antique school, head-clerk, ultimately partner, in the banking firm of Dorrien, Magens,* Dorrien, and Mello, 22, Finch Lane, since amalgamated with Glyn, Mills, Currie, and Co. ; his mother a woman of great force of character, who lived to the age of ninety-six. Only those who now have white hair can recollect when

---

* Son of Nicholas Magens, or Magends, a German merchant settled in London, author of many works on insurance, exchange, etc. ; died 1764.

there were such English mothers as his. The name of Bramwell has been from time immemorial a good yeoman name in the bleak, bracing North Country, about Lowther and Penrith in Westmorland. One of the name, John Bramwell (born 1718, died at Newcastle-on-Tyne, 1790), lived at Penrith, and married in 1742. His wife Anne (born 1724, died 1773) with patriotic precision bore him seven children. The eldest, Thomas, born 1743, seems to have been a Captain in His Majesty's service, and lies buried in Kirkby Lonsdale church-yard. The second son, William, born 1745, by his will dated September, 1786, left 'housing lands and premises' at Beckhead in Witherslack (at one time the home of Addison, of the *Spectator*), as well as personal property. There was a son, George, born to John and Anne Bramwell in 1749. Then came a daughter, Margaret, married in 1784 to Thomas Jackson. A daughter of this marriage, also a Margaret, married to John Smith of the Bury, Stevenage, used often to tell her daughter (Mrs. Margaret Long, living, 1897, at Eye, Peterborough) of having carried Lord Bramwell in her arms when he was a baby of a year or so old—an incident one would not lightly forget. An entry in this lady's diary shows that she was visiting Lord Bramwell's father and mother in London in 1809 and 1810.

Their eldest son, afterwards Lord Bramwell, born within sound of Bow Bells, June 12, 1808, was christened George William Wilshere. At the age of twelve he was sent to Palace School, Enfield, kept by Dr. May.* Thither his younger brother, Harry, went also. When George Bramwell's thirteenth birthday drew nigh, he asked his father for three things : a watch, a large cake, apparently for the purpose of increasing his popularity, and some money. On June 11, 1821, his father wrote :

'With this you will receive a watch, which I hope you will be pleased with, which I request you will not put out of order. The gold seal and key has been added by your mother's desire. I wish you many years of health and happiness to wear the same. I hope you will carefully mark the ebb of time, and make the best use of it, so that you may turn out an honest and clever man. You will also receive a cake, which I think you will find capacious enough for your purpose. As for money, you can want but little, as you will be at home on Thursday. . . . To-morrow your mother, myself & Co. will drink your health, wishing you *many, many* happy returns of the day.'

Among Lord Bramwell's papers, together with letters of fifty or sixty years later, from Peers, Cabinet Ministers, Archbishops, Bishops, Cardinals, Judges, and such famous personages, are a few of his father's letters of this time in faded brown ink, the clumsy old twopenny post-marks on the back. Stray words here and there prove that there was great and diligent affection between father, mother, and children. But no weak indulgence : George and Harry must walk all the way from Enfield to Finch Lane if they will insist on coming home at Easter. One gets a glimpse of matters at Dr. May's from this fine schoolboy letter ; the writer is half sorry at having stepped out into the spacious world, half inclined to patronize Dr. May's 'fellows' :

<hr>

* See note, p. 28.

'*June* 7, 1824.

'MY DEAR GEORGE,

'I received your letter yesterday; I could not receive it before. . . . I am glad to see you are first on the Credit List. I think you deserve it, mind . . . if I were to go back to school again, I should not be so idle as I was formerly. Tell Mr. Jones he would have no occasion to turn me into the middle of the room every prosidy morning. I suppose old Jackson and a few more fill my station? I met old Westwood the other day; he was covered over with black ink, and as dirty as the devil himself. I am quite ruined, so says that old Raven Craw. Tom Spring and Langan fight to-morrow. Success to the best man! Town is quite empty' (the letter is dated Red Lion Square). 'Remember me kindly to old friends and companions. Item to Mr. Bates, Mr. Jones, Mr. Sugden, and Jem. Tell C. Holt I can write better than he now.

'Yours ever,
'COSSAM McRITCHIE.'

George Bramwell must have been a big, silent, self-willed boy at this time, not ornamental, with the superior bull-terrier expression of the true English schoolboy, able to use his two fists a bit, utterly unlikely, therefore, to commit suicide if chaffed by his companions about his opinions. He and his brothers inherited from their mother genius—rare mental powers. Knack of mental concentration, and easy grip of each task before him, put him at the head of the school when he was fifteen. He must early have suspected that he could sail round most schoolbook problems; that difficulties which puzzled and daunted other people need not daunt him. Similar suspicions he modestly kept to himself for ten or twenty years after leaving school. Very quickly solicitors having business within the

Home Circuit shared them.   The future Lord Bramwell never went to a University.   It was impossible—chronologically impossible, of course—for him to 'come under Jowett's influence.'   Perhaps just as well.   At the age of sixteen he was taken into Dorrien's Bank, beginning, no doubt, as ' walk clerk.'   It has been well remarked that what he learnt there must have been useful to him at the Bar in commercial cases.   To lose, by dint of everyday familiarity, one's awe of those bewildering documents bankers deal with is an education in itself. Probably at first he duly went the rounds every morning with bill-case chained to his waist, 'collecting.'   Later, helping at book-keeping and discounting work, he would learn the why and wherefore of bills, cheques, drafts, bottomry bonds, bills of lading, dock warrants, etc., how and where they ought to be endorsed, the stamps and fees required, and so forth. In 1829 he is living at Finch Lane, already a bit of a politician—a Liberal, as most City men were then, rejoicing, he tells us (p. 101) at the passing of the Catholic Relief Bill ; head of the house in the absence of his father, who writes from Margate, September 16, 1829, that he will return to London by seven o'clock, and ' tell Patty to get me a rumpsteak for supper and some stewed eels, and whatever else you like.'   Strange food this for a banker.

In the following year, having no settled prospects, he married (seemingly against the wishes of his family and friends) a lady of Spanish origin, daughter of Bruno Silva.   They loved each other. In 1836 she died.   Whether such a marriage was a wise or a foolish act none can decide, since all tribunals are prejudiced, no evidence obtainable, and the law made *ad hoc* by the parties always. Seemingly, it was considered a very rash thing for a bank clerk to do. After planning various careers for himself, George Bramwell determined to go to the Bar, and in 1830, in order to master that now vanished craft known as 'special pleading,' became pupil of Mr. (afterwards Sir) Fitzroy Kelly— favourite pupil — when it was discovered by that astute master that the quiet, confident young man was good, not only at drudgery, but at high-class brain work. Fifty-eight years afterwards* Lord Bramwell told a British Association audience:

'One could suppose that every educated person would like to have some acquaintance with the laws of his country; certainly that Englishmen would, since they are proud of their laws and responsible for them. But it is said, "The law is so dry." I deny it. No doubt, if you have to learn how to serve a writ, how many days a defendant has before he need plead, and so on, it is wearisome enough. But with respect to study —not of the practice, but of the broad general principles of law —it is quite otherwise. Of the four volumes of "Blackstone's Commentaries," three, to my mind, are most agreeable reading; these general principles should be taught as part of ordinary education.'

Legal maxims, how they came to be invented, and the application of them, had an intellectual fascination for him from the first. His philosophy of law he seems to have constructed by inductive process, going back, step by step, from points raised to rulings, thence to maxims, cited to reinforce

* 'Economics *v.* Socialism,' Pamphlet, L. and P. D. League, 1888.

rulings, until, at the outer circumference, he came upon general principles governing the law of England. The fine, logical completeness of it all appealed to his inherited business instincts. The trade of law which he had taken up was no mere tissue of pedantries ; rather, a methodical scheme for doing the right thing and confounding rogues and fools. Afterwards he could reverse the inductive process, and, with all the more confidence and satisfaction to himself, aided by his own common sense, apply principles by deductive method, the only one Judges are supposed to recognize.

On September 18, 1865, Chief Baron Pollock, who also regarded legal principles from the point of view of an intellectual *gourmet*, wrote :

> ' What is the *pleasure* derived from all this ? I apprehend it is the discovery of a *rule*, or *law*. In mathematics one rarely discovers the rule without discovering the reason. In physics one never reaches *causes ;* it is merely grouping experiences.'

What young Mr. Bramwell had to learn in Mr. Fitzroy Kelly's chambers between 1830 and 1833 may be gathered from these ' Further Suggestions ' (he called them a ' popular, untechnical statement of the rules of Common Law procedure '—they are really an essay on the art of pleading), which Sir George Bramwell submitted to the Judicature Commission, of which Lord Blackburn, Lord Coleridge, and himself were members in 1867 :

> ' The pleadings begin by the plaintiff stating his case— viz., those facts which, if true, show, as he contends, a right to some judgment against the defendant. This statement is

called the declaration. The defendant meets this by denying one or more of the facts; as, for instance, if the action is against the alleged acceptor of a bill, by denying his acceptances, or by admitting the facts and avoiding them, as by saying the plaintiff has released him. This is called the defendant's plea; or by admitting the facts, but denying their legal sufficiency, this is called demurring. The plaintiff's reply is called the replication; and he, like the defendant, denies one or more allegations in the plea, or confesses and avoids it, or demurs to it. In like way there is the defendant's rejoinder, the plaintiff's surrejoinder, the defendant's rebutter, and the plaintiff's surrebutter, beyond which I never knew pleadings extend, nor is there any distinctive name for them. The pleadings stop when neither party has new matter to advance. . . . I may add that a *special* plea is where the defendant pleads specially instead of the general issue, or general denial of the plaintiff's case, and the plaintiff's replication and all subsequent pleadings may be *special* in like way. This is the origin of the expression " special pleading."

'There are two leading features in the science or art of pleading; one is, that pleadings must be single. Originally a plaintiff could support a claim on one ground only. For instance, if he sued the drawer of a dishonoured bill, he could not say in his declaration that he presented the bill, and further say that the defendant exonerated him from presenting it; that was double and wrong ["duplicity"]. He was obliged to rely on one or the other; so defendant could not plead that he did not endorse the bill, and that it was not presented for payment; that was double and wrong. In like way the plaintiff could not reply that the release was not his deed, and that it was obtained by fraud; so of subsequent pleadings. . . . By a statute of Anne, defendants were allowed to plead two or more pleas by leave of the Court; and by the Common Law Procedure Act of 1852, plaintiffs and defendants were allowed to reply and rejoin, surrejoin, rebut and surrebut two or more matters; and defendants and plaintiffs were allowed to plead and demur, leave of a Judge for this double pleading being necessary.

'This last enactment made an end of the substance of the rule against " duplicity "; but the form has continued. For instance, a plaintiff never now puts his case in the double or alternative form, and says, "I presented the bill"; and, further, " Whether I did or not, you exonerated me." Nor does the defendant plead in that way, but pleads each head of defence separately, as : (1) " I did not endorse "; (2) " You did not present "; (3) " A release "—and so on. The consequence is enormous length and complexity. One claim may require four counts, each of which necessitates several pleas, each plea several replications, each replication several rejoinders; so that there may be 4 counts, 16 pleas, 64 replications, and 256 rejoinders; and as every plea, replication, and rejoinder may be denied, there may be 256 issues in law and fact. I cannot say I ever knew of such a case ; but the following case did come before the Court of Exchequer recently :

' It was an action against the Great Indian Peninsular Company for the burning or loss of the luggage of an officer, a passenger on the line. Count 1 said plaintiff was a passenger on defendants' railway with luggage, and that the defendants did not safely carry the luggage. Count 2 said plaintiff was an officer in service of Her Majesty on duty, and was received by defendants with his luggage, being necessaries as an officer on duty, to be carried ; yet they did not safely carry the luggage, nor use due care, but were so negligent that, through their negligence, luggage was burned.

' The pleas were : (1) Not guilty ; (2) denial—defendants were carriers of passengers and luggage ; (3) plaintiff was not a passenger, as alleged ; (4) to count 1, plaintiff was taken as a passenger under a contract with Government, by which defendants were to be under no responsibility for luggage ; (5) to count 1, that the matter complained of was by plaintiff's default ; (6) to count 1, that plaintiff was one of a body of troops, and by their carelessness and wilful misconduct and mutinous act luggage was lost ; (7) to count 2, same as plea 4 ; (8) to count 2, same as plea 5 ; (9) to count 2, same as plea 6 ; (10) to count 1, plaintiff was carried under a contract with Government ; (11) to count 2, same as plea 10. The replications were : (1) A denial of all the pleas ; (2) to plea 4, setting out terms of contract, that luggage was to remain in charge of guard provided by troops, and that luggage was burned through gross negligence ; (3) demurrer to plea 4 ; (4) to plea 7, same as replication to plea 4 ; (5) demurrer to plea 9 ; (6) demurrer to plea 10 ; (7) demurrer to plea 4. (1) Rejoinder denial to replications 2 and 4; (2) demurrer to replication 2; (3) demurrer to replication 4.

'One cause of action had issue 2 counts. The 2 counts had issue 11 pleas, 3 of which applied to both counts ; being in effect, as they might have been in form, 14 in number. The pleas had issue 7 replications, 1 of them being applicable to 10 of the pleas, and being in effect, as they might have been in form, 12 in number ; making, therefore, in the whole, 18. These 18 replications had issue 3 rejoinders, in effect 4. The pleadings raised 12 issues of fact, and 6 issues of law. . . .

'The case of the plaintiff was probably that he was a passenger as an officer under a contract with the Crown, that his baggage was burned either through carelessness of the defendants or otherwise, and that either way they were liable. Probably they had made no contract with the plaintiff, but with the Crown, to whom alone they were accountable ; and that if accountable to the plaintiff, and otherwise liable, the clause in the contract exempted them, or the misconduct of the plaintiff's troops did ; I say probably, and not certainly. For it is a rule of pleading that it is sufficient to prove what it was necessary to state ; the unnecessary fact not proved may be treated as not alleged. The consequence is, the pleader stuffs his pleadings with a quantity of matter to ensure the pleas being good on the face of them, leaving the counsel at the trial to prove as much as he can.

'The other feature of pleading is that, instead of the actual facts being stated, the legal results or implications from them are stated as facts. Thus, the defendant is said to have accepted a bill. The truth is, it is drawn on, and accepted by another person in that other person's name ; but the plaintiff contends that, by reason of the defendant receiving some profits from the business carried on by the acceptor, the defendant is a

partner with him, and liable as acceptor of a bill accepted in
the name in which the business is carried on. So the defendant
is said to break and enter the plaintiff's close if he gives a
warrant to distrain to a broker who enters for that purpose.
So if a man turns his wife out of doors without means of
support, goods supplied to her are said to be sold and delivered
to him, because she had an implied authority to bind him. . . .
I will now point out the mischiefs resulting from this last-
mentioned matter. In the first place, it causes pleadings to
fail in their very objects. They do not state the facts so as
to inform the opposite party, nor evolve the matters in dispute.
. . . The pleadings do not evolve what is in dispute as matter
of fact or matter of law. Hence, as we continually see, as soon
as the plaintiff's case at Nisi Prius is opened, it is found there
is no fact in dispute, and a verdict is taken with leave to move,
or a special case is stated, or the Judge directs a verdict or
nonsuit. In these cases all the expense of the trial, or nearly
so, is wasted. And even where one or more facts are in dispute,
all the preparation to prove the others not in dispute is needless, and immense expense and trouble are incurred in vain.
No doubt this is much mitigated by respectable attorneys who
make reciprocal admissions. But to do this the attorney must
not only be honest and self-denying ; he must also be cool-
headed, and not led away by zeal for his client, and determined
to make his unjust adversary prove everything. This latter is
not so common a virtue. Further, points of law are sprung
on the opposite party and the Judge at the trial, which for want
of preparation and otherwise cannot then be discussed, and
consequently must be reserved, and facts then are disclosed
for the first time, which involves the necessity of new trials on
the ground of surprise. In the next place, mistakes are made,
and justice defeated on technicalities. A plaintiff must not
only make out a good case, but he must show he has used the
right form, that he is in the right in substance, and in the right
in saying his case was one of money had and received. Further,
injustice is worked by this fiction ; there is a form of declaration commonly called " trover," but in which the plaintiff says
the defendant converted the plaintiff's goods to the defendant's

use. It has been held, whether rightly or wrongly is not the question, that, if a man assumes to dispose of another's property, it is a conversion to the use of the person so assuming. I was counsel in a case for the Sheriff where this fiction cost the officer £7,000. The case was this: An attorney named Buchanan Hoare had lent money for a client on some books; he was desirous of selling these books, and thought, why I know not, that he would be safer in selling if he had them seized and sold under a *fi. fa.* at the suit of his client on a judgment which was part of the security. He issued the *fi. fa.*, and took the officer to the place where the books were in his (Hoare's) custody, who accordingly left his man in possession; afterwards the officer had them inventoried, valued, and a bill of sale was made of them to Hoare or his client; the officer then left, leaving the books where and as he found them. Hoare then sold the books. Someone who claimed the books—by what title I forget, nor is it material—brought an action against the Sheriff, who was held liable for a conversion, and had to pay £7,000 damages, and costs. It is impossible he could have been liable for this if the actual facts had been stated. . . . A foreign jurist coming to one of our Courts to be enlightened, instead of hearing principles discussed, would hear the plaintiff's counsel argue there was a conversion, and the defendant's that there was not; and the Judges would gravely discuss the same matter; cases would be cited to show what had been held to be a conversion and what not. The origin of this is, that if a case can be thus solved, trouble is saved to all parties, no principles have to be enunciated nor established, and they are very troublesome things. Lastly, as David Dudley Field said, this mode of pleading is an impediment to a fusion of law and equity. He made the remark as to forms of action; they were abolished in New York. . . . One thing at least is certain— viz., that the Common Law pleading and Equity pleading cannot both be right.'

He does not seem to have made a success of it when he began as a special pleader on his own account, and, as his friend Master Macdonell tells us, earned but a pittance ; had not the right gifts or limitations for some businesses ; made up his mind to go to the Bar, and was 'called' May 4, 1838.   One who was his companion in those trying days says of him : 'Though he had not received a brief, he was always sanguine of success, feeling, as he expressed it, that he had "got it in him," and meant to rise to a seat on the Bench.'   This faith he would impart to his cousin, the late Edward Frith, the ' Ned ' of his father's letters, and to Mr. B. E. Kennedy,* both members of the Stock Exchange, over a cup of bachelor-made coffee—very costly in those days— at his chambers, after a dinner at the Cock, or Rainbow in Fleet Street, they smoking their cigars, he never smoking.   All his life he snatched at chances of picking up information from practical men ; from these friends learnt technicalities and general rules of Stock Exchange business and Committee 'law' (for it *is* law, having the same origin as our Common Law).   They were excellent authorities, both in later days large 'dealers' in the railway market. Thirty years afterwards (December 3, 1868) Sir George Bramwell was one of the Judges who decided the important Stock Exchange case of *Grissell v. Bristowe*, in the Court of Exchequer Chamber, Cockburn, C.J., presiding, the other Judges being Lush, Kelly, Channell, and Pigott ; and Stock Exchange members concluded that the

* Long a member of the Stock Exchange Committee ; now (July, 1898) the oldest living member of the House, having been admitted in March, 1836.

knowledge thus early acquired must have been of assistance to his brother Judges.

Judging from the point of view of 1897, the London of 1837 must have been a dingy and depressing place for a briefless barrister who had quarrelled with his relatives. Dickens pictures the then professional and social life of the middle classes as a blend of dingy formality, vulgarity and *mauvaise honte*. Thackeray tells us that there were no restaurants in the City—nowhere to get a dinner, save the tavern for the rich and the cook-shop for others. Clothes, travelling, books, newspapers, many luxuries now considered indispensable by all classes, were scarce and dear. George Bramwell concluded that if he wanted such things, or more desirable ones, he must work for them. That he could do, and did, to such good purpose that, in 1841, three years after being called, he is described as one of the leaders of the Home Circuit with Shee, Channell, and Lush, rising men being Honyman, Bovill, Frederick Thesiger, Mathew, Parry, and Hawkins (Platt was made a Judge in 1845). The motto he liked best to quote, and formally took in later years, was 'Diligenter.' In order that a detailed account of the work and career of a barrister in good practice shall be interesting, special talents are required—on the part of the reader. It gives a poor and incomplete idea of the enormous mental and physical strain Mr. Bramwell went through between 1841 and 1856 to say how, as a pleader on the Home Circuit, he was entrusted with most important cases, on which depended the fortunes of clients long since dead and gone. Railway construction and industrial expansion, due to Free Trade, were causes at that epoch of much commercial litigation. Mr. Bramwell profited by the new business. Became a power with judges and juries at the Guildhall. City solicitors believed in him.

Although so redoubtable a combatant, carrying far too many guns for most of his opponents in controversy, he had not the combative instinct—did not love fighting for fighting's sake. In later years his expressions of deference for some opponents, such as Mr. George Potter, Mr. Shaw Lefevre, Henry George, etc.—the evidence that their assertions did tell on him a little—is almost aggravating at times. Reasoning, or the product of balanced reasoning, not victory, was the element in discussion which attracted him. Perhaps that accounts for his succeeding best as an advocate with special jurors. The fine British imperviousness of common jurymen discouraged him, while he could not bring himself to befool them nor to work on their prejudices. Although never going quite the length of Roundell Palmer, who refused briefs unless satisfied that they embodied righteous claims, he was never comfortable when he had a doubtful case in hand. An old friend and colleague in the House of Lords—still hale, hearty, and full of fight—once asked him: 'How is it that such a clever fellow as —— doesn't get on in the profession?' 'He is too much of a gentleman to get on at the Bar,' answered Lord Bramwell, which in view of the high consideration he himself had from the Bar sounds almost un-grateful; but it meant that shabby, ungentlemanly, half-honourable things were done now and then by men in haste to get on.

In 1850 he was made a member of the Common Law Procedure Commission, the other Commissioners, all unpaid, being Lord Chief Justice Sir John Jervis, Sir A. Cockburn, Baron Martin, and Mr. Willes. The foremost men in the profession had learnt already that Mr. Bramwell, while thoroughly loyal to English law, was neither a pedant nor an obstructive. No one felt more strongly than the Mr. Bramwell of 1850 that the time had come to refit the ship, alter the rigging, adapt the steering gear to changed conditions, to the latest needs of legal navigation. A school of Judges and practitioners had come to imagine that suitors were created for procedure, not procedure for suitors. Kingly, and all other, threats to English liberty having seemingly disappeared, scant justification remained for legal shibboleths and forms of exorcism, the origin and meaning of which were forgotten. The ancient masters of English Common Law had recognized for centuries a double function, a double duty cast upon them. Besides deciding and enforcing individual claims of right as between suitors, they had also to defend at need popular liberties against the aggression of extra-judicial 'authority,' armed with prerogative or the power of the sword. Thus, at important epochs in the history of English liberty, the best weapons the Judges and pleaders, permanently on frontier service, had—wherewith

to fight the Church, the Barons, or the King—
were precedent, legal fiction, technicalities, gray old
bogies which impressed and frightened oppressors
of a certain kind, just as relics, incantations, fetiches
frighten ignorant savages.*

The school of jurists which was already passing
away in 1856, represented by Thurlow, Eldon,
Stowell, Sidmouth, on the Chancery side, by Parke,
Rolfe, Holroyd, on the Common Law side, did not
explain, possibly did not understand, the origin
and justification of that juridical Conservatism, that
'opposition to historical requirements,' with which
they have been reproached. Charles Dickens, the
inspired prophet of the obvious, and his imitators,
have made plenty of grim fun of Chancery procedure especially. Nothing was easier. All legal
wisdom and 'logic of law' (p. 353) do not date
from the Common Law Procedure Act of 1852, or
the Judicature Acts of 1874 and 1876, any more
than all sound economic legislation dates from the
repeal of the Corn Laws. Joseph was a sound
economist when setting up State granaries in Egypt,
and Edmund Burke was sound, too, when telling
Pitt (and the Indian Famine Relief officers of later
times in deciding) that under modern conditions
Government granaries are a mistake.

* Hakewill's argument in Bates' case is crammed with apparently puerile subtleties, special pleaders' sophistries, which,
howevei, served—as when arguing that the King had indeed
a general right at Common Law to demand benevolences from
a subject, but that Parliament alone could say how much the
benevolence should amount to ; thus, the King had a Common
Law claim to *x* shillings, but not to *one* shilling. See p. 92.

In the United States, where (as American jurists foresaw) the Supreme Court has always been *en barbette*, always on the defensive against popular passion or executive aggression, 'the Common Law of England,' which the framers of the American Constitution annexed *en bloc*, is more esteemed, legal formalities and technicalities are more scrupulously maintained, 'case law' has now far more weight than in this country. In Lord Bramwell's latter years, when 'the New Toryism' and 'some kind of Socialism' seemed to him to threaten a tyranny as pernicious as any that Pym, Burke, Erskine, Brougham, or Romilly had fought against, he, too, fell back upon the entrenchments of the Common Law.

In 1851, after thirteen years of exceedingly hard work as a stuff gownsman, he was made a Q.C. In that year, says a notice of his career by Master Macdonell, he earned £3,414 in fees; in 1852, £4,549. During his last year at the Bar, when acknowledged leader on the Home Circuit, his fees were nearly £8,000. He only once held a brief in a criminal case.

On April 26, 1853, Lord Cranworth, Chancellor in Lord Derby's Government, asked him to serve on a Royal Commission of Inquiry into (1) assimilation of Mercantile Laws of Scotland and England; (2) Partnership Laws, and unlimited liability of Partners, adding, 'I shall consider your services of most essential importance.' These Commissioners were to be paid. From this inquiry came the Companies Act, 1862 (see p. 329). In January,

1856, James Parke, Baron of the Exchequer, afterwards Lord Wensleydale, who had sat on the Bench for twenty-eight years, resigned. The number of Barons was raised from four to five. Partly to reward his services on the two Royal Commissions named, but chiefly to comply with the general wish of the legal profession (and the behest of the *Times*), Lord Cranworth offered the vacant judgeship to Mr. Bramwell, then forty-seven years of age.

CHAPTER II.

JUDGE.

Letters from Baron Parke and from American jurists—Interest taken by latter in English procedure—Notable trials before Baron Bramwell—Charge in *Regina v. Druitt*—Sir William Erle's opinion—Three generations of mastiffs—Letters and counsel from Chief Baron Pollock—Unsettled problems—Murder and manslaughter—Unwelcome duty thrown on Judges by Parliamentary Elections Act, 1868—The official Liberal view—'The Object of the English Criminal Law'—'Riel's Case'—'Passive Obedience'—'Criminal Appeals'—Letters on Geneva Arbitration and indirect claims—Advice to railway men—Takes the part of Judge—Musical joys and sorrows—Quality of Lord Bramwell's humour—Examples—'Serjeants' Inn ' correspondence—Estimate of Sir George Bramwell by public, press, jurymen, and Bar—How arrived at—Signal honour paid to him by Bench and Bar on his retirement in 1881—Raised to the House of Lords—Despatch from Lord Esher.

BARON PARKE wrote to him from Ampthill, January 9, 1856 :

'I rejoice much to hear from the Chancellor that you are to supply my place in the Exchequer; no appointment could be better, and it will be highly·satisfactory to the public.'

Plain words and true, showing insight also, for there was little in common between these two masters, save strong sense of the dread responsibilities of their office; and in after-years Lord Bramwell, having so firm and confident a grasp of the weapons of English law, showed that he could take liberties which Baron Parke had always shrunk from, always remaining, for that reason, bound, in a sense, to the letter of law—the crutch of the man not sure of himself. Besides, it is not safe to say that a well-employed barrister will make a good Judge: Scarlett, unmatched as an advocate, made an indifferent one. The inimitable Sir Richard Bethell did not make a 'good' Chancellor. Sir Alexander Cockburn's judgments are seldom quoted nowadays. The morning Lord Blackburn was raised to the Bench the *Times* asked in a leader 'Who is Mr. Blackburn?' and, December, 1859, Chief Baron Pollock wrote to Sir G. Bramwell:

'What accounts do you hear of the dark horse Colin, who lately won the race and astonished the natives? I expect he will turn out to be "a clever hack" and a "good roadster."'

Among the numerous congratulations to the new Baron at that time from Judges, Q.C.'s, barristers, and solicitors, are the following letters from eminent lawyers in the United States, men free from the bias of comradeship, with no future professional interests or convenience to care for. In respect to jurisprudence and constitutional law the opinion of American lawyers of the first rank is always worth having.* Mr. Charles Curtis, of Boston, is, curiously

* See *post*, p. 193.

enough, almost the only writer who, in congratulating Baron Bramwell, immediately gave him his correct title, noting also the constitutional anomaly involved in Lord Wensleydale's ' life ' peerage. When made Lord Justice of Appeal, Sir George Bramwell had to ask Lord Coleridge whether he was in future to be called *M.* or *N.*, and what clothes he ought to wear. Lord Coleridge replied :

> ' Heaths Court, Ottery St. Mary,
> ' *October* 18, 1874.

' . . . I take it, when you are transferred, you will be known as Sir George Bramwell, *simpliciter*. I was told that was the proper way to speak of Baggallay, and you are now exactly in the same position that he is. Keep the *scarlet* gown for high days and holy days. It is handsome; a very old and historical piece of drapery; knits us on to the past; surely a bond to cling to if we can, without folly or prejudice, do so.'

Mr. Curtis wrote :

> ' Boston,
> ' *February* 18, 1856.

' MY DEAR BARON,

' It is a high honour to sit as a Judge of either of your three Courts ; but to be selected to fill the place vacated by such a magistrate as Baron Parke is a great addition to the distinction. We in the United States look on him as one of the most eminent jurists England has had the good fortune to possess. His judgments are of great weight, and are cited with deference by our most enlightened Judges. Does it ever come into your way to look into American Reports? Those of the Supreme Court of the United States, and those of the Supreme Judicial Court of Massachusetts, will satisfy you that we have made honourable progress in the science of jurisprudence, especially in Commercial Law. You may smile at the vanity which I exhibit when I venture to say that I think the Chief Justice of Massachusetts, Mr. Shaw, is the most accomplished commercial lawyer living.   During a practice of forty years, it has been my duty to acquaint myself with the Reports of the cases decided in your Courts, both ancient and modern ; and I honestly believe that if Chief Justice Shaw had had the same opportunity that Lord Mansfield had of (almost) originating a system of law out of the *indigesta moles,* which the Commercial Law was when he ascended and illustrated the Bench, he would have performed the duty with as much felicity as Mansfield.   I saw the volumes of our Reports in the library of Lincoln's Inn, and I see occasionally references at your Bar to American cases.   I had a letter from Sir James Willes soon after his appointment, which gratified me as to the evidence that he had not forgotten me.

' I observe that Baron Parke has accepted the title of Lord Wensleydale.   I am surprised that he should be willing to sink the name of Mr. Baron Parke.   It is said to be only *for his life.*   This I suppose to be an error.   I have always supposed that a peerage must be an inheritable title, failing, to be sure, if one die without heirs, but still, in its origin, never granted (and I have thought not grantable) for life merely. . . .

'CHARLES P. CURTIS.'*

---

* In contrast are some remarks from Chief Baron Pollock on the Dred-Scott decision, in a letter of March 30, 1857, to Sir George Bramwell, which show a very limited knowledge of the subject referred to ; the ' anomalous power of abrogating laws,' etc., being simply the equal and co-ordinate authority of the United States Supreme Court—' the linch-pin of the American Constitution ': ' . . . Notice has not been taken of that remarkable decision of the Supreme Court of the United States : " That it is of the essence of freedom that a man should have the power of holding others in slavery. . . ." It is an anomalous *power* to give to a Court of Justice—viz., that of abrogating laws agreed to by Congress, Senate, and President —on the ground that they are unconstitutional and inconsistent with the fundamental principles of the Republic.   The present use of the power is more strange than the power itself.   The decision is in substance this : " That it is an infringement of a man's natural liberty to prevent him from having a slave. . . ."'

Mr. Theodore Sidgwick wrote :

' New York,
' *February* 16, 1856.

'Did you receive a letter from me, a magazine, a barrel of apples ? Could *neither* my appeal to your sentiments, personal, critical, or gastric, elicit any response ? I write these few lines to say that I have sent you a magazine article on your law reform (the C.L.P. Act of 1852), and also (much more important) to express my satisfaction that you are on the Bench. It is good for the lamp of legal science, and a fitting reward of a laborious and successful career. . . .'

For the next twenty years Baron Bramwell sat on the Exchequer Bench, 'Her Majesty's peculiar court,' and he survived that august sanctuary which, thanks to the usurpations of successive Barons, had remained accessible to the King's subjects for the apocalyptic number of 666 years. He also was one of those who reformed it out of existence. In 1867, with Mr. Justice Blackburn and Sir J. D. Coleridge, he was made member of the Judicature Commission. In 1876 he was made a Lord Justice of Appeal, and administered the new Acts, fusing Law and Equity for five years. That is the bald record of his service on the Bench. Much wisdom spoken by him there, with profit to the Queen's subjects, lies buried in the Reports.

The first reported case in which he took part as Baron of the Exchequer was *Cook v. Hopewell.* Famous trials before him were the painful libel action of the *Earl of Lucan v. Smith,* raising the story of the Balaclava charge in 1854 ; the garrotting

cases in 1862, which made a profound impression
on the public mind, while the severe sentences
passed on the garrotters, especially by Baron
Channell,* made the same on them ; the famous

* On Baron Channell's retirement, Sir George Bramwell
thus wrote to·him :

'*January* 7, 1873.

'Dear Old Friend,

'So you have left us. Schoolfellows more than half a
century back, friends at the Bar for twenty years, and brothers
on the Bench for sixteen, we now part close company. I don't
like it—I am sure you are right to leave. Your judgment and
heart are too good for you to be wrong. But ours is a very
old association to come to an end. I am satisfied I must be a
good fellow, or we should not have been such friends. I am
sure you can hardly remember a sharp word between us all
this time. I heartily hope you will enjoy yourself ; you have,
at least, everybody's good wishes. What the *Times* said of
you is what all think and say. So farewell for the present, as
I certainly mean to see you again.

'Yours ever,
'G. Bramwell.'

Dr. May's was not Lord Bramwell's first school. When
quite a little chap, he had been a day-boarder at Dr. Reddy's
at Camberwell, where the late Baron Channell, three years his
senior, was head-boy. Of Dr. Reddy, this only is recorded—
that he used to aver that it was he who first taught Jowett
Greek. Baron Channell read for the law in Mr. Colmer's
chambers, and the two schoolfellows scarcely met again until
one day in the year 1839, when Mr. Channell held a brief in a
case at Maidstone Assizes. Consultation with the solicitors
revealed a technical flaw in the pleadings drawn by them,
which in those days would have proved absolutely fatal. The
solicitors could only hope that it would not be discovered.

' Who's against us ?' asked Channell.

' Oh,' was the reply, ' a Mr. Bramwell. Nobody ever heard
of him before.'

insurance case of *Wooley v. Pole*, in which a wealthy half-caste gentleman, tenant of Campden House, was alleged to have committed arson, and the resistance to Wooley's claim was said to have seriously damaged insurance companies' business ; the terrible case of the five pirates of the *Flowery Land*, the last convicts executed in public. August 21, 1867, he presided at the Old Bailey at the trial of G. Druitt, or Drewitt, M. Lawrence, and J. Adamson, officials of an Operative Tailors' Protection Association, indicted for carrying out 'picketing' in an illegal manner and with intimidation during an extensive tailors' strike in the spring of the year. Outrages committed by the Sawgrinders' Union at Sheffield had infamous notoriety at the time. Mr. (now Sir Harry) Poland and Mr. (afterwards Lord) Coleridge defended the three prisoners. Five others, mostly Irishmen, defended by Mr. Hardinge Giffard (now Lord Halsbury) were acquitted. In charging the jury, Baron Bramwell restated, in language which should never be forgotten, the imperishable Common Law rights of British subjects :

' The liberty of a man's mind and will to say how he shall bestow himself and his means, his talents, and his industry, is as much a subject of the law's protection as is that of his body. Generally speaking, the way in which people have endeavoured to control the operation of the minds of men is by putting

---

' Then, gentlemen, we're done,' was the advocate's remark. ' I was at school with that gentleman.'

And done they were. It was Mr. Bramwell's first Assize. In the year 1839 the leaders travelled by stage-coach. He took the steamboat to Gravesend, and walked to Maidstone to save coach fare.

restraints on their bodies, and therefore we have not so many instances in which the liberty of the mind was vindicated as was that of the body. Still, if any set of men agree among themselves to coerce that liberty of mind and thought by compulsion and restraint, they are guilty of a criminal offence—namely, that of conspiring against the liberty of mind and freedom of will of those towards whom they so conducted themselves. I am referring to coercion or compulsion—something that is unpleasant and annoying to the mind operated upon; and I lay it down as clear and undoubted law that if two or more persons agree that they will by such means co-operate together against that liberty, they are guilty of an indictable offence. The public has an interest in the way in which a man disposes of his industry and his capital; and if two or more persons conspire by threats, intimidation, or molestation to deter or influence him in the way in which he should employ his industry, his talents, or his capital, they are guilty of a criminal offence. That is the Common Law of the land, and it has been, in my opinion, re-enacted by an Act of Parliament passed in the sixth year of the reign of George IV., which provides in effect that any person who shall by threats, intimidation, molestation, or any other way obstruct, force, or endeavour to force, any journeyman to depart from his hiring, or prevent any journeyman from hiring, shall be guilty of an offence. That Act was passed forty-one years ago, and, by a statute of 1859, it was enacted that no workman, merely by reason of his endeavouring peaceably and in a reasonable manner and without threat or intimidation, direct or indirect, to persuade others from working or ceasing to work, should be guilty of an offence under the former Act of Parliament. In other words, the second Act said that should not be so if they did what they did in a reasonable and peaceful manner for the purposes of persuasion. . . . I am of opinion that if picketing is done in a way which excites no reasonable alarm, or does not coerce or annoy those who are the subjects of it, it is no offence in law. It is perfectly lawful to endeavour to persuade persons who had not hitherto acted with them to do so, provided that persuasion does not take the shape of compulsion or coercion. . . .'

Druitt, Lawrence and Adamson on Tuesday, and a fresh batch of picketers on Thursday, were found guilty. When they came up for sentence, Friday, August 23, Baron Bramwell, after consulting out of Court with Alderman Lusk, made an appeal to the prisoners in words which, in print, must always convey, to a generation which no longer sees such men as he, but a poor idea of his dignified manner, sonorous voice, and commanding expression, when speaking under strong emotion: '. . . Now I ask you in all kindness to listen to me, to listen to an impartial man . . . because the only interest I can have between you and your masters is that my clothes will cost me a few shillings more or less, which I do not consider will warp my judgment. . . .' Then he went on to point out the unfairness, injustice, and tyranny of their proceedings. In the end he dismissed the prisoners without passing any sentence.

A few days later, August 25, 1867, Sir William Erle wrote on the matter:

'. . . That job was done in a workmanlike manner. I hope it will do good, and am heartily glad you took the duty, for your own credit and the sake of the country. . . . In one of Scott's novels is there not a Bradwardine with motto, "Bewarr the Barr"? I thought you and your dog as photographed might take that motto for the picketers. . . .

'Bramshill, Liphook, *Sunday*.'

He alluded to it again from Bramshill, January 19, 1869:

'All I want to know is, How goes it with your lordship and your brave, sensible, faithful dog? I hope you are hearty and cheery. . . . I have one comfort "great and glorious," as Maw-worm says, and that is, in seeing Willes's sagacity in managing elections, as also in every other possible thing, duly appreciated by the *Times*, and therefore by Her Majesty's public in general. And now good-bye. I wish you health and happiness for many years to come with which to be brave and useful, as you were in *R. v. Druitt and others*, tailors' strike, which we put verbatim into our Report as an exposition of the existing law.'

The fate of the brave, faithful, sensible dog mentioned is told in a letter to the late Mr. Robert Hanbury, of Poles, Herts :

'January 8, 1876.

'DEAR SIR,

'I have received your letter about the Reformatory and Refuge Union. I am afraid it is a lithograph, consequently a circular, which neither calls for an answer nor justifies my writing. But I have as Judge known gentlemen of your name as High Sheriffs in Berks and I think in your county; you may be one of them. So perhaps you have written to me because you have known me, and perhaps I may be warranted in writing to you. If not, forgive me. Some years ago Mr. Blake, of Welwyn, gave me a most beautiful mastiff, bred by a gentleman of your name. I got very fond of him, and when he died of old age, to comfort me I got another, not so handsome, but the gentlest, most affectionate creature possible. He got killed on the railway about six weeks ago, to the great grief of myself and Lady Bramwell. Now to the point. If you are the breeder of these beautiful creatures, and will give or, if you are not will influence me, a puppy I will subscribe a liberal sum to the Union. I very much approve of it, and believe it does great good. In proof of which I venture to hand to you a promise of a small subscription. Pray excuse this : you would if you could tell how we have sorrowed over that dog—though you might think us very silly.

'Very truly yours,
'G. BRAMWELL.'

The result being that he gave Mr. Edgar Hanbury £20 for a robust mastiff puppy, six weeks old. This dog and Lord Bramwell also became great friends.

As a Judge, Baron Bramwell was always learning. His intimate correspondence, lasting for ten or twelve years, with Chief Baron Pollock, shows what these two men were ever most concerned about. February 20, 1859, Sir Frederick, who now and then was perhaps a little too fond of discoursing on Shakespeare and the musical glasses, says :

'. . . In writing to you I always feel as if I could write for ever, and pour out my whole soul through the nib of my pen. . . .'

These letters contain little about either man's own pride, profit, or pleasure ; much about plans for doing their duty in a better way, more wisely, more mercifully. August 7, 1858, Chief Baron Pollock writes :

'. . . It must be remembered that a legal sentence is not a punishment for moral sin (scarcely for legal guilt) ; its object is to deter others with as small an amount of human suffering as will answer that end.'

On August 8, 1857 :

'. . . As to usury, I consider it in the same light as incest. The law does not punish it ; but it is the duty of grave and decent Judges to denounce it when they come across it. . . .'

'*Sunday, April* 5, 1859.

'. . . Our circuit is glimmering in the socket. The Chief* (for I am only the Junior Judge of Assize) is a singularly able, clever man, but of rather undomestic habits. Have never seen him at breakfast ; always had to wait for him at dinner.

---

* Lord Campbell.

He has (as I told him one day) a *sublime contempt* for the *immaterialities of life.* In respect of *ermine* and *gold chains, trumpets* and scarlet cloth, very much of the *Martin* school; likes to get through the rind of the orange and reach the pulp as early as possible. . . .'

Again, July 20, 1860:

'. . . In a Post Office case, I rebelled and refused to give penal servitude to a sorter and deliverer who had been eighteen years in the Post Office, maintaining himself, a wife, and six children with a pound a week, but became a victim to the *wicked* practice of sending *coin* by the post. When Tenterden found that somebody was *always* ready to swear to a " promise to pay " a debt (barred by Statute of Limitations), he introduced a Bill requiring the promise to be in writing. When he saw that a new kind of action had sprung up (for giving a false character), which violated the spirit of the Statute of Frauds, he required all such " characters " to be in writing. . . . Why does not the Post Office lower the charge for Post Office orders, and refuse to convey *coin ?* . . . What is a poor devil to do with starving children, one or two of them sick, money in his *hand*, nothing to protect it but the *envelope ?* It is too bad ; it is scandalous ; it is disgraceful ; it is wicked. I declare war against it. . . .'

'*Tuesday, July* 16, 1861.

' I know little (indeed, nothing) of the discomforts of a Welsh circuit, and I don't mean to learn them. I know not whether I am to condole with you on bad lodgings and stingy magistrates, on drunken and stupid interpreters and incurably obstinate and corrupt jurors, or whether I am to congratulate you on tasting currouch da ! at the summit of Cader Idris.'

'*March* 22, 1863.

'. . . Eighteen months for knocking out brains is not *too much ;* on the contrary, *vastly too little.* But you have endeavoured to shift the question, which is, not whether the punishment was, *per se,* too much or too little, but whether at the end of ten years (and ten may be twenty as well as four) it is right to give the same punishment as would be given at first—all Nature says No in a case of murder. Take Eugene Aram's case, or Governor Wall's (assuming both to have been guilty), you can still do nothing but hang—that is, if you do anything. Governor Wall's case was, however, somewhat questionable, and the Ministry would have spared him if they could have mustered courage to do so, or could have found any excuse for it. . . .'

'March 28, 1863.

'. . . I think physiologically you are quite right about *digestion*. I should certainly take very bad care of *your* digestion.* (I do not take very good care of my own.) But to argue in favour of selfishness on this account is to confound physics and metaphysics, morals and matter.'

'August 31, 1863.

'. . . You are making a prodigious fuss about the abridgment of the long vacation, as if " Bramwell's Abridgment " was an extraordinary work. I remember being engaged at Lancaster in a cause before Bailey in the month of September, and my long vacation consisted of *one* day, which enabled me to travel to London and attend Lord Tenterden's sittings (he was then only Sir Charles Abbott) *the following day*. This was before Scarlett's Bill passed which fixed the terms, secured us a " long vacation " of decent and reasonable length, and gave us a short vacation, commonly called Scarlett's holidays. While the Chief Justice himself received much in fees for business done, his clerk (I believe) a great deal more, and his son (the associate) still more, he worked like a trooper. But when he (and the son) were put on salaries, he was quite content with the " inactivity " to which the statute condemned him, by giving twenty-four days of sitting after each term and no more, unless by consent. It is above thirty years since all this happened, and you (young gentlemen) know little about it. And as to your *stay* at Croydon, I was once three weeks at Guildford myself. The malignant did indeed say that I dawdled on to shirk the Old Bailey. But I sat every day as

---

* See p. 139, " Laissez Faire," pamphlet.

3—2

late as you do now. You are right; it is as late as a Court ought to sit when it sits "*de die, in diem.*"'

'*Monday, August* 28, 1865.

'. . . What a pedant that doubting lawyer must be who at once caused Charlotte Winsor to be respited. Was it Parke, or Rolfe, and why did not the Chancellor* (feeble man !) ask at once the *personal* opinion of the Judges, and act upon the result ? There is no plea to raise the question on a writ of Error. And no point was reserved for the Court of Criminal Appeal, therefore there cannot be a true *judicial* inquiry ; the proceeding must be extra-judicial. No doubt a Court *may* discharge the jury, and in this case it is too late to inquire whether it was done with perfect accuracy or not. Does the blockhead mean to say that if it were *now* discovered that a wrong man served on the jury, the prisoner ought not to be executed ? In Frost's case nine of the Judges thought my objection a good one (that the list of the jury and the copy of the indictment ought to have been delivered "*together*," *simultaneously*), but nine thought the objection was taken *too late*. Oh dear ! oh dear ! when will pedantry and folly cease ? . . .'

'Committee business has attracted —— to London, and he has given up a *Ni. Pri.* brief here in a will case. *Qua propter* they have withdrawn the record. *He* will get one or two hundred guineas. *His client* will be put to the expense of five or six hundred. I don't like the *morale* of this. . . . There *ought* to be some power to notice and check or control such things. If he had said, "I will not remain unless you give me a further fee of 200 guineas," he would have been said to do a very unprofessional thing. As it is, what has he done ? . . . Worse than "not going to church," or than omitting in the sentence of death a prayer for mercy on the soul of the murderer. *You* are right in omitting it—I think so. I always omit it myself. In truth, the introduction of it was an " intrusion " Unless the sentence is certain to be carried into effect—an event never certain, of which I don't complain—it

* Lord Westbury.

is, I think, wrong to utter such a prayer. I am not sure that we are not now ripe for the abolition of the punishment of death—even for murder.'

' *September* 3, 1865.

' . . . The papers have been making a great fuss about the lenient sentences of Judges when women are convicted "*of concealing the birth by putting away the body.*" The fault is in the *Legislature*, which made an *imaginary crime*, and wished to make the Judges parties to the fraud of convicting the accused of *one* thing and punishing her for *another*. I have no doubt the Legislature meant the Judges to give a very severe sentence when there had been foul play with the child, and a nominal sentence almost when there was no suspicion of anything wrong. But the Judges won't be parties to this kind of fraud —one can call it nothing else. . . .

' . . . Why should not a woman who has occasioned the death of her child by carelessness, negligence, some improper conduct (not amounting to murder), be convicted of *man-slaughter?* The State seems to take it for granted that she must be convicted of murder or be acquitted. Is that so? And would not conviction of manslaughter be *some* remedy for the evil ?'*

' *October* 13, 1865.

' . . . *Practically* I quite agree with you as to the imaginary crime of *concealing a birth*. As a fact, it is consistent with perfect innocence of anything, *save want of chastity*. It *may* also be connected with, and arise out of, a foul and cruel murder. All that the jury find is a fact consistent with perfect innocence, or possibly with great crime; then the Judge has to decide *which*. I have a rooted aversion to punish prisoners for a crime of which the *jury* have not found them guilty. You are quite right; I never *did* pass any such sentence as eighteen months' or two years' imprisonment for concealing a birth. It should be for the jury, not the Judge, *to find* that the *child had not fair play*. Our law (it is one of its great defects) has only two

---

* See Voltaire, *Commentaire sur les délits et les peines*, 1766; developing the ideas of the Marchesi di Beccaria.

kinds of *criminal slaying—murder* and *manslaughter*. You may
object to my analogy, that a Judge is bound to look into a case
of manslaughter and decide between a fine of one shilling or
penal servitude for life. But the jury *there* find *criminal slaying*.
Here they do *not*. Next time I have a case that admits of it,
I will leave to the jury to find a verdict of *manslaughter*. Why
not ? " The Court (Bramwell) I am not sure—I agree; but
take a rule." . . .'

Much the same problem is touched on in a letter
from Mr. Robert Lowe, ex-Home Secretary, to
Baron Bramwell :

' 36, Lowndes Square.
'*June* 30, 1874.

'. . . Of course we cannot define murder by reference to
manslaughter, and manslaughter by reference to murder. . . .
There must be a definition of those things which reduce murder
to manslaughter. Perhaps they need *not* be stated, but the
Act might refer to the Common Law. Fitzjames Stephen has
tried his hand, and has so managed that he limits manslaughter
to cases where there was no intention to kill, thus making *all*
killing under provocation murder.'

The Parliamentary Elections Act of 1868 (31 and
32 Vict., c. 125) made election petitions triable
' before a Puisne Judge . . . at Westminster or in
Dublin.' Instinctively Sir Alexander Cockburn,
Baron Bramwell, and others of their colleagues,
saw, although they may not have fully explained
why, that the new work thrown on them was a dis-
tortion of the true functions of the judiciary—
functions which Parliament either could not understand or did not care to preserve intact. Business
in the courts of law had increased with the growth
of the nation, was ever increasing. Behind the
obvious and unanswerable arguments for reform of

procedure which justified sundry legal changes (including, perhaps, the Judicature Acts) of subsequent years, there was a growing ambition within the House of Commons to stretch supervision and direction by the Legislature to a point dangerous to the authority of the judiciary. Maintenance of justice and adjudication of individual claims of right had too long been left to the Judges. Parliament meant to look more minutely after 'social justice' in future. Although, technically, the Elections Act seemed to widen the scope of judicial authority, it was in the true spirit of English jurisprudence that Chief Baron Sir F. Pollock protested, February 21, 1868, against the new policy. The growing indifference of the public to the details of Parliamentary elections and the fate of candidates probably accounts for the nonfulfilment of some of Sir F. Pollock's prophecies. He underestimated, too, public confidence in the perfect impartiality of the Bench.

'. . . 1st. I entirely approve of the Judges declining to do the *dirty* work of the House of Commons. When parties were allowed by consent to dispense with a jury, it was left to the Judge to act upon that consent *or not at his discretion*. My rule was *not* to dispense with the jury when the *facts* were *really in dispute*. In the case of a contested election the *facts alone* are in dispute ninety-nine times out of a hundred. Truth is to be looked for (and not always to be got) in a mass of perjury and corruption, which would defile the mind of a Judge—to look at. Our business is with *principles*, not *fact*. Even in the court business in *Banco*, if a difficult question of fact arose, it was often (by an issue) referred to a jury. And there is good reason for all this. A jury decide "aye" or "no," and give no reasons. No ill-will arises. A Judge would have been expected to do much more; to give the result of his sifting of the case in something like a deliberate judgment, raising a storm of *ill-will, slander,* and *misrepresentation* against himself by saying which of the witnesses he thought had been guilty of perjury.   It seems idle to talk of the *authority of Parliament*, or that the Judges have despised it.   No doubt Parliament might take my estate from me and give it to you.   But what would be thought of a gentleman who asked an upper servant to take care of his books and pictures, and then desired him to scour the stairs, saying he was a servant and bound to do whatever he was told.   A dirty candlestick should not be wiped with a cambric pocket-handkerchief—*assez pour cela.* . . .

'. . . Poor —— died in the morning of the day when you wrote.   He was "an eloquent gentleman," an indifferent *lawyer*, and a very bad *Judge*.'

Meantime, February 19, 1868, Mr. R. Lowe, Chancellor of the Exchequer, in reply to Sir George Bramwell's own remonstrances, put the official Liberal view of that epoch, inspired to some extent by Jacobin enmity to English juridical ideas and by zeal for Parliamentary, official, or departmental ascendency — evil legacies to English Liberalism from Bentham and Austin.   The Judges, Mr. Lowe hints, are superior Civil Servants, Government inspectors in wigs.

'. . . We have no right to overwork you, and I, at least, would not be a party to any proposal which could be shown to have that effect.   Whether the advantages of having the work done by you are overbalanced by the chance of soiling your ermine, I will not argue.   You are not " the judges " of it.   It is the duty of Parliament (not the House of Commons) to hear with respect what you say, and then decide.   Before you the question is, I think, *coram non judice,* invincible repugnance notwithstanding.   As to our having no moral right to impose the duty on you, I should agree, if it were not *ejusdem generis* with the duties you perform already.   You find issues of fact at *Nisi Prius*; in matters of practice your main business is to apply law to fact; I entirely decline so to circumscribe the power of Parliament as to admit that we ought not to require you to deal with other facts or other laws. A much stronger case was the jurisdiction given to the Court of Common Pleas about railways; equally strong the appeal from revising barristers. You don't like the job because it is full of anger and discord. My butler might just as reasonably object to carry the urn because it is hot. I write in a hurry, and with some lack of gravity, but I really cannot admit your arguments. . . .'

On January 12, 1872, the Rev. John Selby Watson, an eminent scholar, was sentenced by Mr. Justice Byles to death (commuted to penal servitude for life) for killing his wife in a fit of passion. At Bow Street one of the prisoner's quotations had been: ' Sæpe olim semper debere nocuit debitori.' Mr. Robert Lowe, it is related, divided the Cabinet on the question whether this was good or bad Latin. The majority said good. Christina Edmunds, sentenced to death, January 16, for poisoning children at Brighton, was reprieved on grounds of insanity.

On February 3, 1872, the Baron wrote to the *Spectator*:

'THE OBJECT OF THE ENGLISH CRIMINAL LAW.

' The two recent trials of Watson and Edmunds have shown the uncertainty and contradiction of opinions on the subject of how far insanity should exempt one who breaks the criminal law from its penalties. The following is an attempt to ascertain the principle:

' Whom should the law punish ? It is obvious that it should punish all whom it threatens, who knowingly break it, and are convicted thereof. To threaten punishment and not punish would be idle. To say that stealing should be punished with three months' imprisonment, arson with eight years' penal servitude, and murder with death, but on conviction not to pass or enforce those sentences, would be nugatory. The question, then, first is, Whom should the law threaten? It seems an obvious answer to say: All on whose minds it may operate, all whom it may deter by its threat. It would be useless to threaten those who could not understand the threat. It would be useless to threaten punishment to an idiot for disobeying the law, doing wrong, or injuring another, if the intellect of that idiot was such that it did not understand the meaning of disobedience of the law, doing wrong, and injuring another. So if a man laboured under a delusion that someone was attempting his life, and believed that facts existed which, if they really existed, would justify his taking that other's life, it would be useless to threaten him. He would say, "I have obeyed your law," and he would have meant to obey it. His mistake would be no reason for punishing him as for wilful breach of a law. It is so in the case of a sane person. If a man shoots another in the apparent act of committing burglary, the shooter is not punishable, though it turns out he was mistaken in supposing burglary was being committed.

'The law, then, should threaten, and consequently punish, those on whose minds it may operate, all whom it may deter. This is the law of England at present as laid down by the Judges in their answers to questions put to them by the House of Lords in McNaghten's case. Should there be any exception to this rule? . . .

'Let us examine the supposed exemption of an offender of unsound mind. It is said mad people ought not to be punished. If not, they ought not to be threatened. But why ought they not to be threatened if the threat may operate on their minds, if it may deter them? It is said that there are certain manias which irresistibly impel to crime, and that though the threat of the law is understood, there is no wilful disobedience of it. Now, what are these manias? The two most frequently heard of in connection with crime are the homicidal mania and the stealing, or kleptomania. A man troubled with these has a strong desire to kill and to steal. These manias, as they are called, do not consist in disease, unsoundness, or a non-sane state of the *mind*, but of the passions or appetites. The homicidal maniac has a morbid craving for taking life. The not doing so is painful to him, the doing so pleasurable. We may wonder that it should be so, but so it is. Not a natural appetite, or source of pain or pleasure, it is so in this man. So of the kleptomaniac. He likes to take from others the property that belongs to them, and have it in his own possession. . . . There are other cases of " mania," supposing that to be the right word. About ten or twelve years ago a man was tried and sentenced at Monmouth under the following circumstances: He was a collier in the employ of the Ebbw Vale Company. Their manager gave him the very best character. He was their best workman, sober, honest, and a deacon at his chapel. But he had this mania: he used to lie in wait on a mountain where a footpath crossed from one valley to another, and then outrage women with circumstances of atrocious cruelty. There were nineteen indictments against him, and many other cases where the sufferers would not come forward. He was convicted on four, and sentenced to penal servitude for life. Why was not this a case of mania? We read in the papers a few days ago of a boy in London, of about fifteen years of age, whose delight was to fracture the skulls of small children. He had done it on several occasions. That was his mania. Now the mad-doctors call these cases cases of moral insanity. But would it not be more correct to call them cases of insane morality; *i.e.*, are they not cases where the desire to do mischief is not counteracted by a morality sound enough to prevent commission of the offences they lead to? Why should the persons who commit offences under the influence of their vicious desires or appetites—or " manias," if that is the right word—not be punished, *i.e.*, not be threatened with punishment? It is said by the mad-doctors and their followers that they, the persons breaking the law under such influences, do not break it wilfully—that they can't help it. " See," it is said; " what is the use of your threat of punishment on this man? He has disregarded it under an irresistible impulse."

' He has disregarded it, no doubt, and the impulse or temptation was too great for the countervailing considerations. The same argument might be used in the case of all offenders, however sane; the temptation has been too great for them. But the justification of punishment, the reason for the threat of punishment, is not to be found in its effect on those whom it does *not* deter, but on those whom it *does*. Watson was not deterred from killing his wife in a most barbarous way by the law's threat that he would be hanged if he did, but are there not many who are? Is there no husband who would like to knock his wife's brains out, but is deterred by knowing what the law says shall happen if he is convicted of doing so? Another way the argument is put is this: "Poor fellow! his case is a hard one; he did not have an equal chance with his fellow-creatures. He knew he was doing wrong; but, then, his intelligence was small, his power of self-control was small, his propensities maniacally vicious, so he is not responsible. To the question, Is such a person as hateful as a person of strong mind and no morbid appetite who deliberately did wrong for his own profit or gain? the answer would readily be, No. But that is not the question. The question is, Should the law not direct its threat against one who stands so much in need of it, who, unless fortified by it, is so likely to do wrong? What would be thought of the law if it should say in so many words: "You have a strong propensity to kill, therefore if you do you shall not be punished; you have a strong propensity to steal, therefore if you do you shall not be punished; and, further, if you, the homicidal maniac, steal, you shall not be punished, because your mind must be feeble. So of you, the kleptomaniac, you may commit robbery with impunity—in short, both of you, having evil propensities, may commit any offence without punishment"? What would be said of a father who should say to his sons: "You, John, are a good boy, but if you rob an orchard in my absence I will flog you; you, Thomas, are a badly-disposed boy, who, when my back is turned, will certainly steal my neighbours' apples if you can, therefore I will not punish you"? And where this argument to stop? I have a homicidal mania, therefore do not punish me for homicide or other offences; I have a kleptomania, therefore do not punish me; I, says the Monmouth offender, have a peculiar physical or mental development, therefore do not punish me; I, says a fourth, am really not a bad man, but have lived all my life among thieves, and am as much inclined to steal as a kleptomaniac; I, says a fifth, am really a good and well-conducted person, but I was in great want, there was no witness near, the owner was rich, so the temptation to steal the watch was irresistible. Irresistible! All we know is that the deterring considerations were not enough. Had a policeman been present when Watson slew his wife, would his temptation have been irresistible? Would Edmunds have given the poisoned sweets to be taken to the confectioner if a policeman had been within hearing? The argument comes to this: Wherever a person is likely, from feeble intelligence or morbid appetite, to commit a crime, wherever the threat of the law is most needed, there the person is to be pitied, and the threat withheld. Why not in every case where the offender is to be pitied?

'It may be said the man ought to be punished, but not so severely as the man of strong mind. Why, the question is, What punishment ought to be *threatened?* Give what is threatened—all or none. Take the two cases I have referred to. Watson's was a most savage, furious murder; not one, but many blows must have been given. Do not furious passions require repression? The other was a most cruel, deliberate murder, undertaken to screen the offender from suspicion of having tried to murder a woman for whose husband she had an adulterous affection. If her insanity tended to this, would it not have been a good thing that she should have had constantly ringing in her ears "The gallows"? Our criminal law is in a curious state. Watson is found guilty, and, as everybody agrees, properly, according to the law as it exists. One of the Judges is said to have expressed an opinion that he ought not to be executed. This seems odd. Let us suggest that the Judges at large vote on such a question. I should think if they had it would have gone hard with that savage murderer. So as to Edmunds, the jury say, and everybody is satisfied, that she is not within the rule the law lays down excepting offenders from punishment on the ground of insanity. It is said that the Judge who tried her doubts if she is not insane, more or less, and Sir W. Gull says she is. What if she is? Her insanity is not the question, but her knowledge that she was doing wrong. Let us not blame the Home Secretary, one of the ablest we have had for many years, and of whose duties none is so difficult as that of advising or withholding mercy. The cases are curious. Watson is "the Rev. Mr. Watson," "Mr. Watson the clergyman," "the venerable-looking prisoner," and so a factitious pity is got up for him in some. As you say, is it clear the same sympathy would have been felt if Mick Connor had knocked his wife's brains out with his pick-axe? And so of Miss Edmunds. Is it certain that no pity was felt for the lady whose relations were so respectable, though of doubtful intellect? These are, as you say, cases that make one wonder if an unconscious feeling for respectable people has not influenced the exertions to save these two most grievous offenders.

' While on this subject, attention may be called to a strange state of the law. Some years ago a commission recommended that unpremeditated murder should not be punished capitally. The report was of such a character (to say no worse of it) that legislation did not follow on it, but the Home Office acts on that recommendation, so that, *pro tanto*, it has repealed the law as to murder.

' The present state of things is most unsatisfactory. If the Home Secretary is not strong enough to deal with these questions (and none is more capable than the present), let some tribunal be constituted which can. At present it is chaos.

' Ex.'

A *Times* letter of October 28, 1885, applies equally stern reasoning to the case of Louis Riel :

' " There is a general expression of editorial opinion," in the United States, that " Riel ought not to be hung." I am of a very different opinion. No man needs severe punishment so much as a defeated patriot who has risen in rebellion against

the State. In ordinary cases of crime disgrace is the consequence of conviction. If a man picks a pocket or steals a
sheep, besides the law's punishment, he loses character. But
see the case of the rebel. If he succeeds he becomes an
emperor, or president, or other distinguished and well-paid
personage. If he fails, he has all the honours of patriotism,
and if punished of martyrdom—" much sympathy " is felt with
him. Then, consider the offence. It is not *one* murder, rape,
arson, wounding, plunder, but many. I say therefore that the
rebel in general needs heavy punishment. But Riel in particular is a very bad rebel. He offered not to rebel if a few
thousand dollars were paid to him. He rebelled for gain.
Further, this is the second time. He has done it before and
been forgiven. Then there is a talk about his insanity. This
was carefully considered by the Court in Canada, and held to
be unfounded. He has done more mischief than a score of
murderers, burglars, and other criminals.

' BRAMWELL.'

In December, 1887, he wrote to *Jus*, an Individualist journal, since discontinued, almost repeating
what P. B. Shelley says in ' Declaration of Rights :'
' No man has a right to disturb the public peace
by personally resisting the execution of a law, however bad. He ought to acquiesce, using at the same
time the utmost powers of his reason to promote its
repeal.' The influence of Godwin (the first of
Radical Unionists) and of Bentham is recognizable
in both passages.

' PASSIVE OBEDIENCE.

' In *Jus* of November 18 appeared a paragraph to which I
respectfully object. I regret to see it in a publication entitled
to authority from its two qualities of ability and honesty. You
say, speaking of children being forcibly vaccinated, " If the
German vaccination law were the law in England, we should
censure the administrator who shrank from enforcing it to the

letter. But we should censure far more severely the craven cur who submitted to such a law. In our opinion it would be the duty of the administrators of the law to carry it out, and the duty of the citizen to shoot the *scoundrel* who attempted to perpetrate the outrage."

'How can this be? How can a man be a scoundrel for doing his duty? How can it be the duty of any man to shoot him for so doing? Please to remember that you do not strengthen your case by calling names. I should be the craven cur you speak of. I should think it my duty to obey the law or leave the country where it existed. The sovereign power honestly and for the good of the community enact a law. Surely it is the duty of the citizen or subject to obey it. Why may not every man disobey any law he disapproves of, if you are right? There are plenty of conscientious crimes; but we punish them of necessity.

'Yours, etc.,
'BRAMWELL.'

The editor appended a note, in which the familiar arguments for the 'sacred right of rebellion,' the other side of this unsolved problem, were ably and ingeniously put.

On April 7, 1883, he thus, in the *Economist*, exposed fallacies which crop up whenever a 'great' murder case looms large in the newspapers:

'CRIMINAL APPEALS.

'The Bill introduced by the Attorney-General on Monday, to allow an appeal to prisoners convicted of capital offences, involves a very great change in English procedure, nothing less than a second trial in all grave criminal cases, for it is absurd to suppose that the appeal can long be confined to capital charges. *Primâ facie* its effect must be injurious. The confidence of the community in the method of trying criminals, now quite perfect, must be weakened; for the public, which judges roughly, will perceive that the courts are not trusted either by Government or Parliament; will not see why, if the first tribunal can go gravely wrong, the second cannot go wrong also. Popular belief in justice, which is quite as important as justice itself, will be impaired, and will not again be strengthened, for the marvellous care now displayed in a capital case is certain to be relaxed. The jury will feel that the ultimate responsibility is not on them; counsel will be much more careless in sifting evidence; above all, witnesses, already heavily punished by the cruel treatment meted out to them, will be twice as reluctant to come forward. They will be kept from their duties and their avocations for weeks on end. Moreover, popular *fear* of justice—which is next to popular *confidence* in justice in importance—will be greatly weakened. Proceedings will be so long, so confused, and so uncertain, owing to the great pressure of opinion which will weigh upon the Appellate Court as it now weighs upon the Home Secretary, that the whole dramatic effect of punishment, in which much of its deterrent power consists, will be lost. Intending criminals will argue that, after all, they have only to run a limited amount of risk, and will have many chances in their favour. That is a most dangerous consequence of the change. Experience shows that while criminals, especially habitual criminals, are daunted by very light punishments, if certain, they will face any punishment, however terrible, even the gallows itself, if there is a visible proportion of chances in their favour. The penalty of death never deterred sheep-stealers, because there was always the chance that juries would be induced by humanity to acquit; they are deterred by the present light punishment, because it is nearly certain to be inflicted. The criminal's impression as to chances, and not the chances themselves, is to be considered. The criminal's impression will be that he is to have two trials, in one of which he may escape; while escape in either means immunity. Terror of the law will be lessened. What with public lenity, dislike to executions, and the increasing cleverness of criminals, it has already been diminished to the farthest limits of expediency. Far-seeing Judges, like Sir Fitzjames Stephen, are asking for greater rigour.

' Such a change should only be made for one of three reasons —to simplify procedure, to secure justice more perfectly, or to protect the innocent.   None of these ends will be attained. Procedure will be far more complicated than at present, for there will be two trials, two sets of expenses, and a double burden laid upon all witnesses.   The dread of commencing a prosecution which constantly—*e.g.*, in poisoning cases—shields the wrong-doer will be grievously, and justly, increased. Delays, always the opprobrium of English justice, will be indefinitely multiplied.   The Attorney-General hinted that the appeal would always be heard during the three weeks now allowed the prisoner to prepare for death; but papers, lawyers, and witnesses must all be brought from distant places to London; Judges are often immersed in other business; postponement will be the first object of the criminal's counsel; the country will be fortunate if three months is ordinarily found sufficient. As for justice, that is not even the object of the Bill.   The main cause of injustice all over the United Kingdom is the readiness of juries to acquit, in defiance of the law.   So injurious is prejudice in favour of the accused, that in England it is next to impossible to obtain a verdict against a woman accused of infanticide.   In Ireland, in times of excitement, persons accused of murder, treason, or outrage threatening life invariably escape.   If the Crown were allowed in such cases to appeal to a superior Court, sitting without juries, the chances of justice being done would be greatly increased.   No such appeal is allowed.   No effort is made to secure conviction when the law has been defeated; every effort is made to secure the criminal, when, after infinite trouble, justice is at last to be done upon him.   The Bill is entirely one-sided.   The claim of the victim, say of a dynamite outrage, which ought to be as strong as the claim of the murderer, is entirely overlooked. Finally, the protection of the innocent is not increased.   Sir Henry James says it will be increased because miscarriages of justice do occur; men are convicted through the prejudice or ignorance of juries.   Sir William Harcourt alone, in his two years of office, has been compelled to pardon twelve men regularly convicted.   Granting that they are rightly pardoned (which is by no means certain), what does that prove, except that the Home Office is a very competent and lenient tribunal, which ought not to be superseded, as it practically would be, by any Court of Appeal? It stands to reason that such should be the fact. The Home Office is constantly, in capital cases, placed in possession of facts, from irregular confessions, which, if examined in Court, would be retracted, from the statements of wives, which cannot be heard at the trial, and from the prisoner's own evidence, which is inadmissible in court, that enable the skilled officials of the department to reach nearer the actual truth than the public tribunal has done. Sir W. Harcourt is helped, not impeded, by his "anomalous" position as an unrecognized Judge, by his ability to hear anything, by the secrecy he can enforce, by his freedom from the fear of setting dangerous precedents ; and, aided as he is by the careful trial below, by the Judge's notes, and by the absence of counsel's eloquence, he becomes much more efficient than any jury. It would be an injury to the innocent to limit his powers, and they will be seriously limited by the new Court of Appeal. He will never like to upset its decisions without giving his reasons ; that may often be impossible, or contrary to the public interest. He will be strongly tempted to examine the case with insufficient care; the accused has had a fair public trial and an appeal, and why, the Home Secretary will think, should he interfere? If he does not interfere Parliament can say nothing. Besides, he can hardly even begin to examine the case until the Appellate Court has heard it, and then either the remaining time will be reduced to hours, or the Home Secretary will be obliged to grant those postponements, which, even if they are not inhuman—and we must recollect the prisoner approves them—diminish the most useful effect of the law, the awe created by a just sentence. They stir up a feeling of pity for the prisoner, which destroys the sense of the justice of the verdict, and will, in the end, help a false public sentiment to render capital sentences impossible. That, indeed, is probably one object of the change, and it is a bad object, the law being already weakened by various causes until the only grand protection of life is the certainty that the wilful murderer will hang. Death frightens a man like Carey the informer, who would face calmly any sentence of imprisonment, with its chances of subsequent pardon, rescue, or escape.'

4—2

In 1867 he had been member of the Neutrality Laws Commission, in 1868 of the Naturalization Laws Commission. This to the third Lord Tenterden, then Permanent Under-Secretary of State for Foreign Affairs, and Lord Granville's reply, bring out some of the divergencies between law, as Lord Bramwell understood it, and that myth ' International Law ' :

' Bodmin,
' *March* 21, 1872.

' There seems to me to be a way out of the *Alabama* difficulty, not only consistent with our honour and interest, but necessary, and one which *must* be taken. . . .

' . . . Let us protest that the arbitrators have no jurisdiction in the matter of indirect damages or claims, and under that protest attend the arbitration. It seems to me we *must* attend in any case. Let us see what would be the position of parties subject to our laws. A and B refer matters to arbitration. On attending before the arbitrators, A prefers a claim which B says is not within the submission and over which the arbitrators have no jurisdiction ; moreover, he says it is not a valid claim. The arbitrators *must* entertain it, and either hold it to be, or not to be, within their jurisdiction ; if they hold it to be within their jurisdiction, they *must* adjudicate it to be well or ill founded. Now, their jurisdiction is in no way affected by B's non-attendance. He had a *right* to attend. He may give up, or refuse to exercise that right, but the jurisdiction of the arbitrators is not affected by his doing so. The arbitrators then will award :

' First, that they have no jurisdiction over this matter.

' Or, secondly, that they have, and that the claim is ill-founded.

' Or, thirdly, that they have, and that the claim is well founded.

' In all of the three events they will adjudicate on the other claims quoted. In the first case, if the submission was conditional, with an *ita quoad*, that the award should be on all matters referred, A, and perhaps B, might contest the validity of the award.   In the second case, it would be binding on both parties.   In the third case, B might contest its validity *quoad* the disputed claim, but would be bound by the rest of the award, unless the matters were so mixed up as not to be separable.

'How does the present case differ from this?   True, we have notice before attending the arbitration that the claim will be made; but that in no way affects the arbitrator's jurisdiction.   Suppose we don't attend, suppose the Americans do; suppose the arbitrators decide, *re* indirect claims, in our favour, but in consequence of our non-attendance, and not putting our case before them, award £10,000,000 for *direct* claims, how can we refuse to pay it?

'It will be said that by attending we acknowledge the jurisdiction of the arbitrators over these indirect claims.   Not so. If there were nothing but these claims in dispute, there might be some ground for such a contention.   But there are other matters, in respect to which we *must* attend.   If, then, we must attend, we must.   What we should be careful to do is to attend under such a protest as shall show we do not admit the arbitrators' jurisdiction over indirect claims.   Now for the result.   The arbitrators say:

'First, they have *no* jurisdiction over indirect claims.

'Or, secondly, they have, and award in our favour.

'Or, thirdly, they have, and award against us, say, £200,000,000.

'In the first two cases we are content.   The third would be awkward.   But, in the first place, it will not happen; nobody, not even Sumner, expects or fears it.   Secondly, it is more likely to happen if we do not attend than if we do.   If it should be said that by our attending we recognize jurisdiction, the answer is the one I have given, viz., that we *must* attend for other matters.   Thirdly, if such an award was made against us, we must refuse to pay on the ground we now take, viz., that we are not liable.

'This may be said to be a lawyer's view of the matter. None the worse for that.   For the law in these matters is good sense, reason, and justice.

'G. Bramwell.'

Earl Granville, then Foreign Secretary, replied :

‘ 16, Bruton Street,
‘ London, W.,
‘ *March* 29, 1872.

‘ I was much interested by your letter to Tenterden, and
should much like to adopt your view, which I suspect would
carry little risk with it. But will it not be said that in civil
matters there is an authority to confirm awards ; the parties
may find themselves bound, if they do not proceed, in case
they differ about the arbitrator’s jurisdiction, or about an
award made *ex parte ?* On the other hand, if the arbitrator
exceeds his jurisdiction, they have their legal remedy in the
Courts, which will treat the award as a nullity.

‘ Among nations there is nothing of this sort. Hence their
usual, and necessary, course has been to treat an agreement as
having fallen through when they differed about its meaning.
The great difficulty of this particular reference is that there
might be an unfavourable award, *really founded more or less on
the indirect claims*, without showing on the face of it that this
was so.’

Roundell, first Earl of Selborne, wrote :

‘ 30, Portland Place,
‘ *October* 18, 1872.

‘ . . . I have to thank you, and I do so very heartily, for
your extremely kind note. I am the more glad that my
reference to your name and authority, at Geneva, gave you
pleasure ; because (as I need hardly say) it was not made
with any other view than to the legitimate purpose of an
argument, in which I did not desire to practise any arts of
advocacy, but merely to contend for what I believed (according
to the best of my light) to be just and true.’

‘ Lord Bramwell’s tastes and habits were of the
simplest,’ writes one who knew him well in his
last years. ‘ He did not care much for club life ;
preferred his own fireside, and a book, or a chat

with a friend. A great lover of billiards, but would put down his cue in the middle of a break to listen to the sorrows of a poor neighbour.' Although he knew everybody worth knowing, and was peer of any living English subject outside the succession, he never was in that fashionable society the delights of which consist of showing one's self off, abusing one's friends, or making love to their relations, none of which things he was able to do.

Here are his ideas in May, 1873, when, presiding at the fourth annual meeting of the South-Eastern Railway Company Provident Savings Bank, he utilized his holiday off the Bench to indulge in a long chat with the company's men, full of homely wisdom and 'the salt of life':

'. . . Of all the good things which this world gives us, the best, in my judgment, are liberty and independence . . . liberty for each man to think and act for himself, and independence which gives him the power to do that which he deems best for his own happiness, and for the happiness of those he cares for. I believe that these good things, like any others, can be acquired in one way only. The best friend you can have, one who never fails you (he is not a very sentimental friend), is a well-filled purse. Without that . . . a man is sure to be somebody's servant; he has not got that which will enable him . . . to exercise his own judgment as to what is best for himself, with whom he shall work, and what work will do for him. . . . But how is a man to acquire this valuable though unsentimental friend? Only in one way—by industry, prudence, and thrift. . . . Of the good things which Nature has provided, there are very few in which we can stretch out our hand merely to collect them. We must labour to get them. . . . The Italians have a saying about "Sweet do-nothing." I do not think that proverb will ever be naturalized in England. Something in the vigorous nature of Englishmen makes a certain amount of work necessary for them. My own feeling is that the greatest punishment I could be doomed to would be to be perfectly idle—it would be the worst thing that could happen to me. I do not, of course, recommend that men should do nothing but work. When one hears of people being sixteen or twenty hours upon an engine, it is lamentable. Where work is extended in such a way as that, a man does not work to live, but is living to work. . . . Now, then, how to keep wealth. People must be prudent. The first way in which prudence is exhibited or may be exhibited—for I am sorry to say a great many people fail in it, especially in agricultural parts of the country—is with respect to marriage. I speak with some knowledge of what takes place in my own neighbourhood near one of our stations. The boys and girls—for I cannot call them men and women—get married when they have not a single shilling to begin housekeeping with, positively without a table or chair or a bed to lie down upon. . . . There is another way in which money is improvidently spent, and that is in dress. Now, we men are not so subject to that infirmity as the other sex. . . . In moderation, I like people to take a pride in their appearance; for, as a rule, people cannot be smart without being clean, and " cleanliness is next to godliness." . . . On the other hand, it is very foolish to waste money upon dress, whatever a man's station in life may be. There is a particular class of people, whom I won't name more particularly, who go round and persuade women to take goods which they have not the means to pay for. I wish I had the making of a law bearing on their cases ;* I would undertake

---

* One finds Lord Bramwell, in 1873, rejoicing because the Legislature had made it rather more expensive for the class who choose to deal with usurers to borrow money, hinting at a 'grandmotherly' Act of Parliament to prevent working men's wives buying shoddy silk from hawkers, also at the need for an inspector empowered to spill half the liquor then drunk by workmen in public-houses. The latter suggestion is especially interesting. But probably if all Sir Wilfrid Lawson's speeches were minutely examined, it would be found that, at some time

that they should not recover a shilling, after they had tempted women in their poverty. . . . I may tell you a thing I heard to-day. I was trying a case of a bill-discounter or money-lender. He was called, and he said, " I have given up business because you cannot put people in prison now, and consequently they don't pay." Upon which I said that it was the greatest compliment to those who passed the Act of Parliament that ever I heard. I should uncommonly like to see the same, or a similar provision made by which these payments should not be extorted from the husband by putting him in prison. . . . But there is another way in which we all spend more than is good for us—in eating and drinking, particularly the latter. . . . It is positively lamentable—one hundred millions a year spent in drink in this country! One hundred millions a year! If the good genius of Englishmen could only stand by the side of those who are doing it and just give their elbow a tilt as every glass goes into their lips! I for one think it would be positively a service to the country if one-half of the entire quantity were spilt. I really think it would be a good thing. " What," you would say, " waste fifty millions of property ?" It *is* wasted now. Why, it could never be wasted so badly as that is which is poured down the throat where it is not wanted. . . . I think it would be a very good thing if the mischief could be obviated by some such good being as I have supposed. It would be a very good thing if, when a man is going to indulge in any vice, or to do anything that was not good for him, if, instead of the pleasant part being put before himself, he could have the other side of the question put to him. A man says to himself, " I am tired; I am out of spirits." Perhaps he hears that the children are crying, or says, " My wife is cross, for it is washing-day," or what not, or some other inconvenience. " I will go to the public-house, for it is warm;

---

or another, he has declared he would rather see a Bishop free than an Archbishop sober. Lord Bramwell certainly was not born a member of the Liberty and Property Defence League ; events drove him in that direction. For his anti-alcoholic bias, see also pp. 114, 118.

I shall find somebody I know. It is much nicer. I really should like a glass of something to comfort me, for it is very damp." That is the bright side of the question ; but suppose, instead of that, he would say to himself, " I will go and lay in a headache for to-morrow. I will make provision for my wife going in rags, and my children with no shoes. I will store up a stock of delirium tremens, and finish my days in a workhouse, if not cut short by a fever or some other disease." You could but say of such a man, then, " Poor fellow ! we must stop him," or if people did not say it themselves, they would think it. That is what those do who forget what it is they are doing; but I am quite certain that it is an infirmity which the depositors in this bank do not labour under. . . . I am going to say something for which I shall perhaps get into trouble. I have not mentioned it to the directors, and very likely they will wish I had not brought it here ; but I have always had a bad habit of saying what ought not to be said. I will tell you what it is. I should like to make you all shareholders in the company very much. Mind, upon better terms than ordinary shareholders, because I should like to make this provision : that your dividends should never be below 4 per cent. upon your deposits ; while, if the shareholders got more, I should like you to do so. . . . We shareholders should not lose by it, because, although every man should do his duty to the best of his ability, whether at work for himself or according to agreement, yet we all know there are two ways of doing one's duty. We know a man never works so zealously as when he is at work for his own benefit. . . . Therefore, if by an arrangement of this description the servants, workpeople, and officers of the company . . . do their duty even more zealously than they do now, the possibility—nay, the probability—is that this apparent sacrifice would be more than made up to the shareholders. . . .'

He was quite free from affectation ; never had the grand manner, often the sole reliance of men not certain (for one reason or another) how they will be received. At the house of Sir Henry

Holland (Lord Knutsford's father), he once acted the part of a Judge in some charades. The word was 'plaintiff'; the last scene was a breach of promise of marriage action. Sir George Bramwell summed up most ferociously, to the great delight of beholders, the children especially. Knowing a great deal about music, and having a fine natural ear, his sufferings, especially when on the Welsh Circuit, from the complimentary performances of the Sheriff's trumpeters under the window of his lodgings, were sometimes acute. In a Welsh town one day, he suddenly threw up the sash, and shouted to the trumpeters in the street below, 'My men, give one good blast, as loud as ever you can, and then pray go home.' He asserted that Mr. Justice Crompton —supposed, literally, not to know 'one tune from another' — did once, and only once, profess to recognize 'God save the Queen.' They both attended some public dinner in Dublin; the band struck up a tune; Mr. Justice Crompton loyally rose to his feet. When the music ceased, Sir George Bramwell explained with great glee to his friend that the band had been playing a tune known to musical experts as 'The Wearing of the Green.' Mr. Justice Crompton, however, used to relate in revenge how, on circuit, they were once shown into a sitting-room at the Judges' lodgings, which, to Crompton's horror, and the delight of Sir George and Mr. Arthur Coleridge, contained a piano. A very unmusical man is sincerely pained by piano-playing, and the prospect was rather dismal, until it was discovered that the piano was locked. Finally, the landlady appeared, and explained, with profuse apologies, that the key was lost also.

He had an abundant subjective sense of the ridiculous ; no ambition to make other people laugh —a penetrating imagination which enabled him to instantly detect grotesque contrasts and absurd consequences arising out of particular situations, assertions, or arguments. Dying in the year 1892, he never had the chance to study and enjoy ' The Law of Employers' Liability at Home and Abroad,' by Mr. A. Birrell, M.P., more especially the suggestion that Lord Holt, ' 200 years ago,' might have ruled that, whenever a lady hires a cook, an 'implied term' must be added to, or inserted in, the contract compelling lady aforesaid to provide cook aforesaid with a bicycle, and the suggestion that it is insurance brokers who pay moneys due on life policies. Some Bramwell letters show that he enjoyed intensely, if demurely, a mental picture of what must ensue should his opponent's wrong logic be yoked to the right facts, or his opponent's wrong facts yoked to right logic. They reproduce, too, in curiously exact fashion, his way of talking. As one reads, one almost hears his voice, and a tinkle of that laughter which writing them excited in him. The man devoid of humour or imagination never knows the subdued joy which it must have given him to write :*

'. . . An ingenious gentleman has suggested that " there is something better than law and order—viz., justice." I agree.

---

* *The Liberal Unionist*, May 4, 1887, article, 'The Crimes Bill.'

"Nourishment is better than victuals and drink." But as we cannot be nourished without food, so we cannot have justice without law and order. . . .'

The value of this passage depends on a man's power to picture to himself the kind of effete person who went about London clubs between 1880 and 1887 saying, 'There is something better than law and order—viz., justice,' as well as the other kind of person who profited by this beautiful aphorism to commit murder, fraud, and outrage in Ireland with impunity. Having frequently dined with the first kind of person, and sentenced the second, Lord Bramwell appreciated both thoroughly. On June 5, 1878, when he presided at the South-Eastern and Metropolitan Railway Savings Bank and Provident Societies' annual meeting, Mr. B. Whitworth, M.P., one of the directors, in recommending total abstinence to the company's servants, had said, 'I am now in my sixty-third year of water-drinking.' Replying to a vote of thanks, Sir George Bramwell wound up :

'. . . Mr. Whitworth has gone a little beyond the exact truth, I should think. Surely the *first* year of those sixty-three he did not drink water. He may have done so since. All I can say is, I hope he likes it. . . .'

The railway men laughed boisterously ; but what he enjoyed was the mental vision of Mr. B. Whitworth solemnly sucking clear cold water from a feeding-bottle in the year 1815.

The notable case of *Bank of England v. Vagliano Brothers*, decided in the House of Lords, March 5,

1891 (Lords Bramwell and Field the minority, Lords Halsbury (Chancellor), Selborne, Herschell, Watson, Macnaghten, and Morris the majority), reversing the decision of Courts below, produced the usual demands, a weekly paper cautiously but earnestly pleading for Parliamentary protection against forgeries by confidential clerks. This very short letter of August, 1891, on the dry topic of 'The Negotiability of Bills of Exchange'—perhaps the last he ever wrote to the press—has much humorous suggestion :

'SIR,

'You most truly say that "if the negotiability of a bill of exchange is to be restricted, that should be done in no ambiguous fashion, but in a way in which the ordinary business man can readily understand."

'Would you favour your readers with a form ?

'Your obedient servant,

'B.'

In this wise, although he was eighty-three years old, he took the trouble to remind people, who would probably soon read his obituary notice, that the Parliamentary interference called for would do far more harm than occasional forgeries. For his own special amusement he sketched with a slight touch the gentlemen who wanted Parliament to interfere, conscientiously trying to invent a harmless form of bill of exchange, applicable, but not embarrassing, to every firm, to every kind of transaction, arising all over the empire every week-day in the year, and yet warranted to prevent confidential Greek clerks forging unpronounceable names.   The editor appended a note to Lord Bramwell's letter: 'When the object is to meet special cases, how can a general form be given?' How indeed?   But the resources of Parliamentary civilization are inexhaustible, and for Lord Bramwell, behind the little question in his letter, arose a mental picture of sundry M.P.'s in a hot committee-room overlooking the Thames trying their hands at forgery-proof, but not really inconvenient, 'forms' for three weeks in July, said M.P.'s consisting of a country gentleman, an authority on Church schools; a banker, an authority on rose-growing and breeding toy-terriers; a very dull Scottish solicitor who had been left a fortune by an uncle in Calcutta, and had thereupon bought a Scottish mining constituency controlled by the Irish vote; an ex-Guardsman who was totally deaf; a handsome young reporter on a Fenian newspaper who had married his Bishop's elderly niece, and so qualified for Parliamentary honours; a gentleman who had written a good deal about stability of ships at sea; a cotton spinner who kept fox-hounds; or a speculator in suburban leaseholds, who had done much for the indigent blind in his time.   Lord Bramwell's letter invited these experts also to try their hands at a form of bill of exchange which, as the newspaper suggested, would 'effectually limit its negotiability, but not in such ambiguous fashion as to lead an ordinary business man astray.'

He never hid his contempt for twisted, dishonest, or question-begging words.   On May 11, 1866, when opposing in the House of Lords the second reading of a Durham Sunday Closing Bill, he said :

'This Bill is to prevent the sale of intoxicating drinks in the county of Durham on Sundays. Wines and spirits are *intoxicating* liquors, and why is one particular property to be singled out? Would your lordships speak of water as a *drowning* element? Yet it undoubtedly is. . . . I ask, What would your lordships think if a man were to come on a Saturday night and demand the key of your cellar . . . and when you said, "Have you any reason to believe that I will make bad use of my liberty to get at the liquor in my cellar?" the man were to reply, "No; but there is a man four doors lower down in the street who will make bad use of his"?'

As he grew older he grew gentler—more tolerant of other people's views, more unwilling to use strong or lethal language. Sometimes very old age is disfigured by very new language. On February 7, 1891, when the Law Lords were listening to the appeal of *Sharp v. Wakefield*, Mr. George Candy, Q.C., argued that licensing magistrates might possibly do that which was 'unfair and unjust.' Lord Bramwell suggested 'harsh and hard' as better words.

The following matter did, however, make him very angry. On December 9, 1884, a *Times* leader dealt with the sale or proposed sale of land and buildings pertaining to Clement's, Barnard's, Clifford's and Staple Inns. A.D. 1837 one of the Pollock family had been born in Serjeants' Inn, which made the proposed sale rather impious. Those structures, the *Times* said, 'lent poetry to the ancient quarter, preserved calm and repose profounder than the fields.' London 'thought them its own possessions in a peculiar manner.' 'Nathaniel Hawthorne,' too, had been 'fascinated by the peculiar tranquillity' of those ancient inns; 'but the persons who had control of the property' had had 'the moral hardihood to wind up and divide the assets'; had exhibited 'a want of equity to their predecessors; had strangled their successors'; had 'lawfully plundered their societies,' 'plunged at the associated funds like a thief at a watch'; had been guilty of 'confiscation' in a 'magnificently rapacious style. . . .' This was strong language for the *Times*—strong enough to have conceivably been written by Abraham Hayward, who in his latter years had for some reason or other once more become a Radical. The *Times* article added that 'the sale of Serjeants' Inn (in 1877) set a flagrant example of analogous spoliation.'

'This statement,' wrote Lord Bramwell to the *Times*, December 11, 1884, 'is quite unjustified. Serjeants' Inn, or, rather, the Society of Judges and Serjeants, was not an Inn of Court. It was not chartered. No one was bound to join it, no one had a right to do so. All candidates were proposed and seconded, and when elected paid an enormous fine—£450, besides annual commons. It never had any duty. It was a purely voluntary society, I suppose, for the purpose of providing chambers and dinners for its members. These objects had ceased to exist. Its members had their chambers in the Temple. The Judges only went to the dinners four times a year, partly in compliment to their brother Serjeants, partly to talk about the affairs of the Inn, partly to settle such important matters as who should go to St. Paul's in Easter and who in Trinity terms. A few choice spirits among the Serjeants still dined—four or five in number—on a few days in each term. But if we should have had successors we should not have sold the property. We were not to have any. No more Serjeants were to be, nor have been, made, and the only effect of our keeping the property would be that it would vest in the last surviving member, his heirs, executors, administrators, and assigns. Worse than this, we could not keep afloat. Our best income came from the fines on admittance, and as they ceased our expenses exceeded our income. We could have paid our way if we had no dinners—that is to say, we could have lived if we gave no sign of life.

'Well, but what about the money? Various suggestions, more or less vague, were made for its disposition. I protested on two grounds: (1) that all the proposals were for mischievous charity; (2) that I object to all corporate charities, being strongly of opinion that a man's almsgiving should come out of his own particular pocket. I received my share, which did not more than return me principal and interest, for the cost of which I had received no return except four dinners annually— dinners in a large hall with our clerks, intolerably long, noisy, and wearisome. Is this spoliation? Who has been spoiled? You say that what was done was probably not illegal. I thought "spoliation" was. Those who want to prevent "spoliation" or to "spoil" had better not say the case is "analogous" to that of Serjeants' Inn. Every member of the society rejoiced at its end. For my own part, my only regret is that my share of the "spoil" was no greater.

'Your obedient servant,

'BRAMWELL.

'P.S.—I would recommend to your notice Serjeant Pulling's "Order of the Coif," chapter v., treating of the Inns of Court and Chancery and of the Inns of the Judges and Serjeants.

'December 9.'

This letter seems to have disposed for the time being of the charge of 'spoliation,' greed, and breach of trust, which Lord Bramwell resented so keenly. In December, 1884, public attention was fixed on franchise and redistribution of seats questions ;

political oratory abounded to an extent quite inconceivable in these tranquil post-Gladstonian times; just then Irish dynamiters tried to blow up London Bridge. Serjeants' Inn was not mentioned again until November 3, 1886, when a lengthy special paper in the *Times* commented on the sale of picturesque Staple Inn to Messrs. Trollope. A passage in this paper caused Lord Bramwell to write, November 6, 1886:

'In your paper it is said, "The Serjeants' Inn, the Inns of Court, the Inns of Chancery, were, in fact, the constituent parts of a legal University, designed to knit closer together the several branches of the Law." I do not know how branches are knit together, nor how Universities knit anything; nor do I believe that there ever was a legal University.'

He was evidently rather angry.

'But assuming that there was, it is untrue that Serjeants' Inn was ever part of it. I use the word "untrue" because the statement is repeated after its untruth has been pointed out.'

Lord Bramwell was, of course, thinking of his previous letter of December 11, 1884. Like the rest of the public, he believed that writers in the *Times* knew its files by heart. If they did, they would be the wisest people in the world.

'The society of Serjeants' Inn was a private society, for the convenience of its members. It had no duties, no powers.'

He then repeats a portion of his former letter, showing how it was a mere club:

'It never was in any way "knitted to," or connected with, any Inn of Court or Chancery. The persons eligible for membership were Serjeants—not Judges only, as said in the article I refer to.'

On November 8 Mr. Baylis, Q.C., wrote to the *Times* at some length, pointing out, *inter alia*, that Blackstone calls Inns of Court 'new Universities, a sort of collegiate order,' etc. He also denied that Serjeants' Inn was a 'private society'; its members had exclusive right of audience in the Court of Common Pleas, etc.

On November 11 Serjeant Pulling wrote, confirming Lord Bramwell's statements, adding that the Society of Serjeants had acquired 'an unprofitable lease of their premises at great expense in 1834,' and had 'quietly and prudently wound up the society in 1877.'

On November 12 Lord Bramwell wrote :

'The letter of Mr. Baylis exhibits a crass ignorance of the subject on which he writes, and a proportionate confidence. Serjeants-at-Law had exclusive audience in the Court of Common Pleas, not because they were members of the Society of Serjeants, or of any Inn, but because they were Serjeants. They were so, not by being elected members of the society, but by command from the Crown. A Serjeant would have been entitled to share in this privilege had he never been, or ceased to be, a member of the society or Inn. This right was not abolished in 1834, as Mr. Baylis says. It existed till 1846, when it was abolished by statute. The " venerable order " of which Blackstone, as cited by Mr. Baylis, speaks, is not the Society of Serjeants, not the Inn, but the Order of Serjeants itself; of which order, I repeat, a man might be a member without being a member of the society or Inn. One of the last Judges of the Court of Common Pleas who was a Serjeant never was a member of the society or Inn. When a man was made a Serjeant he was eligible to the society if it chose to elect him.

'The statute 36 and 37 Vict., c. 66, had nothing to do with Serjeants' Inn. The eighth section was put in because it was contemplated that no more Serjeants should be made. What constitutes a University is, I believe, very uncertain; but I repeat it is untrue that the Society of Serjeants, Serjeants' Inn, or Inns, ever was or were part of any University. I repeat, the Society of Serjeants or Serjeants' Inn had no connection with any Inn of Court or Chancery. It had no duties, no powers. Mr. Baylis asks why, "immediately after the passing of the Act 36 and 37 Vict., the members of Serjeants' Inn sold the property and divided the spoil." I content myself with saying, because they thought fit. The statute removed no impediment to their doing so. They could have done so before had they pleased. Perhaps Mr. Baylis will tell us whom we "spoiled." It is strange he should venture to apply that word to the act of a body of men the least likely in the world to "spoil" anyone, and who knew their rights, which Mr. Baylis does not. Perhaps that accounts for what he says.'

On November 16 Mr. Baylis wrote again, citing many ancient authorities to show that such a thing as a legal University was not inconceivable. Lord Bramwell, who had been restored to good humour by the feebleness of his opponent's argument, wrote finally on the 17th:

' The letter of Mr. Baylis exhibits great research, extending even to the Law List, a most respectable publication. I prefer my own authority for the following reasons. Nearly thirty-one years ago I was made a Serjeant. After that I was elected a member of the Society of Serjeants. Those who elected me might have refused to do so. I suppose this shows that Serjeants and the Society of Serjeants were different. Next, as to the society being part of a University: during the whole thirty-one years it has never done anything in common with any other Inn, any barrister or any student.'

Serjeants' Inn had, in short, become a nineteenth-century club with a sixteenth-century name—a club for which there was no demand, which never could elect any new members.   When the cost of keeping up the club outweighed benefits derived by members, they very properly sold their premises and interest, which otherwise must have become a tontine. Lord Bramwell was, by November, 1886, a conspicuous Liberal Unionist ; party bitterness was then intense.   Gladstonian newspapers, therefore, accused him of dishonourable conduct in the matter, suggesting that the money realized by the sale of Serjeants' Inn ought to have been given to increase the salaries of London Board School teachers, to ' the poor,' etc.

The business of a Judge is to dispense the King's justice, which British subjects have learnt to believe can be nothing but perfect ; in criminal cases superintending the trial of those who are alleged to have wronged their neighbours, defied, profaned the law, and on conviction decreeing the penalty ; in civil actions helping to justly determine disputed claims of individual right.   Beyond this a Judge has no duty to the public—that is to say, no *locus standi* in everyday affairs, no obligation, such as those who instruct, amend, or amuse the public have, to provide a creditable show of some sort.   Therefore a Judge's reputation is made gradually.   Knowledge about him filters through slowly from members of the legal profession, from jurymen and witnesses. The press, very reserved but emphatic on such matters, contributes also.   It was in moulding the actual task-work of justice that Sir George Bramwell's influence was most felt.   ' In court,' says one who knew him well, 'he always held the reins and guided the case.' However eminent the counsel engaged, he was unmistakably captain on his own quarterdeck.

Jurymen, whose opinion counts for a good deal, were glad when he was on the bench, because his summings-up were as terse, clear, easy to understand, as his letters to the newspapers. Some Judges' charges are very diffuse, difficult to follow. Baron Bramwell put the salient points, nothing else, and without verbiage, rhetoric, padding. In summing up he thus (as has been often told) condensed an enormously lengthy argument from counsel in defence of a farmer charged with shooting at a boy who was stealing the farmer's apples: 'Considering the materials he had, I am surprised, gentlemen,' said Sir George, 'that the learned counsel did not make his speech longer. I, however, shall leave the case to you in eight words: The prisoner aimed at nothing, and missed it.' Yet he took great pains with, gave much consideration to, sentences; frankly acknowledged that he welcomed the opinion on that matter 'of any sensible man,' which would show at least how the case struck on-lookers. A prisoner was once convicted before him of a very terrible and repulsive crime, committed under circumstances never likely —indeed, impossible—to recur. Sir George Bramwell saw no necessity for a 'deterrent' sentence; there was no danger of that kind of crime spreading. Accordingly, although it was technically a capital offence, he passed sentence of nine months' im-

prisonment only ; thus, as he told a friend, expressing the law's vengeance or disapprobation—one of
the ingredients in all sentences—without inflicting
needless suffering.   In the profession he had
acquired a reputation for taking a stern rather than
a sentimental or neo-humanitarian view of a Judge's
duty.   On January 7, 1856, Sir John Mellor gave
him this well-meant but really unnecessary warning,
thoroughly characteristic of an English Judge :

'. . . I congratulate you and the profession, but pray do
not go and hang people right and left to please the *Times*.
See article to-day. . . .'

He had that peremptory temper which comes of
acute sensitiveness and capacity for taking keen
interest in every phase of a question, knowing
tolerably well what *was* right, eager to have right
done quickly ; he was apt to get impatient about
anything which seemed to thwart justice.   Now
and then, on the bench, his wrath got the better of
him.   Before sentencing a certain man, convicted
of a series of terrible assaults on young children, he
said : 'Your counsel tells me that four years' penal
servitude will kill you.   I don't care if it does kill
you.'   Such sayings got him the name of an unfeeling Judge.   He did not protest; indeed, he
rather persuaded himself that he had 'no feeling.'
In Flintshire he tried an old woman of seventy,
indicted for the murder of her husband.   Forty
long years they had lived together, the man treating the wife with unbearable cruelty all that time.
Perhaps she was partly to blame ; anyhow, one
night she got a razor and cut her husband's throat,

then cut her own, but did not at once die. When he came to sum up, Sir George Bramwell related to the jury the old woman's life and treatment. By degrees the misery and pathos of the story was too much for him : he put his hands before his face and burst into tears. Recovering himself in a minute or two, he warned the jury to banish from their minds that irrelevancy in his charge. They thereupon found the old woman guilty. She died within a day or two in gaol. 'I can't think,' said Baron Bramwell afterwards to a friend who saw those tears, 'how I came to make such a fool of myself.'

What the Bench and the Bar thought, after knowing him well as Judge of First Instance and of Appeal for twenty-five years was shown by the great compliment paid to him upon his retirement. In the spring and summer of 1881, Lady Bramwell's health had given way. She was a very careful, anxious spouse. The doctors said that she could not stand the English climate in winter. In the middle of September his intended resignation was announced. He actually retired during the long vacation, at the special request of Lord Selborne, to meet official convenience.* At Maidstone, in July, there was a private and informal leave-taking between himself and the members of his old circuit,

* Lord Coleridge wrote, October 19, 1881 : '. . . You are a capital fellow except for what you are going to do on the first of November. . . . You shall try Lefroy if you like it, with all my heart. It might be a very striking last appearance before the footlights. Poor dear Cockburn would hardly have given you such a chance ! . . .'

formerly the Home, now the South-Western. As customary, the Bar entertained the Judges—Lord Justice Bramwell, who presided in the Crown, and Mr. Justice Denman in the Civil Court. The dinner was a notable success, an event in legal annals. 'But such an entertainment,' the *Times* said justly, 'could not satisfy the Bar at large.' A banquet was given to Lord Justice Bramwell in the Inner Temple Hall, November 28, 1881, by all the Judges and by the great body of the Common Law Bar. Twenty-six Judges and 250 members of the Common Law and Chancery Bars, as well as many Government officials of rank, were present. 'All the other Judges then living,' said the *Times*, 'had practised before Sir George Bramwell for years, and consequently could not help looking up to him with the deference due to known experience and the long exercise of authority.' The Hall and the company made a splendid spectacle. No similar honour had ever been paid to an English Judge before.

The Bar of England is the most critical and hard to please of possible juries; yet there had never before been a man so popular with the Bar—none to whom such an honour was so appropriate. Further, there was the foreboding that never again would those old halls and their frequenters look on an English judge with a like record of service. It was suspected that the race which bred such students, the forces which wrought and hammered such a character as his into the shape it had taken, the needs of jurisdiction which for a quarter of a century gave scope on the Bench to his matchless powers and qualities, were passing away, not to return. There would be 'strong men after Agamemnon,' but in future fewer chances for a personality like his, for a mighty exponent of Common Law, since Parliament was plastering over all chinks and crannies with statutes. If another Bramwell did happen to arise, he would have to accept a colonial judgeship in Saturn or Jupiter.

At the time, Sir George Bramwell was, it is true, making way for other men. The new Judicature Act might have rendered Judges immortal. Here was proof that it had not. Allowing for the fact that the most admired, acceptable thing most men ever make is a vacancy, and that there is more real joy over one sinner who resigneth than over ninety-and-nine just appointed men, it is certain that the spoken and written expressions of affection and respect — reverence almost — at that time were perfectly genuine. One of the services which Sir George Bramwell had rendered to the Bar during his twenty-five years on the Bench never could be put into words, without inferentially discrediting other Judges by contrast. He showed always that he understood what pleaders, young or old, confident or nervous, famous or obscure, said or tried to say. Pleading before a dull or weak Judge, like trying to carve for hungry people with a blunt knife, means double work, lost temper, spoilt materials. Nothing is quite so bad as the obtuse man ; he shatters the Bar's faith in the supremacy of natural law in the spiritual world. If you have an ignorant, unfriendly or prejudiced Judge, you can go to the Court of Appeal. If you have to deal with an ill-bred man, you can show your friends how superior your own breeding is. Some of the praise given to Sir George Bramwell for his kindness, consideration, generous help to the profession, meant praise for his knack of always understanding what advocates were driving at. One doesn't really thank a Judge for being 'kind' if he's dull also. Something of this was in the mind of those present at the banquet in November, 1881. It couldn't be fully said, lest some should whisper to themselves, 'Yes; he was *so* unlike A, B, C, or D.'

What the *Times* said, July, 1881, could not be better said :

'. . . Few Judges have been more liked by the Bar than Lord Justice Bramwell. Gifted with great natural vigour of mind and quickness of apprehension, he was yet remarkably patient in listening to their arguments, and showed still more remarkable candour in putting their arguments for them in the strongest and clearest way in which they could possibly be put, so that they could not hope to put them better (a very happy way of repressing undue prolixity), and then if he desired to show their fallacy, he would do so in the Socratic way, by questions so shrewd and keen that no sophistry could evade them, and yet in a good-natured way that never could annoy, and often with a touch of humour that would even amuse, and thus a long argument would often be cut short and its fallacy exposed in the clearest, shortest, and most pleasant and satis- factory way, and without annoyance to anybody. No wonder that the Bar liked a Judge who thus dealt with them—one who had a giant's strength and did not use it tyrannously or unfairly, but with candour and good humour, and racy frankness and thorough kindliness of manner, which made every man feel that he had been able to make the best that could be made of his case, whatever it might be; and it was only very great stupidity, or very great persistency in wrong, which could be proof against his mixture of shrewdness and good humour or rouse his naturally quick temper into anger. . . .'

Whether that unexampled tribute of November 28, 1881, did more honour to the guest or to the givers of the banquet it is not easy to say. As for the guest, the public, from a sort of instinct, had approved each honour or promotion given to him, Only a great people could have been proud of such a man, could have continued, all through the bravest days of the Victorian era, to regard him as one of the pillars of the nation. As for the givers, only men who in their innermost hearts revered most of all honesty, courage, diligence, kindness, truth, could have taken so much trouble, could have paid him that compliment then. Of legal equipment, wit, acuteness, stored learning, gifts of money-making, and success, the Bar had plenty of examples around them. These things the Bench and the Bar of England had never cared to applaud in the same way.

With a fine (perhaps accidental) sense of artistic relief, light and shade, Sir William Harcourt, then Home Secretary, and Lord Coleridge were placed at the dinner-table next and next but one to Sir George Bramwell. Just such speeches as ought to be made were made by Sir Henry James, who was in the chair and proposed the guest's health, and by Lord Coleridge returning thanks for the Bench. Of one sentence in Sir George Bramwell's reply—' I declare that if I had the choice whether to be a great Judge or a good Judge, I should prefer the latter'—the *Times* said, March 10, 1892, the day after his death, that 'it was his rare fortune to be both.' The phrase he used—not perfect, since to be a good Judge means in English so many things, some very commonplace—declared, above all, that it was better to be a good man than a great Judge, the same as Walter Scott's last words on his death-bed meant. Lord Bramwell also said in his speech of thanks, 'I know I have an anxious temperament. I ask pardon of any whom I have offended.'

The *Daily News* had hinted, three months before, that he might be raised to the peerage. Some of the experts in the press, while deploring his retirement as a public misfortune, added that the Common Law autocrat in the Lords, Lord Blackburn, would be none the worse for a colleague. Lord Armstrong wrote to Sir George a warning not to take the suggested title of Lord Edenbridge, lest his family name should be merged, and so forgotten. He was created Baron Bramwell of Hever, February 15, 1882, and took his seat in the House early in that year. For the latter occasion he borrowed Lord Esher's robes, which arrived with this on a scrap of paper :

'MY DEAR LORD AND MASTER,

    'I send you my robes.

'I have not a cocked hat.

'They give you one (I think) at the House of Lords.

'Don't flog me.

                'Ever dutifully yours,

                    'ESHER.'

CHAPTER III.

'THE POLITICAL ECONOMY OF OUR YOUTH.'

Why Lord Bramwell intervened in public affairs—Partial
triumph and acceptance of Free Trade, Free Competition,
Free Contract, between 1846 and 1870—Why ascendancy
of political economists short-lived—Fibres of 'paternalism'
and 'protection' left in soil—*Eppur non si muove*—Growth
of 'new mildness,' and increasing distrust of economic
liberty—Mainly result of new wealth, material prosperity,
humane legislation—Revival of 'some kind of Socialism'
after 1880—Foreign influences—The 'Historical' School
—Spurious ethical sanction for movement—Kinship with
Sacerdotal Economy of Middle Ages—Tendency towards
'some kind of Socialism' also potent on side of jurisprudence.

IT has been questioned by an eminent critic and
sincere admirer of Lord Bramwell's career whether
he was quite as great a success in the Court of
Appeal as he had been in the Court below. An
explanation of the disappointment thus indicated is
suggested by a high authority : It was as Judge of
First Instance that Lord Bramwell's special powers
and gifts showed to most singular advantage, because
the penetration, logical directness, 'high initial
velocity' of his intellect—his workmanlike knack

of mastering facts, assaying evidence, and applying law—acted as solvent to problems, difficulties, doubts, which come before juries, or before a Judge sitting in *banc*. In a sense, those powers and gifts may not be the highest of all ; it happens that they are the rarest. On the other hand, the English judiciary has of late years been rather overendowed with those more subtle and impressive attributes which go to make 'great' Judges of Appeal. To compare him as Judge of Appeal with, for instance, Lord Justice Bowen or Lord Selborne, is like comparing Cobbett and Spinoza. After he went to the House of Lords, Lord Bramwell showed, until the last few months of his life, no symptoms of brain-weariness or failing powers. His judgment in the railway case (p. 148) is a superb example of simplifying questions and clearing the ground. His judgment in the *Bank of England v. Vagliano*, March 5, 1891 (he was eighty-two at the time), was a masterly effort to disentangle the elusive threads of that most difficult case, while the reported judgments of Lords Halsbury, Selborne, and Herschell, especially in the matter of bankers' negligence, remind one that a judicial revolution had been silently going on since the case of *Tucker v. Robartes*, in which Lord Bramwell had taken enormous interest. The ground was slipping from under his feet, and he knew it. 'Probably we' (Lord Field concurring) 'are wrong,' he said.

Lord Bramwell's active, if intermittent, intervention as critic or combatant in that field where jurisprudence and political economy in relation to governmental tactics are causes of war, covers a period of about ten years—from his retirement in 1881 until his death in 1891.

He had a twofold reputation among his countrymen—one might say, two careers. As advocate and master of legal procedure, he rapidly achieved success; on the Bench won additional renown, never dimmed. When already approaching old age, his opinions on public questions came to be familiar to many of his countrymen, who previously had remembered, in a general way, Baron Bramwell, the blunt, wise, witty judge, famous for delivering charges very well from the Bench. His way of taking his holiday—of enjoying that leisure which he had surely earned—was to 'descend into the street,' as French rhetoricians say, to take his chance like the humblest volunteer in the bodyguard of truth, as critic and debater on questions of the day, by means of terse, grave, good-humoured, and not easily answered remonstrances, in the *Times* and elsewhere. From 1880 to 1891, Liberal leaders were trying to banish 'abstract' English ideas about other things besides political economy to Saturn and Jupiter. Handling problems of jurisprudence, Common Law rights, public equity generally, he wrought with a firm, sure hand. Thousands of readers, amused or edified by what he wrote about 'Drink' or 'Land Nationalization,' scarcely noticed his letters, of far greater importance, about contract. His reassertion of the Liberal creed (in a certain and important sense the only one before the nation for many years), although fragmentary, and put forward without any claim to cover the field of discussion, prevented the doing of some things which consistent Liberals had always protested against; was a great encouragement to not a few thinking men inclined to dread, after 1881, that equity, public faith, security of property, and those national characteristics depending on unhampered individual freedom and self-help, were seriously imperilled in this country; told especially upon that undemonstrative class who win not every great electoral contest in this country, but the best two out of three—'the rubber,' so to speak. A Judge or a peer gets a good hearing, especially whenever 'points of lawlessness' are raised by statesmen or politicians, but not necessarily a favourable hearing. That Lord Bramwell's writings got on their merits, solely because his arguments seemed sensible, and very hard to deny.

Why he intervened in controversies of the day, wrote pamphlets, letters to the press, delivered addresses, became a zealous member of the Liberty and Property Defence League, may be asked, because not many men who achieve fame on the English Bench care to step down into the polemical ring to fight with beasts at Ephesus—in Fleet Street and parts adjacent. The English people like to think that not only their Judges, but all men who have once taken official 'vows' to renounce political bias, favour, or partiality, so abstain. A tradition has grown up that one cannot well answer a Judge 'back,' any more than one can a Bishop speaking from the pulpit; therefore, neither has ever been a very welcome controversialist on 'lay' topics. When an English Judge whose political utterances have been freely quoted happens to try a case in which some politician is interested, the average Englishman feels somehow as if he had been non-suited himself. No doubt Lord Bramwell shared the English prejudice in the matter. For many years he scrupulously avoided party politics—one reason why his intervention in purely economic or legal discussions never gave offence or made enemies for him. People saw that he was obviously, painfully honest; wrong, perhaps, but certainly honest, single-minded. Then, Lord Bramwell wasn't wrong often. Some of his reasons for intervening in public controversy were unheroic enough. He had fewer domestic interests and distractions than most men; after 1881 a good deal of time to spare for letter-writing, etc.; an extensive correspondence with clever men, who wrote to him to get his opinion or approval, not for amusement's sake. His letters to the press are often finished works of art—if, following Schiller, one may recognize the true artist 'by what he omits.' Writing to the newspapers was for Lord Bramwell undoubtedly an intellectual gratification, just as sketching is for a receptive draughtsman. He saw points quickly, did not want them lost.

Another reason was, that such a man holding such opinions really couldn't keep silent. Considerable forces were already making for reaction against the ascendency of his friends the political economists when Sir George Bramwell, enjoying the comparative leisure of a Lord Justice of Appeal, found himself drifting into criticism and controversy. They worked more definitely, so soon as Socialists and semi-Socialists in both political camps got their hands on the throttle-valve, to weaken and diminish the nation's respect for principles of jurisprudence, for distinctions between governmental right and wrong, which he held to be fundamental. Even as early as 1870 there were really not many covenanted defenders of political economy left, although it might have been said, between 1840 and 1870, that to root out from the economic and political fields the last vestiges of paternal restraint and capricious inter-ference inculcated by mediæval jurists and economists had been the glory of ' Liberalism.'

A steady, if scarcely perceptible, revolution in public sentiment, a distinct moral change in every grade of civil society, was the result in this country —as De Tocqueville says it was in the United States—of milder laws, increased prosperity, and the peaceful obliteration of class disabilities. Plenty of angry complaints, demands for political change or reform, were still heard ; but already by 1870 a generation of Britons had reached manhood who had never felt, nor even witnessed, infliction of con-scious injustice, hardship or wrong by their 'rulers'; the old savage *intransigeance* of the early part of the century among ' the populace' was becoming a memory only. Commencing with the middle class, the new mildness, tolerance, aversion to harshness or severity in any shape, became factors of great importance in the life of the nation. Slowly but surely they determined popular judgment about the conclusions, or so-called 'laws,' of political economy. Well-to-do communities, with large tax-paying capacity, and assured of just and mild government, can alone afford to indulge in the luxury of applying moral, ethical, or sentimental ideas fashionable at particular dates—but necessarily 'fluid' and varying fundamentally every few years— to serious business of legislation, to problems of jurisprudence, or to economic relations. Such a luxury came more and more within reach of prosperous Britons between 1846 and 1890. The new pity told in a definite way against the 'dismal,' 'unsympathetic,' 'iron' conclusions of *laissez faire.* Savage sports, prize-fighting, duelling, the rigors of the criminal code, imprisonment for debt, cruelty to animals, had been mitigated or abolished by law and general consent; was it impossible to render the iron law of supply and demand, or the remorseless stringency of competition, more humane also? Lord Bramwell, addressing the British Association in 1888,* marvelled whether he was to hear next 'that Euclid's elements are "inhuman."' A fairly numerous class were coming to the front predisposed to so describe them.

Meanwhile thirty years of development in the

---

* Republished as pamphlet, 'Economics *v.* Socialism.' From some points of view it does seem rather unfair that two sides of a triangle should *always* be greater than the third. Mr. Ruskin is, perhaps, the only economist who has dwelt on this. Parliament seems to have done little or nothing for the 'really deserving' third sides of triangles, although few people, except

industrial England begotten of Free Trade had provided abundant objects, problems, enigmas for incoherent exercise of flaccid curiosity, sympathy, pity. The early political economists, dealing with phenomena of their epoch, seem always to have postulated, as their 'wage-earning unit,' a healthy as well as a free man. From the commencement of the century great manufacturing centres, offering promise of good wages and cheap food, had begun to attract, not only the parish apprentices bred under the old poor law, but thousands of healthy country people, ignorant of physiological or sanitary laws, to a town life. If not in the first, certainly in the second or third generation, these new factory and city workers showed signs of physical, and especially nervous, deterioration. The waste heaps and 'tailings' of the great industrial machine, run at ever-increasing speed after 1846, began to present, among certain trades, unhealthy, feeble, and degenerate human types, physically unfit to compete in the struggle ; each successive generation genuinely less and less able to bear nervous strain or physical suffering. Misery, and a man's honest belief that he is enduring misery, are no doubt largely relative. Physical, nervous and mental capacity to endure may deteriorate while material circumstances actually improve. Those horrors of modern city life among the very poor depicted by Charles Booth, G. R.

---

possibly Lord Wemyss and Lord Grimthorpe, would now seriously defend the inhuman judgment pronounced upon them by the followers of Euclid.

Sims, Stead, Sherwell, would probably have neither terrified nor greatly inconvenienced dwellers in the London slums known to Defoe or painted by Hogarth ; while to the working classes of 1780 the food and clothing within reach of the very poorest Londoners in 1880 would represent luxury. What might be called 'the standard of discomfort' had been materially altered during the century, while callousness—or capacity to endure other people's sufferings with equanimity — had simultaneously diminished among the 'better classes.' In his address to the British Association, July, 1888, Lord Bramwell himself confessed as much :

'. . . I once said to Mr. Newmarch, known to many of you as a most able man, "I am a bit of a Socialist." He said, "Yes; every right-minded man has a tendency that way." Our reasons were the same. It is impossible not to have a doubt or misgiving, whether it is right that one man should have in an hour as many pounds sterling as another has in a year ; whether one man should suffer the extreme of misery and privation, and another have every, not only necessity, but superfluity. . . .'

A capriciously sensitive public conscience was evolved among 'the rich,' half ashamed of the fact that they could purchase about 30 per cent. more comforts and luxuries with their money in 1880 than in 1840, and becoming aware in a confused way that the newly enfranchised thousands consisted largely of physical wreckage of the competitive system. By degrees one conception of the early political economists came to be—in perfectly good faith— exactly reversed : 'the ideal wage-earning unit' of our latter-day philanthropists and State Socialists is a physically degenerate man, who also has developed those dependent or servile tendencies observed in low and defective types. Thus, a most important gap gradually opened between what must be called 'the biological standpoint' of the political economist and of the humanitarian. Many economic axioms, true of healthy men and of free men, cease to be true if physically degenerate or artificially pauperized men are in question.

The revival in this country about the year 1880 of avowedly Socialistic theories, of which little had been heard, except in J. S. Mill's 'Autobiography,' after collapse of the Revolutionary movement on the Continent and of Chartism here in 1848-49, moulded opinion and political tactics, even as the breechloader has transformed modern war. In Great Britain those theories represent very largely reaction of improved material conditions upon popular beliefs and ideas—the revolt of the Contented, the *intransigeance* of the Good-natured. Latter-day Socialism—taking its chance in clear air and daylight side by side with free institutions and Free Trade—has had little in common with Continental Socialism or with Bryanism in the United States. Some of its genteel clerical exponents, as well as distinguished wobblers, such as Cliffe Leslie, Jevons, Marshall, Toynbee, J. K. Ingram, Ashley, were for a few years much encouraged by *Katheder* homilies from German professors and by the teaching of the grotesquely named 'Historical' School in Germany, but modern British Socialism,

Collectivism, or 'Idealism,' seems to be a new and distinct culture, thriving and multiplying best in a quite new culture-broth, *i.e.*, under mild government, equal laws, and the general diffusion of wealth. While Socialism from the first took little hold upon the bulk of the working classes—acquiring increased political influence, and conscious that they were better able every year to take care of their own interests—healthy and outdoor trades were early differentiated in respect to the new tendencies from unhealthy, sedentary, and indoor trades. Those persons who from time to time affiliated themselves to Socialist organizations were, as a rule, spontaneously 'selected' types, undersized, weak, and physically unsound. The town-bred worker, who had lost most of his second teeth and was short-sighted and bald at twenty, naturally found the 'present industrial system' unsound, and heard gladly the latest prize-prig from Baliol, duly sand-papered and lacquered by 'The Master,' or the *décadent* poet-philanthropist, who quoted the Sermon on the Mount to prove that the competition of the big man—with sound limbs, nerves, teeth, and eyes— was 'immoral,' and that all the first man's misfortunes, physical or financial, were due to the hellish greed of our brother the capitalist. Discreet permeation went on, 'moderate Collectivism' offering something to everybody, but not everything to anybody. State education, increase in wages, general comfort and prosperity, it was seen, still left much wreckage, many misfits. The new ethical generalizations about economic justice meanwhile provided incoherent sanction and verification, at once secular and theological for certain hates or whims, paltry in substance, but formidable in the aggregate. As has been suggested previously, wise legislation had taken beforehand all revolutionary or irreconcilable sting out of English political movements—perhaps, rather, had made it impossible that disciples should take the advice of apostles seriously. For some reason or other, our latter-day Socialists skipped the eighteenth century altogether and neglected to revive the economic theories of the 'Mercantile School' (almost universally held by latter-day American Socialists). From the start they relied mainly upon the deductive method, creating a *décadent* Ethical Providence, eager for the good of 'Labour' or 'Humanity'; apparently a reincarnation, under another name, of the opportunist 'Deus' of the *corpus juris canonici*, the 'Natural Law' of Locke and Rousseau, or 'the Invisible Hand' (leading to a 'harmonious and beneficent natural order of things') of the physiocrats and of Adam Smith. In the writings of the Historical School, the new Motor-Providence appears as 'Economic Morality.' Each group of two or three Socialists gathered together seems to have evolved an independent and infallible fetich of its own, deductions from his manifest likes and dislikes in regard to economics and jurisprudence acquiring as much authority as decretals of mediæval canonists used to have in past times.

In the United Kingdom the new Socialistic tendencies first found a lodgment 'in the upper story'—that is to say, mainly among well-to-do but not robust people, who had inherited comfortable incomes, the savings of the newly-born commerce and industry. With these people revolt against political economy, and wandering preference for 'some kind of Socialism' as an alternative, seems to have been always more a question of temperament than of intellectual conviction. Latter-day Collectivism in this country has produced no constructive literature, although *ex post facto* attempts to justify Mr. Gladstone's Irish land legislation, denunciations of competition, the institution of private property, unrestricted liberty, and other articles of faith long held sacred by Liberals, appeared after 1881. In that year irritating assertions that the Irish Land Acts violated the principles of political economy were best met by the retort that 'the science' itself was all wrong; everything went smoothly enough afterwards.

It had not escaped latter-day pioneers of 'some kind of' State and municipal Socialism that even in the fortunate absence of a written Constitution ideas about equity and legal rights generally accepted in this country were serious barriers in their way. 'The common law of England' came to be described as an invention of the Tory-landlord-capitalist party, for the purpose of 'defending property against the people.' Of old times Common Law had often been a defence of the poor and helpless against rich, powerful, and unscrupulous aggressors. Contracts were strictly and religiously enforced by patriotic and fearless men, who administered the Common Law in despotic times, because the weak had nothing better to rely upon than superstitious reverence for 'the letter' of agreements. In an age when the poor and friendless had few rights or protectors, 'contract' was an advantage not to the strong, but to the weak. The strong generally got what they wanted without agreements or contracts.

Local and trade charters, deeds, constitutions, treaties, copies of the court roll, are lawyers' gear, binding strong men not to do injustice to weak men. Superstitious and bigoted reverence for custom, for legal ritual and formalism, those apparently meaningless ceremonies and observances still extant as handed down from the 'dark ages,' partly had their origin in a true instinct of self-preservation. They became 'sacred' in the eyes of the people, because if they had been omitted, the steel-clad man with the long sword, who couldn't read, and therefore held documents in awe, would have seized the unarmed man's goods or thrown him into a dungeon, while the King's Judges would have had no memorial to go by. One very natural effect of the redistribution of political power is to discredit ancient and quasi-obsolete safeguards. When all classes were learning to rely upon the franchise, the press, public opinion, and other indirect methods for defence of certain civil rights which nobody seemed likely to interfere with, while a section of the class influenced by 'Labour,' or Socialist-Radical leaders was coming to trust more to violence, terrorism, threats—appeals to the fears, interests or vanity of politicians—for the enforcement of their demands, certain principles underlying English Equity and Common Law, notably in the matter of contracts, began to be regarded by many as mere obstructions to 'social justice.'

CHAPTER IV.

PLAIN WHIG PRINCIPLES.

Lord Bramwell's limited capacity for party politics—Takes active share in business of Parliament after 1881—Respect for his opinion tempered by anxiety there—Letters from eminent men to that effect—His fidelity to Liberalism: rooted aversion to Toryism in Church and State—Letters to him on former from good men, and others—His political confession of faith in 1860—Situation at that date—Reasons why he dreaded leaps in the dark—Splendid fiction of intellectual Liberalism—The dynasty of the professors: why real English people repudiated it —Education Act cheapens culture—His almost isolated loyalty to Liberal creed—Letters on 'Diminished Production'—'Fair Trade'—First address to Liberty and Property Defence League—Pamphlet 'Laissez Faire'—Germs of his criticism of legislation in his judicial rulings.

THE gradual metamorphosis of opinion in progress among those busy millions, whose interest in politics is small, whose momentum in politics is incalculable, long escaped the notice of Lord Bramwell as well as of other orthodox Liberals and political economists in agreement with him. They were loath to believe that the seductive wealth, comfort, and prosperity created by Free Trade must by degrees sap faith in the hard sayings of Free Trade, in the wisdom of the irritatingly infallible men who won it. It was into a new world peopled by strange inhabitants that Lord Bramwell stepped, as legislator, pamphleteer, and letter-writer, down from those serene heights whereon great and successful lawyers affiliated to the best Liberal set were welcome to recline in the early eighties. It is not easy to think of him as a party politician at all.* He was constitutionally unable to be cordial to a humbug. Civil—yes ; but if one lacks capacity to feel genuinely enthusiastic about a well-to-do mediocrity struggling with the practical difficulties of statesmanship, one can never be a thorough-going party man. From December, 1885, on, while the Home Rule pestilence raged, one does indeed see by Lord Bramwell's letters, exposing the flagrant lawlessness of the Gladstonian-Parnellite position, that he too was angrily and anxiously watching the political plague-cart going through the deserted streets. After taking his seat in the House of Lords, he was often consulted by the leaders, made speeches, and influenced legislation a good deal. There he was regarded as standing legal conscience to the Tory or Unionist Party. Tories could not understand when Edmund Burke told them that a vital portion of the old Tory creed was very good Liberalism ; but Radicals, Socialists, Idealists, understood perfectly why Lord Bramwell called the new Liberal creed very bad Toryism, and were wroth

* ' The Judges are, or ought to be, of a reserved and retired character, and wholly unconnected with the political world.'— BURKE, Speech on ' Œconomical Reform,' p. 336, ed. 1803.

with him accordingly. In the Lords he was always rather a terror to the leaders. Awkwardly honest, making a fuss about injustices to people of no political consequence whatever, his formidable knowledge of law, his shrewdness, humour, grasp of facts, gift of plain, convincing speech, took away all chance of his becoming a harmless bore. Besides, he had the run of the *Times.*

Some of the following letters are complimentary devices for keeping Lord Bramwell quiet.*

One of the then Opposition leaders, Mr. W. H. Smith, in sending him a copy of the Corrupt Practices Bill as amended in Committee, added:

' 3, Grosvenor Place,
 ' *July* 18, 1883.

' We, however, regard this Bill, as I have said, from an interested point of view, and we are " unlearned and ignorant men." I should therefore be exceedingly grateful to you if you would look at it both as a legislator and a Judge, and tell me, in confidence, if you please, what you think of it as a piece of workmanship and as a contribution to our laws. I may remark that I may not give a poor man, if he is an elector, five shillings, whatever his trouble may be, for fear it should be held to be bribery; but I may promise, if elected, to double the salaries of Civil Servants at the cost of the State, or to take away half the Duke of Westminster's interest in his property in Westminster and give it to his tenants—my constituents—without being guilty of any offence under the Bill. I think

---

* Chief Baron Pollock had written to him, February 20, 1859: '. . . Of all the forms in which the labour of our office presents itself, by *far, out and cut,* the dullest and most disagreeable is " attending the House of Lords." I am not so bad a listener as Alderson, but I dislike to sit all day like Mum Chance, " saying nothing." '

that there is now no effectual provision against an expenditure for or against me by associations or individuals quite outside the scheduled sum which may be spent. . . .'

On October 7, 1884, one of his most amiable opponents, a statesman who always acquiesces sombrely, but with charming equanimity, whenever the British public throw his political prescriptions out of window instead of swallowing them, wrote, referring to their *Times* letters about the House of Lords and distribution of seats :

'. . . Our controversy will soon settle itself, and it looks as if the Government would give you the victory. So be it. I often think of what old George III. said to somebody : "Sir, politics are a trade for a rascal, and not for a gentleman." By which I mean that if you sat in the House of Commons you would see that intriguing combination plays no small part in things. And Heaven forbid that I should say that all the villainy is on one side! Of course, in the House of Lords all is pure and above-board. Many thanks to you for your good-humoured letter. . . .'

An advanced land reformer wrote :

'*February* 13, 1885.

'. . . Many thanks for your most kind letter. I felt sure you would be pleased at my entering the Cabinet, even though you should fear the tendency of some of my views. . . . I will see about the Report of the Commons Preservation Society. I have told Chamberlain and Dilke that I cannot support their Restitution Bill; indeed, that I do not see how it can be framed. I have always been in favour of forbidding enclosures of commons, except under the sanction of an Act—when due consideration would be given for the public and the labouring people—but I am unable to support a retrospective measure of this kind.'

These views, of August 15, 1885, from a well-known Q.C.,* might, *mutatis mutandis*, have been re-written about the summer of 1897 :

'. . . I really have not, as some suppose, given up Parliament out of pique. I considered the matter well before I decided. . . . As to public grounds, I may say that had my party, or what *was* my party, not succeeded to office, I would have fought tooth and nail to put them there ; but now that they are there, I say, "Confound their politics, frustrate their knavish tricks." I, for one, am wholly unfitted to expound "Tory Democracy" to "Capable Citizens." I have nothing but admiration for Lord Spencer ; and after spending ten years in the House of Commons denouncing Parnell and all his works, I cannot support "Maamtrasna compacts," nor those who stigmatize representatives of the only loyal men in Ireland as "Ulster reactionaries." Still less have I any sympathy with Radical legislation by a Tory Government. There is but small place for men like myself in the present House of Commons, and in the next there will be still less. Not until moderate and sensible men on both sides get together, and send Lord Randolph to seek shelter under Chamberlain's umbrella, will there be any hope for us. . . .'

On April 9, 1887, a most distinguished member of the House of Lords wrote to him :

'. . . I assure you that I am very grateful to you for your amendments on the Tithe Bill. They will be of great value to me. I am not satisfied myself with the 5 per cent. deduction. I fear it will bear hardly in some cases, though in others the change will be worth that to the tithe-owner. I have rather shrunk from the interference with freedom of contract† which you mention, as you have done, on general principles. But I fear some provision of the kind must be inserted.'

---

* J. R. Bulwer, Q.C., M.P.   † See p. 351.

This from a great officer of State:

'. . . The Minister in charge of the Bill would be foolish indeed if he did not avail himself of such knowledge as yours. I am not the Minister in question, but I will take care that he has the opportunity, and I make no doubt he will be only too well pleased to get such help. . . . You are a magistrate for every county in England and Scotland, because "the Lords of the Council" are at the head of every commission; but before acting you require to be sworn in . . . just as ordinary magistrates, when they take out what they call their *dedimus*, require to be sworn in before their brother justices. Do you desire that this should be done? . . .

'. . . I hope you have been well and strong during this long vacation. The newspapers attributed to me that I had gone to Bath to drink the waters, because I was there one night taking back my boy to school, and, of course, I am thus credited with a fit of the gout, which I never have had and hope never to have. I am preparing an answer to you in *Vagliano v. Bank of England.*'

In the *Times*, December 15, 1883, anent the late Mr. Justice Watkin Williams' erratic views about 'Statements by Prisoners,' Lord Bramwell had written:

'. . . I quite agree with your leader that the defendant in a criminal case ought to be able to give evidence if he wishes to do so, on oath and subject to cross-examination. And I agree that the time will come when it will be as much a matter of astonishment that the law was once otherwise, as it now is that the law formerly shut out the evidence of parties to civil cases.'

This principle was in Sir John Holker's Criminal Code Bill of 1878, was recommended by the Criminal Code Commissioners, and has found a place in Bills introduced by Sir Hardinge Giffard, now Chancellor. When in charge of his own 'Justices' Jurisdiction

Bill ' in Committee, House of Lords, March 22, 1886
—passed there in 1884 and 1885—Lord Bramwell
argued that a prisoner should be allowed to tender
himself as a witness, but, subject to the discretion
of the Court, should be cross-examined (as to
credit) like the prosecutor, or any other witness ;
for the jury had a right to know what sort of
character the prisoner-witness had.   This provision,
he considered, would be bad for the guilty, good for
the innocent, etc.

This from an old opponent, one of the last letters
on public affairs he ever received, refers to an Irish
Local Government Bill :

' February 27, 1892.

' . . . I am very much obliged by your note. I think ——'s
point is purely technical. He says an American Legislature is
never actually a defendant before a Court. I believe that this
is true, although in many cases the acts of a Legislature have
been called in question and declared null and void. But there
is no power in an American Court to punish a Legislature
otherwise than by releasing all men from the obligation to
obey its decree. My point was that it was no more insulting
to (an Irish) County Council to make it actually defendant and
to pronounce its acts illegal, than to review the acts of a
Legislature in a suit between private parties and make an
order that these acts are void and should not be obeyed.
With all respect to Mr. ——'s learning, I think he is a pedant,
and cares more for a technicality than he does for the real
issue. . . .'

But political forms or party tactics never had any
real value or interest for Lord Bramwell, except in
so far as they touched certain beliefs to which he
held, without swerving, from early manhood till he

died. He had given complete intellectual consent to 'plain Whig principles.'

Historically the Whigs had Lord Bramwell's gratitude ; they had carried the ark of the law which he revered through the wilderness since 1688. To be a Liberal was in the days of his vigorous youth* and manhood the imperative fashion among 'men of intellect,' and the present generation can hardly realize how easy that was between 1828 and 1868. If he ever hated anything, he hated Toryism, which to him meant those special stupidities, tyrannies, injustices and delusions which he and his great predecessors on the Bench had been often called upon to frustrate, which he himself combated in later life with speech and pen. He had lived near enough to the old times to retain the historic suspicion that the Tories needed watching ; that the judiciary might possibly be again required to shield Englishmen from Toryism of the bad kind in Church and State. Even after December, 1885, when he came, in bitterness of spirit, to believe that his trusted leaders and colleagues had proved traitors to the cause, that the skirmishers had faced about and were firing into their own 'supports,' it was often a wrench and a pang to find himself

* '. . . I remember well the passing of the Catholic Emancipation Act in 1829, and the intense pleasure it gave me. I rejoiced heartily at the laws that removed the offensive and irritating payment of tithes by those of one faith to the ministers of another. I thought, and think, the disestablishment and disendowment of the Irish Church a most just and righteous Act. . . .'—Lord Bramwell in *Liberal Unionist*, August 1, 1888.

acting with Tory peers, squires, and parsons.   The cruellest thing Mr. Gladstone ever did was forcing intellectual Liberal giants, who survived until 1886, to admit to themselves that the Tory pigmies had been the taller men, after all.   No stronger proof of ingrained fidelity to Liberalism could be imagined than Lord Bramwell's confession* that, 'as an old Liberal,' he 'would probably prefer to trust the administration of the Crimes Act, 1887, to Sir George Trevelyan . . .' rather than to some other human beings named.   In matters of religious belief, too, Lord Bramwell had a sort of quarrel with Toryism.   Thirty or forty years ago people used to talk of 'holding liberal views about religion.'   What are 'liberal views about religion'?   Few could tell in these days.   Lord Bramwell held them.   His sympathies were with that band of enlightened and advanced Liberals who, within the memory of man, used to make joyous demonstrations of kid-gloved Agnosticism at annual British Association meetings. It was all long ago.   For one thing, he disliked going to church, a duty Judges have to perform while on circuit.   Although the most generous of men in money matters, he was irritated by the assumption that a Judge, in virtue of his exalted station, ought to put, *nolens volens*, a sovereign or half a sovereign into the collection-plate.   On the Welsh Circuit once the plate was handed to him by a smiling gentleman, with a gold-standard look in his face ; suddenly waking from a reverie, the Baron exclaimed, in a peremptory voice, 'Certainly not!'

* The *Liberal Unionist*, May 4, 1887.

On another occasion, again on the Welsh Circuit, a prisoner indicted for stealing fowls was asked whether he was guilty or not guilty. 'That,' said the prisoner, slowly and deliberately, 'is a question for Almighty God, not for Bramwell.' The man was afterwards found to be a lunatic, and was 'detained'; but it shows somehow that the public suspected Baron Bramwell's orthodoxy.

Writing to Lord Bramwell, October 18, 1877, the late Lord Coleridge thus took pains to vindicate Bishop Butler for his friend's admonition :

'. . . Now as to my great Bishop. I own to being disappointed, and, like you, I will not affect the false modesty of saying that you may be right and I wrong; because I don't think so. Not the clergy and clericals alone feel as I do about the greatness, depth of Butler's mind. Men so very unclerical as Sir James Mackintosh, the Mills, father and son, Tyndall and Huxley, put Butler as the very head of the religious philosophers. These names are only specimens; the list might be multiplied indefinitely. It is, however, true that there are minds such as yours, which do not take to him.

'I should, however, observe two things. First, that it would make no difference in my judgment if, in this, that or the other instance I thought the argument failed or was overdrawn. It is the total effect, the mass, the weight of the whole book, the character of the man himself—his fairness, his perfect fearlessness as to conclusions, his moderation in statement, and yet the deep inherent conviction, the suppressed and reserved enthusiasm of the man—which moved me, and I own I expected would have moved you. Then, his wonderful suggestiveness. Take the chapter called, I think (for I have given away my father's Butler, and have none here), " God's Providence — A Scheme Imperfectly Understood." Then think of who he was, a Bishop in George II.'s time ! And then think of his saying that probably, if we knew more, we should find that earthquakes, storms, famines, and the *produc-*

tion of men of genius, were all governed by as strict and absolute laws as the most ordinary operations of Nature, or as the falling of an apple to the ground. Do you really think that any, save a very great man, could (all things considered) have written that chapter? Secondly, it is only fair to recollect what he was about, and whom he was answering. The unbelievers of Butler's day admitted, nay, contended for, a moral and personal government of the universe. Of course he doesn't set about to prove what all in his day admitted, and *on that assumption* he goes on to show (I must say I think with unequalled power and cogency) that the ordinary objections to Christianity fail of force. I do not know whether *you* would make the full admission which the Deists of Butler's time made ; certainly many men would *not*. Of course to such men Butler's argument is not addressed. You will not—it would be unreasonable to expect you would—find in him proofs or arguments for what in his day was a postulate. . . . Nevertheless the " Analogy " may be, and I think is, well worth reading for the wisdom and force of many parts of it, for the incidental sayings and insight of it.

' Some people prefer the sermons. Very fine they are to my taste. They show often that grave humour and irony which in such a man as Butler is delightful. Do look at the one on the government of the tongue. I prefer the " Analogy," however, as the greater and weightier work. Do look at the letter to a lady on the possession of abbey lands, in the appendix to Reeve's memoir of him, and just remind yourself that the writer was a Bishop. Then say whether it does not show a remarkable freedom and candour of mind, besides being very excellent sense and law. Let me also say that I don't think him *clever*, in the sense in which I understand that word. Jack Jervis* was the *cleverest* man I ever knew, and of that sort of quality I don't think Butler had a grain. He is always grave, severe, earnest. I like his style, too, but that is because he seems to me never to care for style, but only to exactly express his thoughts. I shan't convert you, I dare say, but reverence for Butler is part of my very nature, and I can't give it up.

---

* Sir John Jervis, Chief Justice of the Common Pleas.

'I don't at all want to shirk answering your implied question. Of ecclesiastical Christianity I believe probably as little as you do, but I do believe with my whole soul in a moral governor, and I do heartily believe that Jesus Christ was in some sense—which I don't attempt to define—sent from God; so I can say without hypocrisy the second clause of the Creed. How the human and the Divine met in Him I don't believe any man *can* say, and I certainly don't affect to understand. That Christianity will last, therefore, I believe and hope. I suspect *ecclesiastical* Christianity will last much longer than you think—much longer than is good for the world. . . .'

The two men were more in accord on the subject of the blasphemy laws. Concerning a publisher's case decided in the Court of Queen's Bench, September, 1879, Lord Coleridge wrote:

'*September* 24, 1879.

'. . . Thank you . . . for the criticisms you pass on my judgment, which are quite just, and imply more real compliment than any general praise. My own feeling on the matter and its importance does not differ much from yours. But these things struck me as of more importance when I was young than they do now. I had, besides, at the Bar to argue some difficult cases for which I was, or thought myself, obliged to prepare by reading a good deal of Cockburn's stuff. His judgment struck me as that of an ignorant, or at least superficial, though very clever, man, and as being all wrong. Historically, too, the thing interests me more than perhaps it does you. It reveals to one a curious state of belief and society which has to a great extent passed away, but the shadows of which are upon us still. . . .'

In a subsequent year (July 31, 1883) Lord Bramwell received this letter:

'. . . You are a Judge, and you are accustomed when on the bench to throw your mind into the judicial attitude, both as to facts and principles. I hope you will endeavour to deal with yourself in the same way when you are brought face to face with the problems of what you call theology. You need not quote to me a passage from Sir W. Maxwell in which he refers (probably) to the doings of the Inquisition in Spain or in the Low Countries, for there is an older author than Kier, who has put the matter into terser words—Lucretius: "Tantum Religio potuit suadere malorum." The conclusion from the great fact seems in your mind to be this: "Religions, or religious dogmas, are the source of all evil." If you looked into the question judicially, your conclusion would be very different. It would probably be something like this: 'Men's conduct has in all ages been determined fundamentally by their beliefs. It has been bad in proportion as these beliefs have been false. It has been good in proportion as these beliefs have been true. Consequently the line of Lucretius, and the sentiment of Kier, is equally true when it is made to face the other way: "Tantum Religio potuit suadere bonorum."

'Just as false religion and false dogma have been the source of tremendous evils, so have true religion and true dogma been the source of all that is best and highest in human conduct and in human institutions. This is as much a *fact* as the converse proposition. It is the idlest of all occupations to rail against beliefs. They will exist, and they will exert their power. Even the purely negative belief that there is no true religion, and no knowledge respecting it, is a belief which will have its own tremendous power. I submit, therefore, that the duty of all men is not to despise questions of belief, but to study them, and, as far as may be, to solve them. As a matter of fact, the fundamental institutions of our law are in all their moral aspects more or less directly moulded on Christian belief. I have never yet seen any other foundation even suggested which has the same strength, or the same truth.

'Yours truly,

'ARGYLL.'

And again, August 4, 1883:

'. . . I know the fond imagination of many persons that they can have religion with no theology, and the morals of Christianity without any of its beliefs. There are already plenty of indications what a mess they will make of it, besides the theoretical absurdity involved. You make too much of a pope of my old friend Kier. I knew him pretty well: a cultivated literary man, who knew as much about theology as you told us you knew about astrology. Beyond the region of historical anecdote he is no authority whatever.

' Yours truly,
' ARGYLL.'

On the other hand, the late Professor Huxley wrote to him from Eastbourne about this time:

' . . . I trust before long to deal with that misguided person to whom you refer in a manner which will satisfy your benevolent aspirations on his behalf. He really is not worth powder and shot; but one must think of duty, and not of pleasure . . . though I confess that the practice of that form of virtue carries its own reward. I wonder if G. O. M. and the rest are really so muddle-headed as not to be able to see that poor old Noah's deluge is stated to have happened in a certain manner, at a certain time, and in a certain place; that if their history is to be held true, they have to prove so much; that it really is of no use to show that a good deal of water was spilt over the land in quite another manner, in quite a different place, and at a totally different time? How I wish that Fact versus Noah could be pleaded before you, and that I were counsel for Fact, and these fellows for Noah! M'Lud's summing up would be a thing of joy. But, alas! there sits upon the bench only that prodigious ass, the British public, subscribing to Booth.

' With all good wishes,
' Ever yours very sincerely,
' T. H. HUXLEY.'

This from a man for whom Lord Bramwell had profound respect:

' St. Giles House,
' Cranbourne, Salisbury,
' *October* 20, 1884.

' DEAR LORD BRAMWELL,

' Let me acknowledge the receipt of a copy of the *Sunday Magazine*, which you have been so good as to send me. I must thank you for your kind sentiments and expressions towards myself recorded therein. I have been, I think, much misunderstood. I have very decided opinions on the observance of the Lord's Day, but I should not dream of enforcing them, either by law or public speech. The grievance you refer to, Sunday trains, etc., must be left to the judgment and principle of every individual. I have never interfered, nor shall I interfere, except when labour is to be thrown on the working people, and the day abstracted from repose and enjoyment, to be one of toil and ministration to the pleasures of others. I much fear that the reduction of the seventh day to the category of the other six will bring on that issue, especially at a season when trade is bad, and there is a vastly diminished demand for labour. Then the man must work as they order, or not work at all. You will, however, very soon carry your point in the House of Lords, and also in the House of Commons. *But along with it many other things will be carried.* I myself shall not be long an opponent. My age is great; infirmities are daily increasing upon me.* I can understand many people saying, " So much the better." I heartily wish you well.

' Yours truly,

' Shaftesbury.'

This on the other side of the same question :

' 524, Walnut Street,
' Philadelphia, U.S.A.,
' March 20, 1886.

' Dear Sir,

'Permit me to express to you the general feeling of admiration with which we have received in this city the synopsis of your speech made in the House of Lords on the Sunday Opening Question.

' Here, as in the other leading cities of this country, our academies of fine arts and our public libraries have been long open to the public on that day. We have also in this city halls of public intercourse for the discussion of scientific questions open on that day under a State charter, and it is for

---

* He died April 13, 1886.

the purpose of repeating in one of these your oration that I ask you the favour to mail to me a copy of it *entire*.

'Certainly, if the House of Lords should ever cease the high functions it has exercised through so many centuries, a regret must ever follow that with it must also cease the official advantage of such men as yourself to the country.

'I am, with great respect,

'(Signed) CHARLES S. KEYSER.'

On January 16, 1886, a peer and ex-Judge wrote:

'. . . Why do I support the Church? I once sat opposite to the late Soapy Sam of Oxford and Winchester in a country house, and he said he was "not in favour of anonymous journalism." I had always been of a contrary conviction, and ventured to say, "Well, but why?" A twinkle in his humorous eye: "For various reasons." I won't quite evade your question, then, but will answer it by asking another: "Do you think religion a good thing for a nation, or a bad one?" If you ask yourself this, it is quite possible that while doing so you may stumble over *some* of the reasons why I would uphold the Church. . . .'

Dr. Benson, then Archbishop of Canterbury, wrote:

'Lambeth Palace,
'*February* 29, 1892.

'. . . I am most grateful to you for your kind interest in the Clergy Discipline Bill, and your goodness in writing to me upon it.

'. . . I am thankful that a Judge who is held in such honour should feel humanly that some "assaults" and some "libels" are all but commendable. But this being so, surely no Judge would give hard labour for such offences. If a Recorder did, would not the Crown at once pardon? . . .'

The then Bishop of Rochester (Thorold), enclosing a pamphlet of his on social questions, wrote:

'Selsdon Park, Croydon,
'*October* 15, 1888.

'. . . The Socialists have not welcomed it; they describe me as "a dull Tory with a large income." If the former part of the sentence is no more correct than the latter, the criticism is harmless.

' Faithfully yours,
' A. W. ROFFEN.'

Since Lord Bramwell, prior to his retirement in 1881, steadily declined to take any share in party politics, since in his heart he despised the craft, what little he ever wrote on that particular subject is necessarily marred by 'limitations.'   A very clever man who cordially despises his fellow-men for playing cricket, or for trying to catch trout with a fly, may do very many things very well ; he certainly will never be a successful cricketer or fly-fisher.   One advantage Lord Bramwell's determined 'abstention' gave him—he could indulge in the luxury of being direct, outspoken, or even quite wrong.   About non-party questions he could never afford to be wrong.

A long letter of his to the *Morning Herald*, January 19, 1860, signed 'L. L.,' is in the nature of a political confession of faith, the bitter cry of a Whig jurist troubled about the state of other Whigs' souls.   It says frankly what sundry Liberals were thinking at that curious epoch, when Franchise or 'Reform' problems were forging their way to the front, and Lord Palmerston still blocked the way to political disturbance.   Had they all been equally frank, 'Adullamite' dissension in March, 1866, would not have so taken the nation by surprise.

One may note Sir George Bramwell's prediction about 'eight hours' and 'minimum wage' Bills, restrictions on the use of machinery,* demands for imposing taxation of revenge on the rich minority, with exemption for the ' working classes ' (the latter prediction curiously verified by the Finance Act of 1894).   His trust in the people was tempered by much prudence.

'The Parliament of the Working Classes : its Measures and their Expediency.

' In the next session of Parliament propositions will be made, more or less extensive, for lowering the qualifications to vote for members of the House of Commons, in order to admit to a greater extent what are called the " working classes "—that is, those who live on wages . . . What are their wishes, how would the " working classes " legislate if they had the power ?   Now, there is not one in a thousand of them but would say that they do not get the wages they ought to get, and that they suffer unjustly from the tyranny of capital.   It is in vain to say such an opinion is nonsense, that there is no " ought " or " unjust " in the matter, and that there is no proper connection between any quantity of work and any quantity of pay other than that which is formed where labour and capital are left to adjust their own terms.   Elementary and obvious as this may be, it is not the opinion of the " working classes."   They think, not that 5s. 6d. a day for ten hours' work is less than a carpenter ought to get— probably the majority of the working classes think it enough for him—but the carpenter thinks he ought to have more ; the. dock-labourer thinks he ought to have more than 2s. 6d. a day ; and so every working man thinks he ought to have more, and the whole " working classes " think the capitalist, by some ingenious and wicked contrivance, is depriving them of their rights.

' This opinion they entertain, and this opinion they would

---

* Demanded by the Amalgamated Society of Engineers, understood to be the most enlightened body of trade unionists in the kingdom, thirty-seven years afterwards.

act on. . . . Let us examine what steps they probably would take.

'They might begin with the only harmless, possibly beneficial, piece of legislation the subject would bear—I mean with measures for facilitating the establishment and working of co-operative societies, benefit societies, building societies, money clubs, and similar matters. Summary proceedings would be permitted, summary remedies, with probably savage penalties for frauds by managers and others. No great harm would result from this. Like other laws of a similar description, they would not be enforced, and in time would be set right, having done but little mischief meanwhile. But further measures would be taken. . . .'

The allusion to that extinct type, the dock-labourer at 2s. 6d. a day (further on 'at 14s. a week'), reminds one of the immense rise in the wage of 'mere bodily strength' since 1860. Lord Bramwell could not foresee that, in proportion as their grievances were redressed and the franchise extended to them, trade unionists would come to rely more upon threats, violence, and terrorism than upon legislative sanction, because he was quite unable to imagine that 'the authorities,' Secretaries of State and magistrates, would ever come to connive at such extra-legal methods of enforcing trade union demands. A rather minute forecast of probable legislation, giving to trade union rules, regulations, and restrictions the force of law, is omitted.

'. . . But the mischief,' he continues, 'would not stop there. Every intelligent person, not blinded by a supposed self-interest, knows that the enforcement of such regulations would be most disastrous, and especially so to the "working classes" themselves. But they, instead of being taught thereby to remedy, would be stimulated to increase the mischief. They would suppose that some cunning was re-sorted to by the capitalist, some ingenious device, some shift to make the loss fall on them. The masters would still—at least, some of them—have the luxurious house and carriage which are so much envied, and it would be supposed that their unjust gains still continued, and that further legislation must be resorted to. Even if one could suppose that the " working classes " had bettered themselves by their previous legislation, what reason is there to suppose they would remain content? If this generation thinks 5s. 6d. ought to be paid for nine hours, why should not the next think it ought to be paid for eight? Whether, then, we look on their efforts as successful or (as they certainly would be) unsuccessful, we may be sure that they would proceed, if they had the power, to further measures.

'They would now probably be of a direct character. Those I have supposed would be indirect attempts to obtain a larger share of the joint earnings of capital and labour by an increase of wages. They now would claim to share the profits. The capitalist would still be permitted to carry on his trade as builder, cotton-spinner, ironmaster, or other, but the " working classes " would claim to share his profits. They would say that they, as much as he, earned what was earned; that he got more than he ought, and they less than they ought, and that, therefore, there ought to be a change. Of course, I cannot point out how they would set about this. Perhaps somewhat on the principle of the Income Tax Acts. They would appoint committees of their body, or public officers, to ascertain the average profits of the last three years, and wages would have to be paid accordingly, with a provision that there should be a minimum rate. Other schemes would be adopted. For instance, that the " working classes " should be the manu-facturers or tradesmen, and the capitalist a creditor on the profits.

'Another subject of their enlightened jurisprudence would be machinery. What the " working classes " have thought on this matter and what they have done are well known. Is there any reason to suppose their opinions have changed? None.

Witness the conduct last year of the shoemakers, when the sewing machine was introduced. There is a strong *primà facie* case against a machine which throws a man out of work—so strong that the man himself never can get over it, though to every reflecting and impartial person the ultimate benefit to the public and the man himself is undoubted.

'So much for this kind of legislation. The same views would influence them on other subjects. Taxes on articles they consume would be repealed, and revenue raised by direct taxation ; and, if we suppose them to go no further than their noisy apostle in favour of direct taxation, gin, beer, and tobacco, with perhaps tea and coffee, would be emancipated, and a duty put on property of all kinds—land, railways, funds, and movables. How far that is desirable is another question. I point it out as a consequence of the supremacy of the " working classes." I believe this, for the same reasons I have mentioned before. Ask the " working classes ;" they will tell you it is a shame a poor man's beer should be taxed, while a rich man, who does nothing, can spend £20,000 a year, and keep twenty servants, and ride in carriages. It is idle to say this proceeds on false assumptions and false reasonings. I say it is the opinion they now hold and would act upon.

'But there would be further subjects of legislation. All measures of a levelling and equalizing character would recommend themselves to the " working classes." Of course, the " law of primogeniture " would be abolished ; most probably the power of preferring one child by will or settlement would be taken away ; and the power of tying up landed or other property for any length of time, by settlements for the benefit of children and others, would follow. How far this would be beneficial or mischievous I do not say. I point it out as a consequence. It is a consequence which might be followed by others. The extinction of a territorial aristocracy, of course, might involve that of the House of Peers as at present constituted. It is not impossible to contemplate even an agrarian law and a redistribution of property. I know that it is discussed among the " working classes " whether the State has a right to alienate land and grant it for ever, a question, of course, determined by those who do not, against those who do, possess it.

He then finds that he has stumbled up against the difficulty—besetting those who would base the franchise on 'intelligence'—of demonstrating that one class, which you don't know much about, is inferior in political capacity to another class, of whose intelligence you have a very poor opinion.

'. . . It is said if the working classes would act in this way, why do not the £10 householders? It is asked, are the latter political economists? I say, not necessarily so, any more than the Protectionist Duke who is a £1,000 householder. They may all reason equally badly on the matter. But the difference is this, neither the £10 nor the £1,000 householder thinks there "ought" to be the changes I have mentioned. Neither may be able to give a good reason for his opinion, though it is a right one. Nay, it may be he has no opinion properly so called, but still has the sense to follow that man who is in the right. At all events, he has no supposed self-interest to make him take a wrong opinion. Those Protectionists who voted with Sir Robert Peel for the repeal of the Corn Laws did not change their opinion, but, being accustomed to rely upon his opinion, followed him in spite of the change. . . . Of course, those who think such measures as I have suggested desirable will be at once for universal suffrage as the most likely to bring them about. There may be some who think them undesirable, who nevertheless would give the suffrage. They say that the influence of intelligence and property would still prevail, and that a House of Commons returned by universal suffrage would not be governed in its measures by the opinions of the working classes. No doubt that might be, but why it should I cannot see. The number of those who in this country live on wages far exceeds that of every other class, and why should not the members they choose represent their opinions? Still, though it might, it might not be; then why run the risk?

To this, some people answer, " Every man has a right," etc. Such folly is barely worth an answer, but it may be given thus : " Will it be a good thing they should have the franchise ? If so, give it them, whether there is an abstract right to it or not. Will it be a bad thing? If so, refuse it, for you never can be bound to do evil and cause mischief." I repeat, then, if there is a risk, why run it ? But, then, many say we do not propose universal suffrage ; we propose household suffrage, or £5 or £6 house suffrage. But I say again, if this is to let in the working classes, it is to let in mischievous opinions ; and why run the risk of them ? What good will it do? It is obvious that one reduction of the franchise facilitates a further reduction. It is certain that the £10 householder has more sympathy with the £5 than he has with the £50, and the £5 with universal suffrage than with a qualification. The inferior shopkeeper sympathizes with the workman rather than with the capitalist. He is, in truth, a workman himself ; without capital he works at retailing. Those, therefore, who are prepared for any reduction of the franchise must be prepared for the abolition of all qualification, or for a more difficult struggle for its maintenance than is now necessary to prevent a reduction.'

' Abstract right to the franchise ' was much discussed at the time and later, an abstract right to withhold the franchise being, by the way, always taken for granted. He did not foresee the uprising of the Conservative working man, the wholesale conversion of ' the inferior shopkeeper ' to Conservatism, from about 1870 onwards, nor the list to port given by ' some kind of Socialism ' after 1880. For him the vital question was, How would extension of the franchise affect the House of Commons ? Mental concentration on his own professional work, long years spent in trying to get at the heart of English law, at the best working plan for diminishing injustice (not in the civilized world, but in the matter of A *v.* B), naturally led him to anticipate that the new mischievous tendencies would take set legislative shape.   He asks himself at once what would be the legal effect on A or B.

' A plausible argument is put forward, with which I will now deal. It is said that no class ought to be excluded from Parliament; that the voice of every class ought to be heard there; that all ought to be represented there, and that the " working classes" are not. Never was there a phrase of which a more mischievous, perhaps dishonest, use has been made than there has been of this invidious and inaccurate expression, " working classes "—inaccurate, because it means to exclude all who do not receive wages, and invidious because it supposes that they only work. It supposes a homogeneous body, so that what is true of any of its constituents is true of all. Nothing can be more erroneous. The only thing that those whom it is supposed to describe have in common is that they are paid by wages. There is nothing else in common between the farm-labourer, at from 8s. to 10s. or 12s. a week, and the artist who paints the beautiful fabrics of the potteries. There is nothing else in common between the dock-labourer at 14s. a week, who is paid for nothing but mere bodily strength, and the skilled locomotive driver, who must possess character, firmness, and a knowledge of the complex machine he governs, and be able, perhaps, at a pinch to repair it. There is nothing else in common between the man who carries a hod and the intelligent and skilled workman who can build from drawings. To lower the franchise and admit the better sort of these men is not to make them representatives of the others, or enable their voices to be heard. The hewers of wood and drawers of water would still be outside the " pale of the constitution " (I believe that is the style). Drop the phrase " working classes," and say honestly I propose to lower the franchise, and the proposition is intelligible.

' . . . A change in the constituency, to do good, must improve the representatives. They can only be improved in one or both of two ways, viz., either by being made more honest, or more able, or both. Now, if presumably a man's intelligence and information are in proportion to his education, and his education in proportion to his position, then presumably the lower the position the less the intelligence and information. How lowering the franchise and diluting the intelligence and information of the electors can add to the ability of the elected is hard to see. Then as to their honesty. If it could be pretended that class legislation prevailed, that the lower orders were unfairly dealt with, then indeed would any change be justifiable. But there is no pretence for such a change. Since the Reform Act we have certainly had, in this respect, a self-denying Parliament. It is all very well for a demagogue, incapable of existing without the noisy applause he has been used to, to bawl about profligate expenditure and profligate wars, and shout for the remission of taxes on noxious stimulants ; but those are not the opinions of the intelligent and reflecting part of the community. There is not a measure which the good sense of this country favours which is not certain to become law. . . .'

After denying that electors already enfranchised desired further ' reform,' and deploring the weakness and insincerity of the average opportunist politician, or M.P., Whig or Tory, Lord Bramwell winds up :

' . . . For my own part, I sincerely trust that if the franchise is lowered, it may be as little as possible, and I firmly believe that if those who will have to vote on it vote according to their convictions, a measure which I believe to be the first step to an unmitigated democracy would be avoided.

' L. L.'

Thus did extension of the franchise towards ' democracy' and 'universal suffrage' strike a conscientious intellectual Liberal in 1860, when ' Democracy' had a specially bad name in consequence of events of 1848-'49 on the Continent, the collapse of Republicanism in France, and such scandals as the Brooks - Sumner affair in the United States Senate. Should the House of Commons happen to be ruined, must not the nation be ruined too? Correlation of the sciences in later times has suggested consolations. A free people, like a living organism, instantly begins to throw out protective political substances — horny growths, callous or thickened cuticle, so to speak — when wounded. Compensations were invented to neutralize discreditable consequences for M.P.'s themselves of lowering the franchise in 1832, '68 and '84. The nation, objecting strongly to be 'ruined,' fixed on a new political centre of gravity, and, *pari passu*, developed extra House of Commons methods of expressing its will. Deterioration, demoralization of the elective chamber, was, to Baron Bramwell's mind, the penalty for 'letting in mischievous opinions.' The half-truth, that mischievous opinions are more mischievous out of Parliament than in it, was one of those breezy generalizations which he always distrusted. He did not foresee that advocates of 'mischievous opinions' would lose one of their strongest arguments when it was no longer possible to say to M.P.'s, '*If* the working man only had the vote, such and such measures would be passed quick enough.' It is arguable that a Home Rule Bill would quietly have become law, say about December, 1890, had the Franchise Acts of 1868 and 1884 never been extended to Ireland. Again, it would have been morally impossible to disprove assertions that the entire working classes were enthusiastic for Local

Veto had they not possessed the franchise in recent years.   Apparently Lord Bramwell did not recognize as fully as Burke did[*] the importance of ensuring adequate representation for prejudices and unreasoning instincts.   An elective system which only represented intellect, wisdom, experience—the Sunday-best self of the nation—would be like beer brewed without malt or 'ferment.'   Hop beer has always been much misunderstood.   Practical service the Tories rendered for a century by loyally embodying in the nation's policy the nation's incomparable prejudices.   Had the younger Pitt survived, he would probably have been punished by his party for his dangerous leaning to philosophic culture, a defect which proved fatal to Guizot, Castelar, the two Adamses, Karl Schurz, David Wells, and others in America.   One sees from Lord Bramwell's letter how admission of first the middle and then the working class had been regarded in all sincerity even by many thoughtful Liberals as a favour, a concession, certainly a generous, perhaps a rash act.   Demands for Parliamentary reform after 1832 largely represented a longing among the governors for solidarity in the governing mechanism.   It was the responsible men who for their own sakes wanted responsibility spread over as large a surface as possible.   Never having gone through the political mill himself, Lord Bramwell forgot how the wretched man who governs yearns to find someone else to share blame for the mistakes he knows he is going to commit.   Parliamentary reform in 1832 and after

* 'Reflections,' 4th edition, pp. 129, 143.

was but partly a case of victors dispossessing vanquished, of aggressive reformers snatching power from hands clenched to retain it. The grip of the 'privileged ruling class' upon power had begun to slightly relax even before 1832. What happened between then and 1884 was very much a case of new voters called in to help to rule by a class which was steadily losing not only the art, but the ambition, the sentiment of leadership. Lord Palmerston seems to have refused to the last to admit that the system inherited from 1688, to which Lecky pays a fine tribute in Chap. II., Vol. I., of his ' England in the Eighteenth Century,' had indeed been ended by the Act of 1832 abolishing nomination boroughs, on which the working of the system mainly depended ; there were Calne, Tiverton, Coppock and the prophets still. But the influence of ' the governing families' had been, after all, territorial. No sure method was ever devised (although many were tried) for exercising ' influence ' over the large towns, whose vast populations, products of Free Trade, were becoming in 1860 a factor in politics impossible to neglect. Besides, the task of carrying on the Queen's Government grew heavier and heavier yearly. The British Empire was a tiny thing in 1830 compared to what it was and promised to become in 1860. No wonder those incomparable, extra-human representatives of privilege depicted in the H. B. sketches were secretly anxious to find vulgar partners ready to share responsibility. Democracy is for rulers not the difficult—it is the easiest—form of government. When they make mistakes they can say,

'The people tempted us, and we did eat'; or, in official language, that they had bowed to the evident sense of the nation.   The really nervous, bewildered, anxious man is the despot who never gets mandates from anybody.   Since already in 1860 it was plainly impossible, even if desirable, to rule the working classes, better get them to put their names on the back of the promissory note along with the swells. It was a weak man's argument; but, like the abolition of patronage in the Civil Service, dissemination of responsibility in 1868 and 1884 has saved Ministers and statesmen a great deal of trouble, while salaries have not been affected.

The letter of 1860 shows a certain distrust of his own judgment (a different thing from modesty in assertion) which few of Lord Bramwell's later writings show.   The subtle question of what would happen when that superb fiction, Parliamentary government, reached ultimate conclusions was not his special question.   Neither busy barristers nor professional statesmen easily find out the very truth about classes born, living, dying in the more remote regions of the social continent.   What did the 'working classes' really want, hope, hate, fear, believe?   Often distance lent disenchantment to the view.   Statesmen and leading politicians seek the answers to such questions mainly from 'go-betweens,' agents deemed capable of getting to really 'know' the working man because nobody knows them by sight.   Political newspaper editors and leader-writers, selected because possessing political instinct, do in time acquire the art of 'mastering their brief in the hansom' like a busy Q.C., and in regard to what the working classes think, are not, perhaps, so untrustworthy as 'labour' leaders and M.P.'s, but are less in actual contact with the masses than even Cabinet Ministers. The 'go-between' may be biassed, and he may be stupid. Often he takes to drink. The unavoidable but often misleading prominence given by the press to 'public meetings,' the difficulty for newspaper readers of deciding whether they were genuine or fraudulent expressions of opinion, add elements of miscalculation. Clever men are apt to evolve opinions about less clever men from their own imaginations. After the 1874 election Lord Bramwell probably thought that in 1860 he had done something of the sort; therefore he scarcely ever pronounced judgment on purely party politics again.

Although no politician, he may fairly be classed as one of that phalanx of intellectual Liberals who flourished in the early and middle part of the Victorian era. He never had the jargon of the distinguished fraternity at his fingers' ends; he never could pose; took great interest in the debates of the Political Economy Club, to which he was elected in 1855; always very sound in the faith— so orthodox, *quand même*, that he never failed to say a word in season for that queer old ante-Darwinian, anti-biological delusion of Mill's about prudential checks on population as a remedy for poverty and social dangers—he was first welcomed there as a busy Q.C. who condescends to abstract controversy out of working hours. If not flexible enough for a political economist, he was exceedingly sure always about English law, which was respectable.   That decay of 'authority in matters of opinion' which vexed him in his later years—often the reason why he broke silence on public questions—had to some extent been helped by what was called (because there was no English word for it) 'doctrinaire' bias among intellectual Whigs and Radicals.   Always very mortal, they seem to have unconsciously taken for granted the permanent existence of three classes : (1) Privileged, (2) enlightened, (3) inferior.   The former consisted of landowners or aristocrats who represented privilege, traditional claims to govern, most irrational in the view of people who had not sufficiently studied the origin of institutions from the biological side to understand the genesis of 'privilege'; in any case, invalid, unreasonable nowadays, because opposed to the spirit of the age.

The second, or enlightened, class consisted, in the eyes of philosophic Liberals, of themselves and their friends.   The third, or inferiors, comprised the shopkeeping and working classes, the populace, the ignorant peasantry, objects for just rule, philanthropic amelioration, prudent experiment, gradual enfranchisement.   Out of pure gratitude the third would surely always vote or shout for the second class?   What like, all the time, are the English people?   No Irishman ever knows ; no Scotsman ever cares ; no English party politician ever understands, until he is finally turned out of office.   The man of intellect, the quite perfect member of the Athenæum, has a legendary place of his own, even in the era of force, in the age of chivalry, when the knight is the hero of the piece. In myth and romance one sees the student, the thinker, the clerk, often getting the better of the strong man, the man with the sword. But the thinker is not, after all, the people's ideal leader. In questions of government and leadership warp and weft of the old English stuff are constantly showing through that precious embroidery super-imposed by the wise intellectual men. Mr. Joseph Cowen confesses that his constituents do not want political philosophy from him in 1883; they prefer to talk about that Life Guardsman who hewed off Egyptian heads with his sabre at Khasassin—'a Newcastle man, too.' On Jubilee Day the hoarse spontaneous roar is for the sunburnt man with the empty sleeve, for the men with medals, the real men they opine.

Mighty were the services rendered to humanity by the intellectual Liberal. Without him those same Jubilee celebrations would have been im-possible. On the other hand, his yoke was a narrow one for the English people to bear, and if there was a revolt, to afflict and confound such Liberals as Lord Bramwell, much can be forgiven to a genera-tion whose fathers had been ordered to believe that Nassau Senior could talk wisely about everything, that Henry Reeve was familiar with all those subjects which Nassau Senior overlooked, and that H. T. Buckle's 'History of Civilization' was at once the Bible, Talmud, Koran, and Rig Veda of enlightened

Liberalism.*   Insurrection against Buckle was all the more potent because long ' driven under ground.' For twenty-five years Buckle's influence dominated

* March 23, 1858, Chief Baron Pollock wrote to Lord Bramwell :

' . . . Have you heard of Buckle's lecture? have you read his book? do you believe in statistics? I heard his lecture *vicariously.* . . . My wife, four of my daughters, and a granddaughter, besides Fred . . . my eldest son, were there, and I have had accounts from them all. . . . His philosophy (abundantly set out in his book) is this, that the conclusion to be drawn from all statistics yielding results so similar (which no doubt is the case) is, that some principles are at work which necessarily produce these consequences . . .' etc. Matthew Arnold's captious sneers at the middle class, his attempt to acclimatize amongst us the word " Philistinism "—an involved Teutonic sarcasm, necessitating most complicated gearing of levers, cog-wheels, etc., before it will make one smile—show that the intellectual Liberal in this country had a grudge against the real people, just as " the professors " had in Germany. That discontent with Mr. Gladstone which culminated in the Liberal Unionist Grand Remonstrance was partly (doubtless unconsciously) due to Mr. Gladstone's disloyalty in appealing from the genius of the Athenæum Club, first to the Nonconformists, and then to the masses. In combating pretensions of privilege, birth, land or wealth, philosophic Liberals were not asking for " mob rule," but virtually asserting an alternative claim on their own behalf, on behalf of " enlightenment," believing that the aristocracy of intellect not only ought to rule, but would be accepted as rulers ; the which between 1832 and 1872 seemed likely. Few Liberals then foresaw that, while agricultural depression must reduce the privileged class to a condition of philosophic apathy, alleviated by dealing at the Stores, general spread of education would gradually but surely do away with the once obvious superiority of the man of intellect, ultimately leaving his pretensions baseless and rather the kind of people who write leading articles in Liberal newspapers.

Lord Bramwell looked at what was going on within the Liberal party (in 1882 still the nation's chief law-making organism) from a point of view peculiar to himself. Behind his shrewd, blunt, humorous criticisms was dogged resolve to apply to every new legislative or administrative act trenching on individual rights the same principles of equity, measured expediency, and workaday logic, which guided him on the bench. He cared about political economy a good deal, about justice (as he interpreted it) far more. With him expediency—in politics associated with salary-getting and salary-holding— meant the deliberate judgment of many generations of experienced men trained to weigh evidence.

Already an old man, he had to pick up the threads of a controversy seemingly decided for 'good and all' in his youth, to restate conventional truisms. It had given him an 'awful shock,' no doubt,* to

---

ridiculous. British aristocracy, after all, did represent in a shadowy way historic or legendary claims to lead, based originally on what was in lawless times the most valid title of all—force. The highly-educated politician is found to represent a very shaky title to pre-eminence when once "the populace," deprived of certain illusions by universal education, cheap books and newspapers, begin to suspect, with all the complacency of the half-taught, that there is nothing in intellectual superiority, after all.'

* Addressing the British Association, July, 1888, he said : ' At a meeting of this association nine years ago, it was said, not that political economy was dead, but that it had never lived —that there never was such a science. This was an awful shock

hear that not only was the reign of law a myth, but that political economy had never lived. The main premises of the 'orthodox' school were, to his mind, firmly established. Living not *in vacuo*, not on Mr. Herbert Spencer's now completely deserted 'desert island,' not in Rousseau's 'natural state,' but here in England in a community of free citizens, inheritors of certain rights (acquired and law-clinched, not 'natural'), fairly intelligent, of 'full age,' quite capable of looking after their own interests, he saw that vastly complicated relations between all classes in his day were founded mainly on bargain, on voluntary contracts, each of which is an assertion by the persons concerned of their indefeasible right to vary or refuse the conditions of the proposed bargain. No slave ever enters into contracts ; freemen alone do. Sometimes disputes arise later on about the terms or fulfilment of voluntary con-tracts. To prevent men fighting about such matters, the enforcing of bargains or contracts was thrown upon the tribunals. Something of all that Lord Bramwell may be said to have taken for granted without attributing to him speculative or 'implied'

to me, who for nearly two-thirds of a century have been trying to learn something about it, and who have considered, and do consider, that there is no branch of knowledge more important than that of the truths of political economy. An argument attracted a good deal of notice, but, for my own part, I confess I never understood it. It was said that political economy was not an independent science, but a branch of one more extensive. It seemed to me as bad an argument as one which should say that ornithology was no science because it was only a part of natural history.'

opinions merely because his opponents happened to hold speculative opinions the other way. Of certain deductions made by the orthodox economists, he had never seen any disproof. He had a wholesome British dislike to synthesis-hunting and to metaphysical blind alleys ; no new 'message' of his own to deliver, little to say about controverted questions of the science.*

* In November, 1879, while still Lord Justice of Appeal, he conscientiously, and in all good faith, took part in what might be called a puzzle-competition about 'over-production,' and the suggested quack remedy, 'diminished production.' This controversy (like those about the exclusion of foreign prison-made ice-cream, and the wickedness of dealing in 'grain futures') concerned political astrology rather than political economy. It remains one of the curiosities of British industrial history, a by-product of that confusion of ideas, that bemuddled unrest and feverish (or Shaw-Lefevreish) temper which distinguish the years of economic anarchy between 1870 and 1890—when 'the political economy of our youth' was discredited, before 'some kind of Socialism' had completely fascinated our miscellaneous doubters, dreamers, and Marquises. As with Mr. George Potter's bi-metallist agitation and the Fair Trade movement, a few years of good trade and high wages smothered the 'over-production' heresy. German Social Democrats talk about it to this day. Mr. A. Macdonald, M.P., its Adam Smith, made disciples in 1879 among Scottish colliers, who on his advice threw away weekly wages, perhaps getting sense in exchange. Mr. Frederic Harrison probably gave more consideration to this problem than it was worth ; Mr. John Morley, 'smiling, put the question by' at some length, and Mr. Henry Crompton—interested and hopeful about trade union congresses, conciliation and arbitration schemes in those days—circulated one of Lord Bramwell's letters, 'so that workmen might adopt clearer views and wise action on this important matter.'

Concerning a delusion of the period (1881-83) he wrote to the *Times :*

'Unless all trade is fair, these words [Fair Trade] import that there is some which is, and some which is not—some which is unfair. . . . When a nation buys of another which will not buy in return, is the selling nation 'unfair'? I suppose a butcher who bought bread of a baker, who bought no meat of the butcher, would have no less right to complain of the baker's trading. But has the nation, or butcher, any right to complain ? Suppose we complained of the Americans and French that they sold but would not buy, and that it was unfair, might they not justly say that they had broken no promise, no agreement, falsified no expectation, and that the word 'unfair' was unjust to them ; that we were to take notice that they would continue to deal in the same way, and that, being warned, it would be idle for us to complain in future of

Lord Bramwell denounced the 'diminished production' absurdity, just as he would have done had Mr. A. Macdonald, M.P., demanded that all paupers should be buried in Turkey-red cotton shrouds, in order to raise West Scottish factory hands' wages; he wrote also (November 25, 1879) to the *Scotsman,* and Mr. A. Macdonald replied at great length in his customary style. These papers are scarcely worth reprinting. Many people are as foolish in 1898 as the advocates of 'diminished production' were in 1879, but not in quite the same way. No Bill for compulsorily diminishing production has as yet been introduced into Parliament, even by a Ministry of social reform. Lord Bramwell's letter to Mr. Henry Crompton winds up :

'. . . One word more. It is said that this diminished production is only to be temporary, that prices are to be got up, and when got up, then production to the old extent is to be resumed. This seems to me as reasonable as though someone should say, "Build a tower, and put a house on the top ; then take away the tower, and you will have a castle in the air." . . .'

The latter saying would well serve as a motto for the Works Department of the London County Council.

unfairness ?   Might not our customers laugh at us, and say we dealt with them from no love or goodwill, but because it suited us, and it suited them not to buy of us ? . . .   Further, suppose our customers said, " We do not buy of you, because we want to encourage our own manufactures ;" or, " We must raise a revenue ;" or, " We have a treaty with another country," or other reason. The reasons might be bad, but, if *bonâ fide* entertained, would there be a pretence for saying there was anything " unfair " ?   Might not the baker say to the butcher, " There is a butcher nearer to me than you ;" or, " I have dealt with one for twenty years ;" or, " I kill my own meat ;" or, for other reasons, " I cannot deal with you though you deal with me " ? Is there such a thing, then, as what Fair Traders call " unfair " trade ?   I say " No."

'It may be said that this is a question of words, that " unfair " is perhaps not the right word—it should be "unwise." It is not a question of words only, for if there is anything unfair in those with whom we deal, there is, in itself, a reason for not dealing freely with them. . . .   It is all-important for those having right ideas to use right words, of which no better proof can be given than the misleading effect of the words " Fair Trade." Let us substitute " unwise." Is it unwise to buy where you can get what you want better than elsewhere because the seller will not buy of you? . . .   It is for those who say that such conduct, in the nation or tradesman, is unwise to make it out. *Primâ facie*, it is wise, for they buy more advantageously.

'But it may be " unwise " if anything more advantageous could be done. . . .   If, by ceasing to buy of the nation that will not buy of us, we could make it buy (to avoid loss occasioned by not selling to us), our temporary loss (from buying less advantageously) would be compensated in the long-run by the custom we gained. The butcher, by ceasing to deal with the best or cheapest baker, might drive him to deal with him, the butcher, and in the long-run be more than compensated for his temporary loss in dealing with an inferior baker. In such cases as I have supposed, the nation or tradesman would be wise to apply such a coercion as I have suggested, whether they thought or not that there was unfairness. But is there such a case ? It is for those who call themselves " Fair Traders " to show it. . . .'

Anent this letter, Sir Lyon Playfair wrote to him :

' Your argument as to " Fair " Trade is logical and conclusive. But our " Fair " friends care neither for logic nor for conclusions. So I fear your letter had not the force which it deserves. . . .'

Possibly the Fair Traders had been studying Sir L. Playfair's speeches, or votes on behalf of 'fair rents ' for Irish and Scottish tenants, crofters, etc.

In the *Nineteenth Century*, August, 1881, the late Sir E. Sullivan advocated ' Fair Trade ' in an article ' Isolated Free Trade.'   Lord Bramwell wrote to the *Economist*, August 24 :

' Let us suppose Sir E. Sullivan's notions are right as to what a 5s. tax on wheat would produce (though they are not), and let us follow out his calculations. He says: " It is a large family that consumes twelve 4-lb. loaves in the week, so that a 5s. duty means a food-tax of 6d. per week on every large family." Be it so, though it means much more. Now, there is many a large family the income of which is not above 15s. a week—say £40 a year. A tax of 6d. a week—26s. a year— on that family would be a tax equal to about $10\frac{1}{2}$ days' wages. It would be a tax of $3\frac{1}{4}$ per cent. on the income. It would be as bad nearly as an income tax of 8d. in the £. By the Income Tax Act, incomes under £150 are free from income tax ; and where the income is under £400, the income is not charged on £120. How would Sir Edward deal with the " large family"? It is indeed a " fantastic proposition." It is manifest that wheat alone would not rise in price ; other things—potatoes, for example—would. The power to purchase other articles, clothes, etc., would be diminished in the " large " and small families. Other mischiefs would follow. Sir Edward says,

" This sum of £6,250,000 cannot be considered altogether lost. More than half would have gone into the Treasury." Where would the rest have gone ? Into the pockets of the landlords. I would as soon it should go there as anywhere, for they have been great sufferers, if it is to leave the pockets of the " large families "; but it had better stay in their pockets.'

Lord Elcho, M.P., now Earl of Wemyss and March, was in the summer of 1882 chief promoter of the Liberty and Property Defence League, a Solemn League and Covenant for the purpose of withstanding the works of those backsliding Liberal political economists who either led or followed Mr. Gladstone, it was not clear which. Lord Elcho had attacked the Irish Land Bill of 1870 from the standpoint occupied by Liberal and Radical political economists during the century. His speech of 1870 remains unanswerable ; the remark of Mr. C. Russell during debate on the consequential Land Bill of 1881, that Lord Elcho had 'made his old speech of 1870 over again,' is the only serious attempt to answer it extant. For many years it has been the singular privilege of the Earl of Wemyss and March to bring to the notice of the British public by speeches and letters to the press the fact that latterday Liberals have uneasy consciences ; similarly, the approach of a policeman will often miraculously convince a drunken man reclining on the pavement that he can really move on if he likes. It was at Lord Elcho's suggestion that Lord Bramwell joined the new Liberty and Property Defence League.*

* He wrote : ' DEAR LORD ELCHO,—My opinions of half a century standing are as strong as ever. I like to be governed as little as possible, and what I like for myself I like for others.

At the first general meeting thereof, November 29, 1882, Lord Bramwell said :

'. . . Our wishes and our objects are so easily stated that we ought not to be long in doing it. All we want is to be let alone, so that those who are kind enough to govern the people of this country should have as little trouble as possible in doing it ; that they should mainly concern themselves with keeping order at home and defending us abroad. I am, however, afraid that there is at the present time a very strong disposition to do a great deal more than this—to take a great deal more care of us than we want to have taken ; and if I wanted any authority for that, I should find it in a very excellent speech made by a very distinguished statesman."

Lord Bramwell here read an extract from a speech of Lord Salisbury's at Edinburgh, apparently intended to rebuke those interferences by the Board of Trade in labour disputes, of which much was heard in later years, and then continued :

'. . . Now, I should like, not because he is a noble lord, but because he is a very distinguished noble lord, *who will take a greater share in the future government of this country than he does at the present moment*—I should like to call your attention to a

No one can know my wants as well as myself, and I am pretty sure that no one will take so much pains as I should to gratify them. I am certain it is best to leave what I may call natural causes to operate and bring about natural results. I cannot but think that our present troubles show this. I agree with you ; no party is to blame, though ours—mine—ought to know better. It is the unwisdom of the public generally calling out for legislation and restriction on all occasions. I used to say that the difference between us and foreigners was that we do everything not forbidden, they only do what is permitted. The difference is ceasing. I shall be very glad to be a member of your association.'

speech of Lord Rosebery, in which he says: " I believe at present the people of Great Britain are better off, and happier, and more prosperous than their European neighbours, and this mainly because of their long enjoyment of self-government, which has enabled them to know what they want, and to obtain it." Now, I believe this to be perfectly true ; I believe that the people of this country are better off than the people of any other country of Europe ; or of any other people in the world, except, perhaps, those who inherit our institutions, and have a large amount of unoccupied land—I mean the inhabitants of the United States and the colonies. To whom are you indebted for this prosperity ? Not to the Government or the State. The hundreds of millions which have been laid out upon railways and roads, and other public conveniences, have been laid out by the capitalists, and not by the State. As was well observed by a lecturer the other day, there are about three harbours in England which owe their existence to the Government, and one canal, which does not pay its expenses. Everything that has been done for this country has been done by that new subject of persecution—the capitalist. To a very remarkable measure passed in the former part of this session, the Electric Lighting Act,* I wish to draw your attention. Under that Act men are enabled to venture their capital, if they think fit, in electric lighting companies ; but at the end of fifteen—or I think it was extended to twenty-one—years, the local board or the municipal corporation, within whose district the venture is, is at liberty to take over the work, upon the terms of paying, not the value of the goodwill or anything commensurate to the profits which have been made, but upon the terms of paying the then value of the plant of the electric lighting company, and the local boards and the municipal corporations are to carry on the electric lighting. One did think, at the time when that great writer was studied, whose science is now relegated to Jupiter and Saturn—one did think that the worst possible body for managing such a thing as that

---

* This Act, of course, had to be amended in subsequent years. Its operation had strangled electric lighting enterprise.

was a municipal corporation. However, it was done, and why? Because waterworks and gasworks have been paying concerns, and the only remedy which suggested itself to the minds of those who brought forward this measure was that the thing should be handed over to a municipal corporation or to a local board. I cannot help thinking, by the way, that in addition to the unfitness of these local boards—made up, no doubt, of very respectable men, but who know nothing of electricity—it seems such an undesirable thing that they should have the sort of patronage that they will have, and *that they should have a number of people in their employment who will no doubt agree with the politics of their employers.* Thus, we shall have Liberal lamp-lighters and Conservative turn-cocks, and other functionaries of that description. The sort of reason given for all this is that these things are monopolies. If ever there was a much-abused word in the English language, it is that word "monopoly." (*I have often thought that if people could not talk they would reason much better than they do. They would not be able to communicate their ideas or no ideas as well as they do now, but they would certainly reason much better.*) These things are a sort of monopoly, no doubt, but there are two sorts of monopolies. If a man has to bring his corn to me because no one else may grind it, and has to pay what I ask, no doubt that is a monopoly; but if a man comes to me because I grind his corn cheaper and better and more advantageously in every way than any other miller, what objection is there to that? But people treat railway companies, for example, as if, instead of being public benefactors, they were a set of people who plundered the public. There are several prohibitions, infringements of our liberty of action, in the Metropolitan Boards Act. What the object of this is I do not know, but I give that board credit for being reasonable. Well, then, we come to a very extraordinary Bills of Sale Act. There are all sorts of propositions in it . . . one of them is that there shall be a nullification of a bill of sale under £30. It was supposed that people who dealt with those bills of sale were money-lenders of so extortionate a character that it was necessary to put an end to their proceedings—at all events, when the bills were for less than £30. For my own part, after having looked at the evidence, I cannot think that it was true. *The money-lender carries on a trade, and wants to get a goodwill and a connection, and I don't believe that he would behave in such a way as not to gain the goodwill of his customers.* However, the Act says that bills of sale for less than £30 shall be null. What is the consequence? Does anyone suppose that as long as there are people who want to borrow, and others willing to lend, this will have any effect? Certainly not. The only consequence of putting these impediments in the way of borrowing is that the lender will charge more for the additional inconvenience to which he is put. . . . I have said that the capitalist is an object of alarm and aversion. Next to him is the landlord. It is true that the landlord in England has so dealt with the land as to redeem it from its "prairie" condition, to use an expression which has been used before; but still he is now an object of great aversion and alarm, and it is proposed that there should be an Act of Parliament to say that, though the tenant should stipulate to the contrary, although the terms of his lease should be based on his making no improvements without the landlord's sanction, although he should pay less rent in consequence of having come to that bargain, it is proposed notwithstanding that he should be at liberty to do what is called "improve" the land, and then make the landlord pay for it. So that a man with a temporary interest of I don't know how many years—five, six, ten, or whatever number it may be—is to be able to decide upon improvements which the permanent owner would not adopt, and notwithstanding his own expressed bargain to the contrary. Then the next thing is the proposal that employers and their servants should not be at liberty to contract themselves out of what is called the Employers' Liability Act. Anything more outrageous than this I cannot conceive. That is the worst of these measures—they not only prevent legitimate bargains being entered into, but when they are entered into, in spite of the prohibition or nullification of them, the Act of Parliament tempts a man to be a rogue and to break the solemn engagement that he has entered into. . . . The next thing—and upon my word I think they ought to be ashamed to bring it forward—is that wages are not to be paid in public-houses. Well, I should propose as an amendment to that that any small boys who receive wages shall not be paid in cake-shops, because I suppose the object of this provision is that these men who receive wages shall not be tempted to spend them in the public-houses. I suppose a similar reason would apply to the boys I have spoken of. Then we are to have more factory inspectors—wooden images with red clothing. . . . The last thing to which I will call your attention is that the land is to be nationalized. Now, what that means I don't know. It is a comfort to me that those who propose it don't know also. I have not the slightest doubt in the world that there is not any one of them who can attach a definite idea to that expression—the nationalization of the land. I dare say you remember that Corporal Trim showed that he could attach a definite idea to the commandment to honour his father and mother when he said it meant giving them three half-pence a day out of his pay. That was a definite idea, but I doubt whether those who advocate the nationalization of the land could give you any definite idea of their meaning if they were called upon to do so. So far as I can judge, it means something like the State being the owner of the land. Well, when it is, what is the State to do with the land? Is it to cultivate it? If so, we shall have even more agricultural depression than we have now—a very great deal more. . . . And if the land is to be nationalized, why not chattels, and why not labour? Why is not labour to be nationalized, and why should we not get straight into the very thick of Socialism at once? That is what this argument points to, and to this alone. *I confess, for my own part, I have a sort of sneaking liking for Socialism. I wish we could have it.* One cannot but sometimes feel how much better off one is than the man who gets a few shillings a week, and works hard for it. . . . It is not, I would say in closing, to be supposed that we are opposed to all legislative restraint. I will not attempt to draw any line—indeed, I suppose it would be extremely difficult to do so—where State interference is permissible and where it is not. . . . If the meeting will permit me, I will refer them to a book by the late Mr. Jevons, entitled "The State in Relation to Labour,"* in which what I would bring forward, if I had the ability to do so, is described as well as it possibly can be done. I think there is some necessity for persons to unite and promote the objects we have in view, for in my belief there is a most mischievous tendency abroad.'

Two years later he followed up this line of reasoning in his pamphlet 'Laissez Faire,' published by the Liberty and Property Defence League, 7, Westminster Chambers, London, S.W.:

'The Right Honourable the Chief Commissioner of the Board of Works, the President of the Social Science Congress, in his address to that body told the British public that the old-fashioned notion that people were to take care of themselves was quite gone and ended. He said that he and the other members of the Legislature would do that for us. Now, as to myself, with a single exception there is no one I would so soon trust with such a task as my old friend Mr. ———. I have perfect confidence in his honesty and good nature, and the highest respect for his ability. Still, there is one I should prefer to take care of me, and that is myself; not from any arrogant notion that I could take better care than he of anyone else, but because I think I could of myself. I claim it as a special knowledge in which I excel him. I am sure I know my own wants better than he does. I have also a strong conviction that I should be more zealous in the gratifying of them. Let us put an extreme case. Suppose my friend and I had to care for each other's wants instead of each for his own. I am afraid I should feed him sometimes when he was not hungry, and he occasionally would put me to bed when I was not sleepy. I should take him for his good to the Liberty and Property Defence League, and he would take me for mine to a Social Science Congress, to the edification of neither. Selfishness has something to be said for it. Nature was not altogether wrong when she made our own good our first care. For my

---

* See note, p. 214.

part, then, I decline the help of Mr. —— and other benevolent legislators. I ask to be let alone. *Please govern me as little as possible*. Prevent me doing mischief to others, but let me do it to myself if I like; I shall sometimes, not on purpose, but for want of knowing better. I am afraid more mischief would be done to me from the same cause by others.

'Mr. —— says: "Among the greater number of writers and thinkers there has been a distinct reaction from the views of Adam Smith, and of his successors, Ricardo, McCulloch, J. B. Say, Bastiat, and others. Almost alone, my friend Mr. Herbert Spencer has been left among philosophers to preach the doctrine of *laissez faire*." The gods I have worshipped from my youth are all false gods. Worse than dumb idols, they have been preaching false doctrine. They are not only not right; they are wrong, and I have been their devoted worshipper all this time. It is a comfort to me to think that Mr. Herbert Spencer is "left among philosophers to preach the doctrine of *laissez faire*." "Almost alone," says Mr. ——. The profoundest thinker of the age is "almost alone." So much the worse for the age. How does Mr. —— dispose of the universally lamented Mr. Fawcett? Was he no philosopher? What of Mr. Goschen? Is he none? Then I give up philosophers. But who is there on the other side? Mr. —— says the " movement for extending the action of the State has received much of its impulse from philanthropists, philosophers, and political economists, among the greater number of writers and thinkers," etc., as I have before quoted. Now I will make a demand on Mr. —— which, as a brother lawyer, he will understand. It is a demand very effectual for stopping general and unfounded claims. Please, Mr. ——, "further and better particulars." Who are *your* philanthropists? No; I can do without them. But who are your philosophers, political economists, writers and thinkers? Give their names and their writings. I do not say there are no philanthropists, good men, who would govern us for our good; but unless they possess, besides philanthropy, some philosophy and some political economy, I had rather they had nothing to do with governing me. Mr. —— says: "The more recent school of political economists in this country, and still more on the Continent" (Lassalle, Karl Marx, and the like, I suppose), "have held that while free exchange, free labour and free contract are *important*" (really, now, only do think) "principles to maintain, yet that the State is bound to interfere when individual interests result in the oppression and degradation of the lower classes, and that it is justified in undertaking those works and functions which can be better attained by it than by individual effort."   Now, does Mr. —— really mean that Smith, Ricardo, McCulloch, Say, Bastiat ever expressed contrary opinions? If so, I say again, "Further and better particulars."   Where in their works are such to be found?   Did they ever preach a doctrine different from his own, viz.: "We cannot, I think, oppose to any proposal of legislation, or to the extension of the functions of the State, any rigid doctrine of *laissez faire* based on theoretic objections to the action of society in its corporate capacity, or an abstract view as to the inexpediency of interfering with individuals.   Each case must be dealt with on its merits."   Good.   So say we all.   So said Smith and Ricardo and the others, and so says Mr. Spencer. . . .

'Mr. —— says that freedom of contract is not interfered with when the State permits it to be made, though it refuses to enforce it.   The best answer to make is that there is only real freedom of contract when there is freedom to make an enforceable contract.   Are there two kinds of freedom—one to make enforceable contracts, the other to make unenforceable?   A freedom to make the latter is no freedom.   It is idle.   An unenforceable contract is null in law and in good sense. . . . Mr. —— says: "If on grounds of public·policy, or for the protection of the weak against the strong, the State declines to enforce a particular contract, it does not interfere with freedom of contract, but the reverse!"   Does it not?   Why, it *does*, but does so for a good reason.   The greatest admirer of *laissez faire* never advocated that all contracts should be allowed and enforced; that an agreement between A and B, that B should murder C, should give A a right of action if B did not murder C.   So of an agreement between a man and woman for cohabitation.   All that the advocates of *laissez faire* demand is that freedom of contract shall not be interfered with without good reason. The Truck Acts may perhaps be justified on this ground, but in my judgment it would be better to teach the wage-receivers to take care of themselves.

'Now let us examine what Mr. —— gives as the results of the new philosophy which is to be substituted for *laissez faire* and its old-fashioned teachers, Adam Smith and the others. By the way, he says the Reform Act of 1868 gave "so great an impulse to social legislation," etc. Mr. —— does not say when the new school became of authority and Adam Smith and the others ceased to be. Was it not till the time of passing that Act ? If so, the old school may claim merit for one or two pretty good things done before 1868—Commutation of Tithes, Amendment of the Poor Law, Reform of Municipal Corporations, Abolition of Slavery, Abolition of the Corn Laws, Free Trade generally. These are to the credit of the obsolete school, and some may think will compare well with what has been done since. . . . "There have been two very distinct impulses to legislation, the one in the direction of limiting the powers and duties of the Government—in freeing the action of individuals from the influence and control of the State." . . . The other impulse, we are told, is "in the opposite direction of increasing the intervention of the State in our social arrangements, of multiplying the functions of the Government, and adding greatly to the number of cases where the law prescribes the conduct of individuals or restrains their actions." Let us examine the instances of this "grandmotherly legislation," as Sir W. Harcourt, borrowing from Sir J. Scourfield, called it :

' "Landowners, railway companies, owners of public-houses, ship-owners, factory-owners, and other interests, have been successively dealt with and made to feel that the State is supreme. . . . The domain of private contract has been curtailed. Concurrent with these changes, public opinion, operating through the House of Commons, calls the Ministers to account, and holds them responsible for every act of administration and for the smallest events that occur, to a degree continually increasing." True, "the smallest of events"—things unworthy of notice—things which, if noticed at all, should be asked not of the Ministers in the House of Commons, but of the superior of the person about whom the question is put. The practice is a cowardly way of insinuating a charge without responsibility, and puts on the person the duty, not of showing he was not in the wrong, but more, viz., that he was in the right, which he should be taken to be till a *prima facie* case is made against him. I refused, when a Judge, to notice such questions. . . .

'As to extension of the Factory Acts: "It is necessary for the law to impose limitation as a check on the one hand on the competitive race for profits of the masters, and on the other hand on the greed and ignorance of the parents." Good—agreed. Those who are not their own masters need protection. Mr. —— proceeds: "It has not been necessary to apply these laws to grown-up men. They can protect themselves by combination." Good again. "In some trades, however, of a specially dangerous character, minute and elaborate rules have been laid down by recent Acts for their guidance, 'and are enforced by inspection in the interest of the workmen and the public.'" Cannot the workmen in these trades protect themselves by combination? Why not? As far as they are concerned, the best thing to do would be to teach them ; make them protect themselves from their own "greed and ignorance" instead of treating them like children, prescribing by legislation that a provision of "squash" should be made for them.

'Then Mr. —— mentions the licensing and strict regulation of public-houses, saying that free licensing leads to drunkenness, that reasonable restrictions were good for the trade, as they prevented one man keeping open all the other houses by keeping open his own, and that unrestricted competition leads in some trades to adulteration! So I suppose Parliament, to save us from adulteration, should restrict competition! Mr. —— admits that the monopoly has been strengthened. Police considerations make drink legislation a difficult subject —half-hearted legislation it ever will be. It is not said downright that drink shall not be sold, that people shall not drink intoxicating liquors, but it is made more or less difficult for the sale and drinking to be carried on.   It is as though it was enacted that drink should only be sold in broken glasses or up four pair of stairs, or that the sellers should have a week's solitary confinement once a year.

'Then Mr. —— cites mine regulations.   They certainly seem to him to have been beneficial.   But they have, he says, added to the cost of working; they have created an army of inspectors.   There again we may say that the men ought to have been taught to insist on the improvement.   As to ships, *laissez faire* had better have been left alone.   Mr. —— says: "Notwithstanding this" (meddling), "and in spite of a vast increase of staff, involving an annual charge of £70,000, it is to be feared that no effect has been produced on the loss of ships and the loss of life at sea."   None.   But a grievous effect has been produced on ship-owners by the worry and vexation of these regulations.   Their difficulty of competing with foreigners, bounty helped, has been much increased.   It is most to be deprecated that their troubles should be increased in the present depressed condition of shipping.   As to railways, Mr. —— says: "The Railway Commission is empowered to compel a railway company to alter fares and provide greater facilities for passengers where it is clearly proved the company is treating particular districts unfairly, or neglecting its duty."   Perhaps; I do not know.   But what is the meaning of treating a district *unfairly*, or a railway company neglecting its duty if it acts according to law?   Then we have the Employers' Liability Act.   Mr. —— does not state its effect quite accurately.   He says it *makes* employers liable for the negligence of their agents to their servants.   Not quite so—only for the negligence of those who supply the place of the masters.   And it is not accurate to say it *makes* them liable.   The effect of the Act is this: The master was not liable before unless he and the servant agreed he should be; now he is liable in certain cases unless he and the servant agree he shall not be.   Theoretically, the change is of small consequence.   Practically it is of more, as people do not understand it, and incur a liability they are not aware of.   *The Act does not seem to have done much harm.*

' Then Mr. —— cites the Hares and Rabbits Act. If ever there was a contemptible piece of legislation, it was that. . . .* Then Mr. —— refers to the Agricultural Holdings Act. That Act had many very good provisions in it. But it had one which I think discreditable to the Legislature. A landowner and intending tenant may go over a farm; may agree that one field wants draining and make provision for it, and that another does not, and put down in the lease that it shall not be drained. Yet the tenant may drain it, and call on his landlord for compensation! In other words, he may deliberately violate his engagement, and may do so though he intended to do so when he entered into it. Is this the legislation that Mr. —— admires? A legislation that allows dishonesty; that admits freedom of contract in the making, and freedom of action in the breaking. It may be said, " What matter ? the landlord will only pay the value of the improvement, if there is any." Be it so ; but the matter is this. The landlord thought he had precluded disputes ; he finds himself let in for a lawsuit, with all its worry and uncertainty. He saying there is no improvement, his tenant that there is, the matter to be determined at the cost of the man in the wrong, or, rather, held to be. What is the justification for this ? . . .

' Next Mr. —— cites the Irish Land Act (1881). . . . We can quote Mr. ——, that it was passed not on " economic considerations only, but was of a very exceptional and almost revolutionary character, capable of justification on broad *ethical, historic,* and economical grounds. Its principles were demanded by the almost unanimous voice of Ireland at the last General Election !" Very likely. Something of the same sort was demanded in France about 1790 and the following years. All I would say about it is, that if it was necessary on historic and other grounds to take a deal of landed property from its owners, there was no necessity for not paying them for it. Note the consequences of this Act. English farmers and Scotch crofters, not seeing that the Irish Act is " capable of justification " on " historic " and similar grounds, wish to apply what they conceive to be its principles to their own case.

---

* See pp. 356-9.

' Then Mr. —— recites the Act prohibiting the payment of wages in public-houses. The history of that piece of legislation is instructive and amusing. There was an Act prohibiting such payment in the case of workers at coal-mines. Payment of *their* wages at public-houses never could have been necessary. It occurred to somebody to extend this Act to all wages. And accordingly, with no evidence of any, or what mischief caused by the law as it stood, with no evidence as to what mischief and inconvenience would be caused by a change in the law without any exception or qualification, a Bill was brought in to forbid payment of any and all wages in public-houses. The publican could not pay his own workpeople in his own house ! And the Bill was so ingeniously framed that it prohibited the payment of wages in houses where no intoxicating drink was sold. Some of these things were set right, and the Bill passed. What has been the consequence ? The law has been broken, as all such laws will be. If it is for the convenience alike of master and man to pay and receive at the public-house, it will be done, any law to the contrary notwithstanding. Here, as in like cases, we have a bad commencement of law-breaking.

' Mr. —— says, as to the Employers' Liability Act, " if it should prove to be a fact that large numbers of employers are forcing contracts on their men to elude the liability contemplated by that Act, I should see nothing contrary to principle in refusing to recognise such contracts, unless they contain a fair and reasonable substitute." " Forcing." What is the meaning of that ? How can a *contract* be " forced " on a man ? How can Mr. ——, a lawyer, use such an expression ? How can he, an economist, use it ? Does he not know that what advantages the workman is to have in wages and otherwise is regulated, not by the will of the master, but by the " higgling of the market " for labour ? Does he not know that if the master gives more in one way he *must* give less in others ? I say *must*—to get his fair profit and compete with others. . . .

' Mr. —— would have municipalities provide gas and water at present ; possibly, at a future time, bread, coals, and other things. . . . Mr. —— admits that the good things the State provides us involve an army of inspectors and £300,000 a year. He might add, and a constant worry and intermeddling, causing not only vexation but expense. However, legislation based on the preposterous notion that the State can provide for us better than we can provide for ourselves Mr. —— admires. A legislation which treats people as helpless, and, instead of teaching them to struggle for themselves, adds to their feebleness by a mischievous taking care of them. A legislation which prohibits a valid bargain between two people who wish to make it and perfectly understand it. A legislation which admits the making of the bargain, but permits its breach. A legislation which, it is said, permits freedom of contract in the making, and promotes freedom of action in the breaking of engagements. A legislation which deliberately provides that frauds may be committed with impunity.

'That this should be proposed anywhere is to me a wonder. But that it should be proposed here in England almost passes belief—England, the freest of all countries—the least governed —the most intolerant of control and interference, and the most prosperous; I except colonies and new countries. Not only the most prosperous, but from its very freedom and independence of restraint the first in the world for everything that makes a nation great and good. . . .'

Lord Bramwell, one sees, preferred to touch that side of controversy which really had a fascination for him. He shows how certain specific Acts or Bills passed or proposed from 1880 onwards might injure various real people, A, B or C—people who were nothing on earth to him, whom he had never seen, and was not likely to see. Whether those measures were indispensable to keep 'the party' together or to win votes he did not ask.

Nobody would look for a criticism of the new jurisprudence or of Liberal land legislation — not

only Irish, but English and Scotch—in Lord Bramwell's reported judgments.   Nevertheless, his speech
of July, 1883, in the House of Lords, in the appeal
case of *B—— v. The Manchester, Sheffield, and L.
Railway Co.*,* is an entirely undesigned but very
complete refutation of one of the main principles
underlying the two great Irish Land Acts, the 'most
despicable' Hares and Rabbits Act, the Crofters
and Agricultural Holdings Acts, Leasehold Enfranchisement, Employers' Liability Bills, Railway
Rates Acts, etc.

* B——, a fish-dealer, made a written contract with a railway company relieving them of carrier's liability, in case his
fish was spoilt, owing to the company's servants' delay or other
act, in consideration of freight rates on B——'s fish being
specially reduced from £100 to £80 per ton.   One day B——'s
fish was delayed and spoilt.   Then B—— sued the company,
as common carriers, to recover damages, as though no special
terms had been agreed on.   The company pleaded that their
contract with B—— absolved them, and in the Queen's Bench
Division won the case.   B—— then went to the Court of
Appeal, where, December 19, 1882, the first decision was
reversed, the Judges holding that B—— had been compelled
to make the contract in question—had no alternative but to
make it—since if he had paid £100 per ton (the usual rate) he
could not have competed with rival fish-dealers, etc.   The
Railway and Canal Traffic Act of 1854 had been interpreted
to mean that freight contracts between railways and their
customers must be 'just and reasonable.'

By the Law Lords in July, 1883, it was held, reversing the
decision of the Court of Appeal, that B—— *had* an alternative
—that he needn't have made the contract in question unless
he chose to; that the contract was, in point of fact, 'just and
reasonable,' as required by previous interpretation of the Act
of 1854.

Lord Bramwell said :

' My Lords,—The case of *Peek v. North Staffordshire Railway Company* was decided twenty years ago. At the time it was decided, and from thence continuously until now, I have thought it wrongly decided, as I know it was contrary to the intention of the framers of the Act, and this case confirms me in that opinion ; for here is a contract made by a fishmonger and a carrier of fish who know their business, and whether it is just and reasonable is to be settled by me, who am neither fishmonger nor carrier, nor with any knowledge of their business. And although that (Peek's) case has been in existence for twenty years, and has been acted upon in courts of law, if it were within my competency to overrule it I would do so, because it is impossible to say that people have regulated their contracts in reference to it. They have done nothing of the sort . . . they have entered into contracts, and having had the benefit of them, they have turned round and sought to avoid them. . . . It stands confessedly that B—— (the fishmonger) has put £20 into his pocket by virtue of the contract, and he is now seeking to avoid it as an unjust and unreasonable one, yet keeping the £20. However . . . we must say whether or not this contract is just and reasonable.

' . . . I am not prepared to say at this moment that it is an impossibility that a contract knowingly and voluntarily entered into by two parties could be unjust and unreasonable. If it is not voluntarily entered into, that is a very different thing. But, for my own part, I am prepared to hold that unless some evidence is given to show that a contract voluntarily entered into by two parties is unjust and unreasonable, it ought to be taken that that contract is a just and a reasonable one, the burden of proof being upon the man who says it is unjust and unreasonable.

' First of all, its justice and reasonableness are, *prima facie*, proved against the man by his being a party to it, and if he means to say that what he agreed to is unjust and unreasonable, he must show that it is so. I am prepared to hold, in this particular case, its justness and reasonableness are beyond the slightest doubt, looking at the profit the plaintiff has made by it.   And when it is said, "What an unreasonable thing it is that you (the railway company) should exempt yourselves" —as I own this agreement does—"from all responsibility, even for the wilful default or wilful act of your own servants!" I deny that there is anything necessarily unreasonable.   I say that any man who wants to make out that it is unreasonable must prove it.   I can perfectly understand—as I put in the course of the argument—a man going to a railway company and saying: "Now, I deal with you; you carry fish for me. We often fall out; we have disputes.   Sometimes the fish is late, and oftentimes it is injured; sometimes it is your fault, sometimes it is not.   We get into trouble and into litigation with each other.   If you will make me an abatement of 5 per cent. or 10 per cent. or 20 per cent.," or whatever he thinks fit to ask and they agree to, "I will undertake to hold you not responsible, even if the fish is spoilt or stolen by your servants." I can understand that to be a perfectly reasonable proposal for him to make and for the company to accept.   It seems to me to be perfectly idle, and I cannot understand how it could have been supposed necessary, to require a Judge to say whether an agreement between carriers, of whose business he knows nothing, and fishmongers, of whose business he equally knows nothing, is reasonable or not.   If it is a question, it is one of fact, and evidence should be given to show that the fishmonger and carrier did not understand their business, but made an unjust and unreasonable contract.   However, I am, for my part, prepared to hold . . . that the fact that it (a contract) has been voluntarily entered into is the strongest possible proof that it is a reasonable agreement, and that I should require the strongest possible evidence—something more, even, than a possibility—to show me that that was an *un*reasonable agreement.   Now, in my opinion this was a voluntary agreement . . . the fact that there was an "alternative" is only of importance as showing that the agreement was voluntary.   If there is *no* "alternative," then, although the agreement is come to in terms, yet in truth in a sense it is no agreement between the parties, because there is a compulsion on one of them to enter into it. . . .   Now (in this case) there was most obviously an "alternative." The plaintiff might have sent his fish if he liked, paying 20 per cent. more than he did—that is to say, paying £100 where he paid £80 . . . with liability in the carrier; or he might have sent it upon the terms upon which he did send it. He chose the latter. Really, it is difficult for me to express the opinion which I entertain upon this question with a sufficient appearance of the respect I have for the opinion of those who have thought differently, namely, the learned Judges in the Court below. They seem to say that there is no option (or "alternative") because the terms are too good; the benefit given to the plaintiff is too great; that if a less benefit were given to him, and to all the other senders of fish, if instead of 20 per cent. being taken off the price it were 10, or peradventure 5—for 10 might be too much, for aught I know—then indeed there would be an option. But as the matter stands it is such an irresistible temptation to him —I suppose it is so good a thing for him—that he has (no "alternative" but) to take it. The argument comes to this: The allowance is so just and reasonable to all fish-dealers that it is unjust and unreasonable to each of them. Well, one has heard a great many discussions about freewill, but I protest that this is a novelty; I never heard anything like it before. It is the most extraordinary proposition that I ever heard in my life. The assumption that he (the plaintiff) is obliged to do it (accept the company's terms) because he cannot other- wise compete with his fellow-fishmongers is the most gratuitous one that was ever invented in this world. . . . It is said that because he (plaintiff) has put £20 into his pocket we are to infer that he could not carry on his trade unless he could put that £20 into his pocket; therefore the thing is of a com- pulsory nature. He has no option, no choice (no alternative), consequently his agreement is not voluntary. I repeat that I really do not understand how such a conclusion could have been come to, except by some generous feeling that railway companies ought to be kept for the benefit of fishmongers.

'Now, just let me ask this question, "just and reasonable." Is it "just"? If not, it is *un*just. Is it "*un*just"? Will any human being say that this man has been unjustly treated?

Well, but justice alone is not sufficient; you must not only be just, but you must be reasonable, which, by the way, rather imports that you may be one without the other, I should think . . . an extremely difficult thing. However . . . is it reasonable, too? Why, its very justice shows its reasonableness. I must say that I really do think this is about the plainest case that ever came before your lordships' house.'

To a demand that 'the State' (or a court of law wielding equal power) should 'protect' a fish-dealer, a freeman of full age, against incidental inconveniences arising out of a beneficial contract, the terms of which he had well understood—that the State should break a contract for the benefit of one of the parties to it—Lord Bramwell applied the same plain, direct test which he so consistently applied to certain Liberal legislative proposals after 1870.* The plaintiff B—— was an ideal object for

---

* Addressing the British Association, July, 1888, he said:

'The following specimens of proposed interference with property and freedom of contract may interest you: A Bill to give everyone a right of access to mountain or uncultivated moorland for recreation or study. A Bill that, notwithstanding any agreement to the contrary, a tenant may obtain compensation for *improvements* done against the landlord's consent. A Bill to compel employer to give his servants holidays without deduction from wages. Another Bill to let tenant *improve* without and against his landlord's consent and opinion, and against their agreement. A Bill that a colliery tenant may, *notwithstanding any agreement to the contrary*, have his lease extended if he has been unable to work owing to depressed state of trade. A Bill that everybody may fish in rivers which are highways or along which there is a right of passage. A Bill that property may be taken for labourers' dwellings without payment of compensation for loss of trade, profits, goodwill, etc. Another similar Bill, but one year's profits allowed. A 'the State's' protection, constructively a 'poor man,' therefore, in comparison with that soulless monopoly, a railway company, an object of sympathy. Clearly B—— could not feel comfortable and happy unless allowed to break his contract. The railway company would remain very wealthy in any case. Deeply rooted is that great maxim of natural jurisprudence, 'It is no sin to rob an apparently rich man.' Although few will assert it seriously, many worthy people have acted upon it on a small scale at one time or another. Juries, especially in employers' liability cases, hold it in great repute.

Lord Bramwell refused to fix on the wealthy railway company liability for damage to B——'s fish, after B—— had made money by an agreement exempting the company from liability. He objected also when tenants who had got farms at a rent of 30s. instead of 35s.* per acre—on condition that the landlord reserved the ground game—asked that they should have the ground game also, still paying the lower rent ; objected when tenants holding at 30s. instead of 35s. an acre on condition that they made certain

Bill which may shortly be described as one to introduce into Scotland the mischief of the Irish Land Acts. A Bill that lessees of mines in Cornwall, *notwithstanding any agreement to the contrary*, may remove buildings. A Bill giving general right in Wales and Monmouth to go on lands for recreation, bilberry-gathering, scientific inquiry, sketching, or antiquarian research. A Bill that in every execution against the goods of a household necessary furniture to the value of £20 shall be exempt. In these cases rights of property and freedom of contract are violated.'

* See pp. 203, 356.

improvements, which they well knew would become the property of the landlord at the expiry of the agreement, after benefiting by the improvements and the lower rent, asked Parliament to give all improvements to them.   The judgment in the Court below seems to have been shaped in accordance with the ethical preferences of the day after to-morrow, which in 1882 were beginning to take definite shape.   Lord Bramwell's difficulty was that some struggling railway company might conceivably try to break its contract with a wealthy fish-dealer, pleading that unless it charged £100 per ton (instead of £80 as agreed), it could not compete with rival railways or with sea-carriage.   What on earth was he to do then?   A practical politician would have replied that everybody knew quite well railway companies were not *likely* to try and break contracts.   Nor was a landlord *likely* to sue as aforementioned for rent on the 35s. scale, averring that the tenant had got a bargain, in respect to ground game or improvements, unjust and unreasonable to landlords.

Elasticity, large-hearted caprice, are essential in politics and legislation.   That Lord Bramwell's ideas were inelastic he showed by the remark in the railway case, 'I, neither a fishmonger nor a carrier, am yet asked to say how each should carry on his trade.'   By 1883 M.P.'s were gradually becoming both fishmongers and carriers in the best sense of the term, and could say exactly how tradesmen, professional men, landlords, tenants, employers, or workmen, should bargain with each other.

CHAPTER V.

THE REACTION AGAINST 'PLAIN WHIG PRINCIPLES.'

Mr. Gladstone and Lord Bramwell represent bifurcation of Liberal idea—What the two knew of each other—Patristic and supramundane source of Mr. Gladstone's economic views—Tory political economy always marked 'Made in Heaven'—Canonical or mediæval economics same origin —Clash with rough English Common Law notions— Lord Bramwell loyal champion of latter—Tory party never quite renounce their mediæval or 'paternal' economic ideas—Did Mr. G., after becoming Liberal Leader?—Anxiety among 'orthodox' Liberals caused by reactionary tendencies after 1880.

MR. GLADSTONE seems to have played an important part in that episode of Liberal economic evolution which interested, also vexed, Lord Bramwell in his latter years. Mr. Gladstone has been the cause of many people doing things. These two men, although long members of the same party, very well represent irreconcilable conceptions of political economy and jurisprudence; represent an antagonism underlying the political developments of the last thirty years. They are typical men, notwithstanding that Mr. Gladstone's influence over the nation's policy

was paramount for a generation, Lord Bramwell
being all his life a workman, with nothing to say to
the British public directly during working hours; a
commanding authority on questions which it was
imagined affected lawyers chiefly; an outsider in
respect to statecraft.

Each man was well known to the other. This
letter refers to the Collier episode:

'10, Downing Street, Whitehall,
'*October* 26, 1871.

'DEAR BARON BRAMWELL,

'If it be agreeable to you to accept one of the judge-
ships to be constituted under the Judicial Committee Act of
1871, I shall have great pleasure in submitting your name to
the Queen with that view, and I shall feel, if so permitted,
that I am proposing an arrangement eminently advantageous
to the public service.

'Believe me,
'Faithfully yours,
'W. E. GLADSTONE.'

Lord Bramwell asked for time to consider his
decision. Then Mr. Gladstone wrote again:

'10, Downing Street, Whitehall,
'*October* 30, 1871.

'. . . I appreciate highly the spirit in which your letter is
written, and nothing can on general grounds be more reasonable than your request for time. But we are hard driven by
the difficulties arising from dispersion. The Court meets on
the 6th. A Privy Council meeting must be held at Balmoral
on Friday to swear in. Your acceptance on Wednesday
afternoon would be in ample time; but what would your
negative then be? Allow me to suggest that in this difficulty
you would save time if you could make it convenient to come

up to town at once, so as to be in immediate communication with the Chancellor, as he is the person who will be held responsible by the public and the profession for the starting of the Court in due time and form.   Forgive this officious suggestion, prompted by the pressure of circumstances. . . .'

The public, legal profession, and press, do not seem to have actually held Lord Hatherley, C., responsible.   As early as 1880 Lord Bramwell had formed a clear and emphatic opinion of Mr. Gladstone's characteristics, and once expressed himself thus at Assize time to an Under-Sheriff—still living—of one of the Northern counties, who considered the words worth taking down at the time :

'Gladstone is a man of powerful mind, genius and energy, but of overweening arrogance. As honest as nature allows him to be, he would not do deliberate wrong ; but he is of such a subtle mind as to be able to deceive himself easily into believing black is white. A man utterly regardless of law, and of anything which stands in the way of William Ewart Gladstone.'

When considering how far Mr. Gladstone's influence determined latter-day reaction against 'the political economy of our youth,' it may be noted that after 1869 his activity is by no means wholly political.   As his incomparable influence over his countrymen and his party grows, hesitation is displayed alike by old Liberals, new Radicals and Indifferentists to advance further along that track of economic freedom, self - help and independence of governmental interference surveyed, staked out, and partly levelled by a great cohort of Liberal students and statesmen during the early and middle part of the century.

Designedly or undesignedly, the Liberal party is edged, or cajoled into an attitude half sceptical, half reactionary, towards freedom of contract, freedom of competition, and freedom of trade, which are not three things, but one thing. Since the Tory party had, in such matters, consistently zigzagged or wandered round in a circle, like men lost in the Bush, when the Liberal party went astray the nation went astray.

From 1870 onwards Mr. Gladstone's crypto-Socialistic measures escaped attention because they were so much 'dunnage,' worked, like fustic between mahogany logs, into the interstices of those grand political measures which formed the main cargo of the stately Liberal ship. Lord Bramwell saw the bulk of Mr. Gladstone's followers—already doubting and hesitating to advance—faced, after 1880, to the right-about, and invited to take precisely the opposite road, which led back to mediæval political economy, or sacerdotal Socialism. Thence Mr. Gladstone had originally got much inspiration. Undoubtedly he held at one time that it was the duty of the Crown, the Executive, the Legislature—of the ruling class, however appointed—as vicegerents and representatives on earth of the Almighty, of Divine Providence, to moralize civic relations, to redress inequalities of fortune and condition, to protect unsuccessful adult competitors, the world's failures, against the penalties and inconveniences of failure, to make the lot of the poor and humble less intolerable, even at the expense of the rich and mighty. He had plenty of authorities for that view, from Aristotle to Suarez and Wilson Croker.

One of the radiant fancies of Mr. Gladstone's political youth was that such a policy, tempered by Divinely-Ordered Caprice, would solve economic and social problems in the noblest and worthiest manner. One of the discoveries of his maturer years was that electoral and political changes in this country had turned the poor and humble (whose lot was to be made less intolerable) into the majority, while the rich and mighty (at whose expense bright dreams were to be realized) had become the minority. It may then have been too late for him to reconsider his views. At various epochs in history lofty conceptions of the functions of 'authority,' similar to Mr. Gladstone's early conceptions, have been entertained by various people, who invented for that 'authority' various taking names. In the Middle Ages legists, schoolmen, and sacerdotal economists, following the teachings of early Christian Fathers and commentators on canonical law, had a plan. Socialism, tempered by caprice, was the economic 'note' of the Roman Catholic Church in its day of civic and judicial activity and power. On the Continent of Europe especially, in a society where force and violence determined claims to property, where the tribunals were dependent and the people without local or national liberties, that kind of Socialism, inculcated by the Church primarily as a personal obligation upon all baptized Christians, is now admitted to have been, when embodied in legal codes and procedure, a shield and buttress for the unarmed and ignorant against the oppression of a well-armed ruling class. Pontiffs, councils, legists, while thus rendering unquestionable service to humanity and civilization, always reserved a dispensing power— the right to 'draw the line' if circumstances required, if the growth of commerce, industry, and wealth (or the needs of the Church) made it advisable to waive or suspend Christian economic teaching about speculation, covetousness, usury, fair rents, the living wage, 'the just price,' or private property in land. Similarly Mr. Gladstone has 'drawn the line' when asked to approve land nationalization or Eight Hours Bills. It was largely this element of Divinely-Guided Caprice, this economic dispensing power claimed by the Church, which in England raised that long quarrel between Kings, Barons, and people on the one hand, and representatives of Papal or sacerdotal authority on the other hand. The dramatic story of English law often turns upon a struggle between 'the Latin garrison' who stood for canon law and that succession of very English Englishmen who maintained, against the foreign importation, vital principles of the *leges Angliæ*— a poor thing, but their own. The attrition of English ideas, of custom, of tribal and folk maxims —gathered, as Tacitus declares, 'in the forests of Germany'—moulds these English laws; what they owe to popular tradition, prejudice, precedent, is prudently set forth in coherent, uniform, characteristic rulings by Lord Bramwell's doughty predecessors. Therefore, as English Judge and master of Common Law, he was heir general to a very ancient feud. Consciously or unconsciously, his opinions and writings reflect the historic struggle between those antagonistic conceptions of political economy and jurisprudence, which alone, whatever names they took, have powerfully influenced civilized societies. As his speeches and writings plainly prove, he clamped the gauge at a certain mark. Not by his design — rather automatically, and of necessity in the course of discussion —certain ideas, assertions, schemes which found favour with latter-day Liberals, came to be measured against that standard gauge of his. Probably he never noticed the odd resemblance between canonical ideas about political economy or jurisprudence and Mr. Henry Broadhurst's, Mr. Shaw Lefevre's, or Professor T. H. Green's ideas about the same. Painstaking students such as W. J. Ashley and Cunningham were almost the first to identify, in quite recent years, the essentially dogmatic and theocratic basis of mediæval economic theories. Nevertheless, imbued, saturated, as Lord Bramwell was with the spirit and essence of English jurisprudence, his views, more especially about contract, were necessarily antagonistic to those of canonical philanthropists and their modern plagiarists. He had no respect whatever for Infallible Caprice, either in legal or economic affairs.

It was always impossible for Lord Bramwell to 'join the Tory party,' because when it did dawn upon a few thoughtful Conservatives that liberty of the subject and security of property, real as well as personal, had always been the keystone of that detested 'political economy' which philosophic Radicals discoursed about for a century, the thought was too bewildering to be mastered by the party. Besides, Lord Salisbury apparently has never argued himself out of his dislike to the Manchester School, nor got rid of his early sympathy with those paternal or 'scholastic' theories of political economy dear to 'Young England' Tories.

The Tory party, in which Mr. Gladstone graduated as economist, has never quite renounced its unconscious historic leaning towards 'sacerdotal Socialism,' tempered by incoherent reverence for vested interests. The generous dream among the group of 'Young England' Tories of fifty or sixty years ago—just becoming alive to the grisly inequalities of fortune and opportunity in the modern, high-pressure industrial world, eager to find a solution for social problems more humane and chivalrous than that offered by dogmatists and doctrinaires like Adam Smith, Malthus, Bentham, John Austin, Ricardo, McCulloch, Mill—was substantially a rediscovery of the economic doctrines of Aquinas and the Glossatores.* By 1870 Conservatives had come to acknowledge, frankly if not always cheerfully, the material, £ s. d. success of that Free Trade policy which Liberal economists had enforced twenty-five years before. But it was hardly to be expected that Conservatives who forgot how Edmund Burke had

---

* Aquinas and his disciples taught that to buy in the cheapest and sell in the dearest market was base and sinful.

answered all the speeches Mr. Gladstone would ever make, and were very anxious about purely political matters after 1870, would spring to the defence of ' Liberal principles' against economic Agnostics.*

It is certain that in the face of Europe and the civilized world Mr. Gladstone has ranked for two generations as one of the most illustrious champions of Free Trade. Even so late as 1894 he in effect expressed to M. Léon Say his sorrow at finding that French democracy had banished sound economic

* Tory criticism of the Land Bills of 1870 and 1881 in particular was always weak, random, ineffective, because Mr. Gladstone's Irish economic policy could only be conclusively refuted by those orthodox Liberal arguments which Lord Bramwell (pp. 145, 299) cited. Latter-day Tories, who considered the Irish Land Acts of 1870, 1881, *et seq.*, wholly detestable, never had sufficient intelligence to realize that they were also wholly indefensible. Meanwhile, hostility displayed by Liberal economists to English and Scottish land-owners during a generation—for which Mill and Cairnes are largely responsible—made a defensive alliance between Liberal and Tory land-owners, capitalists, shareholders, employers of labour, and rate and tax payers, difficult even after 1889, when ' Liberal' economic legislation began to take the shape of a random onslaught upon 'capitalism' generally, at the dictation of the Radical-Socialist-Labour minority. It was precisely in respect to land tenure and land legislation that orthodox Liberal economists most frequently abandoned their principles after 1870. Socialists in and out of Parliament were not slow to take advantage of such divisions in the hostile camp whenever destructive legislation affecting others than land-owners came up. It must, however, be remembered that while the Liberal party was switched off the Individualist on to the Socialist track by a very great man, the Tory party (after Lord Bramwell's death) was not.

doctrine to Saturn and Jupiter. It is not clear that Mr. Gladstone, any more than Lord Salisbury, has ever been a stalwart advocate of those principles on which alone Free Trade can be defended. In Mr. Gladstone's Free Trade speeches after 1870 the 'cheap loaf' side of the argument is much dwelt on ; there is usually eloquent denunciation of the Tory party for trying to make the food of the people scarce and dear in order to keep up agricultural rents ; glowing descriptions of increases in exports, imports, manufactures, and national prosperity. His last great Free Trade speech (Leeds, 1882) showed no consistent or hearty repudiation of the basic heresies of Protection. The 'positive' Free Trader who merely tells us that Free Trade has cheapened commodities and increased national wealth is only half a Free Trader.*

* The £ s. d. argument that Free Trade 'pays,' increases exports and imports, stimulates manufactures, adds to national wealth, and benefits consumers, Lord Bramwell did not regard as *the* argument for Free Trade, rather as an 'aside' in the controversy. Assuming that the nation did the right thing in 1846, and that it has 'paid,' *why* was the thing then done right ? Why is protective legislation, direct or indirect, wrong always and everywhere ? He put the matter very clearly in his address to the British Association, 1888 :

'. . . The governing precepts of political economy are few. In my judgment its main one is *laissez faire*—'let be.' As M. Molinari says, "*Notre évangile se résume en quatre mots—'Laissez faire, laissez passer.'*" Leave everyone to seek his own happiness in his own way, provided he does not injure others. Govern as little as possible. Meddle not, interfere not, any more than you can help. Trust to each man knowing his own interest better, and pursuing it more earnestly than the law

Nor is it splitting hairs to ask whether a reputed economist clearly perceives the 'negative' side of the matter also—the reason why 'State' supervision, interference or regulation aiming at 'protection' of any form of human industry or activity must do harm. Mr. Gladstone has seldom said (and it is not clear that he ever believed) that consumers have an indefeasible right to benefit by absolutely free and unrestricted competition among producers everywhere, at home·and abroad, or that, conversely, British manufacturers, farmers, tenants, or adult wage-earners have no claim whatever to be protected, directly or indirectly, by 'the State' against competition in any form. If sundry Acts passed or approved by Mr. Gladstone between 1870 and 1894 are defensible, valid arguments for Free Trade in 'some things' would still remain ; but no answer remains to demands from British farmers and manufacturers, losing money in their business, to be protected against 'nefarious,' cut-throat competition— against that selfishness, money-hunger, and desire for gain which prompt the foreigner to send us

---

can do it for him. I believe this maxim will justify most of the rules that right economists have laid down—let your people buy in the cheapest and sell in the dearest markets. That enjoins Free Trade, for the trader, whether he buys at home or abroad, seeks the cheapest market. If a duty is put on the foreign article to protect the home producers, the trader is interfered with. The consumer is interfered with. The law says he shall not consume that which he can get at the lowest price—that the producers, the capitalists, and labourers shall not employ their capital and labour as they would if left to themselves. . . .'

cheap commodities.   Either all adult freemen are entitled to be protected by 'the State' against competition, or no adult freemen are.   One probable explanation of Mr. Gladstone's share in latter-day reaction against the 'political economy of our youth,' of his crypto-Socialistic legislation after 1870, is that he always disliked the materialistic tendencies of the Manchester School, and therefore very naturally welcomed and availed himself of the growth of milder sentiments and a more highly-sensitized national conscience during the latter quarter of the century.   Besides, Edmund Burke's ideas of a 'representative' had become obsolete; the true function of pilot on board the democratic ship was declared to be, to ever follow that course which steerage passengers prefer.   Those easy-going millions inhabiting prosperous, Free Trade England had perhaps grown afraid or ashamed of naked liberty.   Mr. Gladstone never quite trusted it.   He may have believed after the 1880 election that the time had come to realize the radiant dreams of his Tory youth.   His projection of ethical, quasi-theological ideas belonging to the Age of Faith into the domain of British politics and jurisprudence would have a good deal to do with Lord Bramwell's irreconcilable attitude towards neo-Liberal legislation, assuming that Mr. Gladstone's was the influence which, at a decisive moment, turned the nation back from economic freedom; that it was he who gave the shove downhill—did not make the hill slope, but gave the shove.

Prior to 1870 sundry Liberals—protesters afterwards against the economic aberrations of the party —also anticipated danger to liberty, property, public welfare, mainly from the political side. Mr. Lowe (who had seen something of it in Australia) expressed with academic recklessness his own distrust of 'unmitigated democracy' in 1866. Our institutions might be Americanized by Mr. John Bright. Extreme developments of Radicalism in a purely political direction might land us in Republicanism, weaken the army and navy, destroy the House of Lords, etc. Conservatives said such things openly, philosophic Liberals to each other. Liberal 'Inevitablists,' men who adhered to the party from 1846 till 1886 in order to guide or moderate forces which they dreaded, but believed to be irresistible, never had much faith in the power of their own magical prime mover, Liberty, to right in time small clashing wrongs, to solve new social problems, magnified and exaggerated though they were, by sheer increase in numbers, and in time build up a contented, therefore Conservative, middle and working class.

Mr. Lowe, when warning his party that 'we must educate our masters'—omitted to finish the sentence with the words 'to vote for our opponents.' The proper conclusion of the sentence was not obvious until 1895. Yet after Lord Bramwell was dead it became plain that the instalment of Free Trade won in 1846 and the Elementary Education Acts—measures which Tories feared, and Liberals hoped would make an end of Conservative Ministries altogether —are not only the two most important measures of the century, but are also Conservative measures, since they more than any contributed to the birth and rearing of that novel and unfamiliar phenomenon called—because it certainly isn't anything else, and must be something—latter-day Conservatism. By obliterating the sense of 'inequality,' material and intellectual, they have sterilized the very protoplasm of irreconcilable Radicalism, thus—although in a negative sense chiefly — determining the opinions and political action of the English middle and work-ing classes. Acts extending the franchise, which Tories feared, and Liberals hoped would give im-mense scope to Radical or revolutionary schemes, are seen to have merely readjusted machinery, as it turned out, enabling neo-Conservative equanimity—largely due to Free Trade and Education Acts—to sway the scale in 1874, 1886, and 1895. Franchise extension, while exercising scarcely any direct forma-tive influence upon opinion, probably weakened the prestige, dignity, personal authority, of the House of Commons. The representative system, so soon as it verged upon logical conclusions, began to develop germs hurtful to itself. Men like Lord Bramwell deemed Parliamentary government immortal, while all the time it may only have been robustly immature. Tories, who had a secret grudge against representa-tive government (although never able to put in words the real reasons for distrusting it), imagined their party had nothing to lose by deterioration of the elective House; Liberals of Lord Bramwell's stamp knew that they themselves had everything to lose. Frank dislike to extension of the franchise, which he expressed and others whispered in 1860, was mainly due to prevision that the inroad of 'unmitigated democracy' must mean the disestablishment of that Liberal hierarchy to which he belonged —men like himself being hustled out of the party. Meantime, it did not occur to Liberal doubters (then, indeed, lacking examples from abroad) that the economic bent of all democracies is necessarily reactionary and Protectionist. While current doubts and anxieties were political mainly, the economic revolution initiated by Mr. Gladstone's Irish Land legislation of 1870 and 1881 was sprung on the nation. It had not been ushered in by exhaustive and minute controversy as the new Poor Law, Repeal of the Corn and Navigation Laws, Municipal, Legal, Ecclesiastical Reform, had. Rightly or wrongly, it was an anxious time for those Liberals who sincerely believed that a reactionary policy in the economic field might work irreparable injustice and mischief.

During the years which succeeded that franchise controversy which disquieted Lord Bramwell, it looked as if Palmerston first, and then Gladstone,* would keep matters straight, while avert-

* In 1864 Chief Baron Pollock wrote to Baron Bramwell:

'. . . Palmerston must be a sensible, good-tempered fellow to "keep things together," and *such* things! The present Cabinet reminds me of "the happy family" which a man used to exhibit at Waterloo Bridge, after at Charing Cross. . . .'

And again, March 29, 1868:

'. . . It seems almost funny that this *moribund Parliament* should desire to make the Irish Church a *donatio causa mortis;* it is odd there is so little stir. But I think it not at all unlikely

ing such a bitter alternative as the ascendancy of Disraeli. When Niagara was actually shot in 1868, the falls turned out to be about eight inches high. Lord Bramwell then began to think that the mischief impending was not political at all, mainly economic. Meanwhile, up to a certain point Mr. Gladstone's ingrained economic ideas, thanks to Whig carpentry, dovetailed in very well with the ideas of the new era.

Putting alarmist rhetoric and exaggeration on one side, was there, it may be asked, any good grounds for that anxiety which Opportunist Liberals felt—which Lord Bramwell expressed without waste of words—during 'the transition period' between 1880 and 1893, when the electors enfranchised in 1868 and 1884 were feeling their political feet—learning, as other 'ruling classes' in this country have had to learn, the responsibilities of power? What can nowadays be seen easily enough (after the event) is that the House of Commons, absorbed

---

that although many would not concur in Gladstone's resolution, they entertain *no very high* opinion of the Irish Church. I think I have already told you what I said to John Austin thirty years ago: "The *Irish Church* is a 'nuisance,' but the *Roman Catholic religion* is a *greater*." It is not every nuisance that is to be instantly abated. The River Thames was a few years ago a very great nuisance. . . . One reason for not adopting Gladstone's resolution is that in all great reforms, such as rebuilding a church or a hospital, reconstructing Constitution or a Government, *how* it is to be done, and whether *when so done* it will be an *improvement*, is of the essence of the inquiry. Therefore the details (so to speak) do enter into the *principle* of the measure.'

in Irish affairs for thirteen years, was unable to pass measures which seemed very 'practical politics' indeed in November, 1882, when Lord Bramwell joined the newly - formed Liberty and Property Defence League. Mr. Gladstone's excellent health seemed to portend that the nation had still several years of disturbance ahead. It was difficult at that date to predict that the beneficent activity of Mr. Parnell's followers and their lavish demands upon 'the time of the House' would result in smothering a 'Permissive' or Prohibition Act (without compensation), 'some form' of land nationalization, leasehold enfranchisement, Eight Hours and Early Closing of Shops Acts, penal factory legislation aimed at the ruin of the capitalist, confiscatory taxes levied upon the weakest class, as well as miscellaneous interferences with personal liberty, freedom of contract and exchange, all of which the House of Commons of 1880-85 was, in the opinion of many people, disposed to pass. Judging by what had been done in Ireland, the Liberal majority under Mr. Gladstone's leadership at that date represented the most formidable and efficient instrument of inadvertent wrong-doing and oppression which the nation had seen since 'the Cavalier Parliament' of 1661-79. The Liberal party remained intact in 1880-85, even although its prestige did get a little out of repair. Ostentatious, if grudging, support from the Whig leaders—men of property and high character—lent an air of respectability to every act of the Ministry, inspired a hazy sense of security among capitalists, manufacturers, and business men, especially in the North.   In the constituencies the extreme Radical element, largely consisting of Irish, not yet split into warring factions under rival 'labour,' Social Democratic, clerical, anti-clerical, etc., leaders, contributed a reserve (or at least a useful threat) of physical force, available to back up any Liberal policy of 'thorough.'   The display of Conservative sentiment in 1874 had come to be regarded as a mere accident, a temporary aberration, the result of black magic exercised by Lord Beaconsfield.   Mr. Gladstone's moral prowess, shown by his adhesion to the Concert of Europe, the imprisonment of Mr. Parnell, etc., had, it was thought, banished the possibility of sustained Conservative reaction.   Further, in November, 1882, when Lord Bramwell first addressed the Liberty and Property Defence League, Parliament virtually consisted of one Chamber.   Certain constitutional functions of the House of Lords had remained in abeyance for a generation, while by passing the Arrears Act of June, 1882, in the teeth of Lord Salisbury's remonstrances, the House of Lords had gone as near abolishing itself as any legislative Chamber ever went.   In November, 1882, nobody foresaw that eleven years later Mr. Gladstone would reserve for the House of Lords the privilege of cremating the dead Home Rule Bill (thereby emphasizing the constitutional paradox that the hereditary or non-elective chamber may, after all, be sometimes the truest mirror of public opinion), reviving its authority, and endowing it for the moment with great popularity, respect, and prestige.   In May, 1886, the

House of Lords seemed to have sunk as low as it could sink. It passed the second reading of a Durham 'Sunday Closing' Bill. Seventy members of the House even voted for the third reading—why, it is impossible, after so many years' interval, to ascertain.

Apparently, justification for anxiety and alarm among Liberals which prompted the formation of a League to attempt work which was really the business of Parliament* was found in the circumstances, the very practical effects, of Mr. Gladstone's Irish Land legislation. It must be remembered that prior to 1870-81 there was no instance on record of Parliament deliberately and methodically inflicting wrong and ruin upon one particular class. The enactment of penal laws affecting the property of Roman Catholics and Dissenters under Tudors and Stuarts had at all events the miserable excuse that the proscribed classes had shown themselves to be politically hostile and dangerous at a time when Protestantism and Monarchy were in constant and deadly peril. After 1832 there had often been loose talk about Acts of Parliament amounting to 'robbery,' 'confiscation,' etc., but in the end no deliberate wrong to individuals had been done. People thought it would so continue always. The Irish Land Acts of 1870 and 1881 undeceived them. For the first

* In June, 1882, Sir Charles Trevelyan declined to join the League on the rather imaginative grounds that 'he looked upon Parliament as the protector of liberty and property, and thought that an association of this kind might interfere with Parliament. . . .'

time in English history citizens accused of no offence were deprived of lawfully acquired property without compensation, while hundreds of innocent persons holding land in Ireland who had relied upon the honour, sense of justice, and good faith of Parliament and the nation were ruined. Although Ireland was far away, a pantomime country in the view of many, although the people thus wronged by statute were out of sight, the inference was strong after 1881 that in seeking to remedy old injustices new injustices would be done.

Most of the distinguished and discontented Liberals of 1882 cheerfully jettisoned one doctrine of political economy after another in succeeding years, never realizing how all parts of the edifice of political economy and jurisprudence are inter-dependent—each story or compartment underpinned alike. Lord Brabourne, sound in 1882 about English workmen's right to freely bargain with employers, could not see in 1887* that land-owners had also made a binding bargain with tithe-owners under 6 and 7 Wm. IV., cap. xvii. The Duke of Argyll, orthodox in respect to contracts between landlords and tenants, condoned in later years prohibition of free bargaining between employers and employed, as well as laws prohibiting the sale and purchase of strong drink by his neighbours. Sir William Harcourt, quite orthodox in respect to the gold standard and the causes which influence the price of wheat, came to freely borrow ideas about taxation, the right of property, and the liberty of

* See p. 320.

the subject, from the Fabian Society, the United Kingdom Alliance, etc. Solicitude for that special item of political economy which he did believe in constrained each of these Liberal statesmen in turn to repudiate rights, privileges, and principles which other Liberals believed in.

CHAPTER VI.

CONTRACT OR STATUS?

The Common Law as educator—'A bargain is a bargain'—
Popular sanction for Common Law maxims—Homely
English notions contrasted with foreign or Latin importa-
tions—Reaction in favour of Roman models coincides
with revival of Socialism—'Teaching contract to know
its place'—Ethical, metaphysical, and rule of thumb
derivations of contract—Essentially 'English' bent of
Lord Bramwell's mind—'Freedom of contract' the *Pons
Asinorum* of loose thinkers.

In an age when the ancient doctrine of 'forfeit'
on default was more and more going out of fashion,
when the idea of consequences, penalties, punishment always following misdoing or folly, was
shunned by politicians, attacked by moralists, and
was becoming odious to a good-natured generation,
Lord Bramwell, the kindest-hearted of men, argued
that the letter of the bond must be carried out, that
a bargain is a bargain.

He used to tell a story illustrating the absolute
paralysis which may affect the human mind at trying
moments—in the witness-box, for example. Once
on board a Rhine steamboat he noticed a lady
passenger in the utmost distress, trying by signs to

explain to the officials some matter of consequence. Fancying that she was a countrywoman of his, the Baron went to her assistance, and asked :

' Do you speak English ?'

The poor lady had so lost her head that she could only stammer out : ' *Un peu.*'

Lord Bramwell therefore continued the conversation in French, scarce a word of which the lady understood ; German and Italian gave equally bad results.   Finally the lady muttered audibly to herself :

' How I wish I were safe at home !'

' But surely you *do* speak English ?' asked Baron Bramwell.

' I can't speak anything else,' sobbed the lady, ' and that is what makes me so helpless among these foreigners.'

He had travelled over the greater part of Europe ; had unlimited capacity for taking interest in every sign and exhibit of human activity, energy, or ingenuity which he came across in his journeyings. When on circuit, the moment the Court rose the Baron would be off on a ramble, spying out the objects of interest in the neighbourhood.   He was an insatiable walker, and mountain climber of the amateur kind ; few men knew rural England better than he ; never read in a railway-carriage ; would say to his travelling companion, ' Do put down that newspaper and look at the country we are passing through.'   An immense, child-like faith in the infallibility of the Ordnance Map was one of his orthodox failings, and often led him into adven-

tures which amused him vastly; he always took
with him a section of the Ordnance Map belonging
to the particular circuit he was on, and would insist,
as against the oldest inhabitant, that wherever a
road was marked on the map, there a horse and trap
could go. Occasionally it turned out that the official
road had never been quite made—had been closed
or abandoned for years. In consequence he more
than once landed himself and his travelling companions, late at night, at the end of a sheep-track
on a desolate Yorkshire moor, twenty miles from
the assize town.

It was in later life, perhaps, that he insisted most
rigidly upon the importance of binding men to the
legal consequences of their bargains. The terrors,
threats, 'strong arm' of the law, had, he thought, a
sort of character-strengthening effect. He seems to
have agreed with Holmes that each party to a contract should be held to have contemplated the full
legal consequences attaching to it.

He was inclined to be 'a bit of a Socialist' at
times, which would imply a private theory of his
own of the ethical 'mission' of the judiciary, not,
however, to be fulfilled by conciliating law-breakers.
If people *would* go to law, strict enforcement of
contracts might, at all events, teach one wholesome
lesson : 'If you have been a fool once, don't be
again; take more care next time.' Thus there
would be fewer fools, a gain to the nation.* Men

* In 1888 he said at the British Association meeting :
'. . . Poverty and misery shock us, but they are inevitable.
They could be prevented if you could prevent weakness, and

who love, believe in, and get satisfaction out of their own profession come generally in the end to think that, after all, it may afford the best instrument for improving their neighbours and fellow-countrymen. The German Emperor and Lord Wolseley no doubt think that universal military service is the best Secondary State School; Captain Mahan that Nelson and Admiral Sampson have done most for Dr. Temple's 'education of the world'; a much-be-paragraphed actor or dramatist is bound to point out after dinner that the stage is the true educator. Lord Bramwell sometimes may have felt that at best a 'case' decided, even with perfect wisdom and justice, often merely leaves suitors themselves and everybody else in *statu quo ante.* For the giving of such advice on life and conduct as he often wanted to give, Lord Bramwell, during the best of his days, had no pulpit save the judicial bench. His pet saying, 'A bargain is a bargain,' is also a true English folk-saying—like many broad maxims of Equity and Common Law, a rough English rule of conduct, declaring in common speech that it is only honest, plucky, fair, to stick to your word, and take consequences. Unconsciously, perhaps, our Judges of old adopted such sayings, after

---

sickness, and laziness, and stupidity, and improvidence, not otherwise. To tell the weak, the lazy, and the improvident that they should not suffer for their faults and infirmities would but encourage them to indulge in those faults and infirmities. If it is said that poverty and misery may exist without fault in the sufferer, it is true. But it is but rarely that they do, and the law *cannot discriminate such cases.* To attempt to remedy the disparity of conditions would make the well-off poor, the poor not well off. . . .'

much winnowing, sifting, picking over of English ideas, current from time immemorial in market-place, playground, village green, workshop. When called 'law,' they were just the resultant of English character operating upon the facts of everyday life.* Deep down in the very subsoil are the roots of our Common Law, for the making of which the commonest sort of people provided raw material, the most uncommon sort of people working it up into finished goods, never denying, of course, that the whole thing was borrowed from Justinian.

Never prone to confuse judicial ruling and constitutional theorizing, Lord Bramwell avoided that leaning towards metaphysics which tempted another master of Common Law, Lord Mansfield, to suggest some ' moral obligation' behind contract. Yet the former Judge's charge in Druitt's case (p. 29) makes apparently an enormous concession to the ethical fraternity. The public,' said he, ' have an interest in the way in which a man disposes of his

* One spring day in the year 1889 the local constable at Edenbridge noticed Lord Bramwell intently watching a noisy group of village boys, apparently much excited about something. It was the first day of the cricket season, and they were, in fact, drawing up rules for their cricket club. Fancying they might have annoyed the old lord in some way, the constable approached, and asked whether such was the case.

' No, no,' said Lord Bramwell ; ' those lads have been teaching me something—how the Common Law was invented.'

The constable considered this a remarkable proof of juvenile precocity, and observed :

' It's wonderful what they do learn at school nowadays, my lord—over-education, *I* call it.'

industry and his capital. . . .' Here we have a concise motto for Lord Salisbury and the Fabian Society at once, an argument for a Compulsory Rightmindedness Act. But Lord Bramwell's very next words make plain what is the truth running right through this famous declaration of independence. It turns out, after all, that the public's paramount interest in the matter is to ensure to each individual absolute freedom in disposing of his industry and capital exactly as he pleases. 'And if two or more persons,' he goes on, 'conspire, by threats, intimidation, or molestation, to deter or influence [a man] in the way in which he should employ his industry, his talents, or his capital, they are guilty,' etc., making out that English Law and Equity have always been most concerned with defence of that principle of liberty soldered on to contract from the start.*

* Even Acts of Parliament which 'deter or influence' individual freemen 'in the way they should employ their industry, talents, or capital,' would seem also to be bad. For, granted that 'influencing or molestation,' covered by the charge in Druitt's case, are wrong in themselves, does an Act of Parliament make them right? True, statutory 'influencing' gets rid of many evils—private violence, threats, etc.—but the free man is deprived of his 'liberty of mind and freedom of will' all the same. In *Hilton v. Eckersley* it was said, '*Prima facie* it is the privilege of a trader in a free country . . . to regulate his own mode of carrying on his trade according to his own discretion and choice. . . .' Pollock, 'Contract,' first edition, p. 285 : 'The Supreme Court of Massachusetts condemns contracts "in restraint of trade," firstly, because such contracts injure the parties making them . . . and expose such persons to imposition and aggression. .. . .'

High ideals or ethical tests applied to contract or to economic relations probably seemed to Lord Bramwell as untenable as tests 'deterring, influencing, or molesting' freemen in respect to opinion and religious observance. As to the latter kind of test, the State, at all events, has Holy Scripture, the Koran, the Shorter Catechism, tradition, the wisdom of Popes, Councils, Synods, Convocation, and the religious press to guide it; while ethics is, after all, a fluid and empirical science, constantly undergoing development; the ethical view of the moment being the product of fluctuating sentiment, fashion; frequently dictated by one eloquent, zealous, strong-willed individual, fond of advertisement. Expounders of English Common Law, never admitting any right in Councils and Convocations to dictate in matters of opinion, have similarly refused to dictate to contracting parties in respect to the adequacy of 'consideration.' As a general rule of law, the parties themselves must be sole judges of that.

An analogy has been drawn between Lord Bramwell's view of contract and that assumption to which Rousseau gave the name of *contrat social*. *Contrat* is French for 'contract.' There kinship between Rousseau and Lord Bramwell ends. Those contracts, or 'agreements upon sufficient consideration* to do or not to do a particular thing,' which Lord Bramwell made so much of, were in no way akin to that imaginary treaty, offensive and

---

* Roman jurists laid little or no stress upon 'consideration'; French contract law almost ignores it also.

defensive, between Mankind and the Goddess of Things in General, by which Lycurgus, Milton, Rousseau, the Physiocrats, and even Erskine and Whewell, sought to interpret political, social, and economic phenomena. Rousseau, like the Encyclopædists, was ambitious to cage Cosmos inside a phrase. He was too indolent or ignorant to trace and analyze development of those free English institutions, contract included, which it was the fashion among Encyclopædists to admire. A metaphysical short-cut like the *contrat social* saved a great deal of trouble. It was never an English idea. The sturdy reasonableness of Common Law had even expressly condemned, in anticipation one might say, general contracts, 'binding for uncertainty.' It is significant of wholesome anti-metaphysical bias that no contract, liability, or obligation between the man and the entire community, no such thing as a contract with society, no obligation at Common Law upon 'each' to do anything in particular for 'all,' has ever been recognized by the Judges of the land. 'The man's liability to the community must be a matter of public or statute law.'

Essays in tyranny made in this country have often been inspired by the essentially anti-English idea that a 'general warrant,' issued by society or the State, is good at Common Law against the individual. In money matters, Tudors and Stuarts sought to make good a sweeping obligation, an indefinite moral duty on the freeman to contribute hard cash to the King's exchequer, as when basing exaction of ship-money on extension and development of a dubious local charge existing at the Cinque Ports. There never was any Common Law obligation upon British subjects to give the King, or society, or 'the State'—if 'the State' has any definite meaning on British soil—any of their goods in particular. Their service in keeping the peace or defending the realm the King could claim, but not their goods.* If Brown and Smith, by the man who represents them in Parliament, agree to give the King a specified sum, well and good, so long as they believe that the sum asked for will be spent in the way specified, to the advantage of the King, Brown, and Smith. In recent years all legislative devices for depriving freemen of that 'full and absolute property in their goods and estate,' asserted by the Petition of Right, have been heralded in by arguments that an indefinite contract, a comprehensive bargain with society, binds certain people, property-owners and employers, to be generous, altruistic to tenants and working men. Should the existence of any legal obligation of the sort be denied, Common Law, contract, individual freedom, the right of property, are denounced as immoral, inhuman, anti-social, the which is not new, being merely a very practical rehabilitation, for the profit of one class, of that myth *jus naturale* or *lex naturalis* which Hobbes, Rousseau, and even Adam Smith, built upon. A still older and more elastic fiction, the *lex eterna* of the scholastic and patristic school of political economists,

---

* For centuries Customs duties (levying benevolences on a man's goods simply because he happens to land at a seaport) seem to have been levied upon foreigners only.

reappears as the ' economic morality ' or ' ideal good ' of latter-day collectivists and idealists.   These developments represent a subtle but sinister corruption of the text of English jurisprudence, traces of which, found in Adam Smith's writings, may be attributed to Renaissance influences, Sir Thomas More's among others.   The moral philosophy of the eighteenth century is anti-English and imported. The Puritan movement, on its secular side, was partly a revolt against intrusion of bastard Latin ethics which accompanied Renaissance new learning. Much England owes to that dogged determination among Puritan jurists and Parliamentarians, among the Whig leaders in 1688 also, to revert to English ideas, English precedents, English law.   On these foundations solely Edmund Burke built.   Although metaphysicians might ignore such a mere detail, one defect of Rousseau's *contrat* was that, as Hume, Bentham, Austin, Mill, and Brougham pointed out, it really never had any existence.   For Lord Bramwell, bargains or contracts, as well as implied contracts arising therefrom, always concerned actual English people, Smith and Brown, or partners.   He could at least get material evidence about Smith's or Brown's doings.   They were human beings, not nebulæ.

The note of the new jurisprudence inspired after 1880 by sympathy with ' some kind ' of Socialism, is a denial of national or purely English origin for vital parts of English law and equity.   Erudite German Chauvinists became the fashionable authorities at English Universities for the view that Englishmen imported, in foreign garb, sundry priceless safe-guards of their liberties. German writers—having lost their tails, conscious that their own countrymen failed to preserve ancient liberties and *fueros* which Englishmen did long manage to preserve—naturally try to prove that it is not possible to evolve either the spirit or the letter of modern law from popular notions of right, embodied in tribal or local procedure, custom, tradition, maxim ; jurists of the *pickel-haube* school have a corresponding interest in magnifying the missionary influence, and pan-European ascendancy of Roman Law. Suggestions from these learned men are that our 'crowner's quest' is derived from the Roman *fiscus*, and trial by jury from the prerogatives of Frankish Kings ; who, it is not alleged knew the Digest by heart, but at all events were not Englishmen. It has never been explained how a thirteenth century Sheriff, or Knight of Assize in Wiltshire or Northumberland, acquired any extensive knowledge of, or affection for, Roman Law. Early Judges of the *curia regis*, nearly all ecclesiastics, presumably had much abstract respect for what travelled clerks brought from Bologna or Paris. Considerable independence of Rome and of Roman ideas in civil matters was nevertheless quite possible to an English Bishop, even before the arch traitor Becket's extremely informal execution for high treason. Many of the King's Judges after Evesham were as much Englishmen first and sons of the Church afterwards as sundry Roman Catholics were when the Armada came lumbering up the Channel. Native English stuff, Borough law and Englishry, local procedure, custom, precept, proverb, were in the texture of English Common Law before *Nolumus leges Angliæ mutare* was shouted at Merton, and re-echoed not solely by laymen with long swords who didn't know much Latin, but by English ecclesiastics who did, and doubtless pronounced it all wrong. Habits or characteristics last acquired are the first to be dropped. After Edward III.'s time our Judges begin to drop or shed, bit by bit, many mischievous encrustations derived from the *Jus genti* or the Decretals. What survived and was formative, fruitful, seems to have been that part which was national, English. Roman jurists ingeniously manufactured law for suitors; English Judges compiled rules for the better enforcement of individual claims of right—claims which the fierce English themselves had first made respectable. Although Lord Bramwell quotes the very words of Digest 50 in a *Times* letter about Employers' Liability, it is impossible to evolve either from Roman or from Canon Law that conception of contract which he and his predecessors in comparatively modern times wrought out. The process of evolution is barred at once by the fact that for centuries (until the so-called Conservative leaders repudiated liberty of bargain in 1897) every kind of bargain, except the English kind, was liable to be varied or upset for elastic, capricious reasons. Few people argued with Lord Bramwell about contract; it was much easier not to read, or to forget, what he said and wrote; when they did they had to fling Scævola or Aquinas at his head.

Developing perhaps more rapidly after his death, yet distinctly traversing Lord Bramwell's judgments and opinions on and off the bench, professorial attacks upon the conception of contract held and applied by the great masters of English Common Law, efforts to infuse an ethical spirit into it, to impose fanciful tests, based on some lofty 'ideal of the common good'—all admitting the element of arbitrary caprice—are necessary concomitants of that Socialism of the housetops which marched with the Socialism of the street after 1880. The last word of the new jurisprudence is that, 'if there is to be any law at all, contract must be taught to know its place.'*   This had to be said, because, as T. H. Green, F. C. Montague, and others, frankly pointed out, some kind of Socialism, or Idealism, and Liberty cannot thrive side by side.   The Government official who is to enforce right-mindedness or compulsory altruism, to compel obedience to conceptions of social justice and 'Liberty according to Green,'† obviously must possess despotic powers, absolute authority to crush civil freedom and individual rights.   'If there is to be any law at all' designed to confiscate, nationalize, or municipalize legally acquired private property, alleged to be used in an anti-social way, or 'any law' withdrawing certain objects from the individualistic sphere, on high ethical grounds, the essentially English idea of contract must be repudiated, every contract, bargain,

* Pollock and Maitland's 'History of English Law before Edward I.,' Book II., p. 230.
† R. B. Wallace in *Progressive Review.*

or agreement enforceable at Common Law being primarily an assertion of three acquired (not 'natural') rights, or franchises, inherited, as it so happens, by every individual British and American citizen : (1) A general right to individual freedom ; (2) the consequential right of property, giving particular title to the subject matter of contract, and to the consideration ; (3) the right of free barter, free exchange within the four seas. Notwithstanding that the law has ever been much concerned with it, contract* does not seem to be originally the

* A distinguished living authority has expressed in the earlier editions of a famous book a wish to meet with ' a satis-factory definition of contract,' and straightway goes wool-gathering in the most learned and painstaking way, after the origin of the practice. In later editions of his work, inspired by Continental Katheder Socialists of the *pickel-haube* persuasion, he writes about ' a positive sanction for the expectation of good faith. . . .' That, it seems, is the *grund werk* of contract. Ultimately we do get a translation of *Rechtsverhaltniss*. Yet contract might very well have been invented by freemen them-selves, without waiting for any suggestions from the jurists at all. When the primeval A said to the primeval B, ' Let's swop,' and B. said ' Done '—although, like M. Jourdain, both unaware that they were talking such a fine thing as legal prose—they there and then unwittingly invented contract. Tribunals and Judges do not come in at all for a long time after that. Bracton, proud of having painfully mastered among the schoolmen in Paris what Isidore of Seville knew about Roman law, tells A and B how Justinian suggested that primeval ' swop' of theirs. Still later Dr. Hunter attributes to A and B flattering familiarity with the *nexus* and the *stipulatio*. Finally, Sir Henry Maine's enthusiasm for the splendid symmetry and precision of Roman jurisprudence con-strained him to aver that Englishmen in respect to contract copied Roman models ; only for that it might have been

creation of jurists, courts of law, or 'the State.'
Contracts must have preceded tribunals, or laws

---

deemed a coincidence, two communities of freemen, up to a
certain point, evolving spontaneously, and necessarily, an
analogous practice from analogous social and economic conditions—civil freedom, security of property, a high sense of
civic responsibility and desire to exchange utilities. Trying
to derive from *causa* the primitive English 'conception' of
'consideration'—a thing which the English contract always
has, but Roman contract had not—would be unnecessary if it
could be agreed that contracting Englishmen were quite
capable of inventing 'consideration' for themselves, and so did
—probably because they chose to. When Englishmen came
before the Courts with disputes about contract, somehow
'consideration' was in the affair, so the Judges dealt with it.
They didn't invent it nor add it. Vital, radical severance
between Roman and English conceptions of contract is made
by the political or governmental circumstance, that while
Roman jurists had to meet the case of suitors, some of whom
were dependent, only partially free, English contract always
connotes bargaining between freemen, a distinction which
became of great importance, again, when canonists, finding
the *jus genti* very stretchable indeed, developed their conception of contract on Roman, never on rude English lines. It
would be interesting to trace how the slow, sure decay of
Roman freedom gradually modified, depraved the Roman
view. As the true legal spirit, once present with the people,
dies out, partisans of *jus genti* oust the defenders of *jus civile*,
capricious interference by the Prætor and other grand persons
turns Roman contract into a matter of departmental dispensa-
tion, instead of a phase in free barter. As the Roman citizen
more and [more approaches the *status* of slave, one sees how
contract has its root in freedom ; the paternal red-tape view,
the benevolent slave-owner's view of contract becomes natural,
indispensable.

Theorizing about the origin of contract, tracing the practice
back to Roman sources or to Continental codes slavishly
modelled on Roman examples, are not unlike the domestic

made to guide tribunals, and would doubtless still continue to be made (only enforced in a different way) should tribunals and laws perish. As between individual freemen, capable and of full age, they are selfish private arrangements for each man's supposed benefit. Parties to contract do not start by acknowledging any obligation upon them to guess what expectation 'the State,' the community, or society has made about their good faith or *Rechtsverhaltniss.* Barter is one of the primitive human acts ; definition of the terms of barter brings us to contract ; disputes about terms bring in the vast legal literature on the subject for which one has immense respect. Metaphysicians have had their say about contract; lawyers, and one cannot blame them, have made a professional mystery of it ; Roman jurists, with some reason, riveted all sorts of elaborate pedantries on to it. Contract itself is no thing of mystery ; English contract law is based on an estimate of the average bad faith prevailing among bargainers. If men kept faith without being made to, courts of law would have little to do. One very useful question English law puts—but not before the law is called in by

---

fiction that the family doctor brings the baby in his pocket. Doctors do not 'solely,' nor even 'mainly,' originate babies, although much concerned with them at an early stage. Men who had matters to bargain about did not wait until tribunals were established, and had fully assimilated the Institutes, and then say to each other, 'Here's a Court in working order ; suppose we go in and make a contract.' The origin of British drinking customs is not the Licensing Acts, nor even the public-house. The origin of the British practice of clothes-wearing is not to be sought in that 'institution,' tailors' shops.

A and B as umpire—is, ' Did you both understand what you meant?' Since the vast majority of men are unable to explain in their native tongue what they do mean, legal fortunes have been earned, libraries have been filled, in trying to find out for them.

So soon as parol contracts take the place of solemn religious ceremonial, the King's Courts, the tribunals which supersede the King's justiciary, and, finally, 'the law,' intervene, each as recognized arbitrator—umpire first, champion afterwards—not for society, not because the community has part or lot in the matter, but for the contracting individuals, each of whom thinks he has right on his side, and wants to get justice from the King without fighting for it. The contracting man aggrieved would, in the absence of tribunals, do his best to kill, disable, or punish the other who had not kept to his bargain, a recourse abandoned long ago when the artificial arbitrament of the King's justice came to be willingly substituted by contracting individuals for the primeval, brutal, 'natural' arbitrament of force. Every time they plead contracting individuals express actually (not figuratively, as Rousseau conceived) their willingness to abide by the Court's award. When the elder of the tribe, the wise man, the *earldorman*, the justiciary, and at last the Judge, decides the case and enforces his decision, he simply represents the litigant who is in the right. He thereupon virtually does what the stronger of the two contracting parties would do were tribunals non-existent; only, the Judge is guided by rules (called after awhile 'laws '), not by the mere desire to possess. There is here no question of tribunals at any stage claiming authority to interfere as representatives of some general interest in contract vested in the regulative community, society, or 'State.' English law, like the rider in Æsop's fable, having once been placed in the saddle, called in by disputants about contract, has rightly kept its grip upon contract; has even tried to moralize it, although never to the extent metaphysicians or idealists recommend.

For centuries English Judges were (United States Judges always have been) the least ambitious, least concerned about A's or B's *Rechtsverhaltniss;* hesitated to graft upon contract pompous artificialities and flashy variations out of deference to the Latins; instead adapted their rulings to the circumstances of the common people who probably 'invented' contract.

Lord Bramwell never embittered discussion by his contribution to it; did not speak to the public *ex cathedrâ;* always in a most unassuming way; in open debate, with pen in hand, was as patiently considerate and generous as he used to be on the bench, and just as the honest man can never quite shake off a preconception that the first-comer is honest,* he imagined that every controversialist

* ' Queen's Bench,
 ' *May* 13, 1881.

' MY DEAR BRAMWELL,
      ' Our common friend St. Paul, in that interesting composition which you thought rigmarole, said that he " spoke as

must be as sincere a devotee of truth as he was himself. His letters to the press and other protests about certain matters show indirectly how popular impulses had begun to react upon jurisprudence, evolving, among University professors, and here and there within the legal profession, tepidly anarchical views. The plasticity of the legal, and even the judicial, mind in regard to general rules of law is often forgotten, certainly by the British public, who in respect to the fundamentals of Common Law and Equity probably imagine that *nollumus consuetudines Angliæ mutare* holds good. Certain latter-day theories of contract clashed altogether with those which he sets forth, unpretendingly, as the plain law of the land—virtually the embodiment of English ideas. It proves nothing to call the view one prefers English, the opposite view un-English. Ideas about Equity, about rights and wrongs, which influenced jurists and moulded decisions of the Courts in De Lacy's, Raleighe's, Coke's, Mansfield's day, were English, so also were the ideas which after 1880 arose to confound Lord Bramwell's stalwart counsel. In each instance forces valid and potent in the self-governing community make their imprint upon that plastic medium,

---

a fool " on one occasion. So did I, and I am ashamed and penitent.

' Ever yours,
' COLERIDGE.'

A note in Lord Bramwell's handwriting appears on the margin of this letter :

' This was very magnanimous. I had told him he was unjust to somebody, I forget whom.'

Common Law.   In each instance there is correlation of legal maxims and judicial rulings to actual popular beliefs.   Yet since even the most enlightened of Continental monarchs, councillors, judges, neglected to safeguard popular liberties in the Courts, never establishing or asserting a Common Law, never devising a workaday equivalent for that priceless English word 'reasonable,'* since that misfortune for human freedom was largely due to the formalist's contempt for popular or national beliefs about justice—to a snobbish preference for that grand classical thing Roman law — since insidious but methodical attacks upon what may very well be called Lord Bramwell's position come from a school inspired by foreign prison-made notions,† fashionable

* No word in the language is more illustrious than this one. From those early times when feudal dues were limited at Common Law because not 'reasonable,' down to Lord Esher's judgment in *Hawke v. Dunn*, the word 'reasonable' holds the field.   It is no question-begging term, but is the last word of impartiality, learning and common-sense, interpreting trust-worthy information.   The best human beings can do.   The judicial systems of the world might be divided into those which never knew the word 'reasonable' and so decayed, and those which had it and so flourished.

† During debate on a Workmen's Compensation Bill, July, 1897, Mr. R. B. Haldane bade the House of Commons remember that 'the doctrine of common employment' is not to be found in any Continental system of jurisprudence, and rightly, for no such a 'doctrine' exists, neither in our own country nor elsewhere.   What was novel was the argument that English jurists ought to take example in respect to Common Law from France, Germany, Spain, Greece, etc.

Here is a passage from a letter to Lord Bramwell dated November 22, 1881 :

at our Universities of late years, the essentially
'English' bent of Lord Bramwell's mind is worth
dwelling upon.

Never given to gushing about English freedom
(although, if he had lived in the old troubled times,
likely enough he would have died for it fearlessly),
he argues for freedom in the abstract in his plain
way when insisting that freedom of contract, liberty
to make bargains, is the corner-stone of the social,
industrial, economic edifice, when in letters of May,
1878, of June, 1880, in speech to Liberty and Property Defence League, November, 1882, he describes
as 'most mischievous and outrageous' the proposal
then talked of (actually embodied, at the dictation
of London 'labour leaders' and strike-brokers, in
the Ministerial Bills of 1894 and 1897) to deprive
workmen of liberty to make or to refuse, as they
thought proper, contracts relating to their labour.
The expression 'freedom of contract' may be in a
sense misleading or trappy, the syllable 'free'
suggesting that unless both parties are ideally free
—independent of any strong motive or inclination
to accept the terms offered—bargaining ought not
to be permitted by 'the State.'   At all events, it is
argued, there must be perfect equality; one party

'. . . But there is *one* point on which I think sufficient
stress has not been laid, which has made your judicial position
(in my opinion) unique; it is your *strong loyalty* to English
law, and at the same time your complete freedom from technicality and your unfettered originality of thought. . . .

'Yours very sincerely,

'ARTHUR COHEN.'

must be no more constrained than the other. Arguments from 'defenders of freedom of contract' seem to mean, not that either party to a bargain can be, or ought to be, ideally 'free' to reject the terms, but that British subjects and citizens of the United States,* of full age, have inherited full liberty to decide whether they will accept, refuse, or vary agreements enforceable at Common Law.

Mental confusion due to the expression 'freedom of contract' may be traced through economic legislation and discussion thereof from 1870 to 1897. It was often asked: 'Can the starving worker, contracting with the wealthy employer, ever be said to be really "free"? . . . Were Irish tenants and Scottish Crofters "free" to contract with their landlords? . . . Your boasted "freedom of contract" does not exist *now*,'† etc. Here one finds a reminis-

---

* 'The respective colonies are entitled to the Common Law of England, and to all the rights, liberties, and immunities of free and natural born subjects within the realm of England.'— Declaration of Rights made by American Congress, October 14, 1774.

† Arnold Toynbee, 'Industrial Revolution,' p. 216, wrote: 'Between men who are unequal in material wealth there can be no freedom of contract. . . .' To test the value of this proposition, one has only to become a millionaire and then try to get a hansom cabman to contract to drive one down to the Derby and back for half a crown. On May 17, 1897, a Secretary of State said in the House of Commons: '. . . There is no such thing as freedom of contract in this country or any other. . . .'

Mr. John Coppen, April 10, 1886, wrote from Staines to the *Economist* asking for a Leasehold Enfranchisement Act, because in that vicinity 'on many estates freeholders will not sell, *therefore* freedom of contract does not exist. . . .'

cence of 'duress,' or perhaps of the legal maxim
that there ought to be an 'alternative' to acceptance of a contract.   Constructive 'duress' is indeed
the main argument for recent agrarian and labour
legislation.   Mr. Gladstone had to invent it on
behalf of Irish tenants in 1881.   Certainly, if a man
says to another : ' Agree to sell me your house for £5,
and I will not cut off your leg'; or, 'Spare my life,
and I will give you my purse,' those are contracts,
but voidable at Common Law, since one of the
parties was coerced under duress, and had no
alternative but to accept, or make the offer.   The
stays and guy-ropes of English law well converge
on this point.   ' Duress' of the person vitiates contracts, for the law knows nothing of agreements
outside that paddock where the law ranges.   If you
believe that a man intends not to cheat, but to kill
you, you are both outlawed for the moment and
you may kill him.   You and he will certainly not
exchange 'sufficient consideration.'   Agreements
enforceable at Common Law refer mostly to money
matters, the exchange of utilities, etc.—matters not
likely to cause life and death struggles (which are
beyond the cognizance of civil process).   What is
often forgotten is that if either party to a possible
contract happens to be 'free,' in the sense of being
'indifferent,' no contract is ever made.   In other
words, unless *both* freemen are 'unfree,' to the extent
of being influenced by some strong constraining
motive (such as the value they set upon the subject
matter of agreement or upon the consideration), no
contract is ever made.   The claim, by opponents of

freedom of contract, that Parliament should create equality for buyer and seller—that one should have no stronger motive, no more inclination towards the course of action proposed, than the other—threatens a *reductio ad absurdum*, since if buyer and seller were equally indifferent each would name a fancy consideration, and neither would accept it;* while if both buyer and seller were equally constrained, had no alternative but to deal, another see-saw would result: they could never fix on any sufficient consideration.

* Landlords and employers of labour are never free when bargaining with tenants or with workmen. The fact that real, although indirect, coercion is exercised on employers by workmen in many trades (as, for instance, in the case of slate quarrymen), owing to the trade unionists' monopoly of labour, is no argument against unrestricted bargaining between employers and employed. 'Liberty to make bargains' is perhaps a better phrase than 'freedom of contract.'

CHAPTER VII.

LAND TENURE AND CONTRACT.

Letters to *Times* and *Economist* asserting contractual relation
between English landlords and tenants—Impetus to controversy given by 'Progress and Poverty,' and by Irish
Land Acts—Non-Irish Land Question between 1860 and
1880—Effect of hostile legislation on 'security' and on
investment of capital—Queer agrarian ideas brought out
in *Times* correspondence—Messrs. Hardcastle, McBlank,
Chamberlain and Gee on 'real owner,' 'State autocracy,'
'waste of manors,' 'tenure by poverty,' etc.—The late
Henry George's propaganda in this country—Replies
thereto, and uneasy interest therein, 1880-85—Results in
other English-speaking lands—Letter to Industrial Remuneration Conference of 1883.

A *Times* letter, February 6, 1879—the last paragraph especially—indicates that Lord Bramwell did
not consider English land tenure faultless, nor refuse
to admit that tenants sometimes make dreadfully
bad bargains on paper; but he believed an Englishman who made a bargain ought to show his fellow-
Englishmen that he could stick to his word. The
New Morality, rather in embryo in 1879, replied to
Lord Bramwell that society's moral mission was to
find reasons why men should not stick to their
words.

'Forfeiture of Leases.

'. . . A man takes a lease of a piece of land, agrees to lay out thousands of pounds in building on it, enters into a variety of agreements in relation to land and houses, and this among them—that for any breach of any agreement, however trifling, however reparable, however easily compensated in money, the landlord may avoid the lease and the lessee lose the land and the money he has laid out on it. I say that this is incredible. It is incredible that it should be to the advantage of lessor or lessee to enter into such bargains. Nevertheless it is true. I agree with one of your correspondents that there is not one lease in ten where the landlord has not had the option of forfeiture.

'Of course, so soon as this state of things is made public there is a cry for Parliamentary interference. The Legislature is to prevent foolish bargains in future, and set aside those already made. I send this to express a doubt whether the Legislature should interfere. As to future leases, I suppose it would not be asked that lessors and lessees should be forbidden to enter into any bargain they thought fit, however unreasonable. To forbid that would be to violate a rule which cannot be better expressed than it is in the *Times* of yesterday : " Freedom of contract is so far fixed as a general principle that the very clearest case ought to be made out for every departure from it." The utmost that could be done for the future would be to enact that, unless specially provided to the contrary, provisions causing the forfeiture of a lease should only have that effect when the mischief was irreparable and money would not compensate, or to that effect. In other words, that people should not be taken to mean what they say, but something else. Whether that is desirable I doubt. People had better be taught prudence by suffering from the want of it. As to the past, the proposal to interfere with existing leases is simply a proposal to disregard the homely rule that " a bargain is a bargain." Why should not the Legislature at once say that no bargain should be binding if some Court or tribunal thought it unreasonable ? It would be difficult to legislate on the subject without injustice. Suppose a man is owner of a row of residential houses.   Suppose for the keeping up of its character he has made the lessee of one agree that he will not turn it into a beershop, on pain of forfeiture; and suppose the lessee does.   What damage is the lessor to get ?   He could not get, according to the present law, the damage to the whole row; that would be too remote.   If it was enacted that he should, there would be injustice to the lessee.   Further, the lessor would have a question to try on which there might be different opinions, viz., how much are his damages?   On this he might be beaten and have to pay costs.   As it is, he has made himself safe, and safe without a question.   Still further, if such an alteration in the law would raise the value of leases (and unless it would it would be useless), it would diminish the value of reversions.   Even if not, why should the whole profit go to the lessees?   After all, " a bargain is a bargain."   The lessee has entered into it.   Maybe it is a foolish one, and one which the lessor ought not to have exacted.   But he has, and it seems to me that for the Legislature to rescind it savours of a questionable agrarianism.   It may be said, Is there then no remedy?   I see none, except by the consent of the two parties to the bargain—the lessor and the lessee.   They can consent now by surrender of the old lease and grant of a new. Possibly power might be given to some tribunal to extend this power to lessors and lessees with limited interests.

'B.

' *February* 3.'

By October, 1881, the momentum of Mr. Gladstone's triumphant Irish legislation was not quite exhausted.   The *Economist* on the 29th, reviewing the prospects of land legislation for Great Britain, especially condemned the Land Bill of the Farmers' Alliance ; it would deprive landlords of proprietorial rights without compensation, check improvements, diminish interest in estates, convert contracts of hiring into partition of ownership ; a Land Court on the Irish model was defensible in 'the Irish Alsatia,' not in England, etc., etc.

Commenting on letters from Mr. W. Bear and the Duke of Argyll, Lord Bramwell wrote in the *Economist*, December 3, 1881 :

'TENANTS' RIGHTS.

'Mr. Bear says that "Mr. Gladstone has declared that a tenant has a right to the whole interest in his improvements," and that the Duke of Argyll "maintains that a tenant has a just claim to a portion of that value." Have these distinguished persons said so? If they have, I respectfully ask what they mean. The relation of landlord and tenant, in England at least, is one of contract. That contract may have all its terms stated in words spoken or written, or it may have them partly expressed only, leaving the rest to be supplied by the law or custom. As where the contract in words expressed simply creates a tenancy from year to year, and the law adds that to determine it six months' notice must be given, and custom adds that the tenant shall be paid for ploughings, dressings, etc., how has landlord or tenant a just claim or right against the other for anything not in the contract or added to it by law or custom? Whatever is not so is as much out of the contract as though it was expressly negatived.

'Suppose a tenant takes a farm, and expressly agrees with the landlord that he will improve and not claim compensation. Has he a right or claim to any? It may be said no one would be so foolish. But, if it is foolish, it is done daily; and for a good reason, viz., that the landlord, in consideration thereof, takes less rent.

'To go by steps—suppose the tenant does not agree to improve, but agrees that if he does he will make no demand for compensation. Has he then a "right or just claim" to any? It will, perhaps, be said he has none at law, but that he has morally. What! contrary to his bargain? Suppose it could be shown that the landlord had agreed to take less rent because he knew he had an improving tenant, but declined to have a question of compensation to try at the end of the lease. Would the claim then be just ? Would there be a right, legal or moral? But is the contract to be interpreted, not by what is in it, but by something outside it ?

'Now to the last step—suppose the contract is silent as to compensation, is there then the just claim—the right ? It may be it was not put down in writing, because both parties knew the law added it. I cannot understand a right or just claim to that which has not been agreed for, to that which practically has been tacitly agreed should not exist.

'If it should be said that such agreements negativing a right to compensation, either expressly or by the addition of legal intendment or custom, are mischievous and should be annulled, I deny it. Surely the parties are the best judges of what is for their own good. Surely it is not unreasonable that land-lord and tenant should agree that rather than have a controversy about improvements the rent should be reduced, and the improvements not paid for. To hold otherwise would be to hold that the law can make better contracts for people than they can for themselves. It would annul every building lease. It would tempt every man who had agreed not to claim for improvements to turn rogue, and, having held on favourable terms on account of that agreement, to make a profit in spite of it. All this is very trite and obvious. But, then, why is it not borne in mind ? Why is there a talk of "right" and "just" claims, when the question should be, What have the parties agreed ?

'If, indeed, the question were whether, in the absence of express agreement to the contrary, the law should add an agreement to compensate for improvements, it might be right to say it should, though I doubt it. But that is not the question. The question is whether there is a right or just claim which is not agreed for, and, negatively, is agreed shall not exist.

'B.'

This letter was doubtless unanswerable, unless one appealed from custom, law, contract, to a higher standard ; December 10 W. A. H. so appealed.

'TENANTS' RIGHTS.

' " B's " argument in your issue of last week is a pregnant illustration of the mischievous educational influence of an iniquitous law. The doctrine of English law by which a landlord is allowed to appropriate the property of a tenant as soon as it is mixed with or fixed to the soil has much to answer for, and not least in its corrupting the conscience of land-owners and their friends. If " B " would only revert to the fountains pure and undefiled of Roman jurisprudence, he would get light on some of his problems. Let me give him a case stated by Scævola. A landlord sued a tenant after he was out of his farm for arrears of rent. The tenant pleaded that the claim was against good conscience and fraudulent (*exceptio doli mali*) . . . The tenant, not being bound by the terms of his lease to do so, had nevertheless planted vines, and the land in consequence was let to the next tenant at an increased rent of 10 aurei a year. Was this a good answer to the action for rent? " Yes," was the answer of the jurist, " the landlord must pay compensation to the tenant or he must go without his rent." There can be little doubt that this also would have been the answer of English law if it had not been for the unhappy ignorance of the Judges. . . . The fathers of the common law borrowed one-half of the Roman doctrine—that whatever is fixed in the soil belongs to the owner of the soil, without the corresponding half—that when that is done by a tenant the landlord must pay the value of it. . . .

' . . . The real question of public policy is whether the law ought to sanction a contract whereby a tenant binds himself not to make improvements, or . . . that he shall receive no consideration or compensation for improvements he may execute. The farmers intend to ask the Legislature to make such contracts illegal, and they can hardly fail to have the support of the vast food-consuming population cooped up within our small islands.　　' Yours,　　'W. A. H.'

An interesting letter, not only because of the writer's plan for increasing the nation's food-supply and his frank repudiation of the Liberal theory of contract, but because it shows how modern Radical or Socialist assailants of freedom and of the right of property join hands, *longo intervallo*, with those Roman jurists who found Roman freedom dead or dying, and had to do their best under the circumstances to secure generous treatment for a servile class. On December 17 Lord Bramwell replied:

'TENANTS' RIGHTS.

'Your correspondent, W. A. H., in your paper of the 10th, says that if I "would only revert to the fountains pure and undefiled of Roman jurisprudence I should get light on some of my problems." It certainly never occurred to me to *revert* to a *fountain* to get *light*. Permit me to do what your correspondent calls "revert" to Adam Smith. The legislation nearest to that proposed as to improvements by tenants are the Truck Acts. Adam Smith gives them a doubtful approval, but solely on the ground of the helplessness of the persons for whose benefit they were passed. Are the farmers of England in that condition ?

'It is a mistake to suppose that those who object to the proposed legislation do so on the ground that what is fixed in the soil belongs to the owner of the soil. The objection would be the same as to matters to which that rule does not apply. A tenant may improve a house or land by what are called tenants' fixtures. He may remove them at the end of his term ; he has no right to leave them and make his landlord pay for them. If the improvements are such that he has no right to remove, he has equally no right to demand payment for them. The reason is the same in both cases. He has not bargained for such payment, and has no right to put an improvement on the land to be paid for by the landlord without the landlord consents. The same thing would be equally true of a chattel. Suppose a carriage was let for six months, and the hirer put on a new and better lining, would it be common-sense or justice that the owner should be made to pay for it ?   A bargain is a bargain, and wherever there is no affirmative bargain, there is by implication a negative bargain to the contrary of the absent affirmative.   Why should the tenant be the judge of the propriety of the improvement ?   If that is to be decided by some tribunal, why should the landlord be subject to a trial when the tenant has bargained to the contrary ?   Tenants bargain with their landlords that as a matter of right they shall not be entitled to compensation for improvements.

' B.'

Probably the best-known of Lord Bramwell's writings on the Land Question is his pamphlet published by the Liberty and Property Defence League in 1883, ' Nationalization of Land : a Review of Henry George's " Progress and Poverty."'   The wide dissemination during the next few years of Henry George's book (published in San Francisco, 1879, in London, 1880), and finally the author's visit to this country in 1884, gave specific direction for awhile to ideas about land tenure deep-based upon sentiments, most ancient, endowed with extraordinary vitality, such as class jealousy, envy of persons apparently wealthier, more fortunate, happier than their neighbours.   These sentiments were embittered by the characteristic vices of land-ownership (which always partly explain the personal note in the attack upon landlordism) such as pride, extravagant expenditure and display, irritating exclusiveness, etc., tempting loose thinkers to bestow their ' sympathy ' at random.   Excluding the middle term, there remained the ominous political fact that extension of the franchise in 1832 and 1868 had given considerable impetus to a revolutionary and anarchical campaign against one form of property explicitly safeguarded, in common with all other forms of property, by legal covenant, prescription, etc. Miscellaneous millionaires were scarce in 1880; land, still the most conspicuous, tangible, concrete kind of property in sight, was exalted by tradition and popular imagination into the most enviable kind.

Land-owners—still believed to be well off—were also suspected of the original sin of Toryism. The important point was that the thing in dispute was then deemed well worth fighting about. When a supposed popular demand becomes too vague and chaotic to be expressed by any other formula it is said that 'the question is ripe for solution.' In 1880 (although land reform would 'keep') the English, or rather non-Irish, Land Question was, in an abstract sense, ripe for solution; therefore a thrilling book like ' Progress and Poverty,' described by opponents as 'a model of logical and lucid arrangement,' which induced many people to think about land questions for the first time, was entitled to large circulation. Just as 'authority' has had its Hobbes, its Alison, its Croker, so plausible talkers and writers have never been wanting, eager to give logical or scientific sanction to funda- mental class hatreds and jealousies—often genuinely hoodwinked by their own arguments, confirmed in their honest hatred of injustice by the apparently interested opposition they meet with. Among serious economists, Mill had greatly encouraged abstract revolutionary ideas about land tenure by his 'unearned increment' theory; it is a splendid phrase, and the theory, when first revealed to the average man, is as unanswerable as the Fair Trader's terrible question: 'What is the use of the loaf being cheap if the working-man has no money in his pocket to buy it with?'

The Irish Land Acts of 1870 and 1881 gave considerable stimulus to land agitation in Great Britain, those of the public who took interest in such matters seeing clearly enough—although Mr. Gladstone's partisans pretended not to see—that his Irish agrarian policy had struck a blow at all titles, in reality throwing the whole thing into the melting-pot. Vague and random as were the ideas of extreme land reformers, after 1881 the non-Irish land agitation indirectly contributed to aggravate 'agricultural depression,' then becoming chronic. Consciousness among land-owners that security had been impaired, proposals for partial confiscation openly advocated by leading statesmen, coupled with ever-increasing taxation, which fell first upon tenants, checked the free application of capital to agriculture,* and worked indelible economic mischief. Analogous effects from analogous causes attract more notice in such countries as Cuba, Peru, or the

* 'I believe we have no adequate conception of what the amount of production might be from a limited' (given ?) 'surface of land, provided the amount of capital was sufficient.' . . . 'If you' (British farmers) 'had abundance o capital employed on your farms, and cultivated the soil with the same skill that manufacturers put into their business, you would . . .', etc.—COBDEN, quoted by William Fowler, 'Cobden Club Essays,' second series.

Soudan, where, owing to insecurity of property or bad laws, large tracts of agricultural land go out of cultivation. For a quarter of a century after the repeal of the Corn Laws, British farmers prospered greatly, and farming land steadily rose in value. Had it not been for blows struck at security for Irish, English and Scottish land, and for property in general, by Mr. Gladstone's economic legislation after 1870, British agriculture might have adapted itself to the new conditions produced by Free Trade without friction, without permanent loss to owners or occupiers.

Reproducing what happened when the Irish Land Bills of 1870 and 1881 had to be fought, resistance by English land-owners to destructive agrarian proposals was impeded and weakened by the fact that the Conservative party was historically pledged to misunderstand the basis of political economy— a supposed monopoly of their Liberal opponents. Harassed land-owners and tenants turned to those quack remedies which Lord Bramwell protested against, such as Fair Trade, reduction of tithe rent-charge, Railway Rates Acts, 'marking' foreign mutton chops, bimetallism, re-enactment of the usury laws, stopgap doles from Imperial funds, and un-limited 'State' interference, to heal the mischief which Liberals who repudiated Liberal watchwords —individual freedom and security of property—had done to British agriculture.

One of the most interesting things brought out by Lord Bramwell's press correspondence on this subject is the extent of uncertainty, even among educated men, about the law applying to land tenure in Great Britain.

For example, in a *Times* letter, May, 1883, Lord Bramwell had dissected Mill's famous phrase 'unearned increment:' he hated catch - words, and thought this one.

'Unearned Increment.

'People are now asking for Acts of Parliament to forbid whatever they disapprove of. One gentleman wants a law to forbid the killing of lambs. I should like one to put a stop to something much worse, viz., the making and uttering of phrases, unless, indeed, licensed by competent inspectors. They are often very mischievous. One was started some time ago which led astray a number of worthy people—" Fair Trade." It was very taking. Trade is a good thing; so is fairness. It follows that, put together, they must make something very good. In truth, something very bad was intended. Then we have " a free breakfast-table." Well, a breakfast-table suggests a pleasant, cheerful idea. Refreshed with sleep, clean, bright cloth and crockery, smiling children round—or, what some might prefer, a well-aired copy of the *Times*—then freedom is good, and so a free breakfast-table is very good, and so people have called for it. If the phrase had been dropped, and they had been asked whether they preferred an income-tax or a tax on beer to the duty on tea, few would have said " Yes."

'But there is a worse phrase invented by Mr. J. S. Mill, who seems to have confused a love of his fellow-creatures with a dislike of his superiors in rank and station. The phrase is " unearned increment," as applied to the value of land and to whom it should belong. Let us examine that phrase. " Increment " is " increase," neither more nor less. " Unearned " is " not earned "—a negative. Well, but all negatives are true of anything, unless the affirmative is. A thing is unblue and unhot, unless it is blue or hot. An increase is not earned unless it is earned, it is unsought unless it was sought, unexpected unless expected, uncertain unless certain, and so on.

We may, therefore, leave out the negative " unearned " and all other negatives, and consider the matter with only the word " increase."   Drop the phrase, which has misled a number of right-minded people, and deal with the question thus : " To whom is an increase in the value of a piece of land to belong ?" The answer, I say, is obvious.   " To the same person to whom the increase in the value of any other property should belong, and for the same reason—the owner."   I can understand those who deny the right of property, those who say " *La propriété c'est le vol.*"   They think mankind would be happier if the institution of private property was abolished.   But how those who admit the benefit of that institution can doubt to whom an increase in the value of property should belong, whether earned by the owner or not, I cannot understand.   Why does the institution of private property exist ?   Because it is for the good of the community.   If not, it should be abolished some- how and on some terms.   When it is abolished there will be no question as to whom its increase in value should belong. Meanwhile we will discuss that question on the assumption that the institution of private property is good.   But why is it ?   The answer is plain—because there will be more of the good things of the world for division among the community with that institution than without it.   Each man will work harder for himself to acquire and improve them than he would if the community at large had the fruits of his labour.   But this same reason shows that the increase in the value of land or chattels should belong to their owner.   It is idle to suppose inquiry could be made into the cause of that increase and the owner of the property have it if he had caused it—otherwise not.   Who would trouble himself to improve what he had if the improvement involved an inquiry into whether he had caused it ?   Take a manufacturer of screws and bolts, whose stock rose in value £1,000 because iron or coal rose.   Would he think it reasonable that this increase in value should be taken from him because it was an " unearned increment "? Would the screwmaker care to keep a stock of the " unearned increment " if its value was to be taken from him, especially if its " un-by-himself-caused decrement " was not made up to him when caused by a fall in iron or coal? If this is true of screws and bolts, why is it not of land? Is it because the land-owner does not toil nor spin? But he does. The debt of this country to its land-owners is heavy. Our greatness and the causes of our greatness do not begin in 1832. Our laws and institutions had their origin long before, and are in great part due to and now preserved, maintained, and administered, and the country in great part governed, and well governed, by men who happily are able to disregard the foolish notions of the moment.

'Besides, it is especially untrue that the land has not been improved by its owners. "Managed on the English system" means improved by the owner. But, further, their case, as their enemies put it, is that of the man of screws and bolts, where the increase of value is not of his causing and is un-earned by him. The phrase is invidious and mischievous. Let us drop it. Let the question be, "To whom is an increase in the value of property, land or other, to belong?" Common sense will answer, "To the man most able and interested to bring it about—its owner."

'B.

'P.S.—Does anyone propose to make good to its owner the decrement in value land has suffered?'

In the *Times*, May 22, 1883, Mr. J. A. Hardcastle, after criticizing Lord Bramwell's objections to Mill's phrase 'unearned increment,' thus rebuked the assumption that increase in the value of land should belong to English landlords as 'owners':

'. . . It comes to this, then, that we have to inquire who is "the owner." Doctrines which "B." must think most revolutionary are to be found in a book he may have met with, called "Blackstone's Commentaries"; but I do not wish to go further than to notice that the ultimate ownership of the State in all kinds of property is the only justification for the imposi-tion of taxes, rates, and public charges of whatever description. . . .*   In every case, except where the owner is also the occupier, there are at least two owners to every plot of land. . . . I should say of this phrase " owner," as applied to the landlords, that it is, to use the words of your correspondent, " invidious and mischievous "; that it puts the landlords in a false position, being, as they are, partners with their tenants ; and that the sooner the landlords recognize this truth and answer the question to whom an increase in the value of land ought to go by admitting the just claims of their tenants, the better, not only for those tenants, but for the landlords themselves. . . .

' J. A. HARDCASTLE.

' 54, Queen's Gate Terrace, S.W.,
    ' *May* 18.'

A couple of days later Lord Bramwell replied :

' UNEARNED INCREMENT.

' " A little learning is a dangerous thing."   To judge from Mr. Hardcastle's letter, worse than none, for he certainly would be better without the little, the very little, he has got from Blackstone. Mr. Hardcastle says : " Doctrines which ' B.' must think most revolutionary are to be found in ' Blackstone's Commentaries,' but (why ' but '?) I do not wish to go further than to notice that the ultimate ownership of the State in all kinds of property is the only justification for the imposition of taxes, rates, and public charges of whatever description."

' Now, Blackstone does, indeed, teach that on " feudal principles," no doubt much revered by Mr. Hardcastle, " all the land of the kingdom is supposed to be holden mediately or immediately of the King."   But Blackstone does not say anything so untrue as that that supposition in any way interferes with or affects the use, benefit, or enjoyment of land by its

---

* Jevons, " The State in Relation," etc., p. 8, argues that " taxation is one instance of a man's limited right to his own property."   Lord Bramwell once recommended this book to friends of liberty and property.   See p. 139.

owner. When he and his heirs fail it escheats, but till then he has the full and entire property. And certainly Blackstone does not teach that the State is the ultimate owner of chattels. It is not in any sense. Though what is the meaning of the " ultimate ownership " of what may be eaten or drunk or otherwise consumed, I know not. Nor do I know, nor can I guess, whence Mr. Hardcastle got the notion that " the ultimate ownership of the State in all kinds of property is the only justification for the imposition of taxes, etc." It will be alarming news to the Chancellor of the Exchequer—if he believes it. I have just received a circular that comes so pleasantly once a year, in which I am requested to state how much income I have from foreign railways, with a view to the " imposition of a tax " on it. I suppose this State is not the owner of a French railway. I am glad that Mr. Hardcastle does not wish to go further than he says he does, but I beg to suggest to him respectfully that he should not go so far.

' Your most obedient servant,

' B.

' *May 24, 1883.*'

Thus, one sees that a gentleman living at Queen's Gate Terrace, S.W., presumably belonging to one or two good clubs, accustomed to dine with people of average West-End intelligence, probably destined to become a Liberal Unionist in December, 1885, was sincerely uncertain, in May, 1883, whether English land belonged to the people who had bought or inherited it. The tenant who hired land twenty years ago (or yesterday), might have acquired a moral, legal, actual partnership or share in the ' estate.' Again, the formidable theory is disclosed that ' the State ' in this country, as ultimate owner of all property, real and personal, has unlimited power to ' impose ' taxes, rates, etc.

Early in 1885, Mr. John Morley, replying to Mr.

Wordsworth Donisthorpe in the *Times*, had shown that Mill held almost as extreme views on land tenure as Henry George himself. On February 16 Lord Bramwell returned to the subject :

' MILL'S POLITICAL ECONOMY.

'. . . The quotations from Mill in the *Times* of Saturday, February 7 . . . also show that Mill could talk great nonsense. That is a bold thing to say of that great oracle, but if you will give me space I will convict him of it—or myself.

' He says . . . " There are some things which, if allowed to be articles of commerce at all, cannot be prevented from being monopolized articles. On all such the State has an acknowledged right to limit profits. Railways, for instance, are an inevitable monopoly, and the State accordingly sets a legal limit to the amount of railway fares." Now, this " article of commerce " is not a monopoly. Johnson says a monopoly is an exclusive right of selling. But though this is the etymological meaning, popularly it means all exclusive rights. Railways and their owners have no exclusive rights. Everyone may move himself and his goods by any other mode of conveyance—canal, coach, waggon, ship, balloon, or bicycle. But they prefer the railway. Why? For the same reason that for an advocate they prefer Sir H. James, for a surgeon Sir J. Paget, for a physician Sir W. Gull or Sir Andrew Clark, for a singer Patti, for a fiddler the prince of fiddlers, Joachim— because of their excellence. This is why all who want themselves or their goods carried use the railway, because of its excellence. It is cheaper, faster, easier and safer than any other mode of transport. This is not " monopoly," not an exclusive right, but an exclusive goodness. Nor is it upon any notion of its being a monopoly that the " State sets a legal limit to the amount of railway fares." The undertakers of the railway and the State make a bargain. The State says, " If we give you powers to take the people's land, interfere with highways, and so on, you must charge nothing beyond such and such a sum." The undertakers agree. They have in no sense a "monopoly." There is nothing to prevent the State empowering the making of a second railway alongside the first —a thing the State too often does for want of knowing better, and from not seeing that two railways, where only one is wanted, involve a loss of part of the general wealth of the community, though it comes out of particular pockets.

' Mill says, "On all such articles of commerce the State has an acknowledged right to limit the profits." " Now, land is one of these natural monopolies." . . . Let us look at what seems to be the substance of his meaning. Who has ever doubted the right of the State to deal with all property, land, and chattels, monopoly or not, and with labour? No one says that the land-tax is immoral or unjust. No one doubts the right of the State to expropriate the owner of land wanted for the good of the public, making, as Mill says, " full compensation." The same is true of chattels. The State does not commonly lay a tax on specie or chattels, any more than on land. But if the owner of them does not pay his taxes, he will find the State make free with his chattels, and his land, too, if necessary. So of labour. The hateful conscription is within the State's rights. There can be no doubt that private property is a State or social institution, and exists upon such terms and conditions, and with such rights and liabilities, as the State deems expedient for the good of its members. What need, then, is there for the clap-trap that follows? " The land is the original inheritance of all mankind." " We hold that all property in land is subject to the will of the State." Certainly, and all other property. " Land not having been made by man, but being the gift of Nature to the whole human race, could only be appropriated by the consent, express or tacit, of society, and society remains the interpreter of its own permission with power to make conditions; with power even to revoke its consent on giving due compensation to the interests that it has allowed to grow up." This is better than Mr. George, who says society could not do it, and who would give no compensation. But what Mill says is true, and true not only of land, but of all other property, and labour. But not because it is a gift of Nature. Take land reclaimed from the sea, which, if a gift of Nature, is a very poor one. Does any-one doubt that the State may deal with it as with any other land ? Would Mill's reasoning be more fantastical in Holland than here ?

' Mill says that if certain named very large estates in London " belonged to the municipality of London their income would probably suffice for the whole expense of the local government of the capital." Probably, and for other purposes. " What," says he, " have the possessors done that this increase of wealth produced by other people's labour and enterprise should fall into their mouths as they sleep instead of being applied to the public necessities of those who created it ? It is maintained, therefore, by land reformers, that special taxation may justly be levied upon land property up to, though not exceeding, this unearned increase."

' This is the old " unearned increment " story. Why should those who by their own exertions only have caused this incre-ment have the benefit of it ? What meritorious earning has there been by them ? There has been no exertion of body or mind by them to increase the value of these estates. It is untrue that it has been created by their " labour or enterprise." It would be more reasonable to give the increment to the farmer, who has grown the food, and the railway-owners, who have carried it, and enabled the added population to exist.

' Why does Mill invidiously name the large properties ? Is not what is true of them equally true of small properties— equally true of a property which by unearned increment has become £2,000 from being £1,000 ? But if this reasoning is true of land, why is it not of other things—of railways, for example, whose customers have increased while the share-holders were asleep—of gas companies, water companies ; of persons who have held wheat or hops which have risen in value owing to short crops ? Is the State prepared to make good the loss which has befallen many owners by decrement in value from no fault of theirs ? The truth is that Mill in his hatred, not of gigantic incomes, but of those who possess them, lost sight of the genuine principle that a thing is best improved when its owner has the benefit, and that it would be impossible to inquire either as to land or other things how much of the improvement was due to the owner, and how much to other causes. I have no doubt, too, that he is wrong in saying that the increase in value fell, as he elegantly and amiably expresses it, into the mouths of the owners while they were asleep. Wide enough awake have they been. He is wrong to say there is a right to tax land " up to this unearned increase," and wrong to say " but not further." Unless justice and expediency require it, there is no right up to the increase; if they do require it, it is not limited to that.

' Mill is further quoted as saying that he cannot speak of dividing common lands by any gentler name than robbery of the poor. He proceeds, however, to say that it will be said people cannot be robbed of what is not theirs, and that the commons do not belong to the poor. " Certainly not; our masters have taken care of that; they have taken care that the poor shall not acquire property by custom as all other classes have done." What he means by all other classes " acquiring property by custom," I know not; but why call it robbery, if it is not robbery; why, if the fault is that " our masters " have prevented its acquisition, did not Mill content himself with saying so? Because he was not satisfied with one piece of abuse only, but treated himself as well to the word " robbery." I should be sorry to have it supposed I denied or doubted Mill's great ability and honesty—so far as temper and prejudice let him be honest; but I have a strong opinion that he was one of those who showed their love to their fellow-creatures in general by hating a particular class of them.

' The quotation I have referred to, " The land is the general inheritance of mankind, and is the gift of Nature to the whole human race," may seem to give countenance to the wonderful assertion that " every man was born into the world with a right to a part of the land of his birth." Is he? When is he to take possession? At twenty-one? What is to keep him meanwhile? Here is a set-off. Is he to have a piece of land in prairie condition? No; doubtless improved. Here is another set-off. Is he to have the advantage of the roads and

bridges, and other conveniences that have been made? . . .
If the right is a right at all, it is a right against the whole
world from having been born at all. . . . Directly it is said to
be 'a right against' a particular State, there is a recognition of
that State and its laws.　Rights are what those laws give.'

How ragged were the notions prevalent, even
among politicians with a future before them, so late
as November, 1885, is shown by Mr. J. Chamberlain's speech, Dudley Road Board School, Birmingham, November 9, just before the General Election.
'It is well,' said he, 'that we should have the facts.
. . .　What has been the poor man's portion? . . .
where landlords have been powerful and altogether
independent of public opinion, they have been able
to enclose land without any Act of Parliament at
all. . . .'　Lord Bramwell thus de-coded Mr.
Chamberlain's further ideas in a *Times* letter,
November 12, 1885:

'MR. CHAMBERLAIN AND THE LAND QUESTION.

'You report Mr. Chamberlain as having said at Birmingham
on Monday last that "in the old days, 100 years ago, there
were immense tracts of waste and common land all over the
country.　I dare say it is a good thing that these lands should
be cultivated, but you should remember that when they were
not brought under cultivation they added very greatly to the
comfort and the happiness and the prosperity of the poor in
the neighbourhood in which they were placed.　The poor
people had rights over these commons; they were able to get
fuel, they were able to cut turf, they were able to support
sometimes a cow, sometimes it was geese or poultry, and in
that way they were able to add to their small incomes, and
made altogether a tolerable livelihood.　Well, between the
years 1800 and 1845, in a landlords' Parliament, in which the
land-owners had almost paramount influence, there were no

fewer than 2,000 private Acts of Parliament passed for the enclosure of these commons, and 7,000,000 of acres were thus enclosed—7,000,000 acres that previously belonged to the community, and over which there were public rights, became private property."

'Save that it is true that the Acts were passed and the enclosures made, and that it was a good thing that they should be cultivated, the whole of the above is untrue, every part of it. The land did not belong to the community in any sense; there were no public rights over it except roads and paths; the poor people had no rights over these commons, none to get fuel, cut turf, nor support the cow, geese, or poultry.

'I do not know whether Mr. Chamberlain used the words on purpose; he says they "were able" to do these things. Very likely, and did. Trespasses and encroachments on commons cannot be guarded against. It is well known that people living on large commons were the most lawless and ill-behaved in the kingdom. Good-natured people would not object to geese or poultry on the common, but rights in the poor people there were none. The commons and wastes belonged to the owners of the soil; the rights of common, pasturage, turbary, and others were in owners of property, land-owners, and their tenants in respect of their land-ownership. Enclosures have indeed been made, and the enclosed lands divided among those who had rights to and over them. These enclosures have been most beneficial to the community, turning waste into productive land. To no class have they been more beneficial than to the "poor." A vast quantity of land has been put into a condition in which labour can be employed on it. No labour was employed on commons and wastes.

'You report Mr. Chamberlain also to have said: "Over and above these legal enclosures, there have been a great number for which there has been no legal sanction. In cases where landlords have been powerful and altogether independent of public opinion, they have been able to enclose land without any Act of Parliament; and accordingly you will find in the country districts that roadside land has been taken, that corners of land have been added to great estates, and that little village greens have been taken up and have become private property." " The interests of the poor have been altogether forgotten." He does not understand why the poor man who takes a turnip should go to prison for seven days, and why the greater thief should be able to steal from the community a common or common land.

'This is also untrue. No doubt strips of land by the sides of roads have been taken in and added to the old enclosures. But the strips did not belong to the community, and the enclosures have not been made where they would have interfered with public or private rights—rights of way or rights of common. I do not say never, but as a practice. Where are or were the village greens of which Mr. Chamberlain speaks? Let him name some to begin with—say a dozen. Conduct such as described would soon have found a village Hampden to resent it with the willing help of a solicitor and jury. The " poor " man has no rights over these strips. When he has a cow, or pig, or pony he cannot—in fact, does not—turn out on them, for the things would be impounded as being on the high-ways without anyone in charge of them. These strips no doubt add to the pleasing appearance of the road, but they are of use only to tramps and others with their tents and vans, to the considerable prejudice of neighbouring fences and, as I have heard, hen-roosts. I say nothing of Mr. Chamberlain's language or motives; I only write to you to correct his mis-statements.

'Your obedient servant,
'BRAMWELL.'

At Evesham, November 16, Mr. J. Chamberlain replied :

'Lord Bramwell is known as a very able lawyer, and also as one of the most dogmatic and arbitrary judges that ever sat on the Bench. . . . He has contradicted me with a strength of language and intolerance peculiarly his own.'

Then he read an extract from J. S. Mill's ' Dissertations ' (which Mr. J. Morley apparently had furnished him with in the interval), adding :

'I venture to say we shall have to teach Lord Bramwell, and men like him, that there are rights of the poor, as sacred as, etc.'

On November 19 a *Times* leader said this speech showed that 'Mr. Chamberlain knows as little of Lord Bramwell's career as he does of the rights of commoners.' Notwithstanding this newspaper controversy, the relations between the disputants became cordial in subsequent years.

To other correspondents Lord Bramwell replied :

'MR. CHAMBERLAIN ON THE LAND QUESTION.

'As you have thought Mr. Cook's letter worthy of insertion, I ought to answer it. I suppose he is a barrister or solicitor. I do not find his name in the " Law List " for 1881—the latest I have. I infer from that, and from his letter, that he is very young. I should not have thought anyone was young enough to put such a question as he has. Enclosure Acts were not necessary as between land-owners and commoners on the one hand and the public on the other. They were for the land-owners and commoners *inter se*. Any one unwilling commoner could have prevented an enclosure. In the case of infants, lunatics, or married women, consent could not be given to a voluntary enclosure. Powers, indeed, were necessary to stop up and divert roads. This is the answer to Mr. Cook's question. Mr. Cook is wrong in supposing that strips of land by a highway-side are necessarily a part of it. Sometimes they are, and sometimes they are not. It is downright silly to say their owners have no rights over them. As to Mr. Dodd's letter, I have no doubt that all that Sir H. Maine says is correct. But he would be astonished to find himself quoted to show that there was anything in any sense wrong in the Enclosure Acts. The law as to commons has been in existence 300 years, according even to Mr. Dodd's notions. I believe it was always what it is. It is impossible to go further back ; we might as well see what was the law *tempore* Boadicea.

'Your obedient servant,

'BRAMWELL.'

The public were in an attentive frame of mind at the time, a General Election being to the fore. Perhaps for that reason Lord Bramwell's account of what the law is was read, and little has since been heard of this myth about the rights of ' the poor ' in the abstract, over the waste of manors, commons, etc.

Again, May 27, 1887, a letter in the *Times* described economic effects of the prolonged attack, legislative and polemical, upon landed property in the United Kingdom ; how penal legislation and open threats of further confiscation had checked application of capital to British agriculture, diminished employment and lowered wages ; virtually a homily on Cobden's text, quoted by William Fowler (p. 209), but brought up to date.

On June 1 Mr. H. D. McBlank (let us say), an amiable and erudite economic Agnostic—unable, after much searching of heart and wrestlings, to conscientiously accept that subtle doctrinal statement in the Petition of Right that ' it is the ancient and indubitable right of every freeman that he hath a full and absolute property in his goods and estates '—wrote to the *Times*, pointing out, kindly but firmly, that they erred who described certain great Dukes and other persons as ' owners ' or proprietors of land.

On June 3, 1887, Lord Bramwell wrote to the *Times :*

' Mr. McBlank says in his letter to you: " No private person can have property or absolute ownership in land ; such property or absolute ownership resides exclusively in the State, as represented by the Crown. The greatest Dukes are nothing but tenants of the Crown, and the State has a perfect right to prescribe the terms on which it will allow tenants to enjoy its property." This, so far as England is concerned, is wholly wrong and misleading. Technically, those who hold of nobody else are said to hold of the Crown, but practically they are absolute owners. Not only the greatest Dukes, but the smallest owners, have the right to deal with their land in any way they think fit, without any power in the Crown to interfere. If the owner in fee simple dies without any heirs, the land escheats to the Crown. The owner could have disposed of it, but did not, so the Crown takes it. If this prevents absolute ownership in land by private persons, the same considerations prevent absolute ownership in personal property; for if a man dies intestate with none of kin, the Crown takes his personalty. Will Mr. McBlank give an instance of anything the Crown can do on the fee simple of any subject? If it makes a fresh grant it can prescribe its terms, not otherwise. Mr. McBlank's statement is mischievous, misleading, and so incorrect that I am surprised that he should have made it.'

On June 13 a lengthy reply and protest against the above (dated June 4) from Mr. McBlank appeared in the *Times*. Blackstone, Digby, Littleton, Comyn, Sir Martin Wright, and, lastly, the much-maligned 'Mr. Joshua Williams,' were quoted to show that (as Lord Bramwell said) all English land is technically holden of the Crown. Mr. McBlank added that Lord Bramwell's letter of the 3rd inst. conveyed one impression to legal-minded, quite another to non-legal-minded, readers, and was 'quite misleading.' Some more really irrelevant things were said about feudal tenure generally— about power to devise land depending on statute, not Common Law. The significant distinction between the Crown's right to the reversion of real and of personal estate, in default of heirs or kin, was also pointed out.   Finally, the fabulous claims of the fabulous ' State ' vanished, the writer admitting that the Crown can nowadays do nothing ' on the fee simple of any subject.'   On June 15 Lord Bramwell replied :

' I said of Mr. McBlank's first letter that it was incorrect, misleading, and mischievous.   He has written to you a second letter, in which he appeals to my candour whether I still think his first letter incorrect, misleading, mischievous.   This appeal is made in terms so obliging to myself that it is with some regret I say not that I think, but that I know, that his first letter was incorrect, misleading, and mischievous.

' Mr. McBlank begins his second letter by saying I impugn his statement that by the existing law of England property in, or absolute ownership of, land resides exclusively in the Crown, and that no private person can hold any higher interest in land than a tenancy in fee simple, or perpetual lease, and he cites a number of authorities to prove that this is the law.   I never said anything to the contrary.   So far from it, I expressly said that "technically those who hold of nobody else are said to hold of the Crown."   The statement I did impugn was that "the State *has* a perfect right to prescribe the terms on which it will allow tenants to enjoy its property."   This is what I impeached, and do impeach, as incorrect, misleading, mischievous.   Mr. McBlank in his second letter admits the incorrectness, for he says : "Tenants in fee simple have now, by the consent of the Crown and statute, acquired property or absolute property in their ' estates ' . . . the Crown can no longer interfere with them."   Is that the same thing as what he said before, viz., that "the State has a perfect right to prescribe the terms on which it will allow tenants to enjoy its property"?   Is it not a direct contradiction of it ?   Mr. McBlank says he was not addressing himself to a substantial, but to a technical matter.   But why, then, did he say that "the State has a perfect right to prescribe the terms," as above? . . .   This is incorrect and misleading.   It encourages attacks on property, and is therefore mischievous.'

The following refers to some views not unlike Mr. Chamberlain's, Mr. Hardcastle's, and Mr. McBlank's, expressed in the *Times* by a Welsh agitator :

'17, Cadogan Place,
'*July* 8, 1888.

'DEAR ——,

'I do not think you wrote the article on Gee's last letter. Whether you did or not, I think Gee was not sufficiently castigated. I showed that it is *not* true that a man cannot by law have as large an estate in land as Nature will give him—as large as he can in a chattel. Gee had said that the estate a man can hold is short of this. He was wrong. He does not deny what I said, but shifts his ground, and says that there was a time when *tenure* of land involved services, dues, etc.; but they have been got rid of and the land grabbed. So he, Gee, would take the land, or do something to it. To this there are three answers or remarks: First, what took place was turning vexatious feudal tenures into free and common socage. That took place over two hundred years ago—long enough for any title. Would Gee take the land from a building society on account of a change in the law two hundred years ago? Second, if he is in any sense in the right it would go to show, not that the land should be taken, not that *it* has been grabbed, but that the burthens should be re-imposed. Third, he says that they were dishonestly got rid of, the landed gentry giving no equivalent. The burthens were vexatious and mischievous. It should be remembered that about sixty years before this the law imposed on land the burthen of maintenance of the poor—a deal more onerous. Do pitch into him; I can't.

'Ever yours,
'BRAMWELL.'

Mr. George raised the temperature of the existing yeast-pot of ideas. Land reformers saw that here was an ally gifted with all the fascinating originality of the conventional American tourist. 'Progress and Poverty' had the success of a new American lemon-squeezer, can-opener, or religion; while it was further good-naturedly taken for granted that the author was an original writer, sincere, impassioned, and profoundly touched by the hardships of city workers, by the evils of that nineteenth-century poverty which, lying at our very doors, puzzled and disillusionized two free and wealthy nations.*

* Perhaps Mr. Henry George's strongest point has been his consistent and workmanlike use of the authority of the Almighty as a sort of putty to stop up chinks, knot-holes, and weak spots in his argument. This new polemical device has been terribly overdone since, the Second Person of the Trinity being specially relied upon of quite recent years by sex-novelists and pamphleteers anxious to attract attention to themselves. In 1880-84 Henry George's imitation of Beecher's and Talmage's breezy blasphemies was distinctly new in this country. He writes ('Social Problems,' pp. 282, 286, 288):

'It is the evident intent of the Creator that land values should be the subject of taxation, that rent should be utilized for the benefit of the entire community. . . . When we consider the law of rent . . . the human mind catches glimpses of the Master Workman. . . . By making land private property we defy the Creator's social laws,' etc.

In July, 1893, Dr. William Smart, LL.D., writing from Queen Margaret College, Glasgow, in the *International Journal of Ethics*, about 'The Place of Industry in the Social Organism,' improved on this as follows:

'. . . Ethics and economics are now recognized to have such close relations that . . . the new economist must look at man primarily as a spiritual being, and must look at all men as spiritual beings. In considering the world of working persons, we must take . . . the standpoint of the Almighty Himself.'

Mill, by asserting a claim to 'the land' on behalf of 'the poor' (which presumably would include the poor of all nations), by his saying, in 'Dissertations and Discussions,' that 'land is the original inheritance of mankind,' the gift of Nature to the whole human race, had at first sight anticipated Mr. George. Apart from the fact that 'a gift of Nature' is a rather depressing lay phrase, too often applied to a taste for playing the fiddle or to the potato crop, Mill spoilt everything by insisting that 'due compensation' must be paid to holders of vested interests in land. Other land reformers had declared that the farmers had the best title; others, that the agricultural labourers, the peasantry, ought to be seized of the fee simple in place of actual owners, so called. Henry George proclaimed, in the name of the Most High, that nobody had any right to private property in land. Obviously 'nobody' excluded English landlords; thus the economic theatre was empty, swept and garnished.

In 1883 'Nationalization of Land,' a review of Mr. Henry George's 'Progress and Poverty,' by Lord Bramwell, was published at the central offices of the Liberty and Property Defence League.

'NATIONALIZATION OF LAND.

' Mr. George has, in his book called " Progress and Poverty," discovered that poverty and all its concomitants are in some way or another engendered by progress itself. And he proves it thus : " Go," he says, " into one of the new communities where Anglo-Saxon vigour is first beginning the race of progress, etc.,* and though you will find an absence of wealth,

---

* When I use this 'etc.,' I mean that I omit some of Mr. George's eloquence.

you will find no beggars. The tramp comes with the loco-motive, and almshouses and prisons are as surely the marks of material progress as are costly dwellings, rich warehouses, and magnificent chambers." Apparently, therefore, wealth, the result of progress, is the cause of poverty. Now, Mr. George might just as well say that the sugar hogshead at the grocer's door has brought forth the flies and ragged children that are about it. Did it never occur to Mr. George that the large cities and places where the locomotive has been and where wealth is to be found, attract the idle, the weak, the dishonest, and the thriftless ? Does he not know that the reason they are not found where Anglo-Saxon vigour is just beginning a race of progress, is because the exercise of Anglo-Saxon vigour is unpalatable to them ? Mr. George makes the common mistake of those who boast the virtues of rural districts. Why is there not a professional pickpocket in the small village ? Because there is no scope for his talents ; there are not pockets enough for his industry. Why is there no tramp, no beggar ? Because there are not enough persons of whom to beg.

'But Mr. George is wrong when he says that " the tendency of what we call material progress is in nowise to improve the condition of the lowest class in the essentials of healthy, happy, human life." That is untrue. The great bulk of the people of this country are better off than ever they were. They have more wages, more food, better homes (though far from good enough in towns), and better clothing than ever they had. Everything proves this. Statistics of every sort. The quan-tities consumed ; the quantities of luxuries—drink, tobacco. The diminished number of paupers, the lessened poor rates. Savings banks, benefit societies. What Mr. George means by the lowest class is uncertain. If he means the tramp and beggar, what he says is true, and would be if wealth was multiplied a hundredfold. But it is untrue that increased power of production and increased wealth have not benefited the whole people. What has become of the increased food and clothing ? Have those wicked rich people eaten ten times what they ate before, and worn ten yards of clothing when they formerly used one ? The complaint is untrue and silly. No doubt there are many labourers with large families who could eat, and eat advantageously, more than they do, and so they could if all produce was divided in equal rations. One may wish that every man had his *poulet au pôt*. One may have a misgiving as to whether it is not wrong that one man should ride in his carriage, at a cost which would keep two or three families, while at the same time as many families are underfed. But till we are good enough to work as fairly for the benefit of all as we do each for himself, we are not fit to be Socialists, and the best thing for all is that each should work for himself, though the result may be poverty and wealth, want and have.

' Mr. George, having made this discovery, proceeds to seek the cause—why wealth produces poverty. One would think that an obvious remedy would be to get rid of the wealth, to destroy the locomotive and the great houses, and revert to the log hut, in whose neighbourhood, Mr. George tells us, no beggars are to be found. But Mr. George does not suggest this. He first deals with some economic opinions that have been entertained and promulgated by some of the best and ablest men the world has seen, but which Mr. George denounces as blunders, the result of a perversion of intellect scarcely honest.

' Mr. George proceeds to put his inquiry, which, he says, is, " Why, in spite of increase in productive power, do wages tend to a minimum, which will give but a bare living ?" He assumes the truth of that proposition, which, however, is untrue. For if land increases in productive power, there is not, necessarily, the tendency he mentions. He then proceeds to attack the proposition stated by Mill, and agreed to by all economists but Mr. George, if he calls himself one, viz., " Industry is limited by capital. There can be no more industry than is supplied by materials and food to eat. Self-evident as it is, it is often forgotten that the people of a country are maintained, and have their wants supplied, not by the produce of present labour, but by past." Not so, says Mr. George, with an enviable self-confidence, to feel half which one would be content to be half as wrong. " How," says he, " can that be, if capital is stored labour? How can it be that it existed before labour? And consider the case of the naked savage who lives on shell-fish and fruit, etc." Of course, nobody ever denied that there must have been a time when labour preceded capital. What Mill affirms is not in relation to naked savages living on shell-fish, but in relation to modern highly complex civilization. Let us examine some of Mr. George's arguments to prove, as he says, that " wages, instead of being drawn from capital, are, in reality, drawn from the product of the labour for which they are paid." " See," says he, " the case of a ship which grows in value from day to day while being built. Has the builder lost any of his capital? No; there it is on the increased value of the ship." But the ship is not built of sovereigns or dollars; nor have the workmen fed on the latter. It is built of materials which have been saved or stored, and the workmen are fed and clothed on and with material saved and stored. Mr. George would reason less ill if he could eliminate money from men's transactions and suppose them done by barter. Let us take one of his new communities where Anglo-Saxon vigour is at work. An Anglo-Saxon goes to a settler for work. " Yes, there are three trees to be cut down, but I shall have nothing to give you for six months, when the timber-merchant buys of me." " Well," says the workman, " but I want food and clothing; meanwhile, let us go to the timber-merchant." He is willing to take the timber, but can't give the price or value till the house-builder buys, which will be in six months. Then they go to the builder, who has store of meat and wheat and clothing. He agrees to advance it to the timber-merchant, who advances it to the farmer, who advances it to the labourer, who labours. Does Mr. George say that in this case capital has nothing to do with setting labour to work? But this is the case with all work in civilized societies. It is the case where the capitalist finds the ship, the weapons, and the food of the whale-fisher. Try it thus. Suppose all the machinery in the world suddenly destroyed, or all the stored food, what would become of labour? " Oh, but," says George, " the grain thus held in reserve through the machinery of exchange, and advances passed to the use of the cultivators are set free, in effect, *produced* by the work done for the next crop !" So the work for the next crop *produces* the former crop. If so, the labourer ought to be paid for the production of two crops. Mr. George might say this is a question of words. But it is not ; it is a question of substance and of things ; Mr. George, like many others, would reason better if he used right words. Mr. George asks (chapter v.), " What, then, are the functions of capital ?" He answers : " Capital consists of wealth used for the procurement of more wealth, or, as I think it may be defined, wealth in the course of exchange. Capital, therefore, increases the power of wealth to produce wealth." Why " therefore " ?—but even if so, as a spade and a barrow are as much capital as a locomotive, the admission goes a long way to show that capital sets labour to work—but, in truth, Mr. George (Book III., chapter iii.) answers himself. For he says : " There are three modes of production, in one of which capital may, and in the other two must, aid labour." Mr. George, having attacked the economists about capital, next has a furious tilt at Malthus, and the doctrine connected with his name. And it may well be that the geometrical and arithmetical ratios cannot be justified. But the main proposition is undoubtedly true, viz., that, left undisturbed, population increases, and by increasing presses on the means of subsistence. It is self-evident. It stares one in the face. Why has North America its 70 or 80 millions of European descent, but for this pressure ? Why do the Eastern Americans go West ? Why do hundreds of thousands of emigrants land on American shores yearly? Why does the Chinaman eat the filth and garbage he does ? Not from pressure on the means of subsistence, says Mr. George, for 100 men will produce more than 100 times what one man can. Very likely, in certain cases. Ah, but, says Mr. George, and 100 times 100 men can produce more than 100 times what 100 men can. Well, this brings us to 10,000, and 100 times that is a million, and then we have 100 millions, and then 10,000 millions, all producing more per head than their predecessors. It does not prove this to show that the earth is not full, nor the best use made of it. Besides, suppose it could maintain the 10,000 millions, it could not maintain one hundred times that number. What does Mr. George mean? Why, there would not be standing-room. It is idle to say that increase of population does not press, will not eventually press on the means of subsistence. It does; we all know it, and, oddly enough, it is in part the foundation of Mr. George's argument. And the pressure is comparative, as most things are in this world. Not a pressure that could not be borne, but that could be lessened, and that has been lessened by a diminution of the population through emigration. It is certain that in England, at least, the average well-being of the population is greater than ever it was. But suppose there had not been that emigration, and suppose America had not been peopled, and sent us food! What would have been the condition of things? Would there have been no pressure on subsistence? Could we have produced that half of the wheat we consume which we now import? Some day America will be full. Mr. George admits that there may be "small islands, such as Pitcairn's, cut off from communication from the rest of the world, and from the exchanges which are necessary to the improved modes of production resorted to as population becomes dense, which may seem to offer examples in point. A moment's reflection, however, will show that these exceptional cases are not in point." Will it? I have reflected all the time it took to read the paragraph and to copy it, and that reflection has not shown me that the case is not in point. It is. The world is Pitcairn's Island enlarged. It would have been better if Mr. George had shown why the case is not in point.

' Proceed to consider some of Mr. George's opinions, observing in passing that he has got right notions on the theory of rent. He agrees with Ricardo and Malthus, and owns and shows that the increase of rent is not caused by the landowner, but by the increasing wants of man—in short, by the pressure of population on subsistence.

' Mr. George, in Book III., chapter iii., discusses whether interest is " natural or equitable." And he deals with the case of James and William and the plane. James has a plane which it takes ten days to make, and which will last the 290 working days of the year. William wants the plane, and agrees to give James for it an equally good plane at the end of the year and a plank. Now, asks Mr. George, is that "natural or equitable?" "See," says he, "the case at the end of the year. James, having parted with his plane, occupies ten days in making a new one, and then works for 290 days, at the end of which he will get a new plane from William. James, therefore, at the end of the year, will have done 290 days' work, and possesses a new plane. But that would have been the case if he had kept his own plane, worn it out in 290 days, and then made a new plane in the remaining ten. Why, then, should William give him anything, and so make his own condition worse and James's better?" Wonderful! Mr. George thinks the promise of a plane as good as a plane. But why put a year? Why not ten years? Why should not the promise to return the plane in ten years or a hundred be as good as the plane itself? Mr. George, however, seems to think, as well as can be guessed from some hazy writing, that as a plane might be exchanged for seed, and seed might, if put into the ground, yield an increase not due wholly to labour; therefore a plane may perhaps be reasonably parted with on the terms of getting back a plane and something more. The truth—the common, plain sense—is, that the plane in hand at the beginning of the year is worth to William, in his opinion, and in truth, more than a plane at the end of the year, or more than a plane in the first ten days of the year. Like a sensible man, he agrees to give more for it; and, for corresponding reasons, James will not let him have it unless he does. Does Mr. George think that savings banks, building societies, and others, should pay no interest?

'Mr. George, in Book III., chapter iii., intituled "The Statics of the Problem thus explained"—whatever that may mean—says: "The increase of rent explains why wages and interest do not increase. The cause which gives the land to the land-owner is the cause which denies it to the labourer and capitalist. That wages and interest are higher in new than in old countries is not, as the standard economists say, because Nature makes a greater return to the application of labour and capital, but because land is cheaper." Cheaper than what? I suppose than land elsewhere—in an old country. But what is the meaning of " cheaper "? It is not a question of pounds or dollars. Land is cheaper when it does make "a greater return to the application of labour and capital." And whether it shall or not does not depend on the landlord, as, indeed, Mr. George shows. If one man or ten, or perhaps a thousand men, owned all the land in an isolated territory, they might fix its price ; but, as it is, the price is fixed by Nature. A deal of mischievous and dishonest nonsense has been talked about landlordism. Rent exists in the nature of things, and would exist in substance if we had an agrarian law to-morrow. If one acre of land will produce four quarters of wheat, with the same expenditure of labour and capital as will only produce two quarters on another acre, and it is worth while to cultivate the poorer acre (rentless, perhaps), the first acre will bear and pay a rent of two quarters ; and if, on the agrarian division, it fell to the lot of A. B., he would receive from it two quarters as a return for his labour and capital, and two quarters in the nature of rent. It is true, in a sense (not always, as Mr. George says, but sometimes), that the increase of land values is at the expense of the value of labour, but it is for a reason that no legislation can prevent—viz., the pressure of population on subsistence. Mr. George finishes this Book III. by saying : " To see human beings in the most abject, etc., condition, you must go, not to unfenced prairies, in the backwoods, etc., but to the great cities, where the ownership of a little patch of land is a great fortune." I have dealt with this before. Mr. George might as well have added : but where wages are higher, and the people better fed, clothed, and even housed, than elsewhere.

' Book IV., chapter iii., Mr. George says : " The effect of labour-saving instruments will be to extend the demand." Yes, if there are mouths to be fed, not otherwise—*i.e.*, if population presses on subsistence. Because, but for that pressure, but for an increase in the population, where productive powers were doubled, and only half the land was wanted to feed the population, the competition among the land-owners would reduce rent to nothing.

'In Book VI. Mr. George gives the remedy for these evils. He discusses other possible remedies than his own, and rejects them. I notice one instance, for the sake of Mr. George's style and language. He speaks of the "*robbery* involved in the protective tariff of the United States." That is a word Mr. George is very fond of. Whatever is not right in his judgment is not only wrong, but dishonestly wrong—"robbery." Nobody thinks worse of a protective tariff than I do, but I attribute its existence to an honest want of knowing better—at least, in many cases. Thiers was, and Bismarck is, a Protectionist. Are they "robbers"? Are Mr. George's countrymen "robbers"? Might not some people think the term might be more reasonably applied to those who say, "We must make the land common property," without compensation to present owners, and who advocate its being done covertly, not openly. "To do that would be a needless shock to the present customs and habits of thought, which is to be avoided. Let the individuals who now hold it (land) still retain, if they want to, what they are pleased to call their land; let them continue to call it their land; let them buy and sell and bequeath and devise it. We may safely leave them the shell it we take the kernel. It is not necessary to confiscate land; it is only necessary to confiscate rent." And this Mr. George proposes, and without compensation. He inquires into the "justice of the remedy." He says: "If we are all here by permission of the Creator, we are all here with an equal title to the enjoyment of His bounty, with an equal right to the use of all that Nature so impartially offers. The Almighty, who created the earth for man, and man for the earth, has entailed it upon all the generations of the children of men," etc. It is singular what an acquaintance with the Creator's designs is shown by writers of the stamp of Mr. George. One may be allowed a respectful doubt whether what has so long existed and been permitted was not intended, not that things have gone wrong till Mr. George came to the rescue. At all events, it will be admitted that Benevolence would approve that condition of things which was most for the good of mankind. And if the private ownership of land is so, we may well have it without

Mr. George's Land Act, to get rid of the entail he speaks of. He says: "The poorest child born in London has as much right to the estates of the Duke of Westminster as his eldest son, and the puniest infant that comes wailing, etc., has as much right to the Astor property as the Astors. And he is *robbed* (Mr. George's favourite word) if the right is denied." I am afraid Mr. George's notions of "right" are hazy. I will not say that the man who catches fish or game, or gathers fruit, has not a natural right to do it. Though Mr. George would find it difficult to persuade his Patagonian, if he met the man with the fish or the game, that he (the Patagonian) might not in all right and reason take it. His conscience would not be troubled any more than would be that of the Bedouin if he eased Mr. George of a watch made by him with much labour. However, be it that there are natural rights, that is in a state of Nature, where there is nothing artificial. But men have formed themselves into a social state; all is artificial, and nothing merely natural. In such a state, no rights ought to exist but what are for the general good—all that are, should. And what we have to consider is not any vapouring about "the land being entailed by Providence, the decrees of the Creator, puny infants coming wailing into the world in the squalidest room of the most miserable tenement house," etc.; *but whether private or separate property in land is for the good of the community*. Certainly there is rather a strong *primâ facie* case that it is, since it exists throughout the world. "Oh!" says Mr. George, "tyranny, violence, and usurpation." He quotes M. de Laveleye: "In all primitive societies the soil was the joint property of the tribes, and was subject to periodical distribution among all the families, so that each might live by their labour, as Nature has ordained." And why is it not so now ? Because we are not in a *primitive* state ; because we are older and wiser and know better, as M. de Laveleye ought to do. Periodical distribution ! Is it not absolutely certain that a man will do better with a piece of land, will get more out of it each year, if he has it for two years instead of one, for ten years instead of two, and for all time instead of ten ? If the profit of his care and labour will be his at some time, will he not bestow them when otherwise he would not ?   It cannot be doubted.   Tax him if you like, tax his rent, tax him *ad valorem;* but leave him enough to tempt him to improve.   It is too plain ; separate property in land, as in sheep and oxen, is for the good of the community.   And if so, the quantity that one man may own can no more be limited than can the quantity of sheep or oxen he may own, nor the use he shall make of it. Have an agrarian law, give each man his share ; in ten years the careful, skilful, and provident allottees would be the owners of the share of the careless, unskilful, and improvident.   And it is for the general good it should be so.

' But even if labour alone gave property, the land-owner's case is much better on Mr. George's principles than he admits. Suppose by labour a piece of land was banked and enclosed from the sea — made, in short.   Not a part of the land " originally entailed on the puniest," etc., Mr. George must admit a right to it in the man whose labour made it.   But what is the difference between the case put and land in general, except that in land in general there was before labour was put on it what has been called the " prairie value " ?   That is what, if anything, was " entailed on the puniest," etc.   Tax that— confiscate that, if confiscation is right, but not the stored labour which is on the land.   Mr. George seems to admit this.   What would the tax be ?   Something worth stealing, though not as much as Mr. George thinks.   But confiscation is not right. Separate or private property in land is for the good of the community, and should be respected like any other property, and for the same reason.   There is one passage in the book that may be noticed.   As far as it is intelligible it is, that as a man belongs to himself, so his labour, when put in a concrete form, belongs to him ; and that there can be no other natural rights, as other rights are destructive of this.   Perhaps ! as I do not know what is meant.   But then it would seem that the man who has cut down and stored a hundred trees has inter- fered with my right, as great as his, to cut them down.   How- ever, whatever is meant, I repeat we are concerned with social not natural rights.

' Mr. George speaks of the " justice " of the remedy.   Justice !

A man labours and saves, acquires a piece of land, perhaps taken in payment of a bad debt, dies with the comforting belief he has provided for his widow and orphans. Mr. George calls it "justice" to confiscate it. Another man has been a member of a building society, and built his house, and believes it was his own. But Mr. George would charge him a heavy rent for the land on which it stands, because "every patch of land has become of great value." This is Mr. George's notion of "justice." They are robbers, receivers of stolen goods, knowing they are stolen, and can have no right themselves, nor give any to the widow and orphan. No doubt, to confiscate land and raise the public revenue out of it would be a fine thing for all the community, save the land-owners. But so would confiscating chattels be a fine thing for all but chattel-owners, and the confiscation of labour would be a splendid thing for all but the labourer. It may be there is much to be said for the taxation of land, and that a community would do well if it resolved at the outset to raise its taxation exclusively from land. There is much to be said for it, especially if the taxation is not so excessive as to deprive the land-owner of all interest in improvement; but when the law for ages has allowed private property in land, to take that property from one man and leave property in oxen and horses in another, because the land is stolen goods, and its owner ought to know that—that, I say is "robbery," and repugnant to all notions of fairness. Mr. George does not, indeed, propose to take all the rent. He would leave enough to make it worth the while of land-owners to become tax-collectors. Mr. George says : " In every civilized country the value of the land, taken as a whole, is sufficient to bear the entire expense of government." We flatter ourselves England is a civilized country. If it is, this statement is untrue. The whole agricultural rent, without abatement for collecting it, would not defray those expenses. If the expense were so borne, personal property would be untaxed, and Mr. George, this friend of the poor and the wailing infant, would let the Rothschilds and Astors go untaxed, while he filched the patch of land got by the savings of hard work, which gave a bare subsistence to the widow and orphan.

'I have now gone through the more prominent matters in Mr. George's book. It is a mischievous book, for it holds out expectations that cannot be realized, and proposes their realization by measures most injurious. It is a foolish book, for though Mr. George is anything but a foolish man, his ingenuity is so perverse that his book is filled with foolishness. It is the most arrogant, self-sufficient performance ever seen. No one was right before Mr. George, and some of the best, greatest, and noblest men who ever lived are spoken of with contempt as blunderers and evil disposed. It is also a book which one would think was the work of an ill-conditioned man. According to Mr. George, nobody is mistaken and honest. " Robbers " and " robbery " are his favourite words, and he seems to think he can set the world right and teach it—if he bawls " robbery " loud enough—to practise it. . . .'

On January 3, 1884, Henry George came to London, it was said to lecture there, also in twenty-five principal cities of the United Kingdom. On Wednesday, January 9, a vast audience in St. James's Hall heard Mr. George. Mr. Labouchere, M.P., always watchful to mitigate any tendencies destructive of West - End civilization, presided. Mr. George then stated that land nationalization would provide pensions of £100 a year for 200,000 widows, Queen Victoria among others; but the pivotal passage in his speech was, ' The land of England, by virtue of a grant from the living God, belongs to the whole people of England.'

In the *Times* of January 23, 1884, Lord Bramwell wrote :

'Mr. George in Plain English.

' If a man reclaims a piece of land, " subdues it," cuts down useless trees, extirpates bushes and weeds, removes stones, and makes it valuable, Mr. George says it ought to be taken from him, and that where a man has toiled hard, denied himself and his wife and children luxuries and amusements, belonged to a building society, and become possessed of land with a house on it, he, and his widow and orphans, if he dies, ought to be treated in the same way. Mr. George says there ought to be no compensation, because all property in land has been obtained by "force or fraud." Mr. George puts a limitation on the eighth commandment, and reads it: "Thou shalt not steal anything but land." At least this is dealing with Mr. George in his own style. He cannot understand how anyone can differ from him, without being thief or robber. I think more charitably of Mr. George, and that he is only perversely and wonderfully mistaken.

'His reason for so dealing with land-owners is that "the land of England is God's gift to the people of England." It is astonishing what an intimacy is shown with the Divine counsels by those who would justify what has hitherto been considered murder and robbery. Mr. Parnell's followers justify their proceedings because the land of Ireland is God's gift to the Irish people. If it were fit subject for discussion, one might suggest that what exists was intended, and not that the intention has been frustrated by man, and that it needed Mr. George to set matters right. But I will not rely on this, contenting myself with denying Mr. George's postulate. He relies on nothing else. And reasonably, if right in his postulate and his inferences from it. For we have at once a Divine direction which we should obey, even if we cannot see the reason of it. But if we may suppose that what was intended is for our good, then we may well inquire what that is. The answer is easy. He who makes a thing valuable to mankind, whether it is land or chattels, should have it for his reward to encourage him and others to do the same. Private and separate ownership of everything improvable is necessary to insure its improvement. A late distinguished man, Sir W. Siemens, said that if any invention lay in the gutter, it should be given to a separate owner that he might have an interest in its furtherance and development. All the fish on our coasts and in our rivers are as much given to the people of England as the land of England. Would Mr. George take from the fisherman all he caught? Should he say that there labour has been expended, has it not been on the land? What is land without its improvements? Should Mr. George admit that those who improve should enjoy for a time as their reward, he gives up his principle. For if he once admits that separate ownership may exist for a time, he must admit it may for any and all time. The State gives me a piece of land for ten years at a certain rent, or no rent, and I am to improve it. I say, Give it me for fifty years, and I will improve it more and pay more rent. Would it not be wise in the State to agree, and, having agreed, just to keep its word? And if this is true as to fifty years, is it not true for all time? Has Mr. George ever considered the cruel hardship and wrong that would happen if his opinions prevailed? Two men have each worked hard, saved money under the same law, invested under the same law, one in railway stock, the other in land, and while the first keeps his property, the other has his taken from him and is called "rogue." Why does not Mr. George go to his native country and preach the rights of the red Indians, to whom "the land of America was God's gift"? What would he do with the land when he got it? Farm it? Substitute the State for the struggling farmer? Or let it? And if let it, for how long? If for a year, why not for longer, if it would produce more? And if for a longer time, why not for all time — for "a consideration"? Mr. George's proposal is nonsense. Unfortunately, a good many people have been misled by it.

'Your obedient servant,

' B.'

Perhaps the first among advanced reformers, sympathizing with Mill's land tenure views, to protest against Henry George's rehash of ancient delusions was Mr. Frederic Harrison, who during the year 1883 denounced them to audiences in Edinburgh, Newcastle, and at the London Industrial Remuneration Conference. He disconcerted land nationalizers by pointing out that coal was as much a necessary of life—and so *ex hypothesi* the common property of the human race—as land. On May 16, 1883, he wrote to Lord Bramwell :

'. . . I did not say properly the other night how much I enjoyed your criticism on Henry George, and my scanty thanks to you for sending it recur again to my mind, now that I have been reading it again along with some other pieces on that question. I always have felt that George's book is a mass of sophistry, and your knife has pricked home every windbag that it has touched. On every point you seem to hit, and, indeed, kill. I hope, however, you will do more, and make a further criticism of the whole work. The book, though a mass of sophistry in reasoning, and distorted by prejudice and passion, is still at this moment a very great and dangerous social force in England and in America; and its power is derived from this, that it eloquently displays the appalling facts of actual social injustice and suffering, and in the next place it does offer some remedy, wild as I think that to be. Those who criticize George will never undo the evil George is producing until they admit the disease to be remedied, and offer some remedy of their own; and I hold that the key to George's influence lies in the truth that proprietary rights in the soil need some other social justification than such as applies to movables. Land is a unique form of property, and requires special reasoning of its own. This is a chapter still to be added to your criticism, and also, I think, to the excellent reasoning of B. in the *Times*.'

' The single tax,' although never so exhaustively examined as Mr. Ignatius Donelly's famous Bacon-Shakespeare cryptogram, did produce a great many ' answers ' to ' Progress and Poverty,' indicating the alarm created by Henry George's campaign,

1880-85.* Whether they were or were not works of supererogation is difficult to say. One has a feeling that thinkers 'carried away' by Henry George were very unlikely to read replies to him. If not a formidable political economist, he was certainly a formidable bogie.

On the whole, criticism of his book and propa-

* From the Duke of Argyll, *Nineteenth Century*, vol. xv., p. 537; from Professor R. T. Ely, in 'University Studies,' vol. iii.; from Professor Fawcett, *Macmillan's Magazine*, vol. xlviii., p. 182; from Samuel Smith, M.P., *Contemporary*, vol. xliv., p. 850; in *Quarterly Review*, vol. clv., p. 35 (generally attributed to Mr. W. H. Mallock); in *Edinburgh Review*, vol. clvii., p. 263; *Dublin Review*, vol. xcvii., p. 327; *Banker's Magazine*, vol. xliii., p. 401; *Spectator*, vol. lvii., p. 44; *Saturday Review*, etc. One of the most lengthy criticisms is the late Robert Scott Moffatt's book, 'Mr. Henry George, the Orthodox,' dealing fully with George's attack upon Malthus—the one interesting thing in 'Progress and Poverty.' George, although not a consistent Socialist, finds himself compelled, without knowing why, to assail the Darwinian doctrine of the struggle for existence which Malthus had an inkling of. One may note how all attempts to construct a logical system on Socialistic lines lead up to a collision with Darwin. Mr. Moffatt remarks 'that (in 1885) Henry George had become a great authority in this country.' Wonders where he 'acquired his economic ideas.' In 1896 it was once more admitted by Mr. George himself that the single tax theory, and much of 'Progress and Poverty,' are derived from 'The Elements of Political Science' and 'The Theory of Human Progression,' published prior to 1855 by the late Patrick E. Dove, sometime of Craig; genial, eccentric, and erudite 'Master of Ballantrae'; friend of Hugh Miller, Blackie; Volunteer Colonel, etc. Probably everything in the way of misapplied metaphysics, which ought not to be said, has been said already, in the most unreadable way, by some gifted Scotsman or other.

ganda by Lord Bramwell and others seems to have exercised in this country a 'conservative' influence. The disclosure of demands for sheer confiscation caused many hesitating people to reflect. Serious discussion of land tenure generally was rendered more difficult. The land nationalization crusade, however, ultimately smothered a good many proposals favoured by Radicals, such as leasehold enfranchisement, 'State' creation of peasant proprietorship, abolition of entail, etc. Why turn leaseholder or tenant into a freeholder if the holding bestowed on him was to be nationalized next day? Just as Henry George 'overtrumped' proposals from land-reformers of the school of Mill, Cairns, etc., so his 'single tax' was itself overtrumped by those Socialists, Fabians, etc., who now and then demanded, not the nationalization of land merely, but of all capital, savings bank deposits, railways, factories, the means of production, distribution, and exchange also. The gradual decay of public interest in English land tenure controversies after 1885 seems, however, to have been mainly due to the discovery that English farming on any terms was becoming unprofitable, and that agricultural land was hardly worth confiscating.

That great maxim of natural jurisprudence, ' It is no sin to rob an apparently rich man,' implies a negative popular maxim to the contrary of the above affirmative, viz., that if a man ceases to be rich, it is rather a shame to rob him—a somewhat unheroic termination to controversy about a question 'ripe for solution' in 1880. At that time extension of power to the landless majority seemed to many people to threaten in England and Wales (as in Ireland and northern Scotland) confiscation by statute of property held by a minority under the artificial, fictitious, and by no means impregnable, sanction of legal covenant. The waxing and waning of interest in English agricultural land questions between 1870 and 1890 suggests the case of two Eastern potentates going to war with each other about the possession of a diamond, and finding in the thick of the struggle that the diamond was all the time paste.*

* In other English-speaking countries Henry George's propaganda seems to have left permanent traces. In November, 1895, the Hon. L. F. Heydon, M.L.C. for the colony of New South Wales, told the Institute of Bankers, Sydney:

'Henry George landed on our shores in 1890. In two months after he had left us we suffered from the great maritime strike, singular in its universality and in the ideas which caused it, chiefly those taught by Henry George and Bellamy. Two fatal ideas—first, that there existed some simple political specific, mere enactment of which would render earth a paradise for all men, without necessity for individual effort or self-denial; second, that the working classes, being necessary to all production, could coerce society, and so at any time enact that paradise. In 1891 and 1892 followed the collapse of building societies, in 1893 the closing of banks, disasters directly and mainly due to disturbance of labour and discouragement of capital caused by Henry George's and Bellamy's Socialistic doctrines, and to depreciation of the selling value of land caused by Henry George's special doctrine as to confiscation of land. . . . The introduction of a deadly idea, which would destroy many score of millions of pounds, and degrade, starve, and destroy many hundreds and thousands of our poorer brethren, is smiled upon. We set an active guard to oppose importation of pests dangerous to human, animal, or even

In 1883 an Industrial Remuneration Conference was held in London, and lasted two or three days. The idea was to gauge, and perhaps direct, the opinion of those advanced persons supposed to be

---

vegetable life.   But against free importation of a doctrine more destructive than phylloxera, anthrax, small-pox, cholera, or than all the pests to all sorts of life added together, we appoint no sort of quarantine whatever.

'Pre-eminent among destructive ideas I deem the teachings of Henry George on land nationalization; and I hold our leaders of thought guilty of great *laches* in not having met and repelled this danger at its first introduction among us.'

Of course, there is a good deal of the *propter hoc* fallacy about all this. Before 1890 Australian democracies had shown by their tariff and land legislation that they were quite capable of effecting their own economic ruin without Henry George's help.

In the United States, spite of the fact that Americans quickly took to describing Henry George as a played-out 'crank,' his book and his propaganda touched the public conscience, and whenever the public conscience is profoundly moved anywhere in the United States, the nearest State Legislature tries to pass a law designed to confiscate the wrong man's property. No American citizen who understands business ever actually *is* plundered; the law is generally so badly drafted as to be unintelligible; with great forethought, machinery and trustworthy officials to enforce it are never provided, so that a sharp 'attorney' can always manœuvre a wealthy client out of mischief. Nevertheless, Henry George's writings appealed to that paradoxical and little-appreciated emotionalism which is as valid a characteristic of the people of the United States as shrewdness, energy, or brag. The statute-books of many American States contain laws passed as 'concessions' to George's disciples—laws which have made the poor poorer, the rich richer, wronged and impoverished 'little' capitalists, exalted and strengthened 'big' capitalists, controllers of rings and trusts, railway kings, etc.

influential with working men—at the time hesitating between old Individualist Radicalism and 'some kind of Socialism.' A gentleman present moved that Lord Bramwell (known as a wise and honest Judge, careful about such matters) should be asked : 'Would the more general distribution of capital or land . . . promote or impair the production of wealth and the welfare of the community ?'

Fifteen years have made great changes. The above question may seem an odd one to put to anybody ; similar curiosity is nowadays rare. Possibly Lord Bramwell's reply, made in all good faith, helped to extinguish it. Since many of those inquirers who gravely conferred about 'industrial remuneration' in 1883 are best tranquillized by being given some new thing, more foolish than the old one, to think and talk about, it is probable that the teaching of Fabians, Social Democrats, Independent Labour leaders, etc., has been the means of quenching interest in half-and-half measures for 'promoting the wealth and welfare' of the community, such as 'the more general distribution of capital and land' by those opportunist methods contemplated in the above question.

It was also asked, in parenthesis, whether 'the State management of capital and land would promote or impair the production of wealth and the welfare of, etc. ?'—to all which Lord Bramwell replied :

'. . . The general distribution of capital and land in a community is the result of natural causes, and could be altered only by legislation, which would be mischievous, and impair

the production of wealth and the welfare of the community.

'There are two men—one born healthy, strong, intelligent,
industrious, thrifty; the other sickly, weak, dull, idle, and
improvident. These two men will certainly be differently off
in life. So will their children and children's children, even if
the State should make itself heir to all deceased persons. One
of the two men will be poor, the other rich. How is a more
general distribution of land and capital among such to be
brought about? Is the poor man to be made rich? How?
Is the rich man to be made less rich? That can, indeed, be
done; but can it be done by any means that would promote
the production of wealth and the welfare of the community?
Certainly not!

'I know, of course, that a law might be made bringing
everything into hotchpot, and dividing the mass into equal
shares, one for each member of the community, which certainly
would produce a "more general distribution of land and capital";
but I suppose no one contemplates this. For my own part, I
have no superstitious reverence for the institution of separate
or private property. Show to me that its abolition would be
for the general good, and I would vote for it, letting down the
present possessors gently. . . . If that institution is to be
preserved, it would be useless to make such a distribution as
I have supposed. For at the end of six months there would
be a difference in the wealth of members of the community.
Some would have wasted their shares, some have increased
theirs (unless, indeed, that was forbidden, which would be
most disastrous), and it would result that some would be poor
and some rich. I cannot suppose, then, that a law directly
taking from those who have, and giving to those who want,
is expedient. But unless some such mischievous contrivance
is resorted to, there must be an inequality of conditions, and an
inequality in which there will be the very poor and the very
rich. I say, then, that there are no means by which there can
be a more general distribution of land and capital which would
promote the wealth and welfare of the community. . . .

'I do not say that nothing can be indirectly done to lessen

the inequalities of conditions and improve that of the poor. Heavy taxes might be put on successions which would allow of the diminution of taxes that fall on the poor. Taxes which fall on their luxuries, but which they will pay to the lessening of their means for necessaries. The motive for saving in the rich would be diminished indeed, which is bad, and there would be shifts and evasions to avoid the tax. So, also, more of other taxation might be put on the rich. . . . Abolition of the law of primogeniture would probably in time make the rich less rich, and so tend to reduce inequalities of condition at present existing. Whether this abolition is desirable on political considerations I do not say. That a large number of proprietors, if prosperous, would be most beneficial I doubt not. That they cannot be brought into existence by direct legislation I am certain. That they could make a living I much doubt. . . .

As to the other part of the question, viz., Would the State management of capital or land promote or impair the production of wealth and the welfare of the community, I say, without hesitation, that State management of land or capital would impair such production and welfare. . . . Till men are as honest, some may think as senseless, as the bees, they will not work for the community as zealously as each works for himself. Consequently the total produce will not be as great in the former as in the latter case. When each man knows that the size of his ration will be the same whether he works or not, and knows that others will shirk, he will shirk too, and the poverty and misery of all will follow. Besides, there is the impossibility of managing such a large national farm or factory. Also such a state of things would have a most depressing, deadening effect on all, and make life a dull misery. . . .

' Without going into the question of natural rights, this is true; when men are united in society, all their rules and institutions are artificial, and if any of these is against the general good, it should be abrogated. But I am satisfied that *the institution of private property in land is for the good of society*, as is the right of each man to the benefit of his own labour. It gives each man a motive, and the strongest, to make the best of his means and his work. ¦I agree with the late Sir W. Siemens, who said, "If an invention lay in the gutter unowned, I would give it to a particular owner, that someone might have a particular interest to develop and push it." I believe that the best thing for all is that there should be what I believe the Americans call "the largest pile." Though the shares may be unequal, there will be the greatest bulk to divide, the greatest average share, the greatest amount of enjoyment, the greatest individual wealth, perhaps, but the least individual poverty.

'As to the mischievous nonsense about each child being born with a right to share in the land, the short way of dealing with it is this, is it expedient or not that he should have a share? If expedient, let him have it, whatever his right may be; if inexpedient, refuse it, whatever his right may be. Or rather be sure he has 'no right.' It is nonsense to talk of such a right. As I have said, all rights in a state of society are artificial. It might as well be said he had a 'natural right' to a box at the opera.

'As for the mischief occasioned by farmers having recourse to pasturage instead of tillage, farmers do this because they get the greater profit by it, and would continue to do it for that reason, even if they paid no rent for their land. They now get, or ought to get, the fair reward for their capital and personal labour. If they paid no rent, they would get that rent in addition. But, in consideration of their having to pay no, or less, rent, would they then revert to tillage instead of pasturage, would the gross produce then be greater and the labour employed more? . . . But how bring about this change? By a direct law that the farmer should have such a proportion of his land in tillage? I believe such a thing impracticable. But, farther, how is the farmer to pay no, or less, rent? By confiscation, so that nothing shall be received by the landowner? If A has sold his railway stock and bought land, and B has sold his land and bought railway stock, A shall lose his land, but B keeps his railway stock. Why? It is said that the private ownership of land is robbery, and that every owner of land knows it. This, if honest, is crazy nonsense. All property exists by law, and one is owned as honestly as the other. Are all the members of building societies thieves?

'Only a word as to that part of the question which asks about the State management of capital. It might as well be asked whether the State management of capital and labour at Portland Prison is not as productive and pleasurable as the private management of them. I say capital *and* labour. They cannot be dissociated. Separately they are useless. Those who manage capital must manage labour. . . .

'I answer the second part of the question peremptorily in the negative.'

CHAPTER VIII.

TEETOTAL LOGIC—LEASEHOLD ENFRANCHISE-MENT—LAND LEAGUE JURISPRUDENCE.

His prejudice against that teetotal logic expounded after 1880 —Letter from Lord Shaftesbury—Pamphlet on 'Drink' —Archdeacon Farrar's reply—'Drink, a Rejoinder,' in *Nineteenth Century*—*Times* leader by Lord Bramwell— 'Leasehold Enfranchisement' pamphlet—Its origin— Chief Baron Pollock's remedy—Letters from distinguished Irishmen about distinguished Irishmen—Lord Bramwell's view of Mr. G.'s Irish policy—His jealousy of Nationalist jurisprudence and rules of procedure—The new 'In-stitutes'—Takes an active part in an Irish Defence Union during the *terreur vert*—Letters to secretary of Union and to Sir G. Baden Powell—Article in *Liberal Unionist*— *Times* letter about Mr. G.—Previous one to him from Mr. G.—Criticism of Nationalist administration.

ON March 7, 1883, Earl Stanhope moved the second reading of a Bill prohibiting payment of wages in public-houses. 'An interference with liberty and right of personal option inherent in British subjects,' said Lord Bramwell. He was a lawyer, and there was a disposition to argue that a man acquainted with law should talk about law, and be silent on all other subjects. As for the Trade Union Congress approval of the Bill, 'was Lord

Stanhope going to introduce a Land Nationalization Bill because the Congress also approved of that?' Lord Shaftesbury replied, attacking the recently-formed Liberty and Property Defence League. 'It would be well,' he said, 'if the House did interfere with liberty of the subject for the benefit of the nation'—of course, the old coercive argument of Canonists and Puritans, based on pretended supernatural power to decide what kind of food, clothing, sport or religion actually *is* 'for the benefit' of your neighbour. Socialists were then beginning to claim similar powers, based on profane inspiration. In reply to a remonstrance from Lord Bramwell about the tone of his speech, Lord Shaftesbury wrote next day:

'House of Lords,
'March 8, 1883.

'MY LORD BRAMWELL,

'Your letter has astonished and grieved me. I was not aware that I had been "cross" towards you during the debate on Lord Stanhope's motion, still less that I was "something else." I was not so, I may say, and most surely may affirm that I had no right to be so towards a peer who was discharging his duty conscientiously. That I was alarmed as to the future when I saw and heard an eminent Judge lay down such propositions, I do not deny; but if there was anything in the language I used which any one peer—I care not who—would assert to have been disrespectful to your lordship, I will make an open and ample retraction. Your lordship speaks of yourself as a "very little man" in comparison with me. That is not my estimate, nor the estimate of the public. God knows I have lived long enough, and had experience enough, to learn that my "greatness" is but as "the small dust of the balance."

'Your very faithful servant,
'SHAFTESBURY.'

In February, 1883, some teetotaler, after his kind wrote to the *Times*. This appeared March 1 :

'A LEGISLATIVE NULLITY.

' It is a paradox, but it seems difficult for sincere and earnest people to stick to the truth. Your correspondent is an example, for he is earnest and sincere, as I infer from his letter, but not truthful. He says: " Lords Bramwell, Wemyss, and Brabourne upheld the rights of the employer to compel his men to spend part of their money in drink." He says I forgot several things—among others, that " payment in a public-house tempts men to drink, and leads to actual pressure being put on men to drink."

' Not a word of truth in it. I expressly said that no right-minded employer would lead his men into temptation by paying their wages in a public-house if he could help it. I objected to the Bill on two grounds: First, that it was simply taken from the Mines Regulation Act, and placed before the House without any evidence to show what good it would do, what mischief it would prevent, what inconvenience it would cause, and that the workmen affected by it ought to be taught to take care of themselves, and not be treated like children. Lord Wemyss was not a member of the House. Lord Brabourne said nothing of the kind your correspondent imputes to us. I retain my opinions.

' Your obedient servant,
' BRAMWELL.'

The little pamphlet on ' Drink,' published early in 1885, ran through ever so many editions. It said, not what nine English-speaking men out of ten believe to be the last word on the controversy, but all they care to say by way of contribution to it. The *Times*, April 10, paid Lord Bramwell's pamphlet the compliment of republishing it, adding on the 13th a specially friendly criticism.

'DRINK.

' There are some opinions entertained as honestly, as strongly, and after as much thought, as the opinions to the contrary, which nevertheless are put forth in an apologetic way, as though those who hold them were doing wrong and knew it, or at least doing something they were not sure about; and doubtless where the opinion is one of entire novelty, or where it is contrary to the principles, feelings, and practice of all mankind, one can understand this style in propounding it. If it is possible to suppose an honest and sensible man thinking infanticide or a community of women desirable institutions, one would make sure and think it reasonable that a man so thinking, who put forth such ideas, would do it humbly and in the style of one asking pardon. But this apologetic style is not confined to such cases. It exists in some when the opinion entertained is righteous, just, moral, and in conformity with the practice of all mankind. It exists where those who hold the contrary say, and are permitted by their opponents to say: " We are the righteous, the good, the virtuous, and you are wicked, bad, and vicious." This is what the total abstainers and the like say of themselves and those who do not agree with them. I am one who do not, and I am going to say why, and as I think my opinion as good and virtuous as theirs, with the additional merit of being right, I am going to state it without asking pardon for it or myself.

'Drink—yes, drink! I mean by that drink which cheers and, if you take too much, inebriates—drink as Mr. Justice Maule understood it, when he was asked by the bailiff, who had sworn to give the jurymen "no meat or drink," whether he might give a juryman some water. "Well," said the Judge, "it is not meat, and I should not call it drink—yes, you may."

'Drink! Yes, alcohol, of which if you take too much "you put an enemy in your mouth to steal away your brains." Drink, which makes a man contemptible and ridiculous if under the influence of too much of it. Drink, which ruins the health and kills the unhappy wretch who persistently takes it to excess.

'Drink! Yes; I say it is a good thing, and I think the world would act very foolishly if it gave it up. Why, if it can do all the harm I have mentioned? For this reason: that it does an immense deal more good. I say outright that it does a deal more good, because it gives a vast deal of pleasure and enjoyment to those who take it with good sense and moderation. All over the world, with the exception of the followers of Mahomet, whom we hold wrong, wherever people have had the skill to make alcoholic drink, they have made and drunk it. Wine where wine could be made. Where it could not, and sometimes where it could, beer and spirits have been produced and drunk.

'Is it not true that it is a source of great pleasure and enjoyment? See the thorough relish with which a tired man takes his glass of beer, the keen pleasure of the first glass of sherry at dinner to the man exhausted with the labour of his brain. But besides these keen enjoyments, take the more quiet and sober pleasure of the glass of beer at dinner and at supper, or with the pipe. This is a pleasure had in this country by millions daily—nay, twice daily—and if, instead of the glass of beer or wine, a small quantity of spirit with water is taken, the pleasure is the same and the practice as reasonable.

'I have as yet only mentioned the pleasure of drink, but there is more in its favour. I will not say that it is food, or supplies the place of food. I do not know. Opinions differ. But I will say what Sir James Paget* tells me: "I would maintain this, and all that can reasonably be deduced from it, namely, that the best and, in proportion to numbers, the largest, quantity of brain work has been, and still is being, done by the people of those nations in which the use of alcoholic drinks has been and is habitual. Further, I would maintain that, so far as I can judge of the brain work of different persons, they have done the best and most who have

---

* A letter of March 9 from Sir James Paget commences: ' I think I could not defend so large a statement as "that alcohol is required for the brain. . . ."' He added that for muscular work alcohol was *not* of any value.

habitually and temperately taken alcoholic drinks." And certainly if we compare the brain work of the drinkers of "drink" with the brain work of the Mahometan, we shall find a justification for this opinion.

' This is the case for " Drink "—its pleasure and its utility. Now what is on the other side? A set of enthusiastic gentlemen, very honest, very much in earnest, with a very clever leader, have taken the matter in hand. They say that the world has been in error for all time, that drink is bad, that drinkers are wrong, and that those who do not agree with them are wrong, and not only wrong but viciously wrong, ought to be ashamed of themselves, and their practice and advocacy of drink denounced and put an end to.

' This is hard upon us who think otherwise. A little more charity might be shown us. First of all we are the majority vastly here in this country. Out of it, or, rather, out of Anglo-Saxon influence, there is no minority even. Then we may say to our opponents : " Your fathers drank, and your ancestors as far back as story goes ; let us have time to think it out and see the error of our ways." And this, at least, we may say to our opponents without offence or irreverence. Those of them who are Christians should, in the Eucharist and the miracle of Cana, have found some excuse for those who think that drinking wine is not in itself wicked. But no ! Down with them ! —sinners, drunkards—shut up the shops, and so forth. Is this reasonable, is it fair, is it charitable, even if right ?

' Now let us see what are the grounds of these opinions—no doubt honest. It is said that immense mischief is caused by excessive drink. I own at once that that is true. Disease is brought on, health ruined, insanity and death caused, by excessive drink. Further, the amount spent in drink is enormous, and a large part of it might be better expended, *i.e.*, in the production of more pleasure and enjoyment than are given by drink. Whether as much as £134,000,000 a year is spent on drink, as it is said, may be doubtful. But a good many millions may be taken off, and still a figure remain which is very lamentable—too much for health, too much for comfort, too much for enjoyment. But what does it prove? Not that all the 8,ooo,ooo male adults of the kingdom are doing wrong and are drunkards, but that some are; that some have been drinking to excess, and have swollen the average. There is this, however, to be said, that if that sum is spent in that way, it shows the amount of enjoyment that must be derived from it.

'There is no doubt also that crime is caused by drink. It is certain that more is drunk on Saturdays, and more crime committed on that day than any other. The drunken man is more likely to commit a crime of violence or robbery than the sober. The drunken man, also, is more likely to have a crime committed on him in his helpless state, than is the sober man.

'This is the case against drink, and a very strong one. Now, what is to be done? It seems obvious to answer: Let those who drink in moderation continue to do so, and let others leave it alone or learn to take it moderately. "No," say the total abstainers, or some of them, "that can't be. If drink is to be had, some will take it in excess. Stop it altogether." Now, I do not say that this is beyond the right of society to its members. I do not know what is. If society's right to interfere with individual liberty is limited to cases necessary to secure the object for which society exists, viz., security of person and property from external and internal attacks, then this prohibition of drink is not within the right of society. But, certainly, society does not limit itself in that way. It prohibits disorderly houses and gaming houses. Perhaps on similar considerations it may prohibit the making and sale of alcoholic drink. But if it is within its right, is it fair, is it just, is it reasonable, expedient, because some take it to excess, that it is to be denied to millions to whom it is a daily pleasure and enjoyment with no attendant harm? Does this seem fair? The glass of beer is taken from the whole of fifty men because one of them will take more than is good for him. And take even his case. He drinks and ruins his health. May he not say: "What is that to you? It is my affair; it is my pleasure not to be as good as you. How do I harm you?" Of course, if he is drunk in public, or riotous, or his drinking injures the public, punish him; but it does seem hard that, instead of this, the sober man should be punished—punished I say. For withholding a pleasure and inflicting a pain are equally punishment.

'In truth, these liquor laws are either to make men better who do not want to be made better, or to make men better who have not self-control, and in both cases at the expense of others. "You shall not enjoy a glass of beer; because if you can get it, so can I, and I shall make a beast of myself." Or, "You shall not enjoy one glass of beer, because you take too many." Is that just? Is it a warrantable interference? Then see the mischief of such laws. The public conscience does not go with them. It is certain they will be broken. Everyone knows that stealing is wrong; disgrace follows conviction. But everyone knows that drinking a glass of beer is not wrong; no discredit attaches to it. It is done, and when done against the law, you have the usual mischiefs of law-breaking, smuggling, informations, oaths, perjury, shuffling, and lies. Besides, as a matter of fact, it fails. Nothing can show this more strongly than the failure in Wales of the Sunday Closing Act. Further, what is to be done? Is the sale of drink to be suspended all over the United Kingdom? Impossible. In parts only? Then all the more will be sold elsewhere. On certain days only? Then provision will be made for a store of it, and the drunkard will sot himself at home with no eyes on him to check him. Consider, too, the practical unfairness on men, who, having no cellar, trust to the public-house for what is a reasonable and wholesome enjoyment when not abused.

'Can nothing, then, be done by law to diminish the mischief caused by drink? I say "No." Whether it is desirable to limit the number of drink-shops is a matter as to which I have great doubt and difficulty. But grant that there is the right to forbid it wholly or partially, in place or time, I say it is a right which should not be exercised. To do so is to interfere with the innocent enjoyment of millions in order to lessen the mischief arising from the folly or evil propensities, not of them- selves, but of others. And, further, that such legislation is attended with the mischiefs which always follow from the creation of offences in law which are not so in conscience. Punish the mischievous drunkard — indeed, perhaps, even punish him for being drunk in public, and so a likely source of mischief. Punish, on the same principle, the man who sells drink to the drunken. But go no further. Trust to the good sense and improvement of mankind, and let charity be shown to those who would trust to them rather than to law.'

As a matter of fact Lord Bramwell was singularly partial to water. During his walking expeditions, whenever he came upon a likely pond, if the weather was warm and nobody was looking, he would take off his clothes and have a bathe, drying himself, 'in case of need,' as notaries say, with his pocket-handkerchief. He was no great swimmer, but could float for ever, and delighted to roll and splash in the water. One long vacation, wandering about the west coast of Scotland, he took passage on a steamer which stopped at sundry piers in succession. Learning that at a certain pier the boat was to wait for three-quarters of an hour, the Baron made up his mind to walk along the coast-road, and catch up with the steamer at the next stopping-place. This plan would have worked all right, only that, as soon as the Baron started, a wedding-party came down and bargained with the captain to take them, for ninepence a head, to a certain manse further on, where the wedding ceremony was to be performed at night, as the local custom was. It was a beautiful autumn evening, the sea smooth as glass, and the little steamer kept close in shore. As she gently rounded a promontory, the passengers came upon an object of interest; this was Sir George

Bramwell, standing upon the rocks at a spot where temptation to plunge in the deep, cool water had proved irresistible; he had just emerged from the sea, and was industriously drying himself with the folds of his umbrella.

As for teetotal polemics generally, incoherent rhetoric was at all times exasperating to Lord Bramwell. If very innocuous as well as incoherent, his ready power of appreciating the ludicrous aspect of things put him in good humour again.

In May, 1885, Mr. James Knowles, Editor of the *Nineteenth Century*, reprinted Lord Bramwell's paper on 'Drink,' together with a reply thereto by Archdeacon Farrar, who, instinctively following the Early Fathers of disendowment, said : 'Many of us are sick of this cry about " private rights," which mean " public wrongs."'

Now, what *is* a 'public wrong'? Something objectionable, no doubt; but, then, how can a Common Law right 'wrong' the public? Elsewhere the Archdeacon had said, ' There can be no vested interest in a nation's wrong.' Lord Bramwell probably had come across the latter maxim, to his mind a complete synopsis of chaos; the first bewildering thought about it being that it is true, undeniable ; a truism, indeed, because there *is* no vested interest in 'a nation's wrong '—one can't buy, sell, bequeath, or mortgage it. When behind the richly-upholstered rhetoric an intention to assert something coherent was visible, Lord Bramwell must have been horrified. Apparently, Archdeacon Farrar meant that any property, interest, right, or security, which is alleged, in sufficiently rhetorical terms, to 'wrong a nation,' may be confiscated. Lord Bramwell found himself asked to say that the exercise of an acquired and inherited Common Law right *could* wrong an entire nation. He knew that was impossible. Besides, although there was no visible or tangible plaintiff, judgment was asked by the Archdeacon against the defendant (a real person —Brown or Smith), his goods were to be confiscated, on no evidence, on mere assertion without proof; the imaginary plaintiffs all the time having been, on their own counsel's showing, consenting parties to the ' wrong.'

In the *Nineteenth Century* for the following month —June, 1885—appeared :

Drink : A Rejoinder.

'When I wrote for the Liberty and Property Defence League the paper called "Drink," reprinted in the last number of the *Nineteenth Century*, I was mainly moved to it by a sense of injustice. Alcoholic liquors have been condemned without a hearing. A love of justice, perhaps only an old habit, made me think that "Drink" ought to have its case stated. I thought that in some respects I was a proper person to do so. I do not make drink, nor sell it, nor, if I may be permitted to speak of myself, take much of it ; nor could my paper lose or gain me any votes.

'. . . I am not without hope that I have to some extent got drink a hearing. Archdeacon Farrar has honoured " Drink " with a " Reply " in this review. I have spoken in favour of honest drink temperately taken. The Archdeacon answers by denouncing fraudulent adulterated drink and all drink intemperately taken. So do I, as heartily as he does. I deprecate the unfairness and mischief of an attempt to make people sober by law. . . .

'The Archdeacon says: "Lord Bramwell begins by saying that this cause needs no apology, because it is just and moral and in conformity with the practice of all mankind. If so, what need is there to be so much moved by those whom he evidently regards as a small and wrong-headed minority?" Was I much or at all moved? I think not. I was not conscious of it. Did I say that to drink a glass of beer was "just or moral"? I think not. I think it neither just nor unjust, moral nor immoral, any more than is the eating of an apple. But I think it reasonable, unless the glass is followed by too many others, and I suppose even so harmless a thing as apple-eating might be carried to excess.

'Nor did I, as I have said, call the total abstainers "wrong-headed." I gave them credit for honesty and cleverness, but thought them wrong in renouncing a harmless enjoyment, and doubly wrong in endeavouring, not only to persuade, but to compel others to do so.

'The Archdeacon then quotes me as saying that the opponents of all drink have said, "We are the righteous, the good, and virtuous; you are wicked, bad, vicious." Who, asks the Archdeacon, has ever said this? and he says he never heard anything distantly approaching to such an allegation. On reading this, I sent the Archdeacon a report of a speech at a Blue Ribbon meeting, at which I and drink were spoken of. This speech certainly did, not "*distantly*, approach to such an allegation."

'I will not repeat here what was in it, as I will not help to circulate what the Archdeacon, in a letter he was kind enough to write to me, spoke of thus: "Archdeacon Farrar sincerely hopes that remarks so disgraceful are most exceptional; they might be made by a vulgar-minded person." "Probably," he says in the "Reply," "for lack of education, language may have been used which might constructively be pressed to so *absurd* a conclusion," *i.e.*, that we are denounced as bad while the abstainers claim to be good. Alas! "the disgraceful remarks" which help the *absurd* conclusion, as the Archdeacon obligingly calls it, were made by a clergyman of the Established Church. Another "Reverend," whether of the

Church or a Dissenter I know not, followed in a similar strain. The speeches were very successful, being received with "laughter," "shame," "hisses," and other marks of approval of the speakers and disapproval of me. Now, here is a case for total abstinence. I really should recommend to these reverend gentlemen total abstinence from abuse, for they do not know how to enjoy it with moderation. The same to their auditors. I think they did " condemn and desire to encroach upon the independent judgment and moral liberty of their neighbours."

' In " Drink " I spoke of Mahomet as I think of him—not very respectfully; for I think his religion is very much the cause of the inferior condition of those who profess it. The Archdeacon says : " It is not worth while pausing to inquire whether history will accept this description of the great Prophet of Arabia, or whether his mighty and beneficial influence in saving whole nations from the curse of intemperance does not go far to outweigh many of his errors." Great Prophet ! Well, of course, the Archdeacon does not mean he was really a prophet, an inspired person. But it is as well to use right words. If he was inspired, *cadit quæstio*. If not, he was an impostor or crazy. He enjoined abstinence from drink. Now, I desire to ask Archdeacon Farrar if he prefers Mahomet's teaching to the teaching which did not contain that injunction ? In my paper I respectfully appealed to the Eucharist and miracle of Cana, to prove that drinking wine is not in itself wrong. The Archdeacon says I am "fighting a chimera—no one ever said it was." Indeed ! But I ask, and again appeal to those two instances—and I might appeal to many other texts—does the Archdeacon remember who said, " I am the true vine," and who looked forward to drinking wine new in the kingdom of Heaven ? Is there anything in the New Testament which enjoins total abstinence, or is inconsistent with the moderate use of wine ? and does or does not Archdeacon Farrar prefer that teaching to Mahomet's ? Is Mahomet's teaching right ? If it is, the Gospel teaching is wrong. Is Mahomet's teaching wrong ? Then how can wrong teaching "outweigh many errors " ? What error is.

outweighed ?   The error of polygamy ?   Of course the Archdeacon will admit that is an " error."   Is this an error outweighed ?   Is the " error " which enjoins war on the infidels ?
But the Archdeacon has a regard for "the Prophet."   He
refers to Avicenna and Averrhoes as giving the chief impulse
to philosophy, medicine, and science in the modern world, and
says that Albert the Great and St. Thomas Aquinas did not
disdain to learn from the Arabic commentators on Aristotle.
As Mrs. Shandy said, " That was a hundred years ago."
Does the Archdeacon really think that the brain-work of the
Mahometans now excels that of Christians ?   If so, why does
he not give a few instances more modern than the time of
Albertus Magnus and Thomas Aquinas ?   I do know that
Alcohol is Arabic, as are also Algebra and Alchymy ; but
what of it ?   Enough, however, of "the great Prophet of
Arabia."

'The Archdeacon says : " I challenge the proposition that
because drink gives a great deal of pleasure and enjoyment it
therefore does an immense deal more good than harm.   The
two results are not *in pari materia*."   Then why compare them ?
I meet a thief carrying a bundle of stolen goods.   If I ask him
whether the load on his back or the load on his conscience is
the heavier, he may properly reply that the two are not *in pari
materia*.   But what should we think of his logic if he straightway proceeded to demonstrate that the load on his conscience
was seven times as heavy as that on his back ?   When
Paley described the pleasure of a noble action as " some
multiple of the pleasure of eating a cheesecake," Whewell
objected that the two were not *in pari materia ;* he was too
good a logician to go on and contend that one was greater than
the other.   Not so the Archdeacon.   He goes on and says :
" The good takes the form of a sensuous pleasure, a passing
exhilaration ; the harm takes the form of disease, pain, waste,
insanity, crime, and death.   The pleasure is insignificant, the
harm is deadly."   Now, I did not say " therefore."   A conclusion to the effect stated would be illogical, and, to copy the
Archdeacon, "absurd."   I said, if you sum up the good on one
side and the harm on the other, the good outweighs the harm.

What is the objection ? that the pleasure is sensuous ?   So is the smell of a rose.   Why is not a passing exhilaration good ? What of a thrilling piece of music ?   True, the mischief to an individual from the excess of drink more than outweighs the good of moderate drink to an individual.   But what of the pleasure of the millions who enjoy temperate drinking compared with the misery of the relative few—no doubt far too many—who drink to excess ?   Of what might not that be said which the Archdeacon says of drink ?   Men eat too much, I know.   Sir William Gull has said that more harm was done by over-eating than by over-drinking.   Some men read too much, others are too fond of cricket, some smoke too much. I own that the mischief of excess in these matters is not so bad as the mischief from drink—not nearly as bad ; but there is the excess, and unless the mischief from that excess outweighs the pleasures from moderate indulgence, it is temperance in the enjoyment of, not abstinence from them, that should be enjoined ; and the same is true of drink.   Does the Archdeacon remember what Horace says (Sat. I. ii. 36) about women in general, and Helen ?

‘ The Archdeacon says that “ a Christian in an age of rapid intoxicants, in a country where drinking is the worst national vice ” (have we another ?—what ?) “ may be excused from accepting Lord Bramwell’s conclusions, when he finds that centuries and millenniums ago they were rejected by Jews and pagans, who, though Jews and pagans, thought very differently from the English Judge.”   Innuendo, as a lawyer would say, that an English Judge who did not think at least as well as Jews and pagans did, must be a sad fellow.   But let us see the evidence as to the Jews and pagans, and their thoughts.

‘ The Archdeacon says that some of the Rabbis believed the vine was the forbidden tree.   Now, with all respect for Rabbis, I doubt if their learning has much bearing on the question in hand.   I am glad to believe that their practice was never that of total abstinence.   I fully admit that they know more than I do on the subject on which their opinion is quoted.   Some of them thought the vine was the forbidden tree.   I dare say ; I suppose some thought otherwise ; but even if they all thought so, it seems to me that they paid a great compliment to the vine, for no tree could be more highly spoken of than the one the fruit of which was forbidden. Does the Archdeacon think that the vine was the forbidden tree, or agree with Him who said, "I am the true vine"? And the Archdeacon should remember that the vine does not grow wine, but grapes, and it is the fault of man that grapes are put to a bad purpose, if it is bad. Should the Archdeacon say that a thing is bad which can be put to a bad purpose, I should like him to show me what cannot. And I remind the Archdeacon that he must condemn barley, from which beer is made; and as more people get drunk from that than from wine, it would seem the Rabbis should have made barley the forbidden tree—except for the difficulty that it is not a tree. Then oats, and the potato, and nearly all fruits and vegetables, should be condemned on this ground—even some animal matters might.

' If we do not know exactly what the ancient Rabbis thought or did, we do know what those did from whose writings the Rabbis drew their inspiration. In the Book of Proverbs we read, " Give strong drink unto him that is ready to perish, and wine unto those that be of heavy heart. Let him drink and forget his poverty, and remember his misery no more." In Ecclesiastes, " Blessed art thou, O land, when thy princes eat in due season, and not for drunkenness "; Psalm civ., " Wine that maketh glad the heart of man." Isaiah looks forward to the day when " in this mountain shall the Lord of hosts make unto all people a feast of fat things, a feast of wines on the lees, of fat things full of marrow; of wines on the lees well refined."

' But now we come to formidable matter. The Archdeacon says the discovery of wine in the Scripture is instantly followed by a patriarch's degradation and the son's infamy, and the curse of an entire branch of the human family. In these four verses (Gen. ix. 20-24), says Rabbi Oved the Galilean, there are no less than thirteen vaus, and each vau stands for a woe upon the human race.* I can't deny it, nor could I if Rabbi

---

* In Gerald Griffin's ' The Collegians,' p. 90. When the herdsman is claiming kinship with the gentry, he says, ' My

Oved the Galilean had put the number at five thousand. I
humbly own I never before heard of Rabbi Oved the Galilean,
nor have I the least knowledge why a vau should stand for a
woe on the human race. But, speaking under the correction
of the Rabbi, Noah, who was " drunken," was not punished ;
nor was Ham, whose offence was that he did not honour his
father. Poor Canaan and his posterity were cursed by Noah,
because he had been drunken, and Ham disrespectful. Ham
was not punished himself; so I think " infamy " must be a
strong word to apply to his conduct. I do not know what was
the degradation of Noah, except that he took too much, probably finding it so good and not knowing the mischief. This
also I think too strong a word; I should scruple to say that
Noah was " degraded," though doubtless to be drunken is
degrading. But a dignitary of the Church may perhaps take
such a liberty with a patriarch. The curse of Canaan was
Noah's only. Whether he had authority to curse I know not ;
but as to Canaan and his posterity, if human feeling had
anything to do with the composition of Genesis, it must be
remembered that the Jews had a strong temptation to make
a justification of their treatment of the Canaanites. After all,
it was not he who drank that was punished. Really, is the
important question the Archdeacon discusses to be answered
by the help of these Rabbis and vaus ?

' The Archdeacon, having quoted the Jews, turns to the
pagans. He cites Propertius, Pliny, and a Thracian King ;
but do either of them do more than object to " misused wine "?
We all object to this. But was any one of these pagans a
total abstainer ? Does the Archdeacon deny that all antiquity
praised wine ? He makes a solitary quotation from Propertius,
which I do not understand as condemning drink in moderation,
but in excess. Let me quote to the Archdeacon a passage
recently sent to me out of Horace, who was a sensible
fellow :

grandfather and himself were third cousins. Oh, vo ! vo ! vo !'
A note explains that ' vo ' is equivalent to the French *hélas !*
and the Italian *oime !*

' " Quid non ebrietas designat ? operta recludit ;
Spes jubet esse ratas ; in prœlia trudit inertem ;
Sollicitis animis onus eximit ; addocet artes :
Fecundi calices quem non fecere disertum ?
Contracta quem non in paupertate solutum ?"

'Will the Archdeacon accept Propertius as a *censor morum ?* Does he know that Cuvier said of Pliny that he was "an author without critical judgment whose reflections have no relation to science, but display alternately either the most superstitious credulity or the declarations of a discontented philosophy which finds fault continually with mankind, with Nature, and with the gods themselves"?   Does the Archdeacon agree with his theology ?   The Thracian King, for speaking ill of Bacchus, came to a bad end, to the satisfaction of the whole population of Athens.

'But if we are to have these authorities, why not quote Æsculapius, Hippocrates, and Galen ?   Galen strongly defends the practice of drinking wine, especially for old people.   He says : "Old age is cold and dry, and is to be corrected by cale-facients."   One Greek quotation—Euripides says: " Dionysus introduced among men the liquid draught of the grape, which puts an end to the sorrows of wretched mortals."   This was addressed to his Athenian audience.   Will the Archdeacon consult the Rig Veda ?   "This wine when drunk stimulates my head.   It calls forth the ardent thought."

' The Archdeacon, after the Jews and pagans, quotes Franklin, who advocates temperance.   So do I. . . .

'. . . The Archdeacon says, speaking of me, " Perhaps he may not have tried whether abstinence, undertaken from generous motives, is not a source of even greater pleasure," *i.e.*, than drink.   The question is somewhat personal.   I answer to this extent, I have not tried it.   I never had the opportunity.   But, dropping the personal, I say that if absti-nence on the part of a temperate drinker would reclaim any drunkard, a man of ordinary humanity would practise it as far as considerations of enjoyment were concerned.   I say nothing of myself, for this among other reasons, that I care very little for drink, and could easily renounce it.   I do *not* think that " any number of glasses of beer, or sherry, or gin, could yield a pleasure equivalent to that which we experience when we know by our abstinence we have been blessed in the power to snatch from ruin and degradation so much as even one imperilled life !" Further, I dare say that in many cases drink is a needless luxury, and that many would spend their money better than in its purchase. But that is not the question. There are two questions : one is whether those who can afford it should give it up ; the other is, if they will not, whether they should be made to do so.

' " Sin," says the Archdeacon, " is the worst curse of mankind. It is the one curse of humanity of which we might absolutely cut off the entail." Alas ! the Archdeacon tempts an old lawyer to say we should then be seized in fee simple of this sin, and have the largest possible estate in it.

' The Archdeacon makes a great, I must say a mischievous, mistake when he says : " It is a shameful injustice that the rich should be easily able to keep public-houses from the parks and squares in which they live, while the poor are left helpless and unprotected, to their most fatal temptation." I call this mischievous as a suggestion of ill-usage of the poor, of which there is much too much inflammatory talk already. It is a mistake, because it supposes that there is some law or arrangement which causes it, when it is only the result of this, that a public-house in a square in which the rich live would not pay. What does the Archdeacon say to the injustice of shutting up the place where the poor man gets his beer, and leaving open the rich man's club ?

' The Archdeacon says : " Lord Bramwell bids us trust to the good sense and improvement of mankind. Alas ! we have been doing so for centuries." He refers to the cockatrice on Amiens Cathedral, and cruelly says, " Lord Bramwell once more hangs the desecrated shield of liberty on the signboard of the gin-palace." This is " magnifique, mais ce n'est pas la guerre." It is eloquent—at least, I suppose so—but it is not argument. Why should the Archdeacon distrust mankind and want the aid of the law ? He supposes there are three to four million total abstainers in England. How many were there fifty or twenty years ago? Yet the Archdeacon wants more law. He speaks as though it was now being asked for for the first time. Laws in restraint of drink have existed for nearly three centuries, have been broken more than any others, and have caused more offences than any others. I have tried more cases of perjury arising from them than from any other cause. . . .

' I will not notice Edward IV., the Duke of Burgundy, or Oliver Cromwell, but I will express my agreement with the good and venerated nobleman, Lord Shaftesbury, that " I see the absolute and indispensable necessity of temperance associations," if he means, as I believe, temperance, and not total abstinence—nay, more: if there are men who cannot drink in moderation, but can totally abstain, I heartily agree that they should do the latter. As to Goethe, does the Archdeacon know that one of Goethe's character's quotes, I suppose with Goethe's approval, the following line from an old song :

' " Der Wein erfreut des Menschen Herz."

The Archdeacon may like the rest of the quatrain :

' " Drum gab uns Gott den Wein.
Auf! lasst bei Rebensaft und Scherz
Uns unsers Daseins freun !"

Does the Archdeacon approve the life and conduct of Lacordaire, whom he cites ?

' I have now been through the " Reply." Let us see where we agree and where we differ. I said that " drink " in moderation is a source of great and harmless enjoyment. Does he deny it ? No. He says it causes great mischief. Did I deny that ? No. He thinks the mischief outweighs the good. I think the good outweighs the mischief. So far we differ. I say that, if not, the good may be had without the mischief. I do not understand him to deny that, if people would only be wise. I said it is unjust to deny enjoyment to A and the other letters of the alphabet down to Z because Z abuses the means of enjoyment. Does the Archdeacon deny it ? He complains of adulteration and the vile stuff that is sold as " drink." I did not mention that, but heartily join him, and would punish the makers and sellers as poisoners. He advocates temperance. Have I said a word in favour of intemperance? No. I deprecate compulsory legislation as leading to breaches of the law. This is a subject he leaves untouched. I asked for charity and indulgence for those who think as I do. He does not say we are entitled to it. He appears to think we get as much as we deserve.

'The Archdeacon has called up Mahomet, Noah, his unlucky son Canaan, and all his posterity; the Rabbi Oved the Galilean, and divers other Rabbis; Propertius, Pliny, a legendary Thracian King, Aristotle, Franklin, the Duke of Burgundy, Edward IV., Avicenna, Averrhoes, Albert the Great, Thomas Aquinas, Oliver Cromwell, Milton, Goethe, and finishes with Lord Shaftesbury, who, I warrant, never before found himself in such company. . . .

'BRAMWELL.'

Here is a portion of a *Times* leader written by Lord Bramwell, printed in November, 1885:

'The *Alliance News*, in its number of November 1, says that Lord Bramwell has written that "to prohibit the sale of drink is either to make men better who do not wish to be made better, or it is to protect at the expense of others those who will not protect themselves, and then it is wholly unreasonable." If Lord Bramwell has said so, we are glad of it; but our business is not with him, not with the text, but with the sermon thereon by the *Alliance News*, which is edifying and amusing. Says the *Alliance News*, this "discerns entire unreasonableness in the endeavour to protect at the expense of others those who will not protect themselves. The proprietor, for example, who is induced by public opinion to put at his own charges a railing round his gravel-pit, and that other one who is compelled by law to fence off his machinery, are alike victims of entire unreason. The lady who lets apartments tainted with infectious disease is not to be put to expense in disinfective procedure for the sake of lodgers who, not knowing the facts, will not protect themselves." The writer evidently thinks that people have a propensity to throw themselves down gravel-pits and against machinery, and that people who take infected lodgings, "not knowing the facts," are people who will not protect themselves. The *Alliance News* further says that Lord Bramwell deems it an impertinence to make men better who do not wish to be made better, "however greatly they may need to be improved." So say we, if the making them better is by force. The writer in the *Alliance* says, if it is an impertinence to make them better, it is an impertinence to try to make them better. Not so. If the writer of the article were whipped to make him write better, it would be an impertinence, and worse. He likes his own style, and so do his readers, doubtless; but it would not be an impertinence to try to improve him by gentle means, as we are now doing. He goes on in a singular way. Lord Bramwell is a graduate in a pagan school. "But to seek and save that which is lost is a Divine mission." And then there is a reference to Christianity which we forbear quoting. But this we may say without suspicion of irreverence, that Christianity does not proceed by compulsion, but by persuasion. . . .'

Archdeacon Farrar replied to 'Drink : A Rejoinder,' in the *Nineteenth Century*, July, 1885, and, both being gentlemen, these two controversialists became better, instead of worse, friends. The Archdeacon's side of the question, or some précis of his argument, ought also to be given ; but, firstly, there is no room ; secondly, few people care about the matter nowadays ; thirdly, Archdeacon Farrar seems really to have got the best of it in the end, becoming Chaplain to the Speaker, Dean of Canterbury, and so on.

The June,.1885, number of the *Nineteenth Century* had also contained an article by Mr. Henry Broadhurst about a Leasehold Enfranchisement Bill which he had backed. No doubt Lord Bramwell, after reading—as contributors will do—his own paper, read Mr. Broadhurst's, and in consequence thought a pamphlet on the subject worth writing.

Lord Bramwell begins by thus severely condemning the Bill :

'The Leaseholds (Facilities of Purchase of Fee Simple) Bill lately before Parliament gives power to take a man's property, not for any public purpose, but for the benefit of the taker—without paying a fair compensation to the owner ; avoids all contracts which would prevent the application of the Act ; forbids an intending lessor and lessee to make a binding bargain on such terms as they think suitable. Moreover, it exhibits gross ignorance of the subject with which it deals, and of the law relating to it. . . .'

He then goes on to expose its foolish and contradictory provisions in detail, adding :

'. . . These are some of the objections to this precious attempt at legislation. There are others in matters of detail. But the main objections are what have been mentioned : interference with the rights of property, inadequate compensation for what is taken, and interference with liberty of contract. To justify this some powerful reasons should be given. . . .'

and winds up :

'. . . If property is to be taken, if freedom of contract is to be interfered with, let the terms be fair, and let the interference be for good cause, and not, as in this case, without a reason that will bear examination.'

Ultimately differences arose among advanced land reformers about the matter, Socialists objecting to turn leaseholders into freeholders on any consideration. The Socialist microbe, in other words, ate up the Radical microbe.*

* On July 23, 1859, Chief Baron Pollock had written almost prophetically to Sir George Bramwell :

'. . . I should like to see an " Encyclopædia of Hum-

Other things relative to the matter happened later. In January, 1887, Mr. H. W. Lawson wrote to the *Times* explaining that he had succeeded Mr. H. Broadhurst as President of the Leaseholds Enfranchisement Association. *Inter alia* he recommended 'some form' of leasehold enfranchisement 'as a cure for the evils of overcrowding, insanitary dwellings, and *apathy in the performance of social duties.*' There is still much apathy.

A letter to the *Times* of January 9, 1889, refers to a favourite proposal of the anti-capitalist and Socialist party :

'THE TAXATION OF GROUND-RENTS.

'There ought to be no difficulty about the question of taxing or rating ground-rents. When a man takes a house as tenant from year to year or on a lease (without premium), and pays a rack-rent, that rack-rent is composed of (1) hire of bricks, mortar, labour, etc., used in the building of the house ; (2) hire —compensation for the use of—the land on which the house is built. For example, rack-rent is £50 a year, made up of £40 a year compensation for the house and £10 a year for the land. The tenant pays no ground-rent (so called).

'Suppose he built the house himself at the same cost, but had a lease of the land at £10 a year, he would then pay a ground-rent. Is there any reason why more rates or taxes should be paid in respect of the house in the latter case than if it were occupied at a rack-rent ? Clearly not.

---

bug." . . . I am afraid the probable size of it alarms you, but never fear ; one step towards getting rid of IT is to collect IT together as Jehu did with the priests of Baal when he " destroyed Baal out of Israel." *There are humbugs that destroy each other, like some poisons which are mutual antidotes.* If the whole pile of humbug could be collected, you would see the heap dwindle by action and reaction. . . .'

'But one of your correspondents wants to know why occupiers should pay all rates, etc., and the owner of the ground-rent none ? The answer is, Because the occupier has agreed to do so, or the law has said he should.

'Is it not apparent that, if the burden is put on the owner of ground-rent, it should be taken off the occupier to the same extent ? Otherwise the same value in land and building would pay different rates according to the way it was let.

'Your obedient servant,

'B.'

In his address to the British Association, July, 1888, he had said :

'. . . A man has three pieces of land of the same size, situation, value. On one he builds a house at a cost of £1,000, and lives in it ; on another he builds a house at a cost of £1,000, and lets it at a rack-rent of £65, putting the annual value of his land at £15 ; the third he lets to a tenant at £5 a year for fifty years on the terms that the tenant lays out £1,000 in building a house. He, the land-owner, gives up £10 a year because he will have the house at the end of fifty. The tenant is willing to build the house and give it up at the end of fifty years, because for those fifty years he will have land for £5 a year which is worth £15. Can any human being give a reason why any one of these three houses, or their owners and occupiers in respect of them, should pay more taxes or rates than any other of them ?'

Dissatisfaction, regretful grumbling about the lawlessness of Mr. Gladstone's Irish ideas, Lord Bramwell expressed in the *Times* for years, his letters marking, like a chain of buoys at the estuary of a tidal river, the channel kept and the channel avoided, by the Liberal ship from Burke's day onwards, also the dangerous rocks and shoals. A thorough Englishman in his unwillingness to think much about the Irish Question at any time, he said nothing about the Nationalist or Land League danger until he was forced to.   He differed from an old friend and correspondent, Baron Martin, about the Compensation for Disturbance Bill of 1880, as the following letter shows :

'Crindle, Myroe,
'Londonderry,
'*August* 13, 1880.

'. . . You are right as to Russell. He has turned out much better than I expected. . . . I like what I have seen of Gully, but it was little. As to ——— I never could understand him. He seems to be in Manchester business, and Manchester solicitors are not fools. . . . As to the Irish (Compensation for Disturbance) Bill, I would have voted for it. The Government must know best whether it was necessary. I have a bad opinion of Munster and Connaught landlords. What they let is a site for a house and an acre for potatoes, which fail twice out of three years.

'SAMUEL MARTIN.'

This letter of February 4, 1885, from a genial Irish Judge, known to his friends as 'I. D.,' must have reminded Lord Bramwell that when one Irishman tries his best to speak well of another conscientious difficulties supervene :

'*February* 4, 1885.

'. . . You ask me, Had O'Hagan all the virtues which the *Times* ascribes to him? A question, that, for the public to answer, on which there may be great divergence of opinion. You must not be guided by the press. O'Hagan was from early life a press-man. They never desert each other. I lament him much as one of the last of my old colleagues and a friend from youth to the end. He was really a good man, genial, hospitable to excess ; rarely said an unkind word ; never wilfully

did an unjust act.   Strong and decided in his Liberal political
opinions, tolerant to others, a patriot in the sense of being
influenced by a passionate desire to promote the welfare of his
country.   In religion a most sincere son of " The One and
Only True Church "; probably entertained the sad view that
you and all like you, who wilfully and perversely keep outside
its pale, are doomed (and justly) for all eternity to sulphurous
fires, or to be baked in red-hot steel ovens, or submerged in
boiling tar and petroleum, or perpetually blown to pieces by
dynamite.   Not an educated lawyer.   In a certain sense a
good, popular speaker.   A good presence, an agreeable voice,
and great facility in stringing together platitudes and rotund
sentences, coupled with wonderful industry in getting up his
speeches, made him a success as a popular speaker, and procured for him the character of an orator.   The *Times* characterizes
a speech made by him in 1859, on the occasion of the trial of
the Phœnix conspirators, as " remarkable for its magnitude,
its eloquence, and its denunciation of the Government."   There
was at the time difference of opinion on the subject.   If " magnitude " means " length," the term is properly applied, since
he spoke for eighteen hours.   Mr. Baron Greene, who presided
at the trial, was heard to observe " *every word of that speech
which was not high treason was mere bosh*."   Be that as it may, that
speech procured for him subsequently the representation of
Tralee in Parliament.   On the whole, I think he was much
overestimated.   He had no original genius, no courage, no
backbone, and was a most indifferent administrator.   O'Hagan,
born in the North of Ireland, was brought up with a wholesome
dread of the pernicious effects of Orangeism on the administration of justice.   When Attorney-General, to provide a remedy,
he passed the Irish Jury Act (which the *Times* praised)—his
only real effort as a legislator.   It was a grave mistake; led to
much of our present misfortunes.   He forgot the three other
provinces, and nearly ruined them.   Were it not for two
amending Acts, life in Ireland would be less tolerable even than
it is.   He was, however, a most amiable man, of many virtues,
and succeeded in life largely through his kindness and his
genial temper, which procured and retained for him a wide

popularity. Supposed to possess great influence with the clergy and people, he was in consequence promoted to the highest offices; but it was found by experience that popularity and real political influence were totally different things. It will be difficult to fill his place in Irish Society. Adieu; I have bored you.'

After describing a holiday trip along the Alaska coast and through California, Chief Justice Waite, of the U.S. Supreme Court, wrote from Washington, D.C. :

'June 4, 1887.

'. . . Home Rule is indeed a bother, and I agree with you that our people ought to let it alone. But the Irishman here has his vote, and every politician seems to feel himself under the necessity of making a bid for it. Hence all questions affecting that vote come to the surface and are talked about. As a rule, what you hear comes from politicians in the cities, where, unfortunately, this vote is often controlling. Especially is this so in New York, where it is large and holds the balance of power. I feel quite sure the Fisheries Question will very soon get itself out of the way. Two nations like Great Britain and the United States cannot afford to keep such an irritating subject open to vex them, and some plan will certainly be devised for its settlement; of that I feel confident. I met the "bright young lady" the other evening, and we talked about you. She bid me send you her love, to which I am sure Lady Bramwell will not object. She came over from Baltimore to attend a reception given by her aunt, Mrs. Bancroft Davis, to Sir Edward Thornton, who represented your Government so long at this place. She seemed even more attractive than when you saw her.

Yours very sincerely,
'M. R. WAITE.'

From 1880 to 1885 Lord Bramwell watched Irish hatred and Irish disorder growing from a half-comic thing into an apparently deadly thing.* After December, 1885, contempt and dislike changed into wrath—perhaps exaggeration. English Liberals of Lord Bramwell's stamp, seeing, from the Maamtrasna debate, that the Tories were still the Tories, said, 'We, then, must subdue this deadly thing?' and tried for five years, in their rather blundering way, to subdue it. One day, in December, 1890, 'the disruption' came, and English Liberals concluded that The Thing had outwitted them, after all, by stinging itself to death.

Burke had warned his countrymen of the tendency among revolutionary and destructive groups or combinations in politics to revert to barbarism, to settle questions by savage methods. This reversion proceeds by steps, of which the first is denial, repudiation of law and order—the accoutrements of justice.

That which Lord Bramwell cared most about from first to last was the lawlessness which disfigured, not only the Land League executive and its functionaries in Ireland, but also advocates and apologists for Home Rule, residing out of Ireland. A letter to the *Times*, October 29, 1889, gives the key to his unflinching 'Unionism':

'MR. GLADSTONE AND THE PLAN OF CAMPAIGN.

'I doubt if it is worth while, but there is one matter in Mr. Gladstone's speech reported in the *Times* of yesterday

---

* The Duke of Argyll wrote to him, June 6, 1884:

'. . . The Land Act of 1881 has never been properly *exposed* in its working and operation. I agree with you that the administrators are far less to blame than the legislators. They were given no law, or shadow of a law, to guide them.'

which I think should be noticed. He says: " I believe I am right in saying that the Plan of Campaign has been declared by sufficient legal authority not to be legal. If that be so, I justify nothing that is not legal." He probably means: " If that be so, *since* I justify nothing that is not legal, I do not justify the Plan of Campaign." Why this great master of words did not say so, does not appear. He proceeds: " Mr. Parnell has never given a *distinct* approval to the Plan of Campaign." What does he mean—that an approval of what is not legal is less wrong if indistinct, or that, if Parnell's approval had been distinct, he (Mr. Gladstone) would have approved? Is not Parnell guilty of suffering, permitting, and approving of what he could stop? And even if he is not, are not Mr. Gladstone's confederates—O'Brien, Dillon, and others —guilty of a distinct approval and practice of what he (Mr. Gladstone) will not justify? Mr. Gladstone proceeds: " I admit the Plan of Campaign has something to say for itself," and says the Government and majority in Parliament are the true authors of the Plan of Campaign. " They made it an absolute necessity." If an absolute necessity, how is it possible not to approve of it? How can one disapprove of what could not be helped? . . . But if that is why the Plan of Campaign was *started*, is there any pretence for saying that is why it is kept on foot? If it merited an approval (provided it was not distinct) in 1886, is there any excuse for it now, or in 1887, 1888, and 1889?

' Your obedient servant,

' B.'

Lord Bramwell's view of law and order being the recognized view, and that of the Land League being for a long time also the recognized view, his opinions came to represent a sort of professional jealousy— prejudice in favour of his own trade-brand. The Land or National League—for some years the *de facto* Government over a large part of Ireland—had been compelled to set up—as all Governments must do—a rival system of jurisprudence of its own.   It established tribunals, judges, a *corpus juris Hibernici*, prætors, jurisconsults, police.   If a subject wanted justice from a Land League Court, he could get it, provided he 'stood in' with the parish priest's nephew, feed the principal local Land League organizer, or was on good terms with the adjacent gombeen man's mother-in-law.   Thus there was a legal remedy for every wrong.   This Land League, too, had its Right Honourable Justinian — or Gratian of Chiusi—whose explanatory speeches and writings in defence of Land League jurisprudence between December 1885 and 1892 are Institutes and Decretals combined.   A 'Digest' was drawn up, various *glossæ* and *extravagantes* being added from time to time by independent local agents of the Land, or National League in Ireland itself.   Thereupon Lord Bramwell, like Demetrius the silversmith, began to think his own craft in danger. To the very last the Home Rule spectre (and a vision of the blood for ever wet upon the grass in Phœnix Park) haunted Lord Bramwell, as it did millions of other men in those half-forgotten days between May, 1882, and August, 1893.   The last speech he made in the House of Lords (on a Scottish topic) had a reference to Irish lawlessness.

In October, 1885, an Irish Defence Union was formed in London to checkmate and frustrate the system of boycotting, then unrestrained in Ireland, and to give help to victims.   Like the Pinkerton agency in the United States, an interesting example of those jury-rigged, or makeshift, defences contrived by civilized men when constituted authorities are unable, unwilling or afraid to protect liberty and property. The quaint thing about this Union was Lords Bramwell and Penzance, and any number of magistrates, confederating in a room at 22, Charing Cross to do in their leisure hours what other Judges and magistrates were appointed to do in working hours. The first time Lord Bramwell attended a meeting of the Union at 22, Charing Cross, he was a little late. Excusing himself, he touched on an obscure problem of West-End geography. Said he : ' I suppose I call myself a Londoner—in fact, a Cockney. I thought I knew London pretty well, but I have wandered about for half an hour trying to find 22, Charing Cross. I tried St. Martin's Lane, the Strand, Cockspur Street, and went back to the Athenæum to inquire, but never knew where 22, Charing Cross was till this minute. I always supposed the street running down to the Houses of Parliament was either Whitehall or Parliament Street.' In January, 1886, when he was in the chair at a meeting of this Union, a wealthy Irish merchant present offered to subscribe largely to the fund for coping with boycotting, provided his name was not published, otherwise his own goods would be boycotted, and he would lose heavily. Thereupon Lord Bramwell uttered in a very decided tone this Johnsonian sentiment : ' Sir, you remind me of a soldier who would not mind fighting in a battle, provided it could be guaranteed he was not to be wounded.' Upon this rebuke, the merchant, like Thomas surnamed Didymus, publicly joined the organization.　The late Earl of Pembroke greatly helped the work of the Union.　Lord Bramwell's keen interest in it is shown by the following letters to the zealous honorary secretary, Colonel C. H. Davidson :

> '34, Cadogan Place,
> '*December* 17, 1885.

'Dear Colonel Davidson,

'I return the draft.　I am afraid I have made many alterations, but it is more methodical.　(1) It concerns Britain ; (2) because of trade and in case of war ; (3) it concerns North of Ireland, and so on ; (4) it concerns rent of Ireland, because of plunder ; (5) people are punished who will not assist ; (6) they are compelled to seem to assist ; (7) we must help them, and money is wanted.

'I cannot attend the meeting to-morrow.　I am boycotted by a cold and influenza, bad enough to be Irish, or something else which ends in -ish.

> 'Very truly yours,
> 'Bramwell.'

> 'Four Elms,
> '*December* 26, 1885.

'Dear Colonel Davidson,

'. . . . Could you say something like this, "Force must be used if necessary to prevent this separation"?　That, it will be said, will bring about a rebellion.　A bad thing ; but if there is to be one, it had better be when it suits the followers of law and order, than when it suits the rebels.　At present law and order, and the power of the State, are on our side. After a year or two of Home Rule, all guarantees would be blown away ; property-owners would have been robbed ; law and order would have ceased, and the power of the State in Southern and Western Ireland would be in the rebels.　Rebellion !　Why, there is rebellion now !　The law is powerless. Murder, robbery, outrage, go unpunished, and treasonable intentions are openly avowed.　Give Home Rule, and in a few months rebellion would be manifest and avowed. Let us have it now rather than then. . . .'

'*January* 4, 1886.

'. . . . We should remember: (1) The Irish tenants are for separation as a means of plundering the land-owners. Why should they not ? They do not think it wrong. Their leaders, lay and clerical, say it is right. (2) Though I do not think there is a general hatred of the English, such as existed in Milan and Venice against the Austrians, still, there is a deep and deadly hatred in many toward us, which would make Ireland a hostile country if separated. (3) If the landlords are ruined, separation becomes easier. (4) If the constabulary and police are put in Parnell's hands, we at once have a standing army against us. (5) Self-preservation then compels us to protect the landlords and prevent separation. (6) We cannot abandon Ulster. Lord Cowper says the Land Act [of 1881 ?] was right. I cannot, with sincere respect for him, agree. It established the principle of plunder. The Parnellites are only carrying it further. If there is anything wrong, let the Irish say what it is. I agree with the Duke of Argyll that the Catholics ought to have denominational schools. . . .'

Lord Salisbury, Premier, resigned January 27, 1886. On January 31 Lord Bramwell wrote :

' . . . . I think there is as good reason for a deputation to Gladstone as there was for one to Lord Salisbury. We meant to strengthen him ; we wish to cripple the present fellow. But our object is the same, viz., to prevent a dissolution of the Empire. . . . I do not see that our memorial (I protest against your calling it petition) wants any alteration. It is as true now as then.'

February 12, 1886, a curious letter from Mr. Gladstone to Lord De Vesci invited:

' free communication of views from the various classes and sections most likely to supply full and authentic knowledge of the wants and wishes of the Irish people, I mean of all classes of Irish people, whether belonging to a majority or a minority, and whether they may be connected with the land, with industry, or with property in general. . . ."

The Defence Union accepted the challenge to take part in the Spelling Bee thus suggested, and did send Mr. Gladstone a reply, shortly afterwards, signed by Lords Pembroke and Bramwell.

Meanwhile Lord Bramwell had written, February 18, 1896 :

'. . . I do not suppose it would be the least use to send Gladstone anything—even a message from heaven—so far as influencing him is concerned ; but a good stinging letter to him, if we could get it published, might do good. At all events, it would prevent his saying that he invited information and got none. . . .'

Concerning a proposed deputation to the Lord Mayor in the following year, he wrote, January 7, 1887 :

'. . . You know better than I do who should go. The Duke of Westminster is an impressive speaker, Lord Pembroke is first-rate, Lord Longford is very good, so are Lord Belmore and Lord Powerscourt. Lord Hillingdon is weighty, Sir Whittaker Ellis would be good, so Mr. Grenfell. (Of course, keep these names to yourself.) . . . Our meeting or deputation is an advertisement. We must keep on showing our intents and wants—what we do and why we want to do it. . . .'

May 26, 1889, of a rather florid speaker on his own side, he wrote :

'. . . I do not very much admire ——'s oration. It might be good as one, but is poor as a writing. There is *no* contempt of court in it ; besides, I think everybody is sick of *that* nonsense.'

Enclosing draft of a letter, which appeared in the *Times*, headed 'A Cruel Case of Boycotting,' he wrote :

'*April* 28, 1890.

'. . . All you want me to do is to write to the *Times* saying we have sent Quinlan £20. Surely *you* are the right person to do that as honorary secretary, and I would rather you did. It might be as under. . . . I think we ought not to be receiving money. Take my own case: I shall give nothing this year. How can I receive from others ? . . .'

At the end of 1887 it occurred to Sir George Baden Powell to refute the errors contained in 'A Handbook to the Home Rule Question" by publishing a series of essays by personal friends under the title of 'The Truth about Home Rule,' hence these letters :

'Four Elms,
'Edenbridge, Kent,
'*November* 14, 1887.

'DEAR SIR,
     'I had not heard of the "Handbook of Home Rule." I think it will be a good thing to meet it by a similar work. I will do my best to write something, but I am a bad hand. I can't write unless coxswained by my subject. You must not limit me, therefore. If what I write does not suit you, put it unceremoniously in the waste-paper basket.

'Yours faithfully,
'BRAMWELL.

'G. Baden Powell, Esq., M.P.'

'*November* 20, 1887.

'. . . I send my paper on Home Rule. I am not satisfied with it. It contains nothing new, and does not state what is old with any particular vigour or incisiveness. Do what you please with it. If not good in itself, or not so good as any-

19

thing on the same subject, put it in the waste-paper basket. It is vilely written. I suppose if you determine to print it I must revise the proofs. . . .'

'February 24, 1888.

'. . . I do not know that I can mend my paper in substance, but there are two misprints to correct, and some things would be better expressed, if the expense is not too great. Page 51, "garb" should be in italics. "Probably not the speaker" would be better expressed "probably not the man who used the word." "But the law" should be "but the land." Page 53, strike out the sentence, "If a farm" down to "right for the second," and substitute, "If a farm, over and above a fair return for the capital and labour expended upon it, produces £10, that £10 is rent. . . ."

Some more corrections are added, and the letter winds up :

'. . . I am very glad that the thing has been a success.'

This graceful letter to him of February, 1886, illustrates those fine courtesies which are the anti-septic ingredient in English party politics. But the following article on 'Coercion,' in the *Liberal Unionist*, April 13, 1887, seems to show that, spite of the conventional civilities, a deep gulf was fixed between these two sworn guardians of law and order :

' My dear Baron,

' Pray accept my heartiest thanks. When I was apply-ing to be made Q.C. fourteen years ago, and expressed the obligations I owed to you, you told me that I was the real cause of my own success. I then replied that if I was the *causa causans*, you were the *causa sine qua non*. As that was a step to this, you will see that you are to some extent respon-sible . . . so I hope you will bear this in mind when disposed to be severe on, it may be, political or economical heresies. . . .'

To the third issue of the *Liberal Unionist*, April 13, 1887, Lord Bramwell contributed a paper on :

'Coercion.

'The Executive Government of this country, charged with the maintenance of law and order, has introduced a Bill into Parliament for that purpose. Messrs. Gladstone, Parnell, and their followers persistently and carefully call it a Coercion Bill. It is not, and they know it; but their consciences not troubling them, they are politic and wise in calling it what they do. For coercion is a hateful thing to Englishmen, and the word is a hateful word, and those who think the word truly describes the Bill, and that the Bill is the hateful thing "coercion," will naturally oppose it. What's in a name? Nothing in itself. But if the name is false, and means something other than the truth, there is a great deal in a name. Let us see what is the truth as to this Bill.

'There are parts of Ireland where the law is inoperative, where crimes are committed with impunity—murder, attempts at murder, arson, destroying, burning, and maiming cattle, threatening letters, stealing of arms, midnight attacks on houses, assaults, threats, intimidation. One may mention, as an instance, cutting off the hair of two young women, and covering their heads with tar.

'It is not necessary to go into statistics, not necessary to inquire whether there are more now than at some former time. It is enough to say that these crimes exist in parts of Ireland, unpunished, to such an extent and in such a way that the law is powerless. Power is in the hands of those who break the law; life and property are at their mercy, and peaceable and orderly persons are in constant terror that they and those most dear to them, their persons and the fruits of their industry, may be attacked, injured, and destroyed.

'Of course, no one of repute or authority justifies this— openly. The misguided wretches who commit these crimes may think they are right, and there doubtless are those above them in station who secretly tell them so; but there is a dis-creditable want of condemnation of these barbarous and cruel outrages from those who have still some character to lose. Instead of a loud and indignant denunciation of them, there is something like an attempt to extenuate or palliate them. An English lawyer has said it was some excuse that they are committed to reduce rents! What is that but for gain or profit? And what was the motive of the men who murdered the unfortunate woman in Kentish Town to get her safe and money but gain and profit? This gentleman should remember that those who are the victims of these crimes are satisfied that they are in the right, that they have done nothing which should be punished by law or lawlessness. Does anyone suppose that poor Curtin and his unhappy children had a misgiving that they were doing wrong? Mr. Gladstone has attempted to extenuate the filthy outrage on the girls whose hair was cut, and who were tarred, by saying that the pitch-cap was an invention of the yeomanry, I think, about the year 1798! Well might he pray for a majority at the election in 1885 if he foresaw that for want of it he might be tempted to utter this disgraceful thing. Unfortunate for his character and reputation has been his study of Irish history. With these encouragements, and the feeling of the offenders and parts of the populace, and the approval of the priests, it is hopeless to expect that the crimes I have mentioned will diminish except by force of law. At present that does not exist. Let us see why.

'Crimes are unpunished. Terror prevents their discovery. Terror prevents their prosecution. Terror prevents honest evidence being given, and worse than all, when difficulties are got over, terror or dishonesty prevents a true verdict according to the evidence. There can be no doubt of this. Juries are threatened. They are held up to hatred and scorn and revenge. The names of those who would convict are made public. There can be no doubt that false verdicts of "Not Guilty" are given, and that when that cannot be secured the jury are discharged, because among them was one, perhaps more, who disregarded his oath and refused to say the truth.

'This is the condition of things which the Government Bill seeks to alter. What should be its provisions is a fair subject for discussion. Those in the Bill may be more or less than needed for the object. But they are not "coercion." They are to make the law in Ireland what it is in England and Scotland—respected and obeyed. Unless that respect and obedience are coercion in England, they will not be in Ireland.

' BRAMWELL.'

A letter dated January 11, 1892, from a distinguished man, who differed from him fundamentally on Irish questions, began thus, the reference being to some irritating but quite baseless newspaper criticism :

'MY DEAR LORD BRAMWELL,

'. . . You are the only survivor of the three Judges from whom, in the early days of my utterly friendless struggle at the Bar, I mainly received words of kindness and encouragement ; the others were Mr. Justice Willes and Baron Martin. I should indeed be grieved if any statements . . . should in the least degree dim the good opinion of me which (I believe I am right in thinking) you have hitherto entertained. . . .'

Here is a *Times* letter of no great polemical value—in effect, a contemptuous way of saying: ' Just listen to this man ! What is he not capable of ?'

'MR. GLADSTONE'S ENGLISH.

'In your Monday's paper you say, "There is not the slightest sign that Mr. Gladstone is disposed to drop Home Rule." Not the slightest. He is as bad as ever. In the last number of the *Nineteenth Century* he speaks of the "devilish enginery" of the means employed to bring about the Union (p. 5).

'In the same paragraph are some passages worth notice. "Our judgment on the age that last preceded us should be strictly just." Why on that age in particular ? "But it should be masculine, not timorous ; for if we gild its defects and glorify its errors, we dislocate the axis of the very ground which forms our own point of departure."

'By gilding defects and glorifying errors an axis would be dislocated—that axis is an axis of ground, and that ground forms a point of departure!   Is not this somewhat in the style of a barrister who said to a jury, " Gentlemen, I smell a rat; I hear him brewing in the storm, but his thunder is moonshine"?   Had the barrister any clear notion of what he was talking about?

'Your obedient servant,
'B.'

But memorable as in effect a rebuke from a renowned English Judge and member of the highest Court of Appeal in the Empire to a man who had been three times Prime Minister of England, the same man who six years before had written to Sir George Bramwell at Barcelona :

' 10, Downing Street,
'Whitehall,
'*December* 8, 1881.

'My dear Sir,

'I have the pleasure of proposing to you, with the sanction of Her Majesty, that you should be raised to the peerage.   You will, I hope, accept this offer; and if such be your judgment, you will, I am sure, contribute greatly to the efficiency of the House of Lords in the discharge of its judicial functions; while the honour to be conferred on you will be recognized by the world as no more than a just tribute to your long service and the great eminence attained through your abilities and learning.

' I remain, my dear sir,
' Faithfully yours,
' W. E. Gladstone.

' Rt. Hon. Sir G. W. W. Bramwell.'

Possibly remembering how the Solicitor-Generalship had been 'somewhat strangely vacated' by Sir

R. Collier in October, 1871, Sir George Bramwell
took care to ascertain that Lord Selborne, Chancellor,
had concurred in this offer, before finally accepting
it.   Meanwhile he had written to some faithful
friends at home :

' Avignon,
'*December* 13, 1881.

'. . . What *do* you think ? I got a letter from Gladstone
this morning offering me a peerage, and I have accepted. Of
course I am pleased. Lady B. is very pleased, but for my
sake. I told Gladstone I was on my travels, but I suppose it
can be done in my absence. The thing that pleases me most
is that I shall be kept among old friends and old pursuits. I
shall live all the longer for it. What title shall I take ? I
think it must be " Bramwell." . . . This is all very fine, but
a greater pleasure is that this infernal weather has not given
Lady B. any cough, nor harm, that I can see. . . . Of course,
the offer is no secret, but I don't want people to suppose that
I can't keep quiet about it.

'G. BRAMWELL.'

Most of what Lord Bramwell wrote on the political
or ' Separatist ' aspect of the Home Rule controversy
(next to that about Free Trade, the most elaborate
tournament of opinion the nation has ever seen) is
omitted.   In substance it may be found in contemporary speeches and writings of distinguished
Unionists, and all reads now like old news not yet
ripened into history.   As to the work of steering
public opinion, so well done by Liberal Unionists
(they contributed the brains), some persons may
wonder in these days whether the whole of it was
really needed.   J. A. Froude said, in 1886, of the
Home Rule controversy, that one day John Bull would
wake up, pull on his big boots, and kick somebody ;

which is perhaps what happened in the end, irrespective of all the weighty speeches and letters, many of them only read by specialists and leisured enthusiasts. A long letter of Lord Bramwell's to the *Times*, January, 1891, meant in all good faith to convince Mr. Arthur —— (a gentleman who wrote in the character of an English Nonconformist Home Ruler sincerely anxious to be convinced), makes one suspect that a vast amount of temperate, judicial reasoning, much patiently repeated refutation of the same incredible statements and arguments, may have been wasted by Liberal Unionists in those years.

The *Times* letter of January, 1891, in reply to Mr. ——, indicates that Lord Bramwell held stricter views about breach of marital relations than 'great men' are conventionally supposed to hold.

'. . . Their principal leader . . . has been shown to be party to as filthy a case of adultery as could be conceived. I would not be supposed to palliate adultery. It is always a crime—a crime to the husband, to the woman. But when an unhappy passion has seized the offenders and they give way to it, objects of blame as they are, they are almost objects of pity. In this case a friend's wife is debauched for six years. The filthy intercourse is continued, the woman shared by the adulterer with the husband; every dirty, false pretence resorted to to gratify a lust which showed no respect for the woman. Is this a man to be trusted? Would any decent man shake hands with him, or deal with him, buy of or sell to him? Why trust him as a party leader? . . .'

When one comes upon a *Times* letter of 1885, beginning, ' Lord Hartington said at Belfast, " The people of the United Kingdom will never assent to the practical separation of " . . .' one can, without difficulty, imagine the rest.   A *Times* letter, signed ' B.,' December 3, 1887, on ' Political Prisoners,' deals with a question of constitutional casuistry hotly discussed for centuries, and, as manifestations of public opinion on more recent incidents in South Africa show, quite unsettled still.

' Who or what is a political prisoner ?   Definitions are difficult, but we may give instances.   Guy Fawkes was a political prisoner.   Mr. John Cade would have been, if not otherwise disposed of.   The three men who murdered Sergeant Brett at Manchester for doing his duty were political prisoners.   The man who meant to fling dynamite into the House of Commons is a political prisoner, and so are those who stabbed and stoned the police in Trafalgar Square.   So, I suppose, are the men who murdered Whelehan.

' Now, without attempting a definition, we may draw an inference from these cases, and say that a political prisoner is a man who is dissatisfied with the law or its administration, and who breaks the law to procure a change in it or its execution.

' This definition or description includes all breakers of the law with the object of procuring a change in it or its administration.   There need be no violence.   Treason may be committed very peacefully.   Sedition, holding forbidden assemblies, publishing forbidden publications, are all, like treason, forbidden.   The man who does any of them for the purpose mentioned commits a political crime, and, if in prison for it, is a political prisoner.   Mr. O'Brien, then, is a political prisoner.   So will Mr. C. Graham be if convicted.

' Now, is there any reason why political prisoners should be better treated than others ?   No doubt their offences are less low and dirty than picking pockets.   Perhaps a murder is less revolting when committed for political considerations than when committed for gain.   It may be that the three who murdered Brett, and political criminals generally, are less horrible than those who murder or commit other crime for profit. But they are as mischievous, and much more so. And, paradoxical as it is, the very fact that the crimes do not inspire the same aversion, contempt, and hatred, makes necessary severer punishment.

' If a man picks a pocket or steals a sheep for the gain, he is at once despised by his fellow-creatures—at least, by those whose good opinion he values. But if he murders a policeman who is doing his duty, and is most properly hung for his crime, he is called a martyr, and his memory is honoured by a chief priest and other ministers of his religion, who, I think, must have forgotten the Sixth Commandment, or read it with a qualification, thus: " Thou shalt not kill, unless for political purposes." I ask, in all sad seriousness, is it not certain that the horror of taking life, the feeling that he who does so will be looked on as a Cain, is taken away by this; and with it taken away one of the strongest deterrents from crime, viz., the desire of the good opinion of one's fellow-creatures? And let it be remembered that political crimes, like other crimes, must be dealt with, not according to the opinions and feelings of those who commit them, but according to the opinions and feelings of those against whom they are committed, while power remains with them. " You think it right to shoot a policeman. We think it wrong—most wicked and mischievous. We think it right to hang you, and hang you without providing a silk rope on account of your motives."

' Consider the position of men who rebel—I am not going to repeat the old joke. A successful rebellion almost presumes its justification—at all events, it cannot be punished. But an unsuccessful rebellion, the use of force with the object of rebellion, and of sedition to excite the use of force or terrify those who object—these are the worst of crimes, and involve the possibility of more deaths, wounds, destruction of property, and misery than all other crimes in the code put together.

' And see the temptations to commit them. Let us suppose those mild and orderly gentlemen, the Home Rulers, should be minded to separate Ireland from Britain, which, of course, at present is far from their intention. What would be their reward? Possibly one would be King of Ireland or President of the Irish Republic; others, Commander-in-Chief, Lord Chancellor, Chancellor of the Exchequer, and so forth. If they tried and failed, on the other hand, they would be patriots, perhaps martyrs, beloved by their followers, and honoured with statues and monuments. It is a tempting game—immense profit if successful, great consolation and honour if not.

'This is the political prisoner—the most mischievous of all offenders. Are we to treat him with consideration because he is not ashamed of himself, because he is not a thief, but ten times worse? I say "No," and trust the good sense of our people will not permit it.

'Your obedient servant,
'B.'

A letter of September, 1886, about that Bill of Mr. Parnell's the rejection of which was put forward as an excuse for the Plan of Campaign, shows that Lord Bramwell, after sixteen years' consideration of the Irish Land Act of 1870, held that the principles of political economy and Anglo-Saxon jurisprudence did apply to Ireland, as well as to other parts of the kingdom.

'MR. PARNELL'S BILL.

'I earnestly hope the Government will oppose every part of Mr. Parnell's Bill. It recites that, "having regard to the great depreciation in the prices of agricultural produce since the greater number of judicial rents of tenancies were fixed, it is expedient to make temporary provision for the relief in certain cases of the tenants of such holdings." This is the reason given, and, as you have shown, it is untrue. Next, it enacts that where certain rent has been paid, and the tenant is unable to discharge the remainder without loss of his holding or deprivation of the means necessary for the cultivation and stocking thereof, the Court may make such an abatement of the rent as may seem to them "just and expedient." There is here no restriction to cases where the tenant is unable to pay owing to the fall in the prices of agricultural produce. The tenant's inability may arise from his bad farming, his neglect, his subscription to the League, money paid for drink; but if unable to pay he may have an abatement. If it should be said that the Act is only intended to apply to cases where the inability arises from the depreciation, it had better be so said. But, then, what a question is opened!

'Further, suppose there is a case where the tenant is unable to pay owing to a fall in prices, why should he continue to hold his land at a less rent? Why should he not give it up to his landlord, as he has agreed to do? What would be the case in England or Scotland? Oh, but, says the arch-phrasemonger, there is a "land hunger" in Ireland, and so the tenant must be protected from agreeing to pay the rent he would agree to pay if left to himself. Hence the Land Acts of 1870 and 1881, and in effect the present proposal.

'I believe, myself, that these Acts are at the bottom of the present state of things in Ireland. I once visited a prison and was shown a prisoner who could earn thirty shillings a week at his trade of a shoemaker. I said to him I thought that was better than imprisonment. He looked at me rather contemptuously, and said, "Why should I work for that when I can get twice as much without work another way?" This is the feeling of Mr. Parnell's supporters in the Irish tenantry. Why should they pay their rent when by not doing so, but by murdering, moonlighting, boycotting, and the like, they can plunder their landlords further and get the land for less? By such means they have got their land on the present terms, and by such means they hope to get it for less.

'But there are the Acts; and, as the Marquis of Salisbury has said, it is impossible to repeal them. But at least the mischief can be prevented going further. If the tenant cannot pay the judicial rent, let him give up his land and let the terms on which he shall hold it be matter of bargain between him and his landlord. It is idle to suppose that there would be wholesale evictions even if the rent could not be paid. If the farmer has a hunger for land, the landlord has a hunger for tenants. He can no more do without them than the farmer can do without land.   Let the reasons of good sense and political economy which were flippantly banished to Jupiter and Saturn once again prevail ; let people make their own bargains, and let the law enforce them, and we shall have peace and order again.

'As to the proposal that proceedings to recover rent or possession shall be suspended while an application for reduction of rent is pending, it is monstrous.   What would be thought in England of a law which stayed proceedings to recover rent or possession till the tenant had shown or failed to show that he had agreed to pay too much rent ?   In Ireland it is worse than it would be here, because, as you have said, the landlords by Act of Parliament had a fourth of their rents taken from them, on the terms of being paid the residue, or of having their land restored to them.   Further, there is, as you have pointed out, the power in the County Court Judges of staying execution.   But there is a " land hunger," and there is a League.

' Your obedient servant,

' B.'

CHAPTER IX.

ANTI - RAILWAY AGITATION — TITHE RENT-CHARGE—WATER RATES—COPYHOLD—COMPANIES ACT, 1862.

Attack on railways ; partly an incident in campaign against capitalism — Partly the attempt of harassed farmers and manufacturers to find compensations for injurious legislation — His letters to *Economist* — The ' Preference to Foreigners' mare's nest—Penal legislation in 1888—Its futility—Tithe rent-charge—Land-owners' effort to find compensation for injuries done to them by Parliament—His letter explaining statutory bargain made—Lord Brabourne's plea for some kind of confiscation—Torrens's Act of 1885—Lord Bramwell in *Economist* and *Times* on rights of water companies—Extent of confiscation under Act of 1885 — Copyhold Bills — Echo of campaign against landlordism. Proposals to compel copyholders to become freeholders *nolens volens*—His protest in press and Parliament—Reminiscences of Royal Commission of 1853 and Companies Act, 1862—Word ' limited.'

AGITATION about railway rates between 1874 and 1894, and legislation consequent, have no repulsive elements, no gangrene of injustice to innocent individuals such as the Irish confiscations of 1870, 1881 *et seq.* exhibit. The ' innocent parties ' assailed never actually suffered much, since the economic penalty, direct and indirect, for threats, hostile legislation, etc., has fallen mainly upon those farmers and 'traders' who, between 1874 and 1894, further developed that short-sighted policy initiated by foolish or greedy landowners after 1836. Exactions by the latter class in early days burthened British railways with enormous capital expenditure, interest on which has to be paid for ever in one way or another by the travelling and trading public. So soon as events convinced silly land-owners that railways benefited, instead of damaging them, the still sillier Reformed Parliament took up the work begun by land-owners; ruinous Standing Orders and pettifogging absurdities in Committees between 1836 and 1846 compelled further useless capital outlay, amounting to from ten to fifteen millions sterling, interest upon which also has to be paid for ever by railway-users mainly. After 1870 Parliament turned its attention to land-owners. Increased taxation, statutory breaking of contracts, State-made insecurity of landed property generally (all intended to benefit agricultural tenants) naturally reacted upon English tenants themselves, who, groping about in the dark to find the origin of their misfortunes, were told by persons as uninstructed but more eloquent than themselves, that 'the railways' were to blame. 'Railways' were rich. Parliamentary interference had forced upon them successive combinations in self-defence, thereby, as Stephenson said, making free competition among these carriers impossible. The inland carrying trade on a mighty scale, the determination of millions of freight rates, are difficult matters—

easy, however, for ' traders ' to make misstatements about in grammatical language.   Between 1874 and 1894 agriculturists and ' traders ' asked Parliament, which had done so much to blight British agriculture and was doing the like for industry, to make the most elaborate and successful system of land-transport ever devised more costly, insecure, hazardous, for shareholders, less advantageous to the public ; and asked not in vain.

In July, 1884, professional vote-brokers in the House of Commons had invented a new Standing Order, giving chambers of commerce and agricultural associations a *locus standi* before railway committees, so that they might more effectually blackmail companies seeking new powers under existing Acts—in the way Lord Bramwell describes below. The House of Lords, at that period unwilling to do conscious injustice, altered the Standing Order by limiting ' the trader's ' power of intervention to cases where companies sought new Acts, not new ' powers.' This righteous alteration, the *Economist* said, ' deprived the new Standing Order of much of its value. . . . Parliament could reduce existing railway rates at pleasure,' etc.

On August 2, 1884, Lord Bramwell wrote :

' RAILWAY RATES AND FARES.

' I am sorry the *Economist* disapproves of the alteration made by the Lords in the proposed Standing Order as to railway Bills.   The proposal, to my mind, was most unreasonable.   It amounted to this : if a railway company, doubtless for its own good, asked Parliament for powers the exercise of which would also be for the good of the public, those powers were not to be given unless the company made some sacrifice of its existing rights. I say of its existing rights, because if the complaint is that the company is doing wrong, there is the law to set them right, and I say 'asking for powers the exercise of which would be for the public good,' because unless it would be the powers ought not to be granted, however free from complaint the company might be. See how it would work. A railway company goes to Parliament for powers to enlarge its station, or make a branch line, no doubt having in view its own profit. On inquiry before Committee, it appears that the enlargement of the station or making of the branch line will be a great convenience to the public, but a chamber of commerce has made out that hops are carried on terms lawful, and profitable to the company, but inconvenient to traders. What is the Committee to do? Throw out the Bill unless the company will make more sacrifice? Impossible. They ought no more to do so than if the powers were sought by an independent company. To do so would be to say, " Unless you give up a lawful right you have, we will inconvenience the public." But unless they ought to do so, no one ought to be heard to ask them to do so. The company asks for a boon, but a boon to the public as well as to themselves.

' B.'

In February, 1886, the Gladstone Government had promised a Railway Bill, 'embracing' Railway Commissioners with great powers. At the London and North-Western meeting the chairman pointed out (as had been done often) that if the company did not compete in freights with steamships, goods would be carried to London by water instead of by rail. This, the *Economist* remarked, meant 'if we acted according to the law which forbids discrimination' (there was no such law), 'we should be out of pocket ; therefore we are justified in breaking the law ;' went on to compare the case of a railway company's cashier who complained that he was unable to get rich by stealing the company's money —because stealing was clearly against the law— with the policy of railways and in respect to competing through rates. It was also asserted that companies charged exorbitant way rates to make up for what they lost on through rates—'reduced to benefit the foreigner.'

On February 27 'Inquirer' asked the *Economist* :

'(1) Are low competitive rates given solely to foreigners ? How about coal carried by railway from Durham and South Wales in competition with carriage by sea ? (2) Are " differential " rates really illegal ? (3) Do railways carry on their competitive through traffic at a loss ? If they are prevented by Parliament from carrying such traffic, does it follow that they will lower way freights ? And if so, *why ?*'

No answer has been given to the arguments indicated by these questions.

On March 6 Lord Bramwell wrote :

' When you answer the questions of " Inquirer," will you favour me with an answer to the following :
'(1) If differential rates are wrong, is the wrong to be remedied by lowering the high or raising the low rate? (2) Would not a compulsory lowering of the high rate be unjust and confiscation ? (3) Would raising the low rate benefit the public in any way ?

' Your obedient servant,

' B.'

Same date the *Economist* replied to ' Inquirer,' that railway traffic managers did not themselves know whether competitive through traffic was carried at a loss or not ; and to ' B.,' that lowering or reducing rates should be left to railway companies. For Parliament to compulsorily lower the high rate would be confiscation. Then a question was asked, to which Lord Bramwell replied :

'*March* 13, 1886.

'You ask me whether I think that a railway company is acting within the law which charges 45s. a ton for the carriage of Canadian beef, and 77s. a ton for Scotch beef from Glasgow to London, and are pleased to say that you would value my opinion highly. I should be sorry to give it without hearing what could be said for and against such conduct. If not within the law, I neither uphold it nor defend it; but I may still ask whether those who eat Canadian beef would be benefited by its carriage being raised.

'The case I intended to put to you was one when the differential rates are both perfectly legal, as, for example, the carriage of hops from Boulogne by the South-Eastern Railway Company through Ashford to London, at a less rate than from Ashford only, and I repeat my question : If the company was compelled to reduce the rate from Ashford to the rate from Boulogne, would it not be confiscation ? And if compelled to raise the rate from Boulogne, would hop-consumers benefit thereby ?

'Your obedient servant,

'B.

'["B." says that if differential rates are not within the law, he will neither uphold nor defend them. But, surely, before he talks of confiscation he ought to make sure of their legality, because it is evidently wrong to characterize as confiscatory legislation which aims only at enforcing a statutory obligation.—ED. *Economist.*]'

In May, 1886, a Railway Bill of Mr. Mundella's was read a second time. The *Economist* remarked there could be no confiscation in the Bill since the Stock Exchange did not take alarm. Justice in respect to rates must be obtained from railway companies by force. When Lord Grimthorpe said that railway companies ought to be left to manage their own affairs, he was talking mischievous nonsense ; railways had a State-conferred monopoly. Parliament had expressly reserved the right to enforce revision of rates when it thought fit, etc.

March 27, Mr. J. Buckingham Pope, 'probably a lawyer,' had intervened in the controversy thus :

'The traders say that when Parliament granted monopolies to the railway companies, and compelled private owners to part with their land for railway purposes, it did so in the interests of the State, and that for the due protection of the State certain bargains were made with the railway companies. The traders do not ask for legislation of a confiscating character, but they require and have a right to insist that the terms made by Parliament on their behalf shall be strictly adhered to. . . .'

Subsequently Mr. Pope demanded from the State drastic measures against railway companies. In the spring of 1897 a gentleman of this name, 'going towards Damascus,' was miraculously converted, on the way, to sound individualistic views by the interference of the so-called Conservative Government with freedom of contract as between employers and employed.

On March 20, 1886, Lord Bramwell wrote again :

'One more try for an answer to my question. The South-Eastern Railway carries, or carried, hops from Ashford to London at a certain rate. They also carry, or carried, hops from Boulogne through Ashford to London at a lower rate. Both rates were lawful, and lawful concurrently. My question is, Would the public gain by the raising of the Boulogne rate to that of Ashford ?

' Your obedient servant,

' B.'

' [We should be glad to be referred by " B." to the decision which establishes the legality of the differential rate on hops to which he refers. . . .—Ed. *Economist.*]'

And to the above editorial note as follows (March 27):

' There is no decision which establishes the legality of the differential rates on hops which I mentioned. But there is no doubt about the matter, whatever the hop-growers may hold.'

On May 1 Mr. J. B. Pope wrote again, asking Lord Bramwell to say how he was wrong in his law. On May 8 Lord Bramwell did so :

' Mr. Pope is wrong. " Differential " rates are illegal when they are for the " same services, under the same circumstances "—3 Appeal Cases, 1,029—otherwise not. Even if his construction was right, he would be wrong in saying, as he does, that the rate from Boulogne was illegal. The *higher*, not the *lower*, rate is illegal—where one is. . . .'

In the Session of 1887 a Railway Rates Bill was submitted to Parliament, but withdrawn. On February 9 Lord Bramwell wrote to the *Times :*

' In your paper of Thursday is the following :

' " One speaker said that the Great Eastern Railway charge twice as much for bringing fish from Harwich as they do for bringing it from Rotterdam. If the charge from Rotterdam is remunerative, then they are acting most unfairly and unjustly towards the people at Harwich. If the contrary, then they are carrying foreign fish at a loss which has to be made up by exacting double profits from the home trade." " If they get less than the average profit from the foreigner, then they must get more than the average from the native, who is thus directly taxed to enable his rival to undersell him."

'I venture to dispute the whole of this, which seems to me most unjust to the railway. Suppose they carried no fish from Rotterdam, would there be anything wrong, illegal, or immoral in the charge they make from Harwich ? Certainly not. They charge a sum they have a right by law to charge, a right which they bargained for when they made their railway, a charge which is not excessive, as shown by the price of their stock and the amount of their dividends, which have never yet returned a fair profit on their capital. But if their charge from Harwich is otherwise right, how can it be wrong because they carry from Rotterdam, charging, as doubtless they do, as much as they can get ? They would charge more if they could. But if they did they would not get the traffic. The fish would come direct by sea or not at all. They do not make the Rotterdam rate low to give the Dutch an advantage, but simply because they cannot help it. They do not exact double profits from the home trade to make up a loss on the foreign ; they do not act unfairly and unjustly to the people of Harwich because they make some profit on the foreign trade. Suppose A agrees to carry B to X for 10s., and then C says, "Take me there for 1s.," and A agrees, is any injustice done to B ? A has his carriage and horse, and will make an extra shilling by carrying C. He would not have put to for C's shilling. The railway company has its railway. It would not construct it to carry Rotterdam fish at the price at which it carries it, but, the railway being there, it ekes out its miserable profit by carrying at the rate at which it does.

'You talk of "getting profit from the foreigner." It is the consumer who pays the carriage, and I should like to know whether the consumer would be benefited by the carriage of Dutch fish being raised. If the present state of things is wrong, how is it to be remedied ? Must the railway lower its charge to the Harwich fishermen ? To make it do so would be confiscation. It has bargained for its right. Is it to raise its charge to the Dutchmen ? It simply would not carry for them any longer, to its own loss and that of the consumer. . . .'

In August, 1888, the Railway and Canal Traffic Act was passed. On February 16, 1889, Lord

Bramwell wrote to the *Economist*, which then demanded further interference by the Board of Trade with railway freight charges :

'I regret to read in your paper of the 9th, "Is not the fact that the company is earning its 15 per cent. dividend a proof that there is ample room for a lowering of rates?" Ample room there may be, but would it be just to lower them? In the case of a railway which pays no dividend there is ample room for raising the rates; but would a claim to have them raised for that reason be listened to? And what an injustice would be done to present holders by the suggested lowering! Probably half of them have bought at prices calculated on the belief that the rights given by statute would not be infringed.

'You ask, to my infinite astonishment, "Is it not the business of the authority that hands over a district to the exclusive dominion of one railway company to see that there are not exacted from it profits far in excess of what similar undertakings elsewhere are able to earn?" In the first place, the district is not handed over to an exclusive dominion. There is nothing to prevent Parliament giving powers to another railway company in the same district. In the next place, excessive profits are not exacted from that district. Lastly, there is no "exaction." The railway company has made a good and fortunate bargain with the State, and avails itself of its rights. Confiscation is popular with many, but alas that the *Economist* should be among them!

'B.'

But apparently in the case of gigantic concerns like British railways (and brewery companies) no part of the loss due to hostile or vexatious legislative interference falls directly upon the class struck at— shareholders. Any artificial restraint, or destruction of trade which impoverishes the community does indeed indirectly but surely injure railway companies in the long-run, because they prosper only when their customers prosper.   Nevertheless, one cannot kill a bullock with the same weapon that will slay a caterpillar.   The Board of Trade was not big enough for the mischievous task entrusted to it by Parliament.   Lord Salisbury 'in his Conservative days' had said :

'. . . Parliament is a potent engine. . . .   Its enactments almost always do something ; but . . . seldom . . . what the originators of these enactments meant.   The result, to use a technical phrase, is the resultant of a composition of two forces . . . the enacting force of Parliament and the evading force of the individual.'

The *Economist's* comment upon this was :

'The truths here stated demand the attention of politicians of all shades of opinion, and deserve to be written in letters of gold upon the walls of every Legislature in the civilized world.'

So soon as the Board of Trade schedules under the Act of 1888 were promulgated, railway companies (representing economically Lord Salisbury's 'evading force of the individual') very naturally said :

'Before we put more money into our business, we must wait and see how this new enactment works.   If the right to fix our charges is to pass away from us, we must ascertain what our new masters are willing to vouchsafe us in the shape of remuneration for our services before we risk further capital.'

The answer to this, from the political astrologists, was that 'the State' should compel railway companies to continue their expenditure on improvements, branch lines, etc., under threat that shareholders' rights would be confiscated if they refused.

The anti-tithe agitation of 1886-87 was, in Wales, an attenuated copy of the Irish No-Rent Movement; that indispensable element of racial and religious antipathy which transforms the Welsher into the martyr, being contributed by Nonconformist pastors and their political dependents. In England the agitation was mainly an effort among land-owners and farmers to evade consequences of agricultural depression, the real origin of which they and their political leaders were pledged not to understand. Or, putting it another way, English land-owners harassed, penalized, impoverished by the Legislature, in its anxiety to 'protect' tenants, argued that, Parliament having given tenants power to repudiate contract obligations, surely land-owners might reasonably repudiate their legal obligations to tithe rent-charge owners? Lord Bramwell was more than usually impartial and 'detached' on this question. He did not care about the Church of England; did not constantly write long letters to his unoffending Bishop about nothing—the infallible symptom of enthusiasm for the Anglican Obedience. A very defective and loosely drafted Tithe Rent-Charge Bill brought into the House of Lords in the spring of 1883 was demolished by Lord Bramwell's criticism there. In 1886 the subject cropped up again.

On October 15, 1886, he wrote to the *Times*:

'Tithe Rent-Charge.

' Before the Tithe Commutation Act, tithe was rendered for some things in kind and for others by money payments. The person liable was the occupier, the producer of what was tithed. This mode of rendering and paying was bad : bad for the payer, bad for the receiver—the tithe-owner—and bad for the land-owner. For whatever is bad for the tenant is bad for the landlord. So inconvenient was it, that there was commonly a sum agreed on to be paid by the tenant to the tithe-owner. But though the tenant paid in the first instance, the burden was really borne by the landlord. For a farm tithe-free, or subject only to a small modus for tithe, would let for as much more rent than a farm liable to tithe as the tithe would amount to.

' This state of things was put an end to by the Tithe Commutation Act. That abolished tithe in kind and substituted for it a rent-charge. The amount of this was fixed in some cases by agreement between land-owner and tithe-owner. When they could not agree it was fixed by the Tithe Commissioners. Like other rent-charges, the burden of it is on the land-owner. It was fixed then for ever, for better for worse. If it had been fixed at so much per acre, say 5s. an acre, this would be too clear to be misunderstood. But it was not so fixed. It was supposed that gold might rise or fall in value, so that any fixed sum might be too much or too little. But it was supposed that one year with another wheat, barley, and oats would be of the same value, though their prices might alter, and so the sum to be paid was fixed with reference to the market prices from time to time of those articles.

' But that does not alter the case from what it would have been had the rent-charge been fixed absolutely at so many named shillings or pounds per acre, or farm, or field. It is a mistake to talk of the land-owner's share and the tithe-owner's share of the rent. The tithe-owner is entitled to his tithe, though there is nothing left for the land-owner, just as much as a man to whom the land-owner had granted a rent-charge would be entitled to it, though nothing remained for rent.

' Not only has the land-owner no legal right to deduct any-

thing from the tithe-owner's rent-charge : he has no equitable
or moral right or claim to do so. As I have said, the arrangement was made much to the land-owner's benefit, for better
for worse for all time. If things had turned out differently, as,
for instance, if, though wheat, barley, and oats had fallen,
cattle and sheep had risen in price, the tithe-owner would have
had no claim to have a revision of the arrangement. And it
may be observed that the land-owner is no worse off than he
would be if tithe was still taken in kind. The nine cocks of
hay or shocks of wheat would be as little able to pay rent as
the whole crop is minus the tithe rent-charge.

' I think it important that this should be understood, and it
is clear from some letters in your paper that it is not. The
tithe-owner is entitled to be paid in full, the land-owner is only
entitled to what remains of the rent after paying tithe rent-
charge, when the landlord pays it ; or, when the tenant pays
it, to what rent the tenant in addition pays the landlord. If
the tithe-owner gives up any part of what he is entitled to, it is
a gift, a present to the land-owner.

' But, unhappily, there are cases where the land cannot be
used with profit, if it is to bear the tithe rent-charge. I am
afraid there are many thousand acres in this condition.
Suppose the rent of the land—that is, what would remain after
a fair return for capital and labour bestowed on it—is 4s. an
acre ; suppose the tithe is 5s. an acre. That land is not worth
occupying.

' That does not present a case for legislation, except to
validate reasonable bargains between land and tithe owner—
viz., that the tithe should be reduced either temporarily or
permanently. Legislation for this purpose would be necessary
when the tithe-owner has only a life or other less interest than
the fee-simple. Such bargains would be reasonable and for
the benefit of both parties. Something of the same sort might
be arranged as to rates.

' Your obedient servant,
' BRAMWELL.'

In October, 1886, Mr. James Howard, of Clap-
ham, Beds, advanced in the *Times* the argument,

a very remarkable one coming from such a judicially-minded gentleman, that 'What "the State" had given "the State" can take away.' This argument at once ends all talk about vested interests as well as all indefeasible claims either to civil and religious freedom or to security of property. What people less judicially-minded than Mr. Howard were saying and thinking at the time can be imagined. Canon Blackley replied that 'the State' had never 'given' tithes, or equivalent charges on land, to anybody — a good but almost irrelevant reply. Private individuals, he pointed out, voluntarily charged their private property with such payments.

On October 26 Mr. Howard intimated that Canon Blackley's retort was a half-truth in the nature of a quibble, since 'the State,' if it did not give tithes, graciously consented to enforce payment of tithes. Here one comes across the popular theory of 'the State's' dispensing power : one day it may, another day not, enforce legal rights, protect property ; when it does the latter (as a favour), the freeman ought, in gratitude, to submit to minor confiscations of his goods—for the benefit of 'the State's' protégés. The further argument that rent-charge-owners would get better security, a better title, if they consented to forego a portion of their legal claim had also been used in 1881 to reconcile Irish land-owners and tender-conscienced Liberals to the Land Act of that year.

On October 23 Lord Bramwell wrote to the *Times :*

'Mr. Howard, in reference to my remark that the tithe rent-charge was "fixed for ever, for better for worse," says that he "believes that our Constitution knows nothing of irrevocable decrees; that no Act of Parliament that ever passed possesses the quality of endurance that distinguished the laws of the Medes and Persians." He is quite right; there is no doubt that Parliament has the power to reduce the tithe rent-charge by half or abolish it altogether. But what Mr. Howard overlooks is that what Parliament did was to make, or ratify, a bargain between the land-owner and tithe-owner—a bargain that was meant to be permanent and for ever; a bargain by which the tithe-owner gave up the right to tithe in return for a defined rent-charge, and the land-owner, in return, agreed to pay that rent-charge. The dividend on consols is 3 per cent.; Parliament could make it 2. Would Mr. Howard think that honest because it was possible? If the tithe-owner wanted his rent-charge raised, would he not be told that there was a bargain?

' Dr. Trevor says that there is an inconsistency between my saying that the tithe-owner is entitled to be paid in full, but that where there is not enough to do so it may be worth the tithe-owner's while to take less than his due. There is no inconsistency. It may be worth his while to do so, as otherwise he may get nothing. Take the case he puts—a rent-charge, not tithe, with power of distress. Suppose a tenant could afford a rent of £50 a year, and the rent-charge £60, no one could take the land, and neither landlord nor rent-charger would get anything; but if the rent-charger would take £40 a year, there would be £10 left for the land-owner—something for both. The right of the owner of the tithe rent-charge is to be paid in full, though the landlord may get nothing. It may be worth the while of the owner of the tithe rent-charge to take less when he cannot get more.'

And on February 15 of the following year:

'. . . In your impressive leader of to-day you say: "Nothing will induce the farmer to see that tithes are really not a tax upon him, but a tax upon the landlord." I am afraid that the landlord shares the farmer's opinion, for otherwise his conduct cannot be accounted for.

'The landlord, as you show, is liable for the charge. He appoints his tenant agent to pay it. The agent will not. What is the duty of the landlord? That which is the duty of every man who owes a debt—to pay it; if his appointed agent will not, pay it himself. Some landlords have set the good example of doing so. Is it desirable at the present time to be raising such questions as this state of things gives rise to? It is the duty of the land-owner (and his interest) to pay, or to see that his agent the tenant pays, the tithe-owner.'

On February 26, 1887, J. Laurie replied, as quoted in Lord Bramwell's next letter, suggesting also that 'the tithe is due neither from landlord nor tenant, but from the land itself'—a subtle idealization of the prosaic debtor and creditor relation. A legal difficulty was also propounded: Since neither landlord nor tenant could be sued for tithe, could there be any question of a personal debt? It was not very easy to impale Lord Bramwell on legal chevaux-de-frise. On March 3 he replied:

'I say that when a tenant will not pay the tithe rent-charge, the landlord, as a matter of common honesty, should do so. Your correspondent, J. Laurie, asks: "Should the landlord also pay rates if in arrear?" Certainly not. He does not owe the rates; he does owe tithe rent-charge. It is idle to make a doubt about it; the statute creating tithe rent charges him with it. A tenant distrained on for rent-charge can make his landlord indemnify him, unless he (the tenant) had agreed he would pay, and has a like remedy if distrained on for arrears owed by a former tenant. . . . Tithe rent-charge is *not* "due from the land." Land cannot owe, has no pocket out of which to pay debts. It is a mistake to suppose that there can be no debt, unless an action lies against the debtor. . . .'

On August 12, 1887, replying to Lord Brabourne, he wrote:

'THE TITHE RENT-CHARGE BILL.

'SIR,

'In your paper of Wednesday appeared a letter from Lord Brabourne on the Tithe Rent-Charge Bill, containing some matters that ought to be noticed.

'His lordship says that if the power of distress for tithe rent-charge is taken away distress for rent will follow. Certainly not. The tenant who pays rent knows that he gets his land in return; when he pays tithe he cannot see that he really pays it for his landlord, and pays all the less rent in consequence. He thinks he gets no money value in return, and, if a Dissenter, is disgusted to believe, as he does, that he is supporting a worship to which he objects.

'Lord Brabourne says that what is objected to is the amount of the tithe. Again, certainly not. The tithe-payer wants a reduction, because he wants and gets a reduction of rent, and has not the sense to see that, while it is the interest of his landlord to allow such reduction, the tithe-owner has no such interest. But to the amount of the tithe rent-charge the tenant does not otherwise object.

'Lord Brabourne next speaks of "the undue amount of the charge upon land." To my mind this is unmeaning. Undue amount! What is the due amount? One must begin at the beginning. Formerly tithes were taken in kind. They were a charge then on rent. If a farm was tithe-free, it let for all the more rent. Render or payment of tithe in kind was inconvenient to all parties, and the Tithe Commutation Act was passed, which substituted a rent-charge. By that Act a bargain was made between tithe and land owners by which a money payment was arranged, which was to vary with the prices of wheat, barley, and oats. This was a bargain made for all time, for better for worse. If prices so altered as to make it more burdensome for either party, so much the worse for him. But in such case neither had reserved any right against the other. To alter that bargain without consent of both parties is to do wrong. If anything is done, it should be to give the arrangement up altogether, and remit the tithe-owner to his right to tithe in kind, when he would be much better off than now. But I repeat it was a bargain for all time.

'Lord Brabourne proceeds : The British farmer knows if he takes a farm with £100 a year rent-charge he would have to pay less rent if that charge did not exist. Is this a slip, and should the word be " more," he paying it, or is it meant that if the landlord pays the tithe the tenant would pay less rent if tithe did not exist? Again, certainly not. Do landlords let tithe-free farms at a lower rent than farms liable to tithe, they paying it ?

'Lord Brabourne says that the Government Bill exposes small occupiers to imprisonment if they do not pay their tithe rent-charge. Yes, and large occupiers, too. I am surprised Lord Brabourne should have said this. If judgment is got for any debt, and the defendant can pay, but distinctly and con-tumaciously refuses to pay, not otherwise, he may be sent to prison, and deservedly.

'Lord Brabourne finishes by saying that "land can no longer bear the burden which it was able to bear when pro-tected by legislation," and he speaks of a revaluation of the rent-charge on a "just basis." In plain English, he suggests a departure from the bargain made fifty years ago, and that tithe-owners should be fleeced for the benefit of land-owners.

'I trust the Government will persevere in their Bill, which is a measure of peace and true conservatism, not using the word in its party sense.

'Your obedient servant,

'B.'

Lord Brabourne replied :

'THE TITHE RENT-CHARGE BILL.

'. . . "B." thinks that to speak of "the undue amount of the charge upon the land" is "unmeaning." He would think differently if he owned land the tithe of which equalled or ex-ceeded the rent, or land which he could not let, but upon which he had nevertheless to pay 8s. or 9s. per acre tithe rent-charge. . . . The Tithe Commutation Act was nothing more nor less than the assertion by the State of its right to deal with tithes as national property, at a time when the very existence of that property had become imperilled by the discontent of those from whom it was collected. That right exists equally in 1887 as in 1836, and inasmuch as legislation, rightly or wrongly, has greatly decreased the value of the land, that which was a "due" amount to levy in the one year has become an "undue" amount in the other. To say that any Act of Parliament is to be deemed "a bargain made for all time" appears to me to be taking an untenable position both as regards the power of Parliament and the changes in human affairs, which necessitate the same in legislative enactments. . . .'

Lord Bramwell wrote in August, 1887 :

'I said in my letter to you that imprisonment could not be given for mere non-payment of tithe rent-charge ; that it could only be given as in case of other judgment debts, viz., where judgment had been recovered, and where the defendant had the means of paying, but dishonestly and contumaciously refused to do so. Lord Brabourne does not deny this, but allows himself to repeat his incorrect and misleading statement.

'Lord Brabourne says that the Tithe Commutation Act was nothing more nor less than the assertion by the State of its right to deal with tithes as national property. Is it possible he can believe this? Does he believe that tithes, the property of lay owners, were ever supposed to be national property? If so, he is wholly wrong. But clerical and lay tithes were dealt with in the same way and on the same principles. If clerical tithes are national property, let them be dealt with for the benefit of the nation, not of the land-owner only. Lord Brabourne seems to think that, if there are no charges on a farm, it will be let on terms better for the lessee. Does he suppose that a lessee asks for better terms from a land-owner whose estate is not mortgaged, or on which there are no charges for jointures or children?

'Lord Brabourne says I have but a poor opinion of the tenant farmers. I should have, and they would deserve, a better opinion if they were not misled.

'Your obedient servant,
'B.'

The general attack on 'capitalism,' stimulated by the Radical triumph of 1880, included demands that money should be taken by 'the State' from shareholders in London water companies held to be too rich, too successful. Water, a slippery element, is apt to upset people's political economy and weaken their sense of justice. Sometimes water seems to weigh nothing at all—does not hurt if it falls on people. To pay for the carrying of heavy things like coal, sacks of flour, or paving-stones, which *always* hurt you if they fall on you, seems obviously just ; not so the proposition that London's water-supply needs carrying to the tops of houses, and at great expense. In many country places water costs nothing. Besides, while it never rains coal, flour, or paving-stones, a shower of rain now and then does supply much water gratuitously, which complicates the problem. Finally, Parliament, in early days, had made conditions for the then struggling water companies, which ultimately proved to be favourable to the latter. In 1826 the Grand Junction Company, on the motion of Cropley, sixth Earl of Shaftesbury, Chairman of Committees, got powers inserted in a Bill to charge a certain percentage on *the annual value* of each house supplied. This power, although for years seldom exercised, was embodied, not without protest from Parliamentary Committees, in the Water Works Clauses Act of 1847, in the Act of 1852, and virtually in all private Acts promoted by London water companies. Early in 1885 Lord Camperdown introduced a Water Works Clauses Act Amendment Bill in the Lords (better known as Torrens's Act). Government, rather disingenuously, treated it as a public Bill, and after the most strenuous opposition from Lord Bramwell in the House of Lords (who called it a 'most unjust Bill,' declared that he never held a share in a water company, etc.) it became law in July, 1885.

On May 1 he wrote to the *Times*:

'THE WATER QUESTION.

'The Bill now in the Commons entitled "A Bill to declare and explain the 68th section of the Water Works Clauses Act, 1847," is quite wrong. It can only have been brought in by such gentlemen as those whose names are on the back from a misunderstanding of the judgment of the House of Lords in Dobbs's case. I am told that that misunderstanding exists, and I hope you will help me to correct it. By the Water Works Clauses Consolidation Act of 1847 "the rates shall be payable according to the annual value." That is the real, actual annual value. By the Bill in question, the rates are to be payable on the "net annual value as settled by the local authorities." It is obvious that the two things are different, and certain that the latter will always be less than the former. The only justification for such a provision could be that it would preclude disputes as to value, and that it is to be assumed that local authorities will do their duty honestly, and "settle the net annual value" truly. But the local authorities are persons interested in making the water-rates as low as possible, and therefore, if this Bill becomes law, will be interested in "settling the net annual value" as low as possible; and though we ought to, and must, trust persons in authority, it has not been the practice hitherto to leave it to A to settle how much he shall pay to B. Besides, the "annual value," as settled from time to time by the local authority, is always below the true annual value. This is in order to preclude complaints and appeals. Therefore the annual value as so settled is always different from, and less than, the real, actual annual value. On this (the larger amount) it was held in Dobbs's case the company was entitled to charge. The difference between it and the smaller amount the Bill proposes to confiscate, and without appeal.

'It is absurd that A, rated to the poor rate, might appeal against the rating of B as too low, while the water company could not, though the whole parish should be underrated. Further, there are some tenements, as public buildings, assize courts, and the like, which are not rateable to the poor-rate, which yet must pay for their water. Still further, the local rate may be on a tenement, only a part of which is supplied with water, on the annual value of which part only it would be chargeable—*e.g.*, a railway of several miles is rated to local rates, while the station only is supplied with water. The Bill leaves these cases unprovided for. As to the recital that questions have arisen " whether annual value may not mean other than the ' net annual value ' as settled from time to time by the local authority," I am not aware of any such question having arisen among persons competent to form an opinion on the matter. The rate is payable on the true, real, actual net value; " value " is net value, so settled in Dobbs's case. The Bill is an invasion of property, a confiscation of water companies' rights; an enactment that they shall charge on a value to be fixed instead of on the true value—a value to be fixed by those who will have to pay on it; a value always fixed at less than the true value.

'Your obedient servant,

'B.'

And a month later, June 1, 1885 :

'By inserting the letter of " W." you show you think that the question he so courteously puts to me may properly be put, and therefore should be answered. I answer it willingly; all the more so that it enables me to correct some misapprehensions or misstatements. But I do so with reserve. I could not speak with any certainty unless I knew the rights of the water company and their reasons for what they have done. But assuming that your correspondent is right, and that the company can charge 4 per cent. only on houses not exceeding £200 annual value, and on houses over that value can charge only 3 per cent., and assuming there is nothing in their Act or Acts or otherwise to qualify this, then if his house is over the annual value of £200, the company can only charge him at the rate of 3 per cent. I say "is" over the annual value, because the question is not what he is rated at as the annual value, but what it "is." The company cannot fix a value different from the true value either below or above it, nor can the rating authorities as yet do so as against the water company. "B." never said anything to the contrary, but agrees with your correspondent that it would be a grievous wrong that in fixing the annual value the water companies should use "a law unto themselves," as grievous as it would be that behind their backs, without their being heard on the matter, a value should be fixed against them by those who have to pay them on it. . . .'

Beginning February 14, 1891, four carefully prepared and instructive papers on 'London Water-Supply' appeared in the *Economist*. As to future legislation, the writer laid down the principle that 'so long as the companies exist and fulfil their statutory duties, Parliament cannot equitably alter conditions on the faith of which they have expended their capital' (what Edmund Burke says, 'Reflexions,' sixth edition, pp. 157, 159; what Lord Bramwell had said when arguing with the *Economist* about the anti-railway agitation, 1886-91). It was asked whether Torrens's Act of 1885 did or did not merely embody in a statute the majority vote of the Law Lords in Dobbs's case; in other words, had the water companies for years made illegal charges? The *Economist* rather thought they had.

On February 21 Lord Bramwell wrote to the *Economist* :

'With all respect, you are wrong about Dobbs's case and Torrens's Act. In Dobbs's case the water company tried to charge on what they called the "gross" value—some value over the net value. The House of Lords decided that the charge must be on the "value," *i.e.*, on the net value, that being the value. Torrens's Act limited the right to charge on the rated value or amount—an amount practically five-sixths only of "the value." It was a downright confiscation, and therefore a precedent for another. It caused a loss to the Vauxhall Company of £9,000 a year.

'Your obedient servant,

'BRAMWELL.'

On February 27 Mr. A. Dobbs wrote from West-bourne Park, firmly but temperately pointing out that Lord Bramwell was wrong. Early in 1885 Lord Bramwell had written privately, stating that he could not give Mr. Dobbs the pleasure of a controversy in print, and, on March 7, 1891, he wrote:

'I ought to know something about water-rates. I heard Dobbs's case, and was asked by the other peers to prepare an opinion, which I did. I opposed Torrens's Bill in the House. Nevertheless, I may be wrong when I speak on the subject. I was quite right, however, in the letter I wrote to you. The water company tried to charge Mr. Dobbs—who ought to be much obliged to me for giving him such an opportunity of recounting his exploits—they sought to charge him, I say, on what they called the *gross* value of his house. We held that that was wrong—that the charge should be on *the* value, the *net* value.

'Torrens's Bill said that the charge should be on the amount at which the house is rated. Now, there is a power to rate at five-sixths of the real value, and this is always done; so that the water companies lost a sixth of their possible charges. Your well-informed contributor on water-supply in your last number showed his knowledge of this. He mentioned it as accounting for the water company's receipts the year after Torrens's Act came into operation.

'Your obedient servant,

'BRAMWELL.'

On March 14 Mr. A. Dobbs wrote from Grand Avenue, Brighton, rebuking Lord Bramwell, with the aid of sarcasm. He added scornfully that not even the wisest men in the land could understand the meaning of the last sentence, beginning ' He mentioned it,' in Lord Bramwell's letter of the 7th. Thus Mr. Dobbs reminds one that newspaper readers really do like ' padding ' in letters—miss it when it is not there. Lord Bramwell suppressed all superfluous words, but never omitted essential words. Many readers do not like condensed nutriment ; they prefer something ' filling,' which will distend their minds.

One curious by-product of the war against landlordism, after 1880, was the promotion of various Copyhold Enfranchisement Bills. Copyhold tenure involves some petty inconveniences—in respect to search for and working of minerals, etc. Most of the Bills proposed would have put copyholders to greater trouble and expense than enfranchisement was worth ; this was Lord Bramwell's main reason for objecting in the House of Lords to Lord Hobhouse's Bill when discussed there in 1885 and 1886.

Mr. Waugh alleged as an explanation of Lord Bramwell's opposition, that the latter was ' avowedly briefed by the stewards,' and ' his brief instructing him to get rid of the Bill, his *nisi prius* proclivities suggested the means.' This statement Lord Bramwell retorted, in a *Times* letter, ' is silly and impertinent, which does not matter ;' but ' it is also *false*, which does matter ;' adding, ' I use the word deliberately.' The very point which Lord Bram-

well had made in the House was that, while lord
and copyholder showed by their action they were
indifferent to enfranchisement, the race of stewards
(of whom Mr. Waugh was one) had a decided
personal interest in pushing Lord Hobhouse's Bill
forward, seeing that stewards would realize much
profit from enforced conversion. 'There was,' his
lordship said, 'a third person interested, and that
was the steward, and certainly the Bill would be
a boon to the present generation of stewards; and
when his noble friend said that the Incorporated
Law Society approved of the Bill, he could well
understand that, seeing that there was a great
number of stewards in the society.' 'No one can
deny,' he said, in the course of the debate, 'that
it is desirable to get rid of copyhold tenure.' But
the principle of freedom comes in in another form.
Both or either of the parties concerned could have
obtained enfranchisement, and many of them did
use the power which the law gives them for that
purpose ; but many others, 'avowedly,' as Mr.
Waugh would have said, don't think the advantages
worth the expense.

On March 2, 1886, Mr. (now Sir) A. Arnold wrote
approving of Lord Hobhouse's Bill as an instalment,
adding that Lord Bramwell's proposal, to leave the
matter to the parties concerned, ignored the rights
and interests of the public. When his (Mr. Arnold's)
friends got into power, they would introduce a
'severe measure,' making all copyholders freeholders *d'un coup*, etc.

Whereupon Lord Bramwell wrote to the *Times :*

'Mr. Arthur Arnold says that "to leave it to lord and tenant to decide whether copyhold tenure should be converted into freehold ignores the rights and interests of the public."

'Will he tell us what rights and interests of the public are ignored? Doubtless in some cases the total value of the interests of lord and tenant would be augmented by enfranchisement, but in many cases the expense makes enfranchisement no gain to the parties. Surely, whether it would be or not, the parties are best judges.

'Does Mr. Arnold know that Lord Hobhouse's Bill, after putting them to some trouble and expense, leaves it for them to decide?

'Mr. Arnold suggests that after a certain time, thirty or perhaps ten years, all copyholds shall become freeholds. How? By the lord's rights being extinguished, or the copyholder's. That would be to rob one or the other. The copyholder would be most plundered, but does that matter? It is only a question of *quantum*. Mr. Arnold says it would be a "severe" measure. Very, and something else.'

On May 23, 1888, Lord Bramwell discoursed to the Institute of Bankers on limited liability; gave an account of the curiosities of partnership law as applied to companies existing in the 'old deed of settlement,' and winding up in Chancery, days. 'One strange notion held by the Judges was, that debts were paid out of profits; therefore all persons who took the profits of trade must share in paying the firm's creditors. Debts are really paid, not out of profits, but out of the firm's general means. Common Law always recognized the principles of limited liability. Thus, corporations themselves, not persons composing them, were held liable for corporation debts. Railway companies were from the first limited liability concerns, as were life and fire insurance companies, the reason in the latter case being that policies clearly set forth that companies' funds—not shareholders—were liable. While the policy itself made this plain to insurance companies' customers and creditors, liability in respect to ordinary trading companies was a matter of great doubt.'

Popular belief is that unlimited liability—so cruel an obligation in the case of the Western Bank in November, 1857, and of the Glasgow Bank in October, 1878—was part of the burthen of the in-flexible Common Law, or 'original law,' of the land. Lord Bramwell recalled the fact that unlimited liability was a modern invention of shareholders themselves, who voluntarily extended their liability in order to strengthen the firm's credit. He gave an amusing account of the proceedings of the Law of Partnership Commission of 1853 (p. 21). Two of its members—Sir Cresswell Cresswell and the Irish Master of the Rolls—were 'Tories of a very obsolete character, who thought any change wrong.' The other members, Sir Thomas Bazley, Mr. Slater, Mr. Kirkman Hodgson, of Baring's, and Lord Curriehill, 'thought there was a great deal to be said on both sides.' Mr. Anderson, an English Q.C. and Scottish advocate, backed up Mr. Bramwell's view, which all through was that limitation of liability should be permissive ; this reconciled Mr. Bramwell to the Parliamentary 'interference' with business relations involved. . . . 'A man is none the worse for having an option, although he may sometimes make a bad use of it.' . . . One of the anxieties which troubled certain members was, What sort of business limited liability companies were likely to be engaged in? (Just the sort of thing Royal Commissioners muse over.) Mr. Bramwell replied to them : 'I don't know ; and it is not necessary for us to consider.' Some evidence tendered to the Commission was characteristic. Lord Overstone, for example, thought 'it would be better if capitalists were not interfered with by people clubbing together as bankers to compete with them.' Lord Bramwell did not claim that he was author of the Limited Liability Act ('Lord Sherbrooke, then Mr. Robert Lowe, one of the ablest men the country ever produced,' had a large share in it) but that he himself suggested the addition of the now classic word 'limited.'. No doubt the claim is good, for to insist on letting buyer and seller, debtor and creditor, know exactly how matters stood was always his way.

At eighty years of age he might well have lost some of his old grip of these questions. So we find Saul among the prophets of 'State supervision' in business matters, and gently rebuked by the *Bankers' Magazine*. The fact is, Lord Bramwell's pet piece of constructive legislation—the Act of 1862—while sweeping away monstrous anomalies and hindrances to trade expansion, not only departed too far from his own sound maxim, *Caveat emptor*, but set an example, mischievously copied by the new school of jurists in later years. A penalty had to be paid.*

---

* The *Bankers' Magazine*, June, 1888, criticizing Lord Bramwell's paper, puts very clearly what the most experienced companies' solicitors and secretaries in the city of London say privately in this matter, influenced probably by their experience

that, until a company goes into liquidation, not one investor in a thousand ever studies the statutory 'Agreement for Sale and Purchase' (a far more important document than either the 'Articles' or 'Memorandum of Association'), and always open to the inspection of the public:

'. . . The sheet-anchor of the careful investor is always the Memorandum of Association. He need not buy a pig in a poke, for he can always turn to the Memorandum of Association, and satisfy himself as to the nature of the company whose shares he may be disposed to buy. . . . It is in limited liability companies where the mischief has been. . . . The general investing public have been nursed into a kind of false security under the Acts. . . . They have believed that the law watched over them, that especially the law was down upon fraudulent promoters—that, in short, the buyers of shares were protected by Act of Parliament. . . . It may be asked whether the loss and suffering produced by the too great confidence placed in the Limited Liability Acts have not been as serious, from first to last, as the previous misfortunes brought upon the community by the absence of limitation of the liability of unsuspecting investors.

'On the Memorandum of Association and on limitation of liability under the Act of 1862 . . . advocates of the Act relied mainly for the protection of the public. . . . But "promoters" have wriggled round these buttresses of honesty, straightforwardness, and legality in the matter of the formation of public companies, and it may be doubted whether simple provisions and other impediments to the frauds of unscrupulous promoters are likely to be a whit more successful. . . . Nothing is more astounding . . . than the way in which the public will sometimes entrust hundreds and thousands of pounds to men whose names are printed as directors on a prospectus . . . simply because these Companies' Acts are supposed to give protection to shareholders on the one hand, and to relieve them of the duty of controlling directors on the other.'

CHAPTER X.

THE ARGUMENT FROM COMMON LAW.

Revolt among trade unionists against contract relation between master and servant—Employers' Liability Bill of 1878—Debate and *Times* correspondence thereon—Lord Bramwell's keen interest in the subject—His expositions of Common Law applicable thereto—Letters to *Times* and *Economist*, 1878-80—Pamphlet—Act of latter year—' Hares and Rabbits ' Bill, 1880—Lord Bramwell's protest against further repudiation of contract—' Paternal ' legislation and national character—Complete fusion in his mind of English jurisprudence and Whig principles—The colours he fought under—The law he reverenced.

DISCUSSION of Employers' Liability Bills brought out very plainly how, in respect to contract, the new jurisprudence had parted company with the old. ' The matter is of the greatest importance,' Lord Bramwell wrote, *Times*, April, 1878, and September, 1880, taking extraordinary, and at first sight inexplicable, interest in it. He never protested half so strongly against Irish Land Acts, which did inflict, not theoretical wrong, but palpable ruin, upon many innocent persons. The latter Acts were, however, simply confiscation by statute of one kind of property. It is quite possible for supreme authority, under stress of ignorance, prejudice, terror, blind hate, to plunder or persecute an isolated class—as Anabaptists, Roman Catholics, Quakers, Dissenters, in this country, heretics in Spain, Stundists and Jews in Russia, Armenians and Christians in Turkey —while still conceding a large average measure of personal freedom. . Under local *fueros* in medieval Spain, liberty of the subject was, and in modern Turkey is, far less interfered with in small matters than in the colony of New Zealand to-day. The indirect but far-reaching consequences of repudiation of contract (*i.e.*, of the very principle of liberty) seems to have alarmed Lord Bramwell in the Employers' Liability Bill.

In April, 1878, Mr. A. Macdonald introduced, as a private measure, an Employers' Liability Bill, which was talked out, Ministers promising in both Houses to deal with the matter later, as recommended by the Committee of 1876-77. Mr. Robert Lowe, who had re-enlisted in the Radical Pyrrhic phalanx, because, perhaps, of his dislike to Lord Beaconsfield's Eastern policy, then fiercely questioned, in a speech (which amply justified that dread of the demagogic fallacy he had himself expressed in 1866) charged Lord Abinger with certainly creating, in 1837, in Priestley's case (3 M. and W. 6), a special and novel disability for working men ; English Judges, with evil intent, had 'supposed' or 'invented' contracts ' which never existed,' etc.

On April 13 Lord Shand replied in the *Times*, pointing out among other things that the legal maxim, *Qui facit per alium*, etc., does not apply in this matter.

The *Times* of same date remarked that Lord Abinger had made it clear that, although claims against a master arising out of a fellow-servant's negligence had not arisen before 1837, they might have, and would never have been good at Common Law, while Chief Baron Pollock had also said substantially the same thing.   On April 19 Mr. Robert Lowe, in a long letter, argued that the decision in *Priestley v. Fowler* did not alone originate the grievance of which trade union leaders complained.   The judgment in *Hutchinson v. York*, etc., *Railway* (5 *Exch.* 343) inflicted a worse wrong, because the Judge then laid down that, in the absence of any affirmative contract or agreement, giving a servant claim for damage caused by negligence of a fellow-servant, a negative agreement, positively barring such claim, must be implied.*   English Judges, he said, 'evolved out of their own minds,' or created, 'false contracts . . . notoriously false.'   He wound up with this demagogic fling at English Judges : 'The whole matter was a controversy between rich and poor ; the " sword of Brennus " being thrown into the heavier scale,' etc.   Next day, Sir George Bowyer, an erudite Roman Catholic M.P. and master of misapplied jurisprudence, while agreeing with Lord Bramwell on the whole, quoted Petrus Fabian, Ulpian, and other doctors, to prove that such wrongs as Mr. Lowe alleged would have been differently dealt with by interpreters of Civil and Canon Law. Which was quite true.   Thus, in an interesting way British trade unionism, then, quite unconsciously,

* See p. 207.

reverting to medieval Socialism, found archæological support and assistance.

On April 24, 1878, Lord Bramwell wrote to the *Times,* signing 'G. B.' :

'. . . The proposed extension of a master's liability in case the negligence of one servant causes damage to another servant is uncalled for and mischievous. When it is proposed to alter a law, it matters little how it came into existence. The question is whether the alteration is expedient. Mr. Lowe finds fault with the origin of the present law. He, however, must know very well that many cases are rightly decided, and a principle established, on doubtful reasoning. The cases he refers to, if stated at length, would have a very different aspect to that which he gives them ; would justify the negative opinion that masters and servants have not "contracted" that the master shall be liable for a fellow-servant's negligence. . . . The question is of the greatest importance.

'The fundamental error of those who support the proposed change is to assume that, by some general law or "natural right," everybody has a remedy against a master for the negligence of a servant acting in the master's employment ; that in the nature of things masters are to make good damage done by their servants, and that therefore the law which makes masters not liable for a fellow-servant's negligence is an unjust exception to the general law.

'There is no such general law.

'A master is liable for the negligence of his servant in two classes of cases : (1) Where there is no contract relation between the person injured and the master ; (2) where there is such contract relation.

'In the former class are included such cases as one of the public being injured by the negligent driving of the master's coachman. How this rule originated is not material : some reason or justification is that it has a tendency to ensure care in the selection of servants to whom the means of doing possible mischief are entrusted. If it be said, "Then, make the master liable only when he has been careless in the choice of a coachman," the injured person might say, "I cannot prove that he was; I had no choice in the matter. Unless I give up my right to use the streets, I am exposed to the chance of his coachman being negligent. Let us judge by results, and ensure his being careful by making him liable." Whether that is right I do not say, but it is the reason.

'Injuries to servants by fellow-servants do not, however, come under this head. The servant injured is not merely one of the public; a relation or contract has been established between him and his master. So the case is within the second class. It, again, must be subdivided. Whenever a man undertakes anything, it is understood (unless stipulated to the contrary) that it shall be done with due care and skill. If he does it himself, and fails in care or skill—to the damage of the person he has contracted with—he is liable. If he gets someone to do it for him, and that person (whether servant or not) fails in care or skill, the original contractor is—and in all reason—liable. If A contracts to convey me in a carriage, and I am hurt by his negligence, by that of his servant, or of another coach proprietor employed by A to carry me, A is liable. If I take a ticket from Dover to Liverpool, and am injured by negligence at the Liverpool station (belonging to another line of railway which completes my journey), the Dover Railway Company would be liable to me. The principle of this law is that no man can get rid of his liability by deputing to another, servant or otherwise, the duty which he has undertaken.

'These are the only cases I know where the master is liable for his servant's negligence. The case of a servant injured by a fellow-servant is not within this (second) class. The master has not undertaken to him to do anything with care and skill (like carrying him, shoeing his horse, conducting his lawsuit, and so forth). Yet there *is* a relation between master and servant, created by mutual consent, and it is *not* one of the terms of that relation that the master should be liable for damage occasioned by a fellow-servant. It is proposed to alter this, making the master liable unless the servant, as it is called, "contracts himself out" of it. I believe he will be allowed to do that.

' Why is the master to be liable ?   I believe the burthen of proof is on those who would alter the law.   Why should A, who has done no wrong, who has been careful and just, make good to B damage done by C ?   The reason given in the case of claims by " one of the public " does not apply.   It is open to any servant to enter the service and work with the fellow-servant or not, as he pleases.   He can quit the service ; has more knowledge than the master of his fellow-servant's mode of doing work ; can best guard against it if wrong.   Why in the name of all fairness and reason should the master be liable ?   In my judgment, a great deal more could be said for making servants liable for damage done to a master's property by the negligence of fellow-servants.   Any one with experience knows the recklessness, not specially of workmen, but of undisciplined minds.   I do not suppose that a man will risk life or limb because his widow or he will have a remedy ; but I think it is well to give him as little encouragement that way as possible. . . .   I repeat my question : Why should the master be liable when he has done no wrong ?   The only answer is that he can pay, while the fellow-servant cannot. This is a parry to the " sword of Brennus."   Fie, Mr. Lowe !*

' If a man is a guest at a friend's house, the master is not liable if his servant's negligence damages the guest.   The guest is something more than " one of the public " ; there is a relation between him and his host ; but that the host should be liable for his servant's negligence is no part of that relation. . . .

---

* On May 14, 1880, Mr. Gladstone (born 1809) having come into office, Mr. Robert Lowe (born 1811) wrote to Lord Bramwell :

' . . . Many thanks for your kind congratulations.   There is no one whose opinion I value more.   The worst of it is there is nothing to be congratulated about.   Gladstone told me I was too old for a fresh start.   I could not well retire to the fourth bench, nor resign my seat, having just been elected, so here I am. . . .'

'G. B.' then pleads for 'that liberty of contract which is all-important,' and adds that instead of the then existing law being, as an eminent authority told the Parliamentary Committee of 1876-77, 'a bad exception to a bad rule,' it formed 'no exception to any rule.'

The main points in dispute were somewhat technical, and at least twenty minutes' thought was needed to comprehend them. On the 26th Sir George Bowyer again wrote. Apparently he had been converted from his own to Mr. Lowe's view of the 19th by Lord Bramwell's reply to Mr. Lowe on the 24th, and quoted Alciatus and Menochius to prove that English Judges generally were less trustworthy in regard to the rights of masters and servants than those ancients.

On April 27 'F.' wrote in measured legal phraseology, instancing the maxim *Qui facit*, etc., asserting that Lord Bramwell's doctrines were 'at variance with clear and undoubted law,' and were now 'discarded as downright absurdities'; referred to the law of libel which made masters (publishers or proprietors) liable for the negligence of servants (contributors and compositors), and charged Lord Bramwell with saying that 'a man is only liable for his own acts.'

To 'F.,' 'G. B.' replied in the *Times* at once:

'*Qui facit per alium facit per se* is good law and good sense, but it has absolutely nothing to do with the question of a master's liability for the misconduct of his servant. That liability is beside and in addition to that established by the rule *Qui facit*, etc. If A procures B to murder C, A is guilty of murder, whether B is his servant or not. If A procures B to build a house in such a place and of such a plan that it must and does when built obstruct the light and air to which C is entitled, A is liable, whether B is his servant or a master builder. If A tells B to drive as fast as he can, no matter what mischief he does, and B drives recklessly and injures C, A is liable, whether B is his servant or a cabman hired on the stand. On the other hand, if A tells B to stop trespassers in search of game, and B with an excess of zeal uses unjustifiable force, A would not be liable if B was a policeman, but would be, according to recent cases, if B was his servant. If A employs B to build a house, and the foundations might be dug so as not to injure C, but are wrongfully dug so that they do so, A is not liable if B is a master builder, is liable if B is A's servant. If A tells B to drive him to X, and B negligently drives and injures C, A is not liable if B is an ordinary cabman, is liable if B is A's servant. The reasons for these differences are obvious. In the first three cases I have put, A has caused or procured the injurious act, he has done it by another. In the last three cases he has not caused or procured the wrongful act, he has not done it by another. It is the misconduct of the other that has done it, and A is not liable, unless that other is his servant ; then he is—not because he has done the act *per alium*—but because that other is his servant, acting within the scope of his authority. The matter may be made obvious thus : A employs B to pull down a wall. If the wall belongs to C, A is liable, whether B is his servant or not. If B in pulling the wall down negligently drops a brick on D and hurts him, A is liable to D if B is A's servant ; but if B is not his servant—if, for instance, instead of wages he has agreed to do the job for £5, so that he is not subject to A's orders as to how it shall be done—A is not liable. It is absurd to say that the maxim applies when the wrongful act is in direct opposition to the master's orders. " Drive carefully," is the order. The man drives carelessly. Then, by the maxim, the master drives carelessly (*facit per se*), because the servant (*alius*) did ! The liability of a printer for a libel depends on other considerations. He carries on a trade which may involve the publication of a libel ; he must take care it does not. I do not say this is a good reason, but it is the reason. It is no longer law in all cases. The principle is the same as that which makes a man liable for a nuisance who carries on a trade so as to be a nuisance, though he has not been near the place for years, nor knows of it. It is not a liability for the act of a servant. He would be equally liable if his partners printed the libel or caused the nuisance. Lord Abinger may have made many "irrelevant observations"; but allowance should be made for him and other busy persons who have not had leisure to study so as to lay down "clear and undoubted law," but remain ignorant of "fundamental principles, landmarks, and cardinal principles."

' It is no fiction to say that master and servant do not agree that the master shall be liable for the misconduct of a fellow-servant. It is an actual truth. *Whenever two people come to an agreement, there is negatively an agreement that neither is bound to anything but what is agreed.* In order not to be misunderstood, let me say at once that usual terms are implied and bind as much as if expressed. If I order a coat of a tailor, and he accepts the order, the cloth must be fair and the fit must be fair, and I must pay a fair price, if none was named, and ready money, though none of these things may have been expressed between us. But negatively we agree there are no other terms, whether we express these or not. We do not agree that I shall order a waistcoat of him, nor that he shall have his boots of me. It is manifest that the duty of a master to a servant and the right of a servant against his master depend on agreement, or, if the expression is preferred, agreement and non-agreement. Suppose a servant was hurt in his employment by no fault of anyone—*e.g.*, owing to a defective casting which neither the maker nor anyone else can guard against. Suppose the workman made a claim on the master for compensation : the master would say, " I did not agree to compensate you in such case." But as two are required to an agreement, he should say, " We did not agree that you should be compensated in such case." That is what he says now in the case of a claim for compensation for injury by the negligence of a fellow workman.

'That the question is, what is the agreement between the master and servant, is manifest from this, that the servant might bargain—and he and his master agree—for compensation being paid to him for damage caused by a fellow-servant's negligence.   He would then be entitled to it by the agreement. He is not entitled now because there is no such agreement. And whether there is no such agreement, because there is no agreement on the subject or an agreement to the contrary, is a matter of indifference.   But, as I said before, the question is, not whether this or that maxim applies, or whether the matter has been well reasoned.   "*Qui facit per alium facit per se*" is entitled to all respect, but we must not have a superstitious reverence for it ; and if in some way Judges and lawyers have blundered out of it into something better, let us be thankful and leave the matter where it is.

'I never said that "the general rule of the law of England is that the master is liable only for his own acts," nor anything like it, nor that could be mistaken for it.

'G. B.'

In February, 1880, Lord Cairns, Chancellor, introduced an Employers' Liability Bill, which was referred to a Select Committee.   The Gladstone Government, which came into office April, 1880, lost no time in dealing with the subject.   The working class, believed to have voted mainly Liberal in March, was clearly entitled to the first-fruits of victory.   On no question of the day were official and ostensible leaders of trade unionism more unanimous and persistent, Mr. A. Macdonald, Mr. Broadhurst, and other leaders having for years protested against 'the infamous "doctrine of common employment,"' supposed to have been invented in 1837 in Priestley's case.*   Since trade union

---

* In the House of Lords, July, 1897, Lord Salisbury spoke of the "law" of common employment,' and there was a queer

leaders and their political dependents never managed to understand what the Common Law applicable to the matter really is, their protest has been more than usually sincere.

August 28, 1880, Lord Bramwell wrote to the *Economist :*

'COMMON EMPLOYMENT.

'SIR,

'In your last number is the following : "There can be no doubt that the doctrine of common employment has been pushed to an extreme against the workmen, and that they are entitled to demand that the rule that the principal is liable for the acts of his properly constituted agents, which obtains in other departments of business, shall be made to apply also to the relations between masters and men."

'Permit me with great respect to say this is wrong. I know no other word for it. *There is no such thing as a "doctrine of common employment." I know the phrase is used by lawyers who ought to know better, but it is positively unmeaning.* . . . The reason why the matter to which I call your attention is important is, that at present the workman thinks, as you say, "that the doctrine of common employment has been pushed to an extreme against him"—that some injustice is done him. As long as he thinks so he is bound to struggle against it, and has my entire sympathy. My wish is to show . . . *that the notion is wrong. . . . viz., a notion that there is a doctrine of common employment which is unjust to the workman.* One word more. . . . Why should a master·be liable for negligence by a servant injuring a fellow servant, which he, the master, could not possibly prevent ? Why, if the miner, in order to see more

---

debate on the subject of this myth in the Commons, March 9, 1898. There is, of course no such 'law.' Common employment is a fact rather than a 'doctrine.' The only effectual way to 'abolish' it would be to enact that no employer should ever engage more than one man.

plainly, opens his lamp and causes an explosion, should the master be liable? Why, if liable in such a case, should he not be liable if the explosion was wilfully caused? . . .

' G. BRAMWELL.'

In 1880 the prestige of trade unionism was great. It was supra-political, that is to say, trade unionists were not completely enfranchised; when they were they might go anywhere and do anything. Evidence that their annual Congresses were manipulated for party purposes was not then clear, while the policy embodied in such resolutions as that about the nationalization of Cosmos, passed at the Norwich Congress in 1894, was still in embryo. Demand for an Employers' Liability Bill in 1880 was not so much irresistible as unresisted. Sentiment had a great deal to do with the matter. Barring the Irish horror, England was a pleasant abode for politicians at the time. Mr. Gladstone couldn't live for ever. Prosperous and well-fed M.P.'s did not like to think that poor men, toiling all day long, might break a limb or get smashed and have no remedy. Driving down from his club to the House, the M.P. passed these men going home from work, tired and begrimed; his conscience told him that he really must do a little injustice to employers, to balance matters.* Lord Bramwell's

---

* Judges in the course of their professional duties are not confronted by realistic contrasts of the workaday world in quite the same way, since in a court of justice every layman— plaintiff, defendant, juryman, witness, spectator—looks equally uncomfortable all the time; whether he is a rich or a poor man makes no difference. It is not that English Judges are unfeeling. They would, perhaps, prefer to decide cases by

attempts to get the public to think about the question were not very successful.　He even failed to convince either the *Times* or the *Economist*.　A Judge (off the bench) and a few lawyers took a different abstract view of the law—or rather of the principle announced in Priestley's and Hutchinson's cases—from Lord Bramwell.　Common Law was a little under a cloud at the time, not for Bentham's reason, but for Mr. Ruskin's reason.　The fashion was to apologize for it.　Mr. Sidney Webb wrote in a monthly magazine, January, 1897 :

> 'The lawyer's contention that the wage-earner, by entering into a contract of service, had placed himself in a position different from that of the ordinary citizen was incomprehensible'

to Parliamentary Committees, which is extremely probable.　The Committee of 1876-77 had reported

> '"negligence in the employer or in some person . . . whom he has the power to dismiss must, of course, be shown."　But . . . why should more be required in the case of a workman than in any other case ?　The proposed legislation . . . would be merely the repeal of exceptional exclusion of them from the ordinary protection of the law.'

However, when the leaders of both political parties have all their lives been pledged to reject the principle in a Ministerial measure, while their followers do not take trouble to inquire what that principle is, the measure is described as 'non-contentious.'　Newspaper leader-writers are then

saying to the jury, 'Gentlemen, the only question is, which do you feel *really* sorry for, plaintiff or defendant ?'　After all, an M.P.'s duties are pleasanter than a Judge's.

grateful that they have not to look up the Ten Commandments to see whether the measure is barred there.   Finally, all parties say they will unite to improve it in Committee.   Conservatives, staggered by their smashing defeat in the March previous, were just then wondering in what way Mr. Gladstone's great power would be used to chasten England for her sins : Ireland seemed likely to be the ordained instrument.   In the summer of 1880 the formidable energy of the Land League absorbed people's thoughts.

Mr. Sidney Webb says* the Employers' Liability Bill encountered 'furious opposition from the employers.'   There was much press controversy, many conferences, but no furious Parliamentary opposition, no division in either House.   After some fighting in Committee the Bill became law September 4.

June 9, 1880, Lord Bramwell wrote to Sir Henry Jackson, Bart., M.P., his

' . . . reasons for saying that the common notions of lawyers as well as laymen, as to the reason of the non-liability of the master in cases of common employment, are wrong. . . .'

This letter was afterwards published as a pamphlet by P. S. King, King Street, S.W. :

' ON THE LIABILITY OF MASTERS TO WORKMEN FOR INJURIES FROM FELLOW SERVANTS.

' . . . Those who propose to make a law, in truth propose to alter what exists, and should give a good reason for the

---

* ' The History of Trade Unionism.'

change; ... most certainly ... when the new law is proposed on account of some alleged hardship, or anomaly in the old law. ... It is said that the existing law, as to the liability of employers for negligence of a servant causing damage to a fellow servant, is anomalous, ... an exception to a general rule which makes employers liable for the negligence of their servants, a grievance to workmen, and a grievance without justification. It is somehow supposed that as a matter of natural right (something that exists in the nature of things) employers are liable for injuries occasioned by their servants' negligence, and that to except fellow servants from this rule is unjust and unreasonable.

'Now this is an entire mistake. ... The primary rule is, that a man is liable for his own acts, and not for those of others. A man, as a rule, is no more liable for the wrongs done by another than he is for his debts. Cases in which he *is* liable are exceptions to the rule, not the rule. I will proceed to state the exceptions.

'1. When a man undertakes to do or perform any work, he undertakes that it shall be done or performed with reasonable care and skill. If he does or performs it himself and is negligent or unskilful, and damage results, he is liable. So he is if he does or performs it not himself, but by agent or deputy. For instance, if a smith's servant in shoeing a horse hurts it by negligence, the master is liable; so would he be if he got a neighbouring smith to shoe the horse and *he* injured the horse by *his* negligence. So a railway company that undertakes to carry a passenger from A to B, is liable for damage occasioned to the passenger by the negligence of its own servants ... or of the servants of another company. ... In this case the servant or agent is not liable.

'2. The next case in which a man is liable for the act of another which causes injury is, where he has expressly caused or commanded that act. ... This class of cases also has nothing to do with the relations of masters and servants. The employer is equally liable whether the person who did the act complained of was his servant, or his agent and not his servant. ... The reason of this rule is obvious. The wrong has been done by him who procured it as much as by the actual doer, and the maxim *qui facit per alium facit per se* applies.

' 3. There is a third class of cases in which a man is liable for the act of another. If a servant—acting within the scope of his authority—by negligence—injures one of the outside world (an expression I will explain presently), his master is liable. It will be observed that four things are necessary to constitute this liability. First, the actual doer of the mischief must be a *servant* of the person sought to be made liable. It is not enough if he is employed otherwise than as a servant. If I employ my servant to pull down a wall, and by his negligence he injures a passer-by, I am liable. If I had employed a firm of builders or a working bricklayer to do it, I am not liable. I do not know that it is necessary to define or describe a servant. Shortly, the relation of master and servant exists where the master can not only order the work, but how it shall be done. When the person to do the work may do it as he pleases, then such person is not a servant.

.' Next, my servant, if I am to be held liable, must be acting *within the scope of his employment.* If my coachman takes my carriage and horses to give his wife a ride and is guilty of negligence causing damage, I am not liable. Next, damage to be recoverable against the master must be the result of *negligence.* If caused wilfully, the master is not liable. If my coachman wilfully drives against anyone or his carriage, I am not liable for the damage resulting. Lastly, the master is not liable to anyone with whom he has entered into some relation, *unless such liability was one of the terms of that relation.* The person injured, to have any remedy, must be one I have called "of the outside world." Thus, if my servant drives over a stranger, I am liable. If my friend, having a pleasure drive with me is injured by my servant's negligent driving, I am not liable, because liability is not one of the terms of our relation. If my friend had paid me money to carry him, I should be liable under the first head of liability, because I had contracted with him that he should be carried with care. If my servant leaves a stumbling-block in the street in the course of his work and anybody falls over it, I am liable. If he leaves a trap-door open in my house and my guest falls through, I am not liable. The reason why I am not liable in the cases in which I am not, is the general one I started with, viz., a man as a rule is not liable for the acts of others.

'Another reason ironically given, but which has great practical effect, is, that the master is liable because he is a competent paymaster, while the servant usually is not. There is another reason which exists in fact; whether good or bad, is another matter. A man is walking on the Queen's highway and run over by my servant. He may say, with some colour of fairness, " I was doing what I had a right to do. I was injured by your servant. I had no voice in the choice of him. I could only keep out of the risk of injury from him by foregoing my right to walk in the public streets. Therefore to make you and other masters careful in the choice of servants to whom you give the means of mischief, you and other masters must compensate for that mischief when it happens." Now I do not say that is a sufficient reason, but it is the only one I know of, and it is not a reason applicable to the case of one servant injuring another, for then each servant has a voice in the matter. The master hiring a servant says, " Here is your work, here are your fellow servants, work for me or not as you please." The servant may say, " I do not please so long as so-and-so is in your service, for he is negligent."

'There is, then, no general rule which makes one man liable for the negligence of another. The general rule is the other way. I have described the exceptions, but the case of one servant injuring another is not within those exceptions nor the reason of them, but the contrary. It has been said the servant " contracts himself out of the right to compensation." It would be better to say he does *not* contract himself *into* it. He can if he and his master so agree. Nay, he can stipulate for compensation where there is no negligence. He does not contract that his case shall be an exception to the general rule that a man is not liable for the acts of another. There is no injustice in this. There is in the proposition the other way.

For no one can doubt that the dangers of an employment are taken into account in its wages. No one can doubt that the unpleasantness and risk of a miner's, or a deep sea diver's work add to his wages. Put sixpence out of the miner's daily wage of five shillings as being on account of that risk, a sum which he may save or use as a premium of insurance. What is the proposal of those who would make the employer liable but this, that the servant shall keep the premium in his own pocket and yet treat his master as the insurer ? I do not believe that this is understood, or it would not be asked for ; but it is the truth.

'So much for the existing law, and so much for the reason of it. Now for the proposed change and the reason of it.

'The largest proposed change is, that the master should be liable to his servant for the negligence of a fellow servant. Why? I have shown that the supposed grievance does not exist. That it is not a "natural right" that the master should be liable, nor does such a right exist in the nature of things. That it is reasonable a railway company should be liable to a passenger for the negligence of its servants, because it has so contracted, and that it should not be to one of its own servants, because it has not so contracted. We are to start afresh, then, and make a new rule. Why? I have two servants, A and B ; A injures B and B injures A by negligence ; why should I be liable to both when, if each had injured himself I should not be to either ?* Only one reason can be urged for it, viz. : That on the whole, looking at the interest of the public, the master and the servant, it would be a better state of things than exists at present. Is that so? Now we must start with this, that it is under the present law competent for a servant to stipulate with his master that the master shall be liable for the negligence of a fellow servant, or in respect of any hurt or injury the servant may receive in the service. So that the difference in the law, if changed as proposed, would be this.

---

* 'As has been amusingly asked, why, if the housemaid puts damp sheets on the footman's bed and he leaves the scuttle at the foot of the stairs and she tumbles over it, should the master be liable for the damage ensuing ?'

At present the master is not liable, unless he agrees to be; on the change he would be unless he and the servant agreed he should not be. For *I suppose it is not intended to forbid the master and servant contracting themselves out of the law. . . .** That would be a most mischievous interference with freedom of contract, and would give rise to gross injustice and fraud on the master. I *cannot suppose anything so outrageous*, and proceed to consider what will follow if the liability is optional (but to exist where the parties have not agreed to the contrary). Every prudent employer of labour will immediately draw up a form to be signed by his workmen, that the master shall not be liable for a fellow servant's negligence.

'What good will the new law do? None to the workman, except in such cases as I have last mentioned, cases of surprise and injustice ; for where it is known it will be guarded against. And even if the law were made obligatory, in spite of bargains to the contrary, it would not profit the servant. Because it is certain there is a market rate of wages, one fixed by what neither master nor man can control. If wages are practically added to one way, they will be taken from in another. If a manufacturer whose wages now are £10,000 in the year is made to pay compensation to the amount of £1,000 a year, his wages will fall to £9,000. Were he to charge more for his produce because he has to pay more his sales would diminish and injury be done to the workman in loss of work.

'What good, then, will the change do? . . . The only thing I have ever heard suggested is, that it will make the master more careful in the choice of his servants. I suppose it would. For it would not have an opposite tendency. . . . Now I do *not* say that workmen will injure themselves for the sake of compensation ; but I do say, that whatever tends to lessen their reason for care and good conduct (as compensation would) tends to make them less careful in themselves and more disposed to conceal want of care in others. . . .

'No servant is bound to obey a command attended with danger. . . .

'One word more. It is proposed to guard the master by

---

* Forbidden by Act of 1897.

provisions that he shall not be liable if the servant contributed to the injury. There are other qualifications. In vain. *The untruths told in accident cases are prodigious.* They will be told in such as the Bill will give rise to. I foresee a frightful crop of litigation if it passes.

'G. BRAMWELL.'

In the following month a *Times* leader said :

'A railway collision may be caused by negligence of a signalman or a pointsman. The company is liable for the acts of its servants to all the passengers injured, but the guard, who in most cases is just as much a passenger as any who have paid for their seats, is entirely deprived of compensation. . . . No legal ingenuity can hide the substantial injustice. . . .'

July 19, ' B.' wrote :

'There is no injustice to be hidden by legal or other ingenuity. The company is liable to the ordinary passenger because it bargains with him that due care shall be used in the carrying of him ; is liable whether the accident was caused by the negligence of the company, of its servants or agents, or of another company which continued the carrying begun by the company which received the fare. If there is no such bargain with the company—as, for instance, with a drover travelling with cattle—the company is not liable, not having bargained that they will be. They might make such a bargain as the law stands, but they do not. The proposed law [Bill of 1880] would in some cases create such a bargain between the guard and the railway company . . . How is the guard at present " deprived " of compensation ?'

He wrote again in August, 1880 :

' EMPLOYERS' LIABILITY.

'. . . Mr. Broadhurst, M.P., is reported to have said at the Trades Union Congress " that they only asked for the same rights to be extended to workpeople which were given to all other classes of the community." And he quoted what had been said by an authority than whom there is none higher, that " he could not see what logic of law or public right there was for any number of the public to have full protection and unlimited compensation in cases of accidents, and then to deny it to the workmen." I should doubt if the words quoted were used, but undoubtedly the noble lord referred to did say in substance that which Mr. Broadhurst attributes to him.

'With all submission it is wrong. The matter is important. For if workpeople are treated differently from the rest of the community to their injury they are more than justified in struggling to get the injustice removed. But they are not treated differently, and you will perhaps think me warranted in asking you to let me state what is the law and what is the reason of it, when it will appear that the complaint is unfounded. . . .'

After restating the law, as in previous letters, he adds :

'. . . All I say is . . . that there is " a logic of law " (whatever that may mean) why the public—between whom and a master there is *no* relation—may have rights which the workman, between whom and his master there *is* a relation, has not. . . . It matters little how the law is if master and servant are allowed to make their own bargains. This is objected to by Mr. Broadhurst and others, because the poor fellows, the servants, cannot take care of themselves !'

The prolonged agitation for the Act of 1880 demonstrated the growing ascendancy at a particular epoch of socialistic ideas among trade union leaders. Socialism aims at reducing all workers to a quasi servile *status*, tempered by State doles. The Employers' Liability Act of 1880 conceded one principle insisted on by Socialists — discountenanced to a certain extent that free contract relation existing between employer and employed. Degradation of a particular class, from contract down once more to

status, marks agrarian and economic legislation
after 1870 ; English, Scottish and Irish tenants and
wage-earners being deprived of the right, responsibility—or peril—of making their own bargains with
landlords and employers. Put coarsely, the terms
offered by Liberal statesmen were these : ' We
practically reduce you to the legal, non-contracting
condition of infants, lunatics, or drunken men ; but,
in exchange, we will take some money, or its equivalent, from those with whom you have relations of
hiring, and give it to you.' Although not so expressed, the offer was so understood, and not disliked by such English and Scottish tenants and
workmen as interested themselves in this kind of
legislation. Trade union combination already to
a limited extent did involve the surrender of a
man's absolute liberty of bargain. Joining a trade
union was, however, a voluntary exercise of will,
while the Act of 1880, in a slip-shod, tentative way,
established a new *status* for all workmen. But
since nothing whatever was said in it about 'contracting out,' the old Common Law right stood, and
agreements between masters and servants were still
held good by the courts. Nothing requires cleaner,
neater workmanship than the substitution of Statute
for Common Law ; the Act, however, was very
clumsily put together. Existing relations could
hardly be said to be so flagrantly interfered with as
in the case of tenancies of land, because hiring was
generally by the week. A few large employers of
labour surmised that the Act would benefit them ;
would hamper and injure small employers ; thus in-

directly but surely reducing competition amongst wage-payers, while increasing competition among wage-earners. However, no British working-man was sold into slavery at public auction. Lord Bramwell said in 1884, 'The Act does not seem to have done much harm.'* It is alleged by employers in certain trades to have produced, as Lord Bramwell feared, systematic perjury and conspiracy among workmen to commit perjury; aggravated no doubt by growing contempt for the sacredness of the oath, due to education and progressive views about religion.

The public—and, according to the testimony of recent spokesmen for 'labour,' the bulk of the working-classes also—never cared much about the Liability Act of 1880. Lord Bramwell thought the matter important, and tried to make people understand why, believing that those entrenchments crowned and fortified by the Common Law of England were the first—and that with him meant the impregnable—line of defence against infringements of civil freedom, against wrong or delusion, small or great, threatening employers or employed. In a sense he was right; that his idea must win in the long-run we must all believe. Wrong he was in a sense, because the new, prosperous, good-natured England, which had come into being since Lord Bramwell's early days, preferred new ways of doing the right thing, of mitigating injustice, more hazy and roundabout, less direct and clean-cut than his way.

A plea for contract, insistence upon the ex-

* 'Laissez Faire,' p. 144.

pediency of allowing men to freely regulate their dealings by means of it, was once more made by Lord Bramwell in the matter of the Ground Game Act of 1880, better known as the 'Hares and Rabbits Act.' The political history of this rather paltry measure may be safely neglected. More interesting is the demand for it in some quarters as a genuine specific for 'increasing the productiveness of English land,' while compensating the British farmer for the pressure of foreign competition in agricultural produce, at the time becoming more and more perceptible. Many people honestly believed that ground game ate up enough grain and other food-stuffs to make a sensible difference in food production. Although he never shot hares or rabbits,* it was indignation at this particular measure which actually led Lord Bramwell to join the Liberty and Property Defence League. In the *Times* of June, 1880, he wrote :

'I am very sorry that the Hares and Rabbits Bill has the approval of the *Times*. I most earnestly deprecate its becoming law. Let me say why : A land-owner's terms for a farm are £100 a year if he has the game, £120 if he has not. A farmer is willing to take on either condition. Both prefer the former. The proposed law is to prevent them making a binding bargain

---

* His only performance with the gun was during a visit to Lord Westbury's country house, about the year 1865. Pigeon-shooting was the fashion in those days, and the Bethell family of that epoch possessed, in a rare degree, the instincts of this difficult sport. Sir George Bramwell fired at a pigeon, blew it to pieces, and didn't like it at all. Never went out shooting again. Up to about the age of fifty he used to ride in the Park now and then, but was never a good horseman.

to that effect. They make such a bargain, in fact, but as soon as they have the farmer may break it, and, having got his land cheap because he was not to have the game, may nevertheless take it. What excuse or justification is there for this? Only one, which the *Times* has very ingeniously invented—viz., that it is for the interest of the public at large that the occupier of land should have an inalienable right to destroy ground game. If that were so, if it were so to a sensible extent, and there was no other remedy, so as to justify an interference not merely with freedom of contract, but with the use and enjoyment of property, I agree such a law would be right, but it would be an entire novelty. The law forbids, and, if it did not, ought to forbid, the use of land in a way harmful to the public; but it has never prescribed the way it should be used and enjoyed on any such ground as public profit. Where is such legislation to stop? Are deer-forests to be turned into sheep-walks, parks to be ploughed up for turnips, flower-gardens to grow cabbages? If this were the reason of the legislation, Parliament should go direct to its object, and not merely permit, but order, the killing of the ground game. But it is not the reason the farmers put forward; and this Bill owes its origin partly to that mischievous meddling which prompts interference by the Legislature in matters which ought to be left to private agreement, and partly, I am afraid, to a desire to conciliate the farmer. It may have been necessary to legislate to protect factory children, women, possibly men grown up, as by the Truck Acts, sailors who cannot judge for themselves as to the safety of ships, and perhaps in other cases; but the British farmer! Is he to be put among the feeble and helpless who require to be taken care of, because he cannot take care of himself? He should be ashamed to ask for such protection, especially now, when the landlords, for want of tenants, are at his mercy. How is it forced on him to let his landlord have the game? If he ought not to have it, why does not the farmer say so like a man and refuse the tenancy? It is shocking to think of the moral feebleness such legislation encourages. It is all very well to say that the landlord wants two profits: the rent of the land from the farmer, and the use of the land for the game. It is more true to say that the farmer wants two profits—viz., the land cheap on account of the mischief done by the game, and compensation afterwards for that mischief. Should the Bill pass, it will be evaded and give rise to disputes and frauds. If the farmer is the helpless creature supposed (and unless he is, this legislation is not required), he will agree that his landlord shall have the game. If he breaks that agreement, he will do a dishonest thing, and he will be turned out after profiting for a short time by his fraud. If he cannot be turned out, the law will invite him to cheat, and reward him for doing so. Landlords will turn their tenants into bailiffs ; other devices will be resorted to. Is the occupier to take out a licence to kill game ? I will not ask for more of your valuable space. I know nothing as to whether by the proposed law we shall have more or less hares, rabbits, pheasants, and foxes. I do not write in the interest of landlords against tenants, preferring, indeed, the latter as more numerous, and because I am more interested in their prosperity than in the love of sport and killing.

' B.'

One effect of the Act of 1880 is alleged to have been exactly the opposite to that intended. Rabbits breed and pass most of their lives close to or inside copses or coverts, but no provision in the Act empowered farmers to enter plantations in pursuit of game. Rabbits seem to have increased in numbers since the Act came into operation. Farmers, their sons and their friends, are not sorry for this, since rabbit-shooting is good enough sport. Sometimes farmers let the shooting (to the ' one gun ' permitted by the Act) on the quiet. Hares, which breed in open fields or by hedgerows, being more defenceless, have been reduced, according to various authorities, by from 50 to 75 per cent. since 1880. It is said that rabbits kill young leverets, and that hares will not feed on ground where rabbits have fed. Whether the Act has increased the productiveness of farms is uncertain. The whole thing is still described as a paltry and unjustifiable interference with land-owners' rights. But no land-owner has died of starvation in consequence. Most of the people who advocated it have forgotten all about the Hares and Rabbits Act of 1880. An Act compelling all insurance agents to wear yellow waistcoats on Good Friday, although an interference with personal freedom, would not affect the general prosperity of the nation. Business would go on much the same as usual afterwards—a truth forgotten by many people who talk as though repeal of laws guaranteeing liberty of the subject—the Habeas Corpus Act, etc. —must at once compel chaos.

Lord Bramwell was, however, very angry about this Hares and Rabbits Act, just as he was about injustices done to utterly uninteresting speculators in town property under the Disused Burial Grounds Act —angry about unfairness to persons he never knew, nor cared to know. He did not on that account join the pessimists, according to some authorities, people eager to prove that their neighbour must share that ruin which they have brought on themselves by private misconduct. The condition of the thinker's nerves and internal organs may have something to do with it too. Lord Bramwell was born of too healthy a stock, worked too hard, was too free from remorse, to be a pessimist.

He was a big, burly man, sound and strong; never had any of those ailments which induce a man to pity himself, and make cures, systems of diet, and so on, important everyday questions. All his life he was an early riser, a habit which is probably quite as much an effect as a cause of physical and nervous healthiness; after he was fifty years of age he generally went to bed at ten o'clock, and could sleep nine hours on a stretch. On fine summer mornings he would leave his bedroom at six o'clock, carrying his coat and waistcoat over his arm. On the stairs he usually finished tying his neckcloth, at the breakfast-room door put on his coat. At Edenbridge and in Cadogan Place, if there were no guests and the weather was hot, he would sit at table in his shirt-sleeves—the servants, no doubt, shocked and awed, for he inspired awe. Coat or no coat, he always had that emphatic, kingly air and manner—nowadays all but extinct—which one fancies the figures in some of the old historic portraits must have had.

Lord Bramwell knew nothing about 'the ruin of England.' Having travelled so much, he doubtless saw that it is not easy to ruin England. It is a very big firm, but there is some evidence that national character, which built up the firm and is all our own to experiment with, can be 'ruined,' can, by taking thought, be slowly enfeebled. Mischief wrought by petty but frequent interferences with personal freedom, especially with liberty of bargain, estimated in terms of national character, gives, as result, diminished initiative and self-reliance, less capacity to take responsibility, increased disposition to clutch the apron-strings of 'Government.' These things tell in competition with foreigners. The roving Englishman misses those public luxuries and sops which, when at home, he gets from ' the State,' or the municipality, and cannot, there is some reason to believe, hold his own *contra mundum* as of old. Traces of mischief may be identified in that direction, rather than in the Board of Trade returns ; for the wealth accumulated under Free Trade has enabled the nation to buy its way out of the consequences of those many treasons to Free Trade which Lord Bramwell protested against. Britons still find sundry ways of evading the ethical ingenuity of our legislators and inspectors. Again, that which appears to be an ' effect ' of State inter-ference, grandmotherly government, and ' some kind of Socialism ' in legislation, may all the time be a ' cause.' Possibly legislation hurtful in the long-run to national character was submitted to, welcomed, just because many civic virtues were already things of the past, before latter-day British legislators set to work at all. Children and grand-children of the pauper hordes bred under the old Poor Law, concentrated in working-class centres and enfranchised, gave Mr. Gladstone his mandate in 1868 and 1880. If free from the coarse vices, they lacked the rugged virtues of ' the populace ' who shouted for Sacheverell, Wilkes, or Fox, who fought under Wolfe, Moore, Nelson, Wellington ; or they represented a crop of Britons, large, certainly, but, like those bulky crops grown on sewage farms, not sound at the core. When Lord Bramwell appealed in vain to ancient British prejudice in favour of liberty of the subject, the right of property, independence, self-help, etc., perhaps it was not so much that the Britons he had in mind were deaf or hostile—they were merely dead.

He was very jealous in his old-fashioned way for justice—a perfect fanatic about it, as Pym, Wilkes, Cobbet, the Napiers were. His laborious legal training, much thankless drudgery in the courts, never cured him in the least of his habit of vexing himself about things which he might easily have left alone, when he got a regular income. Anybody's wrong was his own personal wrong. As also happened to a long, long array of men who went before him in the same place, dying in due time, having their reward, we conclude, although we are not sure what it was, Lord Bramwell had absorbed into his blood that animating spirit and quality of English justice which has never departed far from the King's Courts. He was proud of his office and its traditions, as the sailor is of his ship flying the white ensign, as the soldier is of the regimental colours, or of the silver cross, sanctified by the names of many battles fought in outlandish places— long ago and far away. All these men alike work for something more than their pay. Precisely what it is Englishmen are slow to say; also slow to believe, amid the drone, drone, drone of dusty, foggy courts of law, that worn, bent, weary old men one sees sitting on the bench there worked and struggled and wore themselves out, buoyed up by the very same spirit which sends often mere lads, full of life, to challenge death in front of their comrades—some dying on the deep sea, some in the snow, in the thick woods, or up among the rocks.

Many who had the right spirit have died without witness or honour, leaving no record of their fidelity, except among a few who remember. Lord Bramwell had great honour in his long, peaceful lifetime, and was much loved. By-and-by, those who care to remember him as he used to be will pass away also. What will outlive all memories of his personality—because a transmissible, imperishable quality—is his single-minded loyalty and consistent adhesion to that English way which he had learnt was the only sure way to compass justice. He was consistent, to the point of fanaticism, about apparently trifling things, not because he was a pedant fitted to one groove, but because he early learnt, and never forgot, that the man who delivers judgment must never swerve.

He well knew that it would not do for him to say from the bench: 'On Mondays, Wednesdays, and Fridays I will decide according to evidence and law; on Tuesdays, Thursdays, and Saturdays we will inquire into the " right - mindedness " (or " wrong-headedness ") of the parties, and decide according to the higher ethic, deep, spiritual ideals, wider conceptions of the needs of humanity and social justice.* I do not know what social justice

---

* During debate in the House of Commons, in July, 1897, Mr. Asquith mentioned two new kinds of justice, 'ethical justice' and 'political justice.' 'Diamond Jubilee justice' also began to be heard of at this date. A landlord having tried to eject a defaulting tenant, a barrister (apparently) wrote from the Junior Carlton Club, May 25, 1897, to one of the

means, neither do you, but we nourish the large hope.'   He could not say that, although it is an easy formula ; and expressed good intentions, not bad.   He could never see why a poor voter should have fuller measure than a rich taxpayer.   When Mr. Henry George happened to declare in ‘ Progress and Poverty ’ that the Almighty had given ‘ the puniest babe that comes wailing into the world ’ as good a title to Mr. Astor's or the Duke of Westminster's estates as the legal owners have, Lord Bramwell remained unsympathetic.   If another man had written a book to prove that the Almighty yearned to have Mr. Henry George hanged, Lord Bramwell would never on that evidence have non-suited the American economist.   When invited to admit that the property of landlords, of tithe rent-charge owners, of shareholders in various companies, ought to be expropriated without compensation and given to other persons, who either did not like to pay what they had contracted to pay, or suffered from ‘ earth hunger,’ or committed outrages, or had many votes, the effect upon Lord Bramwell was precisely the same as if the Lord Lieutenant of some county had taken a seat beside him on the bench during Assizes when a farm-labourer was on trial for assaulting a policeman, and said : ‘ I see, Sir George, there is no evidence against this prisoner, and the

newspapers : ‘. . . After all, to uphold the landlord's undoubted right is to enforce the morality (the Common Law) of a past age, while to adhere to the letter of Section 106 is to practise the morality of the Diamond Jubilee Year, 1897.'

jury will probably acquit him; but I want you to give him a year's imprisonment, all the same. The fact is, the fellow's uncle is a tenant of mine, and an incorrigible poacher. It will be an example to the dangerous classes.' Why should an unconvicted man be sentenced because his uncle is a poacher?

Of others, as well as of Lord Bramwell, it can be said that they had (or swore to themselves that they had) a passion for justice. Nevertheless, they went astray and did infinite mischief. What measure and gauge did Lord Bramwell apply to test fidelity to this same 'justice'? Was his a good or a bad standard?

His letters, addresses, everything he said or wrote on public questions, enable us to contrast his method of determining questions of personal right with those methods which were revived and became fashionable under Mr. Gladstone's influence. All extra-reasonable, or supra-legal systems and theories of judicial, economic, or social relations, from Confucianism to Fabianism, have been driven to rely upon alleged superhuman sanction or inspiration; are necessarily capricious, one day hot, another day cold, because subject to ever-variable interpretation by self-constituted high-priests and medicine-men, who pretend to know what their fetish likes or dislikes. Canonists pronounced certain business transactions between buyer and seller, landlord and tenant, 'idolatry,' contrary to *jus naturale* or *lex divina*. Ultimately that gave a most dangerous latitude; for all the time it was only one man guessing at the will of Nature or the Almighty—a guess perhaps given with intention to do justice. But as years went on other canonists and legists came along, of whom one might have bought his office from a great man's mistress, while another had poisoned his seniors and so risen. They also, by virtue of the essentially extra-reasonable, or superhuman, sanction attributed to their rulings, were able to declare, just as sententiously, that such and such commercial transactions or claims of personal right were ' idolatry ' and displeasing to God ; but this time because they had been bribed to say so. When you have bribed the Almighty, it is no use for the other man to go to the Court of Appeal. Knowing all that, the English would never recognize Canon law, preferring to go before their own men, who decided according to precedent, or to what had been done in their father's time ; at all events, by some reasonable rule which a plain man could understand.

CHAPTER XI.

THE LAST CHAPTER.

Last speech in the House of Lords—Sticks to the same story
—Letters to him—Not wanted, and yet much needed,
in the House of Lords—Goes there no more—May 9,
1892.

FRIDAY, March 6, 1891, the Earl of Wemyss called
attention to the strike of railway servants in Scotland, 'to the system of picketing, and the outrages
by which it was accompanied,' and asked the
Government whether they would take such measures
as would in all future strikes ensure due protection
to unionists willing to work and to non-union workmen ?

Lord Bramwell thus spoke towards the close of
the debate :

'I wish to say a few words to your lordships upon this
subject, more to lament the existence of what I believe to be a
very great evil and mischief than to suggest a remedy for it.
I have always said and held that by the Common Law of the
land there is nothing unlawful in a trade union. And now
there is nothing unlawful in it by statute. I have said the
same thing of strikes; they are not unlawful, and they are not
even without, in many cases, great justification. I see nothing
immoral in them where the only object is to raise the wages

of the strikers, and, as you have heard, I have said and do say, there is nothing unlawful in picketing provided that it is lawfully practised. But that is what it never is. I do not know the particulars of the Scotch strike or of the Scotch picketing, but I do not see how your lordships should reasonably have been led into a discussion whether it was a laudable strike and laudable picketing or not, because some of that picketing of which we have heard could not have been lawful under any provocation. If the men received any provocation, about which I express no opinion, the remedy was not to break the heads of those who did not choose to join them, or throw stones at engines and demolish stations. Their remedy was a different one. If the picketers had only done what they pretend and nothing more, that is to say, if they had merely met their fellow-workmen in a friendly way and asked them to join, with nothing but a kind of persuasiveness in their manner, nobody could have objected to it; they would have a perfect right to propagate their own opinions, and try to get persons to ally themselves with them. But that picketing would not pay; it would not be worth the trouble to picket in that way. The picketing must be of such a character as to inspire terror. That is the object of picketing, and it is attained tolerably well in many cases. Your lordships have heard that I tried—I am sure I do not know how many years, I believe twenty years ago—a picket case in connection with a tailors' strike, which, as far as I remember, was for no other reason than an increase of wages. They would, I dare say, have said that they had picketed in the mildest possible way. My noble and learned friend on the woolsack [then Mr. Hardinge Giffard, Q.C.] was one of the counsel that defended one of the picketers, and got him off, and he will be able to tell your lordships whether I am exaggerating. The men who had not joined in the strike were in such terror of these pickets that they did not dare to take their work home to the master tailors; they got their wives to do it in many cases, and it was pitiable to see the women in the witness-box—they were in the greatest possible terror, and described the treatment they had met with to be of such a character that it was not surprising they were in that condition of alarm in which they exhibited themselves. It matters not that there is no blow given—though I believe there are few cases of extensive picketing in which there is no blow given ; if the conduct of the pickets was such as to excite terror in the minds of those picketed, and to deter them from doing their lawful work, I say it is an intolerable wrong and mischief both to the men who desire to work and to the community at large. It would be bad enough if it were some benevolent, intelligent autocrat who terrorized over people in this way ; but when you consider that the tyranny is exercised by people who are actuated by ignorance and greed, it is insufferable, even though there may be no blow provable. I have said I do not know what the remedy for this is. You could not put down trades unions if you would, and I for one would not ; on the contrary, I take the liberty of saying before your lordships, what I have said before in open court : if I were a working-man, I should be a unionist. I think that trades unions are useful institutions, and I would strike for good cause. You cannot get rid either of trades unions or of strikes. You have got now an excellent law against unreasonable intimidation—if one may use such an expression—if we can suppose there ever was any reasonable intimidation ; the difficulty is in reaching the offenders and protecting those persons who are injured and oppressed by it, and the only thing that I can suggest as a remedy for what I believe to be a most serious mischief is that the persons picketed, those who do not agree with the pickets, should be carefully protected, and that that remedy should be applied which the noble Marquess has so well administered elsewhere, namely, that the law should be enforced, and people taught that they could not safely break it.'

This was the last speech he made in the House of Lords, most ancient abiding-place of the *Aula Regis*. No man who ever sat there was better qualified than he to keep alive such of its reverend traditions as survive. Men have schemed, flattered, paid large sums to obtain a peerage and a coronet, which they well knew would give them the only kind of elevation they were ever likely to get. When Lord Bramwell went up to the House of Lords his patent gave him nothing that he had not before ; rather he brought honour, added honour, strength to that assembly during the ten years he was there.   His last words, it will be seen, were what Lord Salisbury would call 'a sermon' on the text ever present to him.

> ' Let the laws of your own land,
>   Good or ill, between ye stand,
>   Hand to hand, and foot to foot,
>   Arbiters of the dispute.

*   *   *   *   *

> ' The old laws of England, they
>   Whose reverend heads with age are gray ;
>   Children of a wiser day ;
>   And whose solemn voice must be
>   Thine own echo—Liberty.'

So Shelley wrote, allegiance to ancient English precept being in the imagination of the mutinous, diseased young English aristocrat, also deep in the mind of the laborious student—stalwart champion of English institutions.   During the remainder of the session of 1891 Lord Bramwell was in London, hale and hearty enough, but seldom attending in the House of Lords.   His old foes, enemies of liberty and property, were nearly rid of him.

At this time he received this letter from a writer of world-wide celebrity, who was not always quite so wrong, since he happened to write a great deal about the Irish Question :

'November 2, 1891.

'. . . We had an instance the other day of the liabilities of the present connection. To gain a majority in the Canadian elections (which he brought on mainly for the purpose of forestalling certain awkward disclosures), Sir John Macdonald appealed to Canadian dislike and distrust of the Americans. His followers, of course, outran their chief. The platforms rang with abuse of our neighbours, and the walls were covered with placards and caricatures insulting to their character and flag. The Americans, of course, noted all these things in their book. They had, as I understand, special reports of the speeches of Sir John Macdonald and Sir Charles Tupper, so that they could not be deceived with the official versions afterwards put forth. To cap it all, Lord Salisbury cabled Sir John Macdonald his congratulations on the victory. This was at the time when negotiations about the Fisheries Question and the Behring Sea Question were going on at Washington. No wonder the British Ambassador has trouble!

'As to the mode of terminating the connection, what I would like to see is a petition of the Parliament of Canada granted by the Government and Parliament of Great Britain. Heaven forbid that the parting should be violent or otherwise than amicable!

'The American Revolution, I am persuaded, did the Americans themselves a good deal of harm.

'If you get into a war with a maritime power, and the Atlantic trade of Canada is seriously interrupted, the end will come. A war with Russia would very likely do the business.

'Since the disclosures of corruption and the census there has been a considerable growth of feeling in favour of political union with the United States. . . .'

This letter he never read :

'22, Gramercy Park, New York,
'*April* 27, 1892.

'DEAR LORD BRAMWELL,

'It grieves me to hear of your bodily afflictions. The face of the fine photograph that you have sent me does not betray suffering. Judging by that, I should prophesy that you are good for some years more. I have sent the picture to be framed, and shall hang it in my library. Thus I shall ever look into the eyes of a great jurist. Notwithstanding your depression of spirit, I hope you will mend and regain the wonted vigour of earlier years. Count me always as one who has great admiration for your life and labours, and believe me,

'Most faithfully yours,

'DAVID DUDLEY FIELD.'

At the end of May, 1883, during debate on a feeble proposal of Lord Stanhope's to break contracts and half confiscate some private rights, Lord Rosebery plaintively observed: 'Any attempt at legislation is at a great disadvantage when the noble and learned Lord (Bramwell) criticizes it '—a graceful way of testifying that folly is not always ironclad, and that between 1882 and 1892 Lord Bramwell did indeed prevent the passing of more than one measure intended to conciliate foolish or spiteful people, noisy at the moment, but long since forgotten. After he died, in respect to many questions, it was dunce's high holiday in the House of Lords. The old race of legal giants—who made such debates as those on the creation of life peerages, in 1856, an education in constitutional lore — had passed away. There was nobody left with sufficient grasp of law, courage, zeal, power of logical statement, to analyze, from Lord Bramwell's point of view, proposals aimed by the leaders of both political parties at security of property and liberty of the subject. What was everybody's business became nobody's business. The peers, indeed, pulled themselves together one afternoon in August, 1893, and made short work of the Home Rule imposture. When the Finance Bill of the following year, in an offhand sort of way, repealed the Petition of Right, when Lord Salisbury in 1897 talked about 'the "law" of common employment,' Lord Bramwell was not there to trouble his noble colleagues. Trial of the Appeal case *Sharp* v. *Wakefield* having brought to light some flagrant injustices possible under the Licensing Acts, Lord Bramwell drafted a short Bill to remedy those injustices ; and prior to the General Election of 1895, Lord Salisbury promised, if returned to power, to support this Bill. He was returned to power.

One foggy evening in the early spring of 1892 a friend went to Lord Bramwell's house in Cadogan Place ; there by flickering firelight he saw the old lord sitting all alone at the piano, his hands wandering feebly over the keys, recalling some ancient airs, as he once wrote, 'to comfort him.' At that hour darkness was surely setting in. On Easter Sunday, 1892, for his last journey, he left London, where he was born, going to Four Elms, by Edenbridge, growing weaker there daily. On May 9, 1892, he died at that house. His ashes were buried at Woking. English dust to English dust.

INDEX

Lord Bramwell's pamphlets, letters, sayings, etc., are indexed in italics.

THE END.

MACMILLAN & CO.'S STANDARD BIOGRAPHIES.

ALFRED, LORD TENNYSON. A Memoir. By his SON. With Photogravure Portraits of LORD TENNYSON, LADY TENNYSON, etc. Facsimiles of portions of Poems, and Illustrations after pictures by G. F. WATTS, R.A., SAMUEL LAURENCE, Mrs. ALLINGHAM, RICHARD DOYLE, BISCOMBE GARDNER, etc. 2 vols., medium 8vo., 36s. net.

BISMARCK, SOME SECRET PAGES OF HIS HISTORY. Being a Diary kept by Dr. MORITZ BUSCH during Twenty-five Years' Official and Private Intercourse with the great Chancellor. 3 vols., 8vo., 30s. net.

FORTY-ONE YEARS IN INDIA. From Subaltern to Commander-in-Chief. By Field-Marshal the Right Hon. LORD ROBERTS of Kandahar, V.C., K.P., G.C.B., G.C.S.I., G.C.I.E. Containing Forty-four Illustrations and Plans. Thirtieth and Cheaper Edition. Extra crown 8vo., cloth, 10s. net.

LIFE AND LETTERS OF EDWARD THRING. By GEORGE R. PARKIN, M.A. With Portraits 2 vols., extra crown 8vo., 17s. net.

A MEMORY OF EDWARD THRING. By J. H. SKRINE. Crown 8vo., 6s.

LIFE OF NAPOLEON BONAPARTE. By Professor W. M. SLOANE, Ph.D., L.H.D. Illustrated. 4 vols., imperial 4to., 96s. net.

LIFE AND LETTERS OF FREDERICK WALKER, A.R.A. By JOHN GEORGE MARKS. With Illustrations and 13 Photogravures. 4to., 31s. 6d. net.

THE YOKE OF EMPIRE. Sketches of the Queen's Prime Ministers. By REGINALD B. BRETT. With 7 Photogravure Portraits. Crown 8vo., 6s.

CYPRIAN: HIS LIFE, HIS TIMES, HIS WORK. By EDWARD WHITE BENSON, D.D., D.C.L., sometime Archbishop of Canterbury. 8vo., 21s. net.

LIFE AND LETTERS OF WILLIAM JOHN BUTLER, late Dean of Lincoln and sometime Vicar of Wantage. With Portraits. Demy 8vo., 12s. 6d. net.

MEMORIALS (Part I.) FAMILY AND PERSONAL, 1766—1865. (Part II.) POLITICAL. ROUNDELL PALMER, Earl of Selborne. With Portraits and Illustrations. 2 vols., demy 8vo., 25s. net each part.

LIFE AND LETTERS OF FENTON JOHN ANTHONY HORT, D.D., D.C.L., LL.D. By his Son, ARTHUR FENTON HORT, late Fellow of Trinity College, Cambridge. With Portraits. Extra crown 8vo., 17s. net.

THE LIFE OF CARDINAL MANNING, ARCHBISHOP OF WESTMINSTER. By EDMUND SHERIDAN PURCELL. With Portraits. Fourth Thousand. 2 vols., 8vo., 30s. net.

THE LETTERS OF MATTHEW ARNOLD, 1848—1888. Collected and Arranged by GEORGE W. E. RUSSELL. 2 vols., crown 8vo., 15s. net.

ALFRED THE GREAT. By THOMAS HUGHES. Crown 8vo., 6s.

SAMUEL TAYLOR COLERIDGE. A Narrative of the Events of his Life. By JAMES DYKES CAMPBELL. With Portrait. With a Memoir of the Author by LESLIE STEPHEN. Demy 8vo., 10s. 6d.

A MEMOIR OF RALPH WALDO EMERSON. By JAMES ELLIOTT CABOT. 2 vols., crown 8vo., 18s.

LETTERS AND LITERARY REMAINS OF EDWARD FITZGERALD, Edited by WILLIAM ALDIS WRIGHT. 3 vols., crown 8vo, 31s. 6d.

RICHARD BRINSLEY SHERIDAN. Including much Information derived from New Sources. By W. FRASER RAE. With an Introduction by Sheridan's Great-Grandson, the MARQUIS OF DUFFERIN AND AVA, K.P., G.C.B. With Portraits and other Illustrations. 2 vols., demy 8vo., 26s.

THE LIVES OF WITS AND HUMOURISTS. Swift, Foote, Steele, Goldsmith, Sheridan, Sydney Smith, Theodore Hook, etc. By JOHN TIMBS. 2 vols, crown 8vo., 12s.

MACMILLAN AND CO., LTD., LONDON.

MACMILLAN & CO.'S STANDARD BIOGRAPHIES.

THE LIFE OF JOHN CHURCHILL, FIRST DUKE OF MARLBOROUGH. Vols. I. and II.—To the Accession of Queen Anne. By Field-Marshal Viscount WOLSELEY, K.P., G.C.B., G.C.M.G., Commander-in-Chief. Demy 8vo., with Portraits of the Duke and Duchess of Marlborough, James II., William III., the Duke of Monmouth, Duchess of Cleveland, and other Illustrations and Plans. Fourth Edition. 32s.

THE LIFE OF HENRY JOHN TEMPLE, VISCOUNT PALMERSTON. With Selections from his Diaries and Correspondence. By the Hon. EVELYN ASHLEY, M.P. 2 vols., crown 8vo., with Frontispiece to each volume, 12s.

LIFE AND LETTERS OF HENRY CECIL RAIKES, late Her Majesty's Postmaster-General. By HENRY ST. JOHN RAIKES. With Portrait. 8vo., 10s. net.

FRANCIS OF ASSISI. By Mrs. OLIPHANT. Crown 8vo., 6s.

THE NEW CALENDAR OF GREAT MEN. Biographies of the 558 Worthies of all Ages and Countries in the Positivist Calendar of Auguste Comte. Edited by FREDERIC HARRISON. Extra crown 8vo., 7s. 6d. net.

LIVES OF THE ARCHBISHOPS OF CANTERBURY, FROM ST. AUGUSTINE TO JUXON. By the Very Rev. WALTER FARQUHAR HOOK, D.D., Dean of Chichester. Demy 8vo. The Volumes are sold as follows: Vol. I., 15s.; Vol. II., 15s.; Vol. V., 15s.; Vols. VI. and VII., 30s.; Vol. VIII., 15s.; Vol. X., 15s.; Vol. XI., 15s.; Vol. XII., 15s.

LIFE OF ARCHIBALD CAMPBELL TAIT, ARCHBISHOP OF CANTERBURY. By RANDALL THOMAS, Bishop of Rochester, and WILLIAM BENHAM, B.D., Hon. Canon of Canterbury. With Portraits. Third Edition. 2 vols., crown 8vo., 10s. net.

CATHARINE AND CRAUFURD TAIT, WIFE AND SON OF ARCHIBALD CAMPBELL, ARCHBISHOP OF CANTERBURY: a Memoir. Edited by Rev. W. BENHAM, B.D. Crown 8vo., 6s. Popular Edition, abridged. Crown 8vo., 2s. 6d.

JAMES FRASER, SECOND BISHOP OF MANCHESTER: a Memoir. By T. HUGHES, Q.C. Crown 8vo., 6s.

LIFE AND LETTERS OF E. A. FREEMAN. By W. R. W. STEPHENS. 2 vols., 8vo., 17s. net.

DEAN HOOK: HIS LIFE AND LETTERS. Edited by the Very Rev. W. R. W. STEPHENS, D.D., F.S.A., Dean of Winchester, Author of 'Life of St. John Chrysostom,' etc. The POPULAR EDITION, 1 vol., crown 8vo., with Index and Portraits, 6s.

LETTERS AND MEMORIES OF THE LIFE OF CHARLES KINGSLEY. Edited by his WIFE. 2 vols., crown 8vo., 12s. Cheap Edition, 1 vol., 6s.

BISHOP LIGHTFOOT. Reprinted from the *Quarterly Review*. With a Prefatory Note by the Bishop of Durham. With Portrait. Crown 8vo., 3s. 6d.

LIFE OF FREDERICK DENISON MAURICE. By his Son, F. MAURICE. 2 vols., 8vo., 36s. Popular Edition, 2 vols., crown 8vo., 16s.

THE LIFE OF JOHN MILTON. By Professor DAVID MASSON, Vol. I., 21s.; Vol. II., 16s.; Vol. III., 18s.; Vols. IV. and V., 32s.; Vol. VI., with Portrait, 21s.; Index to 6 vols., 16s.

LIFE OF SIR A. C. RAMSAY. By Sir A. GEIKIE, F.R.S. 8vo., 12s. 6d. net.

CHAPTERS FROM SOME MEMOIRS. By ANNE RITCHIE. 8vo., 10s. 6d.

LIFE OF ADAM SMITH. By JOHN RAE, Author of 'Eight Hours for Work.' 8vo., 12s. 6d. net.

A RECORD OF ELLEN WATSON. Arranged and Edited by ANNA BUCKLAND. With a Portrait. Third Edition. Crown 8vo., 6s.

RECOLLECTIONS OF A LITERARY LIFE. By MARY RUSSELL MITFORD. Crown 8vo., with Portraits, 6s.

MACMILLAN AND CO., LTD., LONDON.